New Yiddish Library

The New Yiddish Library is a joint project of the Fund for the Translation of Jewish Literature and the National Yiddish Book Center.

Additional support comes from The Kaplen Foundation, the Felix Posen Fund for the Translation of Modern Yiddish Literature, and Ben and Sarah Torchinsky.

SERIES EDITOR: DAVID G. ROSKIES

The End of Everything

DAVID BERGELSON

TRANSLATED AND WITH

AN INTRODUCTION BY

JOSEPH SHERMAN

YALE UNIVERSITY PRESS

NEW HAVEN AND LONDON

Set in Scala and Scala Sans type by The Composing Room of Michigan, Inc.
Printed in the United States of America.

Library of Congress Cataloging-in-Publication Data

Bergelson, David, 1884–1952.
[Nokh alemen. English]
The end of everything / David Bergelson ; translated and with an introduction by Joseph Sherman.
     p.   cm. — (New Yiddish library)
Includes bibliographical references.
ISBN 978-0-300-11067-8 (pbk.: alk. paper)
1. Sherman, Joseph.   II. Title.
PJ5129.B45N613 2010
839'.133—dc22
2009022478

A catalogue record for this book is available from the British Library.

This paper meets the requirements of ANSI/NISO Z39.48-1992 (Permanence of Paper).

10 9 8 7 6 5 4 3 2 1

♦ ♦ ♦ Contents

♦ ♦ ♦ *Introduction*

JOSEPH SHERMAN

1.

Shortly before world war and revolution swept away the established
European sociopolitical order, the year 1913 brought to public attention
a number of significant works of twentieth-century art. No sooner had
the Armory Show, which exposed American viewers for the first time
to Impressionist, Cubist, and Fauve painting, distressed New York con-
servatives in February, than *The Rite of Spring,* a modernist ballet composed by Igor Stravinsky (1882–1971) and staged by Sergei Diaghilev's
Ballets Russes, caused a riot at its premiere in Paris in May. During the
rest of the year, many lovers of literature were shocked by the appearance of the first, heavily censored version of D. H. Lawrence's semiau-
tobiographical novel *Sons and Lovers,* were perplexed by Franz Kafka's
short story "Das Urteil" (The Judgment), and—among those who read
Yiddish—were either infuriated or enraptured by the appearance of
Nokh alemen (*The End of Everything*), David Bergelson's first novel,
completed after two years of intense work.

Those familiar with Bergelson's earlier stories had now to accustom
themselves to—or reject—a more extensive deployment of a style that
set out to be consciously literary. They were obliged to confront writing
that moved as far away as possible from the oral tradition that charac-

terized the immensely popular work of Sholem Aleichem, and immerse themselves in prose that was less concerned with action than with mood, that had little use for conventionally conceived plot, that slowed down events to focus on the interior life of characters yet refused to offer any conclusions about them. In all these respects, Bergelson's work reflected the instability that accompanied radical sociocultural change from an old world that was dying to a new world that had not yet fully come into being.

Born in 1884 in Okhrimovo (Sarny) near Uman in the tsarist province of Kiev, Bergelson was the youngest of nine children born to wealthy and pious parents, and he received a private education that combined traditional Jewish learning with secular subjects. His father, Rafail, died when he was only nine, and his mother, Dreyze, an avid reader with a marked gift for storytelling, died five years later. At the age of fourteen, therefore, the orphaned Bergelson went to live with an older married brother in Kiev, the costs of his board and lodging being deducted from his share of the family inheritance. Although he was intellectually and artistically gifted—he became an accomplished violinist and reciter—his unsystematic education handicapped his attempts to acquire higher qualifications. An external student at the university in Kiev in 1901, and again in 1907–1908 when he audited classes at the dental school, he failed all his examinations and gave up formal study without earning a diploma.

Bergelson started writing very young, first in Hebrew and then in Russian, but soon returned to Yiddish. By his own admission, in a memoir published in 1934, he had difficulty in finding a Yiddish diction suited to his artistic aims. Although he was a younger contemporary of Mendele Moykher Sforim (1836–1917), Sholem Aleichem (1859–1916), and Yitskhok-Leybush Peretz (1852–1915), the pioneers of modern Yiddish literature, Bergelson was determined to produce fiction fundamentally different from theirs in both conception and execution. He found Mendele's style alien, and considered Peretz's Polish dialect a dead end. Only in the writing of Sholem Aleichem, also a native of the Ukraine, did he find a Yiddish familiar to him, but Sholem Aleichem's "volubility" was, he recorded, useless for his own artistic goals. To convey his vision of the fading world of Russian Jewry, Bergelson was obliged to create his own language and style.

That the literary innovations he introduced were initially unwelcome to all but the most sophisticated of his readers is proved by the difficulty he experienced in getting his earliest work published. His stories were regularly returned by editors who refused to take risks, so by the age of twenty Bergelson had already written some of his best work without having seen any of it in print. By 1907 he had completed *Arum vokzal* (*At the Depot*), the novella that established his literary reputation, but it was published—in Warsaw in 1909—only after he had personally defrayed half the printing costs, the other half being subsidized by a group of friends led by the writer and critic Nakhmen Mayzel (1887–1966).[1] The work received enthusiastic reviews from highbrow critics, and a year later Mayzel, encouraged by its success, brought out two more of Bergelson's short stories, "Der toyber" (The Deaf Man) and "Tsvey vegn" (Two Roads),[2] in the first volume of a literary miscellany entitled *Der yidisher almanakh* (*The Yiddish Miscellany*).

From 1905 until the outbreak of World War I, Warsaw and Vilna led the field of Yiddish publishing throughout Eastern Europe, each capital catering to a different reading public: Warsaw fed the popular taste, whereas Vilna appealed to the intelligentsia. From 1910, the chief patron of Yiddish belles lettres in Vilna was Boris Kletskin (1875–1937), a wealthy Bundist who joined publishing forces with Mayzel. In 1913, Kletskin's visionary entrepreneurship finally brought out and called to public attention *The End of Everything*, the novel through which Bergelson hoped to bring Yiddish literature into the mainstream of European letters. As much as this novel mirrored contemporary international literary trends, it also marked a sweeping departure from the conventions hitherto established for modern Yiddish prose fiction, and thus spoke to its author's extensive literary ambitions.

All Bergelson's work before World War I is dominated by the concerns common to European modernism: skepticism of all ideological systems, perplexity about the function of art, and a quest for individualistic new forms. His first novel was startling not only in subject matter but also in style, and its crowning achievement was—and remains—its indirect narrative technique, which consciously separates speaker from speech. Language is reduced to bare essentials, punctuated by silences that create a sense of alienation. The reader is made to pass, without being fully aware of the transition, from seemingly objective reality to the subjective vision of the protagonist without any kind of mediation. The society Bergelson knew best and on which his authorial gaze fastened at first was that of the Russified Jewish nouveaux riches, no longer exclusively Yiddish-speaking provincials but sophisticates able to move to and from great metropolises, attracted by growing industrialization and enlarged economic opportunities. From among the educated of such people Bergelson drew not only his subject matter but also his most fervent admirers. When war broke out in 1914, tsarist censorship was reintroduced, with particular ferocity in Kiev, where all Yiddish outlets were closed down in March–April 1915. The general tension that accompanied the deteriorating situation at the front erupted into the turmoil of the Russian Revolution, and sharpened Bergelson's sense of futility, since the Bolshevik victory after October 1917 swept away the well-to-do Jewish shtetl bourgeoisie who formed both his subject matter and his chief readership. At a stroke, Bergelson had lost the subject matter he knew best, and his most avid readers.

The sense of fragmentation that Bergelson felt at the disappearance of the life he knew best was exacerbated by the medium in which he wrote. Yiddish was a language respected neither by the assimilated nor by the leaders of the Zionist movement. The former demanded linguistic acculturation to their countries of adoption; the latter insisted on the revival of Hebrew as a precondition for fulfilling Jewish national-political aspirations that Bergelson regarded as pipe dreams. In response to this social turmoil, many Jewish intellectuals, Bergelson among them, came to believe that the Yiddish language could be made the central component of a secular, modern culture. This conception, known as "Yiddishism," perceived the Jewish people as a world nation whose essential distinguishing characteristic was its extraterritoriality. This emerging conception of modern Yiddish culture was given a chance to bloom after the Pale of Settlement had been abolished in February 1917 and a group of nationalists, declaring Ukraine independent, set up the moderate socialist Central *Rada,* which survived until April 1918.

In Odessa in 1917 Bergelson met and married Tsiporah (Tsipe) Kutzenogaya, a recent graduate of the Odessa high school for girls. A year later, on 8 August 1918, just as pogroms began raging across Ukraine, the Bergelsons' only child, their son Lev, was born in Heisin, near Vinnitsa, a town on the Bug River that was Tsipe Bergelson's birthplace, and Bergelson sought and found employment in Kiev, the capital of Ukraine, where he and his family lived in 1919–1920. For Yiddish writers in the period, Kiev was a welcoming place despite the surrounding sociopolitical turmoil. The *Rada* gave emerging Yiddish culture its best chance by adopting a policy of national autonomy. All four of the competing Jewish political parties that functioned in Kiev after the Revolution joined forces to serve a pan-Yiddishist ideal and nominated representatives, Bergelson among them, to the central committee of the *Kultur-lige* (League of Culture), created in January 1918 as a suprapolitical Yiddishist body that sought to cover all areas of cultural activity in the former tsarist empire. Many who worked with the *Kultur-lige* shared little beyond being socialist, non-Zionist, and Yiddishist, but they cooperated with zeal in organizing a school system, a teachers' training college, and two publishing houses, the *Kiever farlag* and the *Folksfarlag,* which produced politically engagé journals like *Oyfgang* (Sunrise) and *Baginen* (Dawn), both published during 1919, as well as the modernist miscellany *Eygns* (Our Own, Kiev 1918, 1920). Bergelson's story "In eynem a zumer" (During a Certain Summer) appeared in *Oyfgang,* and he wrote a story for children, entitled "Mayse-bikhl" (Little Story Book), for the educational wing of the *Kultur-lige.*

The most substantial of the works Bergelson published at this time was his novella *Opgang* (*Descent*), begun in his annus mirabilis of 1913 but abandoned at the beginning of the war. A variation on some of the themes of *The End of Everything,* but with a dead and failed revolutionary as its central character, this novella first appeared in the second issue of the journal *Eygns* (1920).[3] War and revolution demanded a wholly new intellectual and artistic synthesis from Bergelson if he was to develop as a writer, however. The world he had known had been swept away and he was now obliged to come to terms with what had replaced it.

Although all the writers associated with the *Kultur-lige*—who in time became known as the "Kiev Group"—were sympathetic to the aims of socialism, most were reluctant to subordinate their work to the dictates of the Bolshevik Party.[4] Instead they belonged to that cluster of intellectuals labeled "fellow-travelers," supporters of the Revolution who were neither members of the party nor of proletarian origin but who hoped to enjoy the kind of literary freedom familiar in the West. Euphoria soon gave way to pessimism, however, as these young modernists confronted the realities of escalating political instability and the absence of discerning readers among the "masses" with whom the Revolution demanded they engage. The Civil War of 1919–1920, accompanied by brutal pogroms, dispelled many of their utopian illusions. By the beginning of 1921 the Red Army had decisively recaptured Kiev, and the Bolshevik government took over the *Kultur-lige*, severely curtailing its educational and cultural activities.

With this withering of his work, a despondent Bergelson joined other Yiddish writers in seeking better opportunities in Moscow, officially proclaimed the Soviet capital in March 1920. From 1918 on, Yiddish literary activity had gone forward in Moscow under the umbrella of the specially created "Jewish Commissariat," which published the Yiddish daily *Der emes* (The Truth) and the journal *Di komunistishe velt* (The Communist World). In the earliest post-Revolution days, political differences had been widely tolerated, since both Bolshevik and non-Bolshevik Yiddish activists shared the common dream of synthesizing universal with Jewish-Yiddish culture. In 1920, however, just as significant numbers of writers had relocated from Kiev, the Jewish Commissariat was replaced by the *Yevsekstia*, the Jewish Section of the Communist Party, which on 7 November 1920 relaunched *Der emes* as its central organ, introducing with it the politicized new Soviet orthographical code for Yiddish, which aimed to make the language an instrument through which the Soviet Jewish nation could develop a particularistic Soviet Jewish culture.[5] The *Yevsektsia* employed Bergelson as an editor of Yiddish and Russian literature, but since it was staffed

by seasoned party functionaries, it demanded a considerable degree of political conformity to the dogmas of Bolshevism.

Soviet Yiddish literature consequently split into two ideologically opposed camps. The first followed the ideals of the Kiev Group, supporting the Revolution while encouraging an autonomous and polyphonic literature. In opposition, a group of "proletarian" writers strove to create what they defined as "a poster-like literature, militant in character, affirmative in tone, and accessible to simple readers," written with a high degree of "realism." Leading this faction were the doctrinaire journalist Moyshe Litvakov (1875–1937), and the poets Itsik Fefer (1900–1952) and Izzi Kharik (1898–1937).

The individualistic and essentially skeptical Bergelson evidently rejected the yoking of Yiddish creative endeavor to a fixed ideological agenda. In early 1921 he left the starving capital to take up the invitation of the publisher Zev-Wolf Latzky-Bertholdi (1881–1940) to join him, Der Nister (1884–1950), and Leyb Kvitko (1890–1952) in Berlin, then a hive of émigré cultural activity. His first major publication there was the appearance of his *Gezamlte verk* (*Collected Work*) in six volumes under the imprint of the firm Wostock (East). For this edition, Bergelson completed and published, in its final form, the novella *Yoysef Shor,* which emerged from the material of the aborted novel *In fartunklte tsaytn* (*In Darkened Times*), on which Bergelson had been working on and off for nearly ten years. Though Bergelson was impressed by the sophistication of Berlin, he found the city impersonal and rootless. In a series of stories set there,[6] he presented the city as driven by capitalist self-interest and postwar decadence in which its émigrés suffer the dislocating effects of exile.

In his early days in Weimar Berlin, Bergelson earned well from his contributions to New York's Yiddish socialist but anti-Communist daily *Forverts,* although his family still relied on his wife's earnings as a typist. He continued to publish in unaffiliated journals like Warsaw's *Moment,* which in 1921 carried his subtle story "Yordim" (The Déclassés),[7] but kept his options open by writing for Soviet publications: in 1922 he contributed to the Moscow journal *Shtrom* (Stream) his Civil War story "Botchko: fragment fun a roman" (Botchko: A Frag-

ment of a Novel).[8] That same year Bergelson and Der Nister co-edited the first issue of *Milgroym* (Pomegranate), a highbrow illustrated periodical with a Hebrew counterpart titled *Rimon*. To the first issue of the Yiddish edition Bergelson contributed a literary-critical essay paying tribute to the young Russian-Yiddish poets and expressing regret that non-Soviet critics ignored their work, as well as a brief but powerful sketch depicting the terror of the anti-Jewish massacres of 1919–1921.[9] In October 1923, however, Litvakov savagely denounced *Milgroym* as "petit-bourgeois," and both Bergelson and Der Nister resigned from its editorial board, announcing through a joint open letter in the third issue of *Shtrom* that they had done so to show solidarity with their Soviet colleagues.

By 1925 Bergelson had grown enthusiastic about the Soviet regime's officially announced decision to settle, by the end of 1926, about half a million Jews in a still-to-be-determined region of the USSR that, it was hoped, would in time be declared an autonomous Jewish republic. Despite Zionist opposition, this plan was enthusiastically accepted by many Soviet and Western Yiddish intellectuals dazzled by the prospect of a region where Yiddish would be the official language of government, education, press, and literature. On 2 March 1926 Bergelson published in *Der emes* a letter in which he openly expressed the desire to become a committed Soviet writer. Despite having only just published two fine stories in *Forverts*, "Altvarg" (Obsolescence) in March, and "Tsvey rotskhim" (Two Murderers)[10] in April, he now switched his allegiance to New York's pro-Communist Yiddish daily, *Frayhayt*. One of his earliest pieces there, published on 29 May 1926, was a propaganda effort entitled "Vi azoy vet oyszen dos yidishe lebn in Rusland shpeter mit etlekhe yor" (How life in Russia will look in a few years' time). The very next day he followed this with an openly pro-Bolshevik story called "Hersh [later Hershl] Toker,"[11] which was simultaneously serialized in *Der emes* with a note explaining his ideological reasons for breaking with *Forverts*. Even more significantly, he worked hard to establish the pro-Soviet journal *In shpan* (In Harness).

In a vigorous programmatic essay entitled "Dray tsentern" (Three Centers),[12] which appeared in this journal's first issue, Bergelson called on the Yiddish literary world to move its center of gravity to the

Soviet Union. Dismissing America as a country of selfish opportunism and Poland as a reactionary outpost of religious orthodoxy, he claimed that those who, because they stood closest to the proletarian Jewish masses, could most effectively perpetuate Yiddish culture were to be found in the Soviet Union only. At a time when Yiddish-speaking communities worldwide were dwindling through assimilation, he argued, the Soviet Union was home to two million Jews whose home language was Yiddish; it supported Yiddish educational and cultural institutions and sponsored newspapers and publishing houses. In attempting to define a new direction for Yiddish culture, Bergelson's essay exposed a fundamental contradiction between what Yiddish literature had already achieved, and what party functionaries now demanded it should accomplish. Predictably, therefore, his manifesto pleased neither the Left nor the Right.

On 20 June 1926, by extraordinary coincidence, reviews of *In shpan* appeared simultaneously in two Yiddish dailies sundered ideologically and geographically: one by Litvakov in *Der emes,* and the other by Shmuel Niger (1883–1955) in New York's liberal daily, *Der tog* (The Day). Litvakov, censuring Bergelson for being still "very far from true Communism," categorically denied that his new journal was of any use to the party and its purposes. For diametrically opposite reasons, Niger assailed Bergelson's tendentious stance by warning of the dangers to artistic creativity of harnessing individual talents to doctrinaire demands. Both attacks exposed the ideological bind in which Bergelson found himself. However much he might empathize with the ideals of the revolution, he was fundamentally a bourgeois intellectual, and *In shpan* itself, published jointly in Vilna and Berlin, was effectively an émigré publication. Nevertheless he was acutely aware that, having lost not only the subject matter of his earlier fiction but also his primary readership, he was urgently obliged to find both different themes and a secondary readership, which he thought he could best accomplish by becoming an apologist for the Soviet regime.

Like all the most gifted of his Soviet Yiddish writer-colleagues, and thousands of Yiddish-speaking Jews worldwide, Bergelson steadily came to believe that only in the Soviet Union, the government of which both recognized and supported Yiddish, could the treasured ideal of defining Jewish identity through the promotion of Yiddish culture be realized. For this reason it was particularly significant that both issues of *In shpan* (April and May 1926) carried substantial extracts from his new novel *Mides ha-din* (*The Full Severity of the Law*), published in full three years later. While this novel can be read as a Bolshevik interpretation of the Civil War, in a deeper sense it is, typically for Bergelson, a metaphysical exploration of the forces of history, in which individuals remain uniquely incapable of fitting predetermined formulas.

Since Bergelson had elected to put himself under its aegis, the Communist Party started making demands. In August 1926, during a visit to the Soviet Union, he attended a reception in Moscow at which Litvakov, the main speaker, stressed that Bergelson as a Soviet writer had to desist from writing what he insultingly called "entertaining light literature." Angered more by Litvakov's trivializing disparagement of his work than by his ideological censure, Bergelson nevertheless publicly declared that "the instructions that have been imparted to me on this evening, from beginning to end, I accept with love and deference." He had come to believe that conforming to the party line was the only way he could continue contributing to Yiddish literary culture. To demonstrate his new commitment, in Kiev the following year he published the first edition of a new collection of engagé stories under the title *Shturemteg* (*Days of Storm*, 1927), which met with a mixed reception. The scandal provoked by his political reorientation greatly boosted his fame, however: in Russian and Ukrainian translation his work proved enormously popular in the Soviet Union, his name began to appear as a separate entry in Soviet literary encyclopedias, and between 1928 and 1930 Kletskin in Vilna published his collected Yiddish work in eight volumes.

From November 1928 until May 1929 *Frayhayt* sponsored Bergelson on a tour of the United States, where he expressed shock at the country's inflated commercialism and its intense mechanization of human life. Urged by American Communists to treasure his citizenship of the world's first socialist state, and personally antipathetic to Zionist settlement in Palestine, Bergelson returned to Berlin. Barely five months later, the collapse of the New York stock exchange that precipitated the Great Depression confirmed in him his rejection of capitalism. In other respects, however, 1929 was a highly productive year. He republished *The Full Severity of the Law,* and his old friend Mayzel, now the editor of Warsaw's *Literarishe bleter* (Literary Pages), dedicated an entire issue (Number 37) to Bergelson's twenty years of literary achievement in which he featured one chapter from Bergelson's newly begun novel, later known by its collective title *Baym Dnyeper* (*On the Dnieper*).

Bergelson's artistic sensibility instinctively inclined to subtlety and allusion, to speculation rather than to assurance, to the individual rather than to the collective. Soviet state propaganda, on the other hand, demanded art that worked in precisely the opposite way. In seeking to accommodate the party line, therefore, Bergelson was forced to work against his own artistic grain. The extent to which he succeeded in producing work of some quality even within the restrictions imposed by the party line demonstrated how far he was able to reinvent himself. The possibilities for continuing to do so were steadily closed off, however, by intensifying demands for conformity to the increasingly inflexible demands of Stalinist doctrine.

By 1929, the climate in Yiddish literary circles changed abruptly in proportion to the change in Soviet society as a whole. Stalin had consolidated his grip on absolute power, and his demand for ideological conformity was first seen in a destructive political campaign waged against Russian-language writers who published abroad.[13] To show unquestioning solidarity with the new party line, the functionaries of the *Yevsektsia* launched an analogous attack on Yiddish writers.[14] At the same time, relations with the Jews in the West grew strained after *Frayhayt,* under pressure from Moscow, justified the Arab riots against Jewish settlers in Palestine as a revolt against the joint oppressions of Zionism and British imperialism. Like all Jewish left-wingers, Bergelson was compelled to reconsider his position. He chose to remain with *Frayhayt,* thus implicitly siding with stridently pro-Soviet colleagues and making a choice that grew increasingly irrevocable.

In January 1932, after a further three-month visit to the Soviet Union, he announced his decision to return there permanently, a decision precipitated by Hitler's accession to power in January 1933, when Bergelson and his family learned at first hand what Nazism meant. His son Lev, at that time a schoolboy of fifteen, was beaten in the streets, and the family's apartment was searched. His wife and son left Germany almost immediately, and Bergelson joined them in Copenhagen. Although he found Denmark congenial, that country had no Yiddish-speaking community and its Jews had no interest in Yiddish belles lettres. Although his wife was reluctant to return to the Soviet Union, their son needed the acceptance of boys of his own age, and only the Soviet Union could guarantee him a university place. Consequently, at the beginning of 1934 Bergelson returned to the USSR, first visiting Birobidzhan, where a house had been built especially for him. Always an urban rather than a rural writer, however, he preferred to live in the capital.

In Moscow, Bergelson enjoyed fame and prosperity for close to fifteen years. His books, protected like those of his Russian colleagues by the state-supported Writers' Union, were printed in standard runs of thousands of copies, for which he received handsome royalties. In the spring of 1934, expectations that the Soviet Union would permit greater expansion of Yiddish culture were heightened when, on 7 May, the same day as the official opening of the important Kiev Yiddish Language Conference, the government upgraded the status of Birobidzhan from Jewish National District to Jewish Autonomous Region, a change widely seen as another step toward the creation of a Jewish Autonomous Republic. Later that year Bergelson was chosen as one of the representatives of Moscow Yiddish literature at the First All-Union Congress of Soviet Writers, a propaganda parade of unity between men of letters and the party leadership, over the course of which Bergelson was several times openly praised. Behind its gala façade, however, this Congress was convened to enforce Stalin's literary doctrine of "socialist realism," which aimed to render the discourse of Soviet literature in all languages inseparable from the discourse of the regime. As only one of four Yiddish writers permitted formally to address the Congress, Bergelson in his speech welcomed Stalin's directive that writers should become "engineers of human souls." He had no choice now but to write according to party rules.

Turning boilerplate party rhetoric into literary form, Bergelson now published a collection of stories titled *Birebidzhaner* (*People of Birobidzhan*), purportedly based on the glowing impressions he had gained during his visits there. This volume, unlike anything he had published before, startled Western readers. Its language, replete with Yiddishized acronyms for collective state enterprises, relied heavily on colloquialisms while the schematized plots and pasteboard personages of its tales predictably pitted progressive Soviet heroes against reactionary bourgeois villains. More than anything else, the collection's uncritical exaggeration made it clear that it had been written to order. Bergelson then revised a number of his earlier stories to bring them into line with acceptable party doctrine, and these "adjustments" were reissued together with a few new stories in such later volumes as *Trot nokh trot* (*Step by Step*, 1938).

A more complex problem beset Bergelson's last major work, his ambitious, quasi-autobiographical novel *On the Dnieper*, of which only two of a planned five volumes finally appeared: the first, titled by the name of its chief character as *Penek* (1932), and the second, titled *Yunge yorn* (*Years of Youth*, 1940). On one hand, the novel at its best showed Bergelson at the height of his powers, re-creating the prerevolutionary period he understood perfectly; on the other, the actions and reactions of his characters were now predetermined by ideological imperatives. The plot sought to demonstrate how the rejected youngest son of a wealthy merchant could instinctually grow up fully equipped to assimilate into proletarian society. Although it went through five Yiddish and four Russian editions and was included in the Soviet literary canon, this novel was clearly the work of a writer divided against himself. In an essay published in 1937, Bergelson argued that Yiddish writers who so skillfully used folk idioms and oral constructions to depict traditional modes of Jewish life were regrettably at a loss when their characters left the shtetl. While this essay was intended to encourage Yiddish writers to present party-approved stereotypes in party-approved clichés, it unconsciously highlighted the catastrophic effect of ideological repression on literary art in general and on Yiddish writing in particular. Jewish writers, using an exclusively Jewish vernacular, were being asked to divorce themselves from the cultural world from which they derived both their language and their inspiration in order to write about life and events that—in accordance with party ideology—had no national-cultural distinctiveness and therefore required only an impersonal, universal monotone. Bergelson had honed his remarkable gifts for the precise purpose of depicting the upper-middle classes of the decaying shtetl. Prevented by ideology from concerning himself with this "dead" world, he was left at a loss, not least because he excelled at irony and satire, and socialist realism was hostile to both. Though tightening repression did not initially affect Bergelson directly, the price he was forced to pay—like all the best of his Soviet contemporaries, whether they wrote in Yiddish or in Russian—was his artistic integrity.

In 1937, the year in which Stalin set in motion the bloodbath known as the Great Terror, many prominent voices in Soviet Yiddish letters were silenced in a wave of arrests and judicial murders. Like many who feared for their lives, Bergelson found it necessary to endorse the purge trials, and from Birobidzhan he sent to Moscow a strident denunciation of the arraigned defendants. In the bitterest of ironies, among the earliest to be purged was the fanatically doctrinaire Moyshe Litvakov, absurdly accused of belonging to the same anti-Soviet terror group in Minsk as his bitterest ideological opponents, while other writers, notably those from Kiev—like Bergelson—who had been criticized for years as petit-bourgeois nationalists, were left unharmed for another decade because the strategy pursued at this period required some token preservation of national cultures. All the same, repression was everywhere. Foreign travel and emigration was forbidden; Yiddish education was significantly reduced. This negative trend was partially reversed after the Molotov-Ribbentrop Pact in September 1939, when first eastern Poland, and then the Baltic States, Bessarabia, and northern Bukovina, fell under Soviet rule, swelling the Jewish population of the USSR from three to more than five million. For its own propaganda purposes, the regime then made use of Yiddish education and media in those areas with deep-rooted Jewish life. Though sporadic arrests of Yiddish activists continued, Soviet Yiddish literature as a whole was granted a reprieve in the years leading up to and including World War II.[15]

When Germany invaded the Soviet Union in June 1941 Bergelson was among many other Yiddish intellectuals, writers, and artists—including the whole of GOSET, the Moscow State Yiddish Theatre—evacuated to Tashkent, the capital of Uzbekistan, where they remained until October 1943.[16] There he was appointed one of the editors of *Eynikayt* (Unity), a new Yiddish periodical created to rally the world's Yiddish speakers to the cause of what Soviet terminology called "the Great Patriotic War." He also served as a member of the Jewish Antifascist Committee (JAFC), a body set up by Stalin in April 1942 under the chairmanship of the GOSET's director Solomon Mikhoels to foster international Jewish support for the USSR. As reports of Nazi extermination atrocities began pouring in, Bergelson, under pressure from Mikhoels, returned to writing plays expressing solidarity with the war effort in general and with the national identity of the Jewish people in particular. In 1943 he produced *Ikh'l lebn* (*I Will Live*), a play set in contemporary Soviet times asserting an indomitable Jewish determination to survive, while in 1946 he completed *Prints Ruveni* (*Prince Reuveni*), first published, by virtue of the wartime alliance with the West, in the New York left-wing journal *Yidishe kultur* and reissued shortly thereafter in book form.[17] While *Ikh'l lebn* was never performed in the USSR, *Prints Ruveni*, a historical drama based on the life of a sixteenth-century messianic figure who urged the Jewish people to self-redemption through force of arms, was in its final stage of rehearsal when Mikhoels was summoned to Minsk, where he was murdered on 13 January 1948 in an elaborately faked motor accident on direct orders from Stalin. Though Bergelson was no dramatist, and his plays were uniformly unsuccessful, the pain of contemporary events moved him to pen powerful expressions of Jewish national consciousness in the face of genocide.

Bergelson had embraced the Soviet Union and its ideology because he believed it offered the best chance for both the survival and the promotion of Yiddish culture through which he believed Jewish national identity in the modern world could be defined. In the aftermath of Hitler's genocide, he found a way through the iron carapace of Stalinist ideology to assert a pride in Jewish identity. The stories Bergelson wrote in response to the Holocaust, first published in *Eynikayt* and thus subject to censorship, were partially assembled and published in book form under the title *Geven iz nakht un gevorn iz tog* (*Night Fell and Day Followed*) in Moscow in 1943; a further volume appeared in Moscow four years later under the title *Naye dertseylungen* (*New Stories*). To get this work past the censors, Bergelson carefully deployed his gifts for understatement and literary allusiveness. He offered no blatant depictions of violence; instead he used individual experiences as metonyms for mass murders. The party-pleasing, antireligious contempt for Judaism's observances he had expressed in *On the Dnieper*—for which many of his readers never forgave him—were here replaced by a warm respect for Jewish pain, subtly highlighted in the context of generalized Soviet suffering at the hands of a common enemy. In several tales Bergelson consciously employs phrases from Judaism's mourning tradition, citing from its Hebrew liturgy; in other stories he drew on the teachings of Hasidic rabbis, on Jewish legend and folklore in skillful allusions evident only to fellow Jews.[18]

After the war, in company with all other members of the JAFC, Bergelson was awarded the state medal "For Valiant Labor During the Great Patriotic War, 1941–1945." Such public acknowledgment of the work of the JAFC—and of how far the JAFC and its members openly identified themselves as Jews—exacted a heavy price. Both during and after the war, Soviet government policy was strict denial that the Nazis had singled out the Jews for special persecution; all citizens of the Soviet Union, it was claimed, had suffered equally in Hitler's war of aggression. Yet by virtue of its official responsibilities, the JAFC had access to more information about the fate of Europe's Jews than was made public in the USSR. It was impossible for them not to be overwhelmed by a sense of national catastrophe, but equally impossible to show such feelings openly. Only in secret, among trusted friends, could such prohibited emotions be shared. To the general Jewish public, the Soviet Union's vote in favor of the partition of Palestine at the United Nations on 29 November 1947 suggested a change in official Jewish policy, but in reality by early 1948 Stalin had decided to eradicate Jewish culture from the USSR. Pretexts were created to place the JAFC under suspicion as a subversive organization working with American and British spies; the very agencies in the West with which it had been specifically charged to deal during the war years were now used to incriminate it. Steps were progressively taken to restrict the activities of the JAFC. In August 1946 it was placed under the control of the Central Committee Foreign Policy Division; in November its praise for the role of Jews in Soviet and world history was labeled a "chauvin-istic-Jewish deviation." Its closure was recommended because it had taken on a "nationalist and Zionist character." During the second half of 1947, increasingly vehement anti-Zionist attacks on Jewish nation-alism were launched, and Mikhoels was murdered the following Janu-ary. Despite official attempts to present his death as an accident and the lavish state funeral he was accorded, it was clear to all, Bergelson in-cluded, that there would be no renewed acceptance of Jewish national identity. On 20 November 1948, the JAFC and its organ *Eynikayt* were shut down together with three other Yiddish periodicals in Moscow, Kiev, and Birobidzhan; *Der emes*, the sole Yiddish publishing house, was disbanded; and Yiddish publications in Ukraine and Byelorussia were banned. With the abolition of most other Jewish cultural institu-tions, mass arrests of principal Yiddish cultural figures began in Sep-tember 1948 and continued until June 1949.

Bergelson was seized on the night of 23 January 1949, a week to the day after the first anniversary of Mikhoels's state funeral. Together with his fellow accused, he lingered in prison for over three years, until his trial in May 1952. Fifteen defendants, including the poets Peretz Mark-ish, David Hofshteyn, Itsik Fefer, and Leyb Kvitko, were charged with capital offenses, ranging from treason and espionage to "bourgeois na-tionalism."

At their secret trial, the principal charge brought against the leaders of the JAFC was rooted in the "Crimea question." To solve the prob-lems of dispossession and anti-Jewish hostility in the aftermath of the Holocaust, Mikhoels and others had proposed making the Crimea, where Jews had established some small agricultural colonies in the 1920s, a Soviet Jewish republic. This proposal had been strongly sup-ported, according to a report from the security services, by Bergelson, who had argued that a Jewish republic in the Crimea would be wel-comed both by the Jewish population of the Soviet Union as a whole, and by other Soviet nationalities who were reluctant to see Jews "using their talents to take over choice regions in other parts of the USSR."[19] At first the regime pretended to treat this proposal seriously, but Lazar Kaganovich, the only Jew in Stalin's Politburo, expressed its true atti-tude when he told Mikhoels that "only actors and poets" could dream up something so absurd.[20] With the start of the Cold War, Stalin chose to believe that this proposal originated with the American Joint Distribution Committee (JDC), in his view a front organization for American imperialism, which aimed to establish a Jewish homeland in the Crimea as a "bridgehead" from which to implement a long-term strategy of dismembering the Soviet Union. This plan, it was now alleged, had been devised with the JDC by Fefer and Mikhoels during their official visit to New York in 1943, and had been developed during the approved postwar visits to the USSR of the left-wing Americans Peysekh (Paul) Novick, the editor of New York's *Morgn-frayhayt,* and Sholem Aleichem's son-in-law, the Yiddish journalist Benzion Goldberg. Anxious to assess the prospects for Jewish reconstruction after the war, these two journalists had naturally spent most of their time with Yiddish-speaking colleagues at the JAFC. Now security investigators perverted their visit into an accusation that they had been American espionage agents collecting secret economic and political information from Zionist traitors.

Most of the defendants in this mock trial were brutally treated. Only Fefer, who had been the executive secretary of the JAFC and an informer for the Ministry of Internal Affairs (MVD) since at least 1943, cooperated with the investigation immediately, detailing a multitude of baseless allegations used to frame the indictment. Right to the end, Fefer was led to believe that, if he continued to cooperate, his life would be spared. Although the original intention was to conduct an open "show trial" like those of the Great Terror in 1937–1938, more urgent matters intervened and individual defendants, held in isolation for over three years, began to retract their testimony. When they were finally brought before a military tribunal in May 1952, they were required to speak in turn to "confessions" extorted under duress. Those who during the war had been explicitly entrusted with rousing international Jewish support for the Soviet war effort were now accused of replacing "proletarian internationalism" with "cosmopolitanism." The fact that four of the five writers charged had lived abroad during the 1920s—Markish in Poland and France; Hofshteyn in Palestine; Kvitko and Bergelson in Germany—was adduced as proof of their long-standing treachery. In the face of hostile questioning from the presiding judge, most could not avoid debasing themselves in a desperate attempt to save their lives, Bergelson included. Nevertheless, his testimony proved that, whether or not he was dedicated to the ideology of Communism, he was certainly dedicated to fostering Jewish national identity through the medium of Yiddish.

Jews of Bergelson's generation had been defined from childhood by a multitude of religious observances that he was now required to condemn. Forced to confess that these constituted "nationalism," he exposed the impossibility of simultaneously being an identifying Jew and an ideologically conforming Communist: "I was raised and educated in a spirit of strict nationalism [. . .] There is a day that falls in August when the Temple of Solomon was burned [Tisha B'Av, the Ninth of Av]. On this day all Jews fast for twenty-four hours, even the children. They go to the cemetery for an entire day and pray there 'together with the dead.' I was so immersed in the atmosphere of that temple being burned—people talked about it a great deal in the community—that when I was six or seven years old it seemed to me that I could smell the fumes and the fire."[21]

In the act of seemingly denouncing a boy's indoctrination in "Jewish nationalism," Bergelson actually defines a bond with the very traditions he supposedly abjures. Why elaborate on the atmosphere of Tisha B'Av to a hostile Gentile judge ignorant of Jewish law and custom? Why not denigrate the Passover Seder instead, or the twenty-four-hour liturgy of Yom Kippur, or the blessing of Levantine fruits and leaves on Sukkot? Why specifically name a fast that commemorates the Destruction of the Temple and the dispersion of the Jewish people? Jewish national mourning on this day is as much an expression of political as of religious loss. Given the extent to which Yiddish writers in the USSR, like their Russian-language counterparts, had been increasingly compelled to deploy Aesopian language to escape the censors, it is possible to read Bergelson's testimony both as an encoded equation of Bolshevik with Roman repression, and as an encoded assertion of national pride that, at one point, was explicit in Bergelson's response to the overt Jew hatred that increasingly emerged during the hearing. Taken as a whole, Bergelson's testimony could be said to exemplify, in bitter reality, the same kind of affirmation in denial that he had fictionally dramatized in some of his "Berlin" stories twenty years earlier.[22]

He admitted to the "crime" of promoting Yiddish culture, speaking feelingly of the concern he and his colleagues had felt at the closure of Yiddish schools, and at the growing refusal of Jewish parents to place their children in the few remaining schools. Pointing—consciously or not—to the success of the state's policy of forced assimilation, he highlighted his fear for the future of Soviet Yiddish culture, and admitted—because previously sanctioned conduct had now become a felony—that the Yiddish Section of the Soviet Writers' Union had repeatedly sent its members to various cities to promote Yiddish culture. The presumed encouragement of Yiddish culture by the Bolshevik regime was what had drawn him back to the USSR; that regime's malevolence in now destroying those who had taken its promises at face value was repeatedly exposed in his testimony, and that of others, in defending the work of the JAFC. To fulfill the task with which the state had charged it, the Committee had no alternative but to disseminate material specifically highlighting Soviet Jewish activities, because American Jewish institutions would publish nothing else. Similarly, the Committee had only been doing its duty by playing up the role of Jews who distinguished themselves at the front and behind the lines in reports for *Eynikayt,* since the newspaper had been specifically established to boost the morale of Yiddish-speaking Soviet Jews. How could it now be just to regard such activities as "essentially nationalistic propaganda"? Above all, Bergelson defended his right to be a Jew and to feel kinship with the Jewish people worldwide. "The anti-fascist Jews of the Soviet Union," he said, "were appealing to Jews of all countries during the war. [. . .] This was a time when people with nationalistic feelings were included in the struggle. There are many such expressions [like 'I am a child of the Jewish people'] which were permitted at the time and were appropriate then, whereas now they would be considered highly nationalistic. There was an expression 'Brother Jews.' I don't see anything wrong with this expression. [. . .] There cannot be anything criminal in the phrase 'I am a Jew.' If I approach someone and say, 'I am a Jew,' what could be bad about that?"[23]

The most ironic moment in Bergelson's testimony came when, accused by the presiding judge of "slanderously" suggesting that anti-Semitism was still rife in Ukraine, he was told that during his interrogation he had said that he wanted to leave for the Jewish autonomous district, where, as he put it, he "could die in peace." To this Bergelson replied quite simply, "The last sentence is true. I talked about wanting to move to Birobidzhan and settle there." All he now hoped for was to be allowed to die as a Jew in a Jewish place. By this time, Bergelson, like all his colleagues, must have known that he had served a lie, but in his final appeal to the court, he tried to save his life by repeating his pride in it: "I ask the court to take note of the fact that not one of the Yiddish writers of my age has entered the ranks of Soviet literature [. . .] I am the only one of that entire generation of writers who accepted the ideas of Comrades Lenin and Stalin and devoted the last thirty years to Soviet themes. I was headed toward attaining the level of a real Soviet man, but did not quite reach it, and of that I am guilty."[24]

The indictment, and Fefer's testimony on which it was founded, were so often exposed as fabrications by the defendants, in particular by Solomon Lozovsky—a former member of the Central Committee and deputy chairman of the Soviet Information Bureau (Sovinformburo)—that the authority of the security services was undermined. As Lozovsky incisively noted in one of his own interventions, "What is on trial here is the Yiddish language." To cover this judicial sham—and to protect himself—the presiding judge halted the proceedings for almost a week, appealing for further investigation. Georgii Malenkov, at that time the second man in the government, personally instructed the wavering judge to "carry out the Politburo's resolution." He did so, and prearranged death sentences were handed down on 18 July. On 12 August 1952, his sixty-eighth birthday, Bergelson was one of thirteen defendants, including two women, to be shot.[25] At the time of his arrest, the NKVD confiscated three sacks of manuscripts that, his widow believed, contained work that he had written with an increasing concern that it would never be published.

For some fifty years, the tensions of the Cold War, coupled with Shmuel Niger's critical strictures, made it easy to dismiss most of Bergelson's post-Revolution work as Stalinist propaganda. This prejudice has been deep and lasting; there are many readers, even today, unwilling to admit that some work produced under the constraints of "socialist realism" has artistic worth. Most readers of Yiddish prose associate Bergelson exclusively with the oblique and allusive style he perfected in his earliest writing, of which *The End of Everything* is the supreme example. Anything else he produced, to which the label "impressionist" cannot be attached, has been neglected, thus limiting perception of the extent of his versatility and the ways in which, throughout a long creative career, he continually reinvented himself as a writer. His political reorientation linked genuinely held socialist principles to the conviction that Yiddish culture, trapped between the assimilation demanded in the West, and the antagonism toward Yiddish in Jewish Palestine, could grow only in the Soviet Union. Yet, significantly, Bergelson returned to live in Moscow only when no other options were open to him. Whether driven by what he accepted as the irresistible forces of history, or by the yearning to live among Yiddish-speaking Jews, after thirteen years of emigration abroad, he rejected the West and returned home. In willfully blinding himself to the dangers that lurked there, he was one of thousands caught in a tragic lie. During the agonizing years he and his fellow writers spent in prison, and again through the shocking weeks of the rigged "trial," the extent of this lie would have certainly become clear to them. Their aims—to promote Yiddish language and culture by exercising their considerable talents as writers and poets—had been noble; how far they were to blame for trying to survive in a despotic system that grew increasingly more murderous and from which they could not escape is a question readers must answer for themselves.

In 1961, nine years after his death, a volume of Bergelson's selected work was published in Moscow during the Khrushchev "thaw."[26] This book, one of only six in Yiddish allowed into print between 1959 and 1961, is significant because it marked Bergelson's official Soviet "rehabilitation" and identified those of his works that were acceptable to the party line of the 1960s. Among them, interestingly, was *The End of Everything,* which was republished in its entirety. The appreciation of a masterpiece, it would seem, can survive even the most brutal vicissitudes of ideology.

2.

Set in and around the unnamed but easily identifiable city of Kiev, with its action shifting between metropolis and shtetl during a period of intense capitalist growth between 1905 and 1914, *When All Is Said and Done* views the coterminous decay of tsarist rule and traditional Eastern European Jewish life through the tangled emotions of its depressive chief character, Mirel Hurvits. She is briefly jolted out of her near-total self-absorption by the decline in fortunes of her father, Reb Gedalye, a refined and learned Jew whose old-fashioned business methods cannot compete with those of aggressive nouveaux riches like Avrom-Moyshe Burnes[27] and Yankev-Yosl Zaydenovski. In a society dominated by material values, Reb Gedalye Hurvits's bankruptcy becomes an embarrassment that renders him dead even while he is still alive: at his funeral his bier is rushed off to the cemetery "like something that ought to be hidden from sight as quickly as possible" (4.1).

Though the outward pattern of Jewish life in both shtetl and city continues to follow the rhythm of the liturgical year, and the externals of festivals are carefully observed, religious observance has essentially been reduced to a means of acquiring or retaining social status. Thus only in prosperous middle age does the unlearned Avrom-Moyshe Burnes feel the necessity to start attending prayers regularly (1.1), while the crafty Yankev-Yosl Zaydenovski leads prayers in the synagogue chiefly to indulge the same vanity (2.9) that makes him entertain lavishly on Sabbaths and festivals (3.3). Even Reb Gedalye's Judaism is more intellectual than spiritual: he reads such works of medieval Jewish philosophy as the *Kuzari* by the poet and thinker Judah Halevi, but he fails to bring up his daughter with any sense of religion (3.11). Avreml, the shtetl rabbi, is a figure of limited influence, reductively designated only by the diminutive of his personal name and daily undermined by his marriage to a commonplace social climber with a malicious streak.

Mirel, a beautiful, hypersensitive young woman around whom every action in the novel turns, is continually in search of some undefined alternative to the tedium of bourgeois life both in the shtetl and in the metropolis.[28] Her hopeless search for some meaning—the "central, overriding concern" she repeatedly mentions—and her failure to find a place for herself in a vacuous world certainly embodies the demoralization of an entire generation of young Russian Jews on the eve of revolution, yet her personal choices limit her life even further. She is not part of the intelligentsia, since she is scantily educated, has no desire to pursue further study, reads in a superficial and desultory manner, and remains rooted in a privileged class. At the age of seventeen, as Mirel herself recounts (2.3), she is betrothed to Velvl Burnes, an engagement that drags on for four years before it is broken off, making her twenty-one when the novel opens. Since its events play out over a carefully marked period of two years, she is only twenty-four when she finally disappears without a trace. In so far as she rejects what she does not want without defining any clear alternative for herself to pursue, she justifies Herz's dismissal of her as "a provincial tragedy" (2.11).

Created in the shadow of Flaubert's Emma Bovary and Tolstoy's Anna Karenina, Mirel might seem at first glance to be a proto-feminist avant la lettre. On the surface she does many things radical for her sex, time, and class. Her closest friend in the shtetl is the fiercely independent midwife Schatz; she pursues at least one extramarital affair that is sexual, and scandalously undergoes an abortion to rid herself of an unwanted child; one of the books she reads suggests some intellectual interest in the position of women in society. Yet unlike her only female friend, who is a dedicated midwife, Mirel is totally self-centered and does nothing to establish an independent life for herself. She agrees to accept as her husband Shmulik Zaydenovski, a rich young man from the metropolis who is besotted with her, in a momentary access of pity for her ruined and desperately ill father, yet she can hardly be said to sacrifice herself for him, since she seeks to cancel her betrothal almost immediately after she has agreed to it. As soon as Shmulik tearfully resists, she submits (2.13) even as she absurdly attempts to preserve her liberty by demanding the right to a celibate marriage, from which she insists she must be free to leave whenever she chooses. She subsequently permits her husband to have conjugal relations with her for the same reason she marries him—indifference rather than choice. The narrative repeatedly stresses the extent to which, as an only child, she is both spoiled and selfish; she lacks any defining moral values and is wholly unable to empathize with others. Yet her conduct does not exclusively derive from caprice: a depressive personality, she is genuinely in a state of what the twentieth century called "existential angst."

Mirel's relationships with men are always paralyzed by her image of life after marriage, which presents itself to her as a vision of endless boredom, isolation, and hopelessness, nowhere more vividly than at the party held to celebrate her betrothal to Shmulik Zaydenovski:

> The conversation flowed from sixty eating and drinking mouths simultaneously, but none of this prevented Mirel from feeling as isolated as she'd felt before when she thought of the great provincial capital where she'd live with Shmulik in three or four rooms, and imagined the streets she'd once visited there as a child with Reb Gedalye.
>
> —There one summer evening they'd stroll out somewhere as a couple, would walk slowly and have nothing to say to each other, would return home and again have nothing to speak about there. [2.9]

All Mirel seems to require of men is wealth and good looks, requirements ironically emphasized by her choice of the crippled medical student Lipkis as an interim companion. Lipkis is poor and unattractive as well as crippled, and Mirel clearly uses him to spite the rest of the shtetl. She finds the blond Shmulik physically acceptable because he looks "like a European" (2.5), but she has a sexual affair with the swarthy but handsome idler Nosn Heler, who looks "like a Romanian" (2.8). When Heler starts to bore her, she breaks off with him, realizing that a sexual liaison is not what she is looking for. Yet she rejects two other alternatives available to women of her time: the conventional role of wife and mother personified by the former revolutionary Miriam Lyubashits, and the promiscuous existence of a "free spirit" lived by her rich and dissolute cousin Ida Shpolianski. She seems always to be living between a break with one man and awakening affection for another.[29] While still engaged to Velvl she has an affair with Heler; she then separates from Velvl to take up with Lipkis, and drops Lipkis in favor of the jaded but good-looking Hebrew poet Herz. For a time she seems to long for serious love, yet reminds herself that although "other people were living fully. [. . .] For a long time now, it seemed, they'd known that love wasn't the most essential concern in life. [. . .] But then where was the most essential concern in life? Did life perhaps offer some hidden corner where a few words about it might be heard?" (2.11).

Seemingly indifferent to her own life, she struggles to establish a connection with others whom she believes to be suffering as she does, seeing reflections of her own situation in trains and their assorted passengers (2.2). Yet she is fully conscious of "the alluring power of her graceful figure" (2.6), which attracts even the Burnes family's callow young tutor, who is "captivated" by her voice, "modulated by the enervated tones of one who'd lived through a great deal yet remained stubbornly loyal to some private ideal and paid no mind to the opinions of others" (4.4). Mirel never hesitates to use her beauty to attract those she feels can assist her in some way. Thus where Heler provides her with the opportunity to explore her sexuality, Herz offers her the possibility of acquiring some intellectual insight. Setting out to capture his interest, she sees in him only what she wants to see—another directionless soul suffering in solitude. Herz's response to life is the detached cynicism of an outsider, however. He wanders about questioning the peasants like an anthropologist (2.3), yet he tends to view the world of the shtetl with neoromantic idealization: one Sabbath eve he interprets the lassitude of twilight as a manifestation of what has been identified as "historical Jewishness,"[30] an affectation undercut by Mirel's realistic awareness of its quotidian tedium (2.15).

Detached from social engagement, perhaps through disappointment at past failure, Herz withdraws completely from any practical commitment to life by writing poetry in Hebrew, an activity that embarrasses him by its futile evasion of reality at a time of revolutionary change: "Two years ago he'd poked fun at himself and told her: To write during the day was a disgrace to him personally, as well as to the entire Jewish population of the shtetl who had no need of it, so he wrote only at night, when people were asleep. At night, he said, everyone's sense of shame was diminished. And then he'd smiled and held his peace. Nothing else was left to him, he said, except this smiling silence" (2.3). His helpless disillusionment finds vivid expression in his symbolic evocation, in his "Dead City" prose poem, of "bodies clutching stones tightly in their fists. Before their deaths they had, it seemed, desired to hurl these stones at someone" (2.3). Poseur and cynic that he is, he keeps the needy Mirel at an emotional distance by ignoring her letters for a long time, so that when he eventually does respond—twice (3.16 and 4.4)—to her desperate summons, he is no longer able to help her, even if he wanted to.

For all his devotion, Mirel's husband Shmulik is the most pitiable of the men with whom she has a relationship. Though Mirel tells him frankly that, despite their betrothal, she can never love him and will always treat him badly (2.12), he nevertheless insists on going through with the marriage and then suffers bitter consequences he could easily have avoided. Emotionally immature, prepared to accept any degradation at Mirel's hands only to keep her, he lacks the dignified stoicism of Velvl Burnes, who loves Mirel just as deeply and tracks her doings with just as close an interest, but who accepts the inevitable. Mirel is vaguely aware of how badly she treats both of them but is too self-absorbed to consider their feelings. She continually pursues illusions so that, when Shmulik agrees to give her a divorce, she feels free, seemingly "recogniz[ing] on the horizon the important new life she sought" and fleetingly believing that "there was only one small thing she still needed to grasp [. . .] and the essence of her life, that which she'd been seeking for so long, from the time she'd been a child, would be clear to her" (3.10).

Shmulik's cousin Montchik, the last of the six men in the novel infatuated with Mirel, is the one with the most balanced awareness of what she is and the dead-end into which any relationship with her must lead. Fascinated by her beauty and her ever-present "sadness"— a key word almost always attached to any description of her—Montchik understands her need for "something" that no one can provide for her, but is honorably clear that, because she is the wife of another man—and one of whom he is very fond—he can be nothing more to her than a good friend, an office he loyally performs.

3.

The novel develops its theme through contrasts and parallels between the social worlds of the shtetl on one hand and the metropolis on the other. Mirel is the force that disrupts the settled rhythm of life in both, leaving no one with whom she comes into contact untouched or unchanged. Her most resolute enemy is finally not her dull-witted, self-satisfied mother-in-law but her namesake, the former student radical turned bourgeois homemaker, Miriam Lyubashits. Where Herz's frustration sluices away in mocking indifference, Miriam's thwarted zeal channels itself into the maintenance of the domestic status quo which insists that the only acceptable way of life for a woman is marriage and child-rearing, conditions that stand in total opposition to the personal autonomy Mirel demands. Having chosen the option Mirel is determined to avoid, Miriam speaks for the established social order in judging Mirel as "no longer a normal person" (3.8).[31]

The values of an all-embracing bourgeois society and the all-pervasive reach of its limited provincialism are also bodied forth in such fleetingly marginal figures as Heler's bachelor uncle who speaks Russian badly "like a dentist" and "sat on interminably in the salon with Mirel and, in the big-city manner, bored her until nightfall" (2.8); the rabbi's mother, who has a sixth finger and is mortified by this divergence from the norm (2.9); or one of the guests at a late-night drinking party in Schatz's cottage, "some teacher or other from a nearby shtetl, a shabby thirty-eight-year-old fellow in a blue peasant blouse who'd once had rabbinical ordination and the daughter of a ritual slaughterer for a wife, but was now in love with a prosperous shopkeeper's daughter not yet seventeen years of age" (2.14).

Often these subsidiary figures serve as a kind of chorus, commenting obliquely on the main action: the cutting remark of Schatz's aged grandmother; for example—"Whoever talks less about herself talks less foolishness" (2.3)—makes a sharp comment on the unremitting solipsism of both Schatz and Mirel. Similarly, a group of boisterous young tailors' apprentices undercut Mirel's pretensions by mocking her (2.5), and stress the irrevocable passing of the old order by accidentally breaking some windows in her father's abandoned house (4.2). Members of the small-town intelligentsia that surround Mirel, like the pharmacist's assistant Safyan, the student from Paris, Esther Finkel, and the local Hebrew teacher Shabad (2.11), are all indifferent to her besetting preoccupations, while her search for independence identifies her to the shtetl's young bachelors merely as a woman of easy virtue and thus exposes her to lewd insults like that offered by the lascivious polytechnic student at Tarabay's party (2.6). In the city, her beauty is objectified—on a streetcar it reminds an officer of his lost first love and his present unsatisfactory marriage (3.1)—and simply makes her conscious of what seems to be near-universal promiscuity (3.1).

Characters are largely identified by recurring and judgmental epithets marking their distinguishing characteristics. For instance, Velvl —like Mirel's father—always thinks of her in the affectionate diminutive as "Mirele," Reb Gedalye is always presented as a pointed nose and gold-rimmed glasses, and Montchik has huge black eyes. Shmulik's mother, whose personal name, Mindel, is mentioned only once (2.4), is always designated "the mother-in-law" regardless of the different relationship in which she stands to other characters. Themes, too, are developed through descriptions of the physical world that consistently reflect psychological interiority. Mirel's horror of the frozenness of life in the shtetl, for example, is powerfully inferred from the anthropomorphism of the narrative's presentation of its winter landscapes:

> Like great beasts, houses hunkered down ponderously under their heavy, snow-covered roofs and dozed in an unending reverie.
>
> It seemed:
>
> These houses had ears, hidden, highly attentive ears, continually listening to the great silence that bore down on everything around both from close by and from far away.
>
> It seemed:
>
> They were ready, in response to the slightest, most remote rustle from the fields, to spring up and in great rage and haste rush to confront it, like those starving dogs that race forward to challenge some alien intruder of their own species, an unwelcome guest. [2.2]

Inanimate objects denote material and social standing, like the contrasting sleighs of the Hurvits and Burnes families en route to Tarabay's party (2.6), or the expensive, imported curtains and velvet runners in the Hurvits house, which are signs of past prosperity and reminders of present decay (2.4); they are later invested with human emotions, seemingly mourning for the loveless marriage that will destroy Mirel and her family (2.15). Both in the shtetl and in the "quiet suburb" of the metropolis, the windows of houses are personified as eyes either looking out brightly or shut in darkness; almost always, those who stand outside are cut off from any emotional warmth, their emotions mirrored in the harsh elements outdoors, as with Shmulik:

> That night, walking round his house, he came to that part of the garden on which the windows of Mirel's room looked out. The place was sodden. An autumn shower, driven by a gust of wind, streamed down diagonally while the cherry trees shuddered, were soaked, and protested faintly against something. A row of old poplar trees standing at one end of the orchard all bowed their crowns in the same direction, gesturing despondently to the heavily overcast corner of the sky from which the wind was driving the clouds:
>
> —From over there . . . That's where the misfortune's coming from.
>
> The shutters of Mirel's room were fastened from within, but the glow of a burning lamp striking through their cracks indicated that she was still awake. [3.9]

The subjective, emotional nature of reactions and reflections—those of other characters as much as Mirel's—are frequently conveyed in this metaphorical correspondence between the physical and the emotional. A vivid illustration is the way the yearning for one character by another is conveyed almost cinematically by the use of light. Keen to see Herz again but unwilling to admit it even to herself, Mirel unexpectedly runs into him:

> A little while later, when she emerged from the pharmacy, the distant flame-red sun hung low on the western horizon like a great golden coin, and standing alone on the outskirts of a shtetl poised to receive the Sabbath was Herz. [. . .] With his face wholly steeped in the glow of the setting sun, he appeared to be made of gold. [2.15]

A parallel description conveys Nosn Heler's desperate desire to see Mirel once more:

> Every now and then he screwed up his eyes and gazed intently toward the farthest end of the street on which the distant low-hanging sun still blazed

down, inflaming the yellowing leaves on the surrounding trees and the roofs on the nearby houses. From time to time some gilded person emblazoned with red-gold sunshine approached from that direction—but it wasn't Mirel. When he did finally catch sight of her coming toward him, he failed to recognize her and didn't believe that it could really be she. [3.2]

The narrative's repeated use of verbal markers of imprecision like "apparently," "seemingly," "thought" suggests that situations offered to the reader are perceived through some unnamed filtering consciousness. Indirect sentences using impersonal pronouns and the passive voice deliberately avoid identifying the perceiver and blur together the third-person narrative voice with the thoughts and speech of individual characters, as in Heler's desperation to make Mirel commit herself to him, for example:

> He was still unable to gather the thread of his thoughts. Fancying that Mirel was looking at him as though he were a babbling idiot, he grew even more agitated; he was overcome with a powerful resentment against her that helped him to pull himself together and quite suddenly to say what he wanted, without fully anticipating it himself.
>
> —This was what he wanted to know: did Mirel love him? She couldn't deny it. So he asked only one thing of her: why didn't she want to divorce her husband and marry him, Heler?
>
> Mirel heard him out, shrugged her shoulders, and glanced down at the lines she'd scratched out on the ground with the tip of her parasol:
>
> —Well, and afterward, after the wedding . . . ? [3.2]

The capacity of the novel's allusive, indirect discourse to create a polyphony of voices that make it difficult if not impossible to determine not only who is speaking but what is being said—and the implications of what is supposedly said—is well illustrated in the ambiguity of Reb Gedalye's dying words. These are not directly heard but are reported by a third party:

> Holding his glass of whiskey, the rabbi spoke to those assembled about Reb Gedalye of blessed memory:
>
> —This is what happened . . . Right at the end, this is what happened: he said to me, Avreml, he said to me, why are you weeping? . . . Foolish fel-

low: if I felt I were leaving anyone behind me, I'd make the journey there as readily as going to a dance.

All those who stood round heard and were silent. Only one man, an emaciated, timid sycophant who was unemployed, edged unobtrusively closer to someone at the back and smiled foolishly in consequence of the liquor he'd drunk. Wanting to make some allusion to the many young men whom Mirel had always dragged around with her as she wandered over the shtetl and to the fact that she'd not come down to the shtetl here after her father's death, he remarked snidely:

—Evidently Reb Gedalye knew his own daughter, eh? Evidently he knew very well what she was. [4.2]

This remark is puzzling, because its meaning is not straightforward. Strictly speaking, Reb Gedalye does "leave someone behind": his daughter Mirel, who should be his heir. But Mirel is both unwilling and unable to inherit anything, whether material or spiritual, from her father. Her estrangement from her parents is clear even before her marriage, and intensifies after it. Does Reb Gedalye recognize on his deathbed that his daughter is as brutally unfeeling as the nasty bystander suggests to the rabbi's listeners? Is Reb Gedalye mourning because his name will never be perpetuated through a male heir? Are these in truth Reb Gedalye's last words, or are they a pious fabrication retailed by the rabbi? The fact that his purported remark fits any or all of these possibilities is part of the purpose of the narrative discourse, which subtly transforms ambiguous individual remarks into thematic statements. To accept only one of these possible meanings would restrict the implication of what has been said, and would make obvious and one-sided what the narrative insists is complex, indirect, and diffuse. Reb Gedalye's ambivalent remark moves the particular to the general and the personal to the communal. The house he lives in becomes a metaphor for the society of which he was once a leading representative; it has no heir to take it over but remains deserted and desolate because the world it inhabits is dead. The polyphonic narrative discourse thus transforms the purported dying words of one individual into a metaphorical sigh of regret for the death of an entire world and way of life. The vision of a "dead city" expressed through the voice of the poet Herz can be read as a lament for the sociopolitical stagnancy that appeared to have taken permanent hold in Russia after the failure of the 1905 revolution. It may also be said to define the essential pessimism of Bergelson's oeuvre. The characters crowding his fiction remain as perplexing to themselves as to others. Their speech and actions are never unambiguous: speech is often an intrusion upon more eloquent silence; actions are generally reactions to circumstances over which they have no control. In Bergelson's early work, no particular actions are privileged above others; the events of his fiction, sometimes banal, sometimes violent, are presented with equal emphasis.

To articulate this elusiveness, Bergelson developed a style characterized by the choric repetition of set phrases and sentences and the general subordination of direct to reported speech, a mode resembling the use of the free indirect discourse devised by the French novelist Gustave Flaubert (1821–1880) for *Madame Bovary*, which appeared in Russian translation in 1858, one year after it was first published in French.[32] What is said by an individual character and what is observed by the third-person narrative voice frequently become indistinguishable, a process that Bergelson advances by his repeated use of the passive voice to cloud the possibility of ascribing judgments exclusively to the character from whom they ostensibly emanate.

Typical of this technique is a moment early in the novel when Mirel's frustration at the tedium of shtetl existence is generalized in a passage of description that deliberately blurs the source of the feelings described:

> Short damp days followed in quick succession, driving the shtetl ever deeper into winter. Neither indoors nor outdoors offered anything to awaken interest, stirring instead the same indifferent discontent toward everything around, so that one might as well stop every overgrown girl who occasionally strolled down the main street in smartly dressed self-importance, vent one's frustration on her, and rebuke her in the voice of an older, deeply discontented woman:
>
> —Why are you so choosy, you? . . . Why don't you get married? Why?
> [2.2]

Above all, by creating vivid images through unexpected use of language, Bergelson's style presents the reader with new ways of seeing and feeling. So, for example, the grief that overcomes Mirel when she finally recognizes the futility of all her struggles is perceived as an all-embracing anguish that has a manifest physical presence: "The whole house was dark, silent and forlorn. The night had utterly enveloped it, had everywhere coiled itself around the extinguished shtetl and far beyond, encircling the surrounding fields where the desolation of all those asleep beat quietly on the ground" (4.5). Encouraging a nonlinear reading, the densely layered narrative steadily suggests an ever-widening range of alternatives for comprehending superficially commonplace situations.

The actual phrase *nokh alemen,* "the end of everything," is used only three times in the novel, twice near the beginning and once at the end. In Part 1, reluctantly recognizing that he has lost Mirel for good, Velvl muses: "Did this mean that the betrothal was really over, that this was the end of everything?" (1.4). When Mirel makes the irretrievable decision to marry Shmulik, a man she dislikes, she enters her father's deserted house late in the afternoon of the Fast of Esther and is confronted by a vision of utter desolation: "Mirel could see no one. No one stopped her, no one was made happier by her arrival. Something, it seemed, was too late here, had already ended" (2.8). Finally, in Part 4 the phrase, in stressing the void left by the death of Mirel's father, anticipates her own ultimate effacement: "the desolation that follows when everything has ended clung to the walls and ceiling, calling again to mind that Reb Gedalye was now dead and that Gitele had now no single place on earth" (4.2).

In seeking to assess what is left after profound change, this phrase, from which the novel draws its title, defines the frustration of almost all the major characters, who realize by the end of all their searching that what they thought would make them happy is, when all is said and done, unattainable. The extent to which each is able to accept that he will never achieve the happiness he seeks is what finally determines his capacity or incapacity to go on living.

NOTES

1. David Bergelson, *At the Depot,* in *A Shtetl and Other Yiddish Novellas,* ed. and trans. Ruth Wisse (New York: Behrman House, 1973), 79–139; repr. Detroit: Wayne State University Press, 1986, 79–139.

2. David Bergelson, "The Deaf Man" and "Two Roads," in *No Star Too Beautiful: Yiddish Stories from 1382 to the Present,* ed. and trans. Joachim Neugroschel (New York: W. W. Norton, 2002), 416–18; 424–43.

3. In English as "Departing," in *The Stories of David Bergelson: Yiddish Short Fiction from Russia,* trans. Golda Werman (Syracuse: Syracuse University Press, 1996), 25–154; as *Descent,* trans. Joseph Sherman (New York: Modern Language Association, Texts and Translations Series, 1999).

4. For more about the *Kultur-lige,* see Hillel Kazovsky, *The Artists of the Kultur-lige* (English and Russian) (Jerusalem-Moscow: Michael Greenberg, 2003).

5. For more detail, see David Shneer, *Yiddish and the Creation of Soviet Jewish Culture, 1918–1930* (Cambridge: Cambridge University Press, 2004), 60–87.

6. Some of these have recently been published in English translation; see Joachim Neugroschel, trans., *The Shadows of Berlin: The Berlin Stories of Dovid Bergelson* (San Francisco: City Lights Books, 2005).

7. There are two English versions of this story: "Impoverished," in *The Stories of David Bergelson,* trans. Golda Werman, 14–24; and "The Déclassés," in *The Mendele Review (TMR),* trans. Joseph Sherman, Vol. 09.009, http://www2.trincoll.edu/~mendele/tmrtoc09.htm.

8. A reworked version of this piece appears in English as "Civil War," in *Ashes Out of Hope: Fiction by Soviet Yiddish Writers,* ed. Irving Howe and Eliezer Greenberg, trans. Seth Wolitz (New York: Schocken, 1977), 84–123.

9. English translation, under this title, by Joseph Sherman in *Midstream* 54, no. 4 (July/August 2008): 39–40.

10. "Two Murderers," translated by Joachim Neugroschel, in *The Shadows of Berlin,* 1–8; "Old Age," translated by Joachim Neugroschel, in *The Shadows of Berlin,* 9–20; "Obsolescence," translated by Joseph Sherman, *Midstream* 38, no. 5 (July/August 2002): 37–42.

11. "Hershl Toker," translated by Joseph Sherman, *Midstream* 37, no. 8 (December 2001): 24–29. I have critically examined this story in some detail; see Joseph Sherman, "'Who Is Pulling the Cart?' Bergelson and the Party Line, 1919–1927,' *Jews in Russia and Eastern Europe* 1, no. 52 (2004): 5–36.

12. An English translation of this essay can be found in Joseph Sherman and Gennady Estraikh, eds., *David Bergelson: From Modernism to Socialist Realism* (Oxford: Legenda, 2007), 347–55.

13. Yevgeny Zamyatin (1884–1937) had published his dystopian satire *We* in Prague, while in Berlin Boris Pilnyak (1894–1937) had brought out his novella *Mahogany*, which satirizes NEP-men—unscrupulous profiteers who exploited the capitalistic aspects of Lenin's New Economic Policy (NEP, 1921–29) for personal gain—who descend on a provincial town seeking to snap up mahogany furniture from impoverished townspeople, and offers a sympathetic depiction of a Trotskyite who is unhappy with the changes he finds here, his hometown. Both were viciously persecuted.

14. To ensure his survival, the young Yiddish writer Shmuel Gordon (1909–1998), who had ingenuously published some poems in *Literarishe bleter*, was compelled to make a groveling public apology for this lapse.

15. For a fuller discussion, see Gennady Estraikh, *In Harness: Yiddish Writers' Romance with Communism* (Syracuse: Syracuse University Press, 2005).

16. See Jeffrey Veidlinger, *The Moscow State Yiddish Theater: Jewish Culture on the Soviet Stage* (Bloomington: Indiana University Press, 2000), 216, 235–40.

17. For a detailed analysis of this play see Jeffrey Veidlinger, "*Du lebst, mayn folk: Prints Ruveni* in Historical Context," in Sherman and Estraikh, eds., *David Bergelson*, 248–68.

18. For a fuller discussion, see Joseph Sherman, "'Jewish Nationalism' in Bergelson's Last Book," in Sherman and Estraikh, eds., *David Bergelson*, 285–305.

19. See Shimon Redlich, *War, Holocaust and Stalinism* (Luxembourg: Harwood Academic Publishers, 1995), 45.

20. Joshua Rubenstein and Vladimir P. Naumov, eds., *Stalin's Secret Pogrom: The Postwar Inquisition of the Jewish Anti-Fascist Committee* (New Haven: Yale University Press, 2001), 20–21.

21. Rubenstein and Naumov, *Secret Pogrom*, 150–51.

22. For an analysis of one such story, see Joseph Sherman, "A Note on Bergelson's 'Obsolescence,'" *Midstream* 38, no. 5 (July/August 2002): 37–42.

23. Rubenstein and Naumov, *Secret Pogrom*, 157–58.

24. Ibid., 478.

25. All fifteen were condemned, fourteen to death and one to a term of exile, but one died in prison before the sentence could be carried out.

26. Hirsh Remenik, ed., *Dovid Bergelson: Oysgeveylte verk* (Moscow: Melukhe-farlag fun kinstlerisher literatur, 1961).

27. His surname is pronounced "Boor-ness."

28. See, for instance, Mikhail Krutikov, *Yiddish Fiction and the Crisis of Modernity, 1905–1914* (Stanford: Stanford University Press, 2001), 190–200.

29. These are among a number of illuminating insights offered in an analysis of the novel by Susan Ann Slotnick, "The Novel Form in the Works of David Bergelson," Ph.D. diss., Columbia University, 1978, 55–171.

30. This is suggested in a severely Marxist reading of the novel by Yekheskel Dobrushin, *Dovid Bergelson* (Moscow: Emes, 1947), 67–69.

31. Slotnick, "The Novel Form," 167–69.

32. For a fuller discussion of this influence, see Daniela Mantovan, "Language and Style in *Nokh alemen* (1913): Bergelson's Debt to Flaubert," in Sherman and Estraikh, *David Bergelson,* 89–112.

The End of Everything

1.1

For four long years the provincial, small-town engagement dragged on between them, and ended in the following way.

She, Reb* Gedalye Hurvits's only child Mirele, eventually returned the betrothal contract and once more took to keeping company with the crippled student Lipkis.

The rejected fiancé's nouveau-riche father, enormously wealthy and genteelly taciturn, constantly paced about in his study with a cigarette between his lips, musing on his three great estates and wondering whether it was perhaps unbecoming for him to remember either the name of the man to whom he'd almost become related by marriage or the returned betrothal contract. Dark and tall, he was an unlearned individual who, having acquired a veneer of refinement, had, at the age of forty-eight, started regularly attending both afternoon and evening prayer services in the nearby study house.

And his mother, a squat, obese woman whose asthma obliged her to breathe hoarsely and with difficulty, like a force-fed goose, first became

---

Reb is a Yiddish title of respect accorded to older men or strangers; it is the equivalent of the Polish term *Pan*.

aware of the returned contract considerably later when, sunburned and disconsolate, she returned from abroad without having found any cure at all. Quietly and dolefully she cursed the former fiancée in virtually the same breath as that dismal Marienbad* which had frittered away her strength and spirits to no effect. Repeatedly shaking and rubbing one of her rheumatic legs, she brooded silently:

—God knew whether she'd ever live to see her son's wedding.

One evening, when she was hosting out-of-town guests in her house, she caught sight of Mirele and the crippled student passing the open window nearby. No longer able to contain herself, she thrust her head outside, and shouted after Mirele at the top of her hoarse and breathless voice:

—He's a pauper already, that father of hers!—and that's the way he'll always be! So why's she still frisking about like a bitch in heat, that one?—Yes, her, that one right over there!

And he, the tall, handsome twenty-seven-year-old bachelor, could not endure it. Then and there he rebuked his mother:

—Hush! Hush! Just look at her.

By nature he was a patient and quiet young man, loved his nouveau-riche, genteelly reserved father, and wanted everything to be conducted as quietly and courteously in their own home as in the homes of the Gentile landowners with whom, through his father, he'd been involved in business dealings from the time he was sixteen years old. However, since he found it distasteful to remain in the shtetl and watch Mirele strolling about every evening with the crippled student, his father leased the Bitznev farm in the nearby village for him† and he moved

---

*Marienbad is a spa town in the Carlsbad region of what is today the Czech Republic. During the second half of the nineteenth century, when the town was part of the Austro-Hungarian Empire, many European celebrities and aristocrats came to enjoy its curative carbon dioxide springs. Wealthy and assimilated Jews went there to seek well-connected matches for their daughters and sons. Before World War I it averaged about twenty thousand visitors every year.

†This kind of large farm, known in Polish as a *folwark,* was operated in the Polish-Lithuanian Commonwealth from the fourteenth until well into the twentieth centuries to produce surplus grain for export. The first *folwarks* were created on church-owned land; later they were adopted by both the Polish nobility (*szlachta*)

there, not too far away, settling into the whitewashed landowner's cottage, which shared the same courtyard as the house of the village priest.

Here in the quiet, deserted village the Gentiles called him *Panicz*, 'little master,' and doffed their caps to him, and his two younger sisters with their overweight, wheezing mother often came to visit, bringing him gifts of home-baked pastries. In his own home he always smiled at his sisters because they were being tutored by a university student and because they were still meeting her, the young woman who'd returned the betrothal contract to him. He pressed their hands and asked them:

—How are you? How are you getting on?

Here in his own home he wanted to show his mother exactly the same respect that mothers received in the homes of those landowners who ran estates they either owned or leased in the neighborhood. He always remained standing in her presence, and since courtesy dictated that he could address her in neither the familiar nor the formal mode, he always spoke to her in the third person:

—Would Mother like to drink tea? Would Mother perhaps like to lie down?

Only when, complaining about her illness and bewailing the fact that he didn't get married, she began cursing her, the young woman who'd returned the betrothal contract, was he displeased, and pulling a somewhat sour face he rebuked her angrily but politely in the same way he would rebuke her angrily and politely in his father's house:

—Hush! Hush! Just look at her.

He seldom returned to his parents' home and then only when business made it necessary. There he conducted himself courteously and quietly, like a welcome guest from out of town, smiling politely as he stood opposite his sisters, or slowly lifted the little boy who ran past, placed him on the table, stroked his grubby cheeks, and asked winningly:

—What are you doing, eh? Are you running around?

He spent almost all his time there with his father in the small, per-

---

and rich Polish peasants, and the export grain they produced was a central part of the economy.

petually smoke-filled study, discussing various commercial transactions, thinking of the dowry money—his six thousand and Mirele's three thousand rubles, all still on deposit with the old Count of Kashperivke—and fearful that his father would soon start in again:

—Yes, those six thousand rubles still lying with the Count . . . What'll become of those six thousand rubles on deposit with the old Count of Kashperivke?

At that time Reb Gedalye Hurvits, the man who was to have been his father-in-law, an absent-minded Torah scholar of distinguished lineage with little head for business, was in serious financial difficulty, and his creditors stood about in the marketplace every afternoon openly calculating what he was worth:

—It seems that he's invested five thousand rubles in the Kashperivke woods . . . and three thousand in Zhorzhovke poppy seed. And what about the mill? How much did he lose in that unlucky Ternov mill after Shavuot?*

Why Reb Gedalye didn't withdraw his three thousand rubles from the Count was impossible to fathom, and, as Velvl sat in the small study, he wanted his father to go on smoking his cigarettes in silence, to go on pacing back and forth for as long as possible, and to go on thinking as he did about the man who would have been his father-in-law:

Apparently he understood his only child very well . . . To this day he'd apparently not given up hope about making the match.

Once, late on a Sunday afternoon, when the whole house stood almost deserted awaiting the return of those of its occupants who'd gone out, he lingered longer than usual in that dark little study with his father. At length he heard his younger sister, who'd only just returned from her walk, taking off her corset in an adjoining room and wondering aloud about something.

—How do you like that Mirele? Can you understand her?

---

*Shavuot, the Feast of Weeks, coincides with the harvest festival and is celebrated, according to the Hebrew calendar, on the sixth day of the month of Sivan (usually corresponding to the secular month of June).

Obviously Mirele had met his sister on the promenade only a moment before, had stopped her there, and had asked her something, which was why here, in this half-darkened room, his heart leapt and he abruptly forgot what he'd just been discussing with his father. Perhaps three times he repeated the same pointless words, overcome with a powerful desire to join his sister in her room and question her about her encounter, but he composed himself, remained where he was in the study, and in the end asked nothing of her. Later, with other members of the household, his sister came out with him, saw him seat himself in his buggy and drive off to spend the night on his farm. As he pulled away from the house, he merely smiled at her and nodded somewhat too vigorously. He knew that Mirele, escorted by the crippled student, was quite capable of accosting his sister on the promenade and shamelessly inquiring after him, her former fiancé:

—What's Velvl doing at present?

—Why don't we ever see Velvl in town?

Anything was possible with Mirele. That other incident, for example—when had it taken place? Only the other day, in company with the crippled student, she'd gone into the town's only grocery store in the middle of the marketplace regardless of the fact that she'd recognized his buggy waiting for him outside and knew that he must be inside himself. At the time he'd been overcome with confusion, had wanted to get out of the shop as quickly as possible, and had asked the shopkeeper more loudly than normal:

—Please see that the account is prepared by Sunday . . . at least not later than Sunday.

And then, without hesitation, she'd stopped him to ask:

—Did he really think it suited him, that soft light beard he'd recently permitted himself to grow?

The crippled student, standing with someone in the doorway of the shop, wanted to show that he wasn't in the slightest concerned that Mirele was talking to her former fiancé, so he shouted out rather too loudly:

—Who says that a through draft can be harmful? Does it say so in black and white in the medical textbooks?

As Velvl's perfectly healthy young man's heart began beating abnormally fast, he imagined that he did well to smile and answer with a barb:

—Some people like beards, and some do not.

Anyway, he made known that he still had his pride and was quite capable of defending himself. And the main thing . . . the main thing was that he'd done well to repeat loudly to the shopkeeper:

—Could he be certain that his account would be prepared by Sunday?

In this way he'd at least given her to understand that he was a busy man wholly engrossed by his farm, and cared very little for the idle chatter she engaged in every day with the crippled student.

All the way home he'd been greatly agitated and had reflected:

—Practically all the grain on his fields had sprouted and was already starting to turn green.

The grain looked promising, but even without it he'd still earn tolerably that year. In the winter, when trodden snow lay frozen on the ground and his workerless farm stood silent and dormant, he'd buy a polished sleigh and a fur coat with a detachable collar and, traveling into town, would frequently come upon Mirele with the student on their way to visit an acquaintance somewhere.

1.2

The time for harvesting and gathering in the grain soon came. The work on the farm intensified, and he had no time even to think about going into town.

Peasants, men and women alike, with scythes in their hands, were deployed across his fields, and wagons, both his own and those he'd borrowed, carted the dried sheaves uphill to the barn, where a steam-driven machine positioned between huge haystacks had been puffing away since very early that morning, whistling every time the water in its boiler evaporated, cheerfully threshing the full, dry ears of wheat.

All day long he galloped about on horseback, busy everywhere, supervising the reapers and the farm laborers who cleaned and weighed the grain in the gloomy low-roofed sheds, snatching time in order also to visit the steam threshing machine, where he rebuked the lazy, smiling peasant girls.

Almost every day during that period he rose at first light and fell asleep as the sun set, dropping onto his bed dusty and exhausted, content that the warm night gave promise of a fine, clear day to follow.

That was the time when he usually slept fully clothed, dreaming virtually uninterruptedly of his noisy, bustling barn and his newly furnished cottage in which, astonishingly, Mirele seemed somehow to be wandering about, smiling at those townsfolk who'd come to buy his wheat and suggesting, from her chair near the ever-ready samovar:

—Velvl, perhaps these men would like to take a glass of tea with us?

The all-embracing air, the huge barns filled with hay, and the great heaps of threshed grain all mutely suggested that his tireless work— his galloping about, his lack of sleep, and the money he was earning— had some kind of intimate connection with Mirele and the crippled student who spent days on end wandering about the shtetl together; all of it also suggested that possibly it would all lead to important changes ultimately, that in Reb Gedalye Hurvits's house there would be considerable regret about the broken engagement, and every time his buggy was seen through the window, those inside would comment to each other:

—Velvl's only just driven past; he's come by with a new pair of horses.

And when the work and the commotion that attended it had finally ended and the entire harvest of threshed grain had filled all his low-roofed sheds, only then, as though awakening from a dream, did he begin to look about him and to realize:

The hottest two and a half months of the summer had already passed and the days had grown noticeably shorter and cooler; he himself was exhausted and too often slept fully dressed both by day and by night, starting awake at the sound of the slightest spurt of rain that came clattering down on his tin roof from the overcast skies, and then lying half-asleep with eyes wide open, thinking:

—His beets* . . . they were growing . . . they were growing . . .

---

*Because the root of the sugar beet contains a high concentration of sucrose, it was grown commercially for sugar in the tsarist empire.

In this way, fully dressed, he slept through one of the Gentile holidays. When he awoke, it was already dark and chilly outdoors, and here and there in the village houses the first fires of night were trembling into life. The dark air was heavy with silence, and only the light breeze outside knew sorrowful stories about the day that had died. Through the darkness it gusted in toward him from the open window, and once inside, it grieved despondently:

—The day has finally ended . . . finally ended . . .

Well rested and composed, he bathed, donned white collar and cuffs, slowly drank some tea, and ordered his buggy harnessed:

—It's high time, it seems, to take a trip into town . . . eh? Certainly, high time.

He'd not been there for so long and yearned for it.

Sitting in his buggy, he unhurriedly considered whether he ought to instruct his driver to urge the horses on faster; that if he were to do so he might still reach the shtetl early enough to ensure that, from among the strolling couples at the head of the street, Mirele and the crippled student might yet recognize him.

But he said not a word to the driver, allowing him to travel the whole way at a dignified and leisurely pace. Once, when the driver was irritated at the right-hand horse and lashed it unnecessarily in anger, he rebuked him in the tone of a highly regarded householder, a prominent man of affairs:

—Gently! Gently! There's no reason to hurry.

Though a little annoyed, he was calm and sedate, thinking constantly of Mirele and shrugging his shoulders as he did so:

—Really, someone might think that he needed her . . . that he was running after her.

Not far from the town, however, filled with more than usual yearning, his heart started beating faster, and in confusion he began casting agitated glances at the couples strolling past, heedless of the fact that it was almost totally dark outdoors and thus difficult to distinguish the features of people even from close by. He was angry at himself for continually turning to look at these couples, was loath to watch them, yet went on staring anyway, brooding all the while:

—She wasn't there . . . Not that it made any difference to him . . . But she was definitely not there.

From various corners of the town, early evening fires gazed pensively at his passing buggy. They reminded him of how much time had elapsed since he'd been here even once, intensified his longing for his former fiancée, and made dearer the remembrance of her sorrowful features, so long unseen.

Thoughts arose:

Now she was undoubtedly sitting over there, in one of those brightly lit town houses, sad and indifferent to the people surrounding her, her blue eyes fixed on the lamp, saying nothing.

And were there to be some talk of Velvl Burnes, were someone over there to say,

"He'll earn a considerable sum this year . . . without doubt a considerable sum . . ."

she would, for a moment, tear her sad eyes away from the lamp and ask, "Who? Velvl Burnes?" and then she'd go on staring sadly at the lamp for a long time and in silence, and no one would know whether she regretted returning the betrothal contract or not.

Unexpectedly, someone stopped his buggy near the first of the town's houses and began yelling out to him:

—They weren't at home, his father and mother . . . Very early yesterday morning they'd gone off to the provincial capital.

He turned round swiftly and saw:

A young man who worked as a steward, a commonplace steward, on one of his father's estates who was returning to the village for the night.

And for some reason there seemed something disrespectful in the fact that over some triviality this young man in the high boots had stopped him here at the very edge of town; in the fact that, without his knowledge, his parents had for motives of their own gone off to the provincial capital very early the day before.

One person among the strolling couples seemed to pause and laugh at his discomfiture, so in annoyance he yelled back at the steward:

—So what? Does it matter that they're not at home?

And he immediately poked his driver in the back and ordered him to drive on faster. He was agitated and distracted, and as his buggy drew steadily nearer the center of town, he continued to brood:

—What a fool that steward was . . . What a stupid idiot of a steward . . .

But approaching his father's house, which was situated opposite the marketplace, he saw all the windows of the salon brightly illuminated and beaming festively out into the night. All at once forgetting his own agitation, he was astonished:

—Could there really be guests there? . . . What kind of guests could possibly be calling now?

Thinking immediately of Mirele, he stole a glance at her father's house, the darkened windows of which looked out in this direction from the opposite side of the street, and felt his heart pounding within him:

—Mirele was capable of anything! Even now she might've called on his sisters.

In the brightly lit entrance hall he slowly took off his dust coat. He was in no rush, and even had time to smile at the elderly woman, their cook, who was hurrying through the dining room. He felt personally very satisfied with this smile.

—Whatever the case, it behooved him now to be composed and cautious, and the main thing . . . the main thing was to be in no rush, and to give no indication that he was pleased at her coming.

Various voices carried from the salon into the dining room, which he finally entered. Much theorizing and disagreement was going on there, and the crippled student, who was also present, was trying to shout above everyone else:

—Just a minute: how much have the metaphysicians given us up until now?

A child, one of Velvl's little brothers, coming out of the salon into the dining room by chance, caught sight of him, rushed over and threw his arms around his knees; Velvl lifted him up and smilingly stood him on a chair:

—You're running around, eh? Running around?

But the door of the salon had been left open behind the little boy, and from time to time Velvl's eyes were stealthily drawn in that direction where they saw:

Apart from the crippled Lipkis, also seated there were the big-city university student whom his father had employed as a tutor to the children not long before, one of his younger sisters, and a large, unknown young woman. His sister and this young woman were sitting on the soft divan while the two students were standing opposite each other with flushed faces, deeply absorbed in their dispute.

He finally went in, learned something from his sister about his parents' departure, crossed over to the big-city student and, offering him his hand, politely inquired:

—How was he? How was life treating him?

The student, however, was so carried away by his own theorizing that he made no reply, continuing to shout at the crippled Lipkis instead:

—What about love, then? . . . What about every thought that's transmuted into *oshchushchenie*, into sensation, into feeling?

Here in his father's house these two students didn't notice him, spent the whole evening theorizing about matters he didn't understand, and even forgot that he was hovering about near them. For his own part, he was obliged to stay the night there and, returning to his farm at nine o'clock the next morning, had to pass through the western end of the town and see:

Mirele, dressed for an outing, sitting in a phaeton* hired from the capital and waiting near a neighboring house for the crippled student Lipkis, waiting in pleasurable anticipation and smiling. And he, the crippled Lipkis . . .

He was limping in great haste toward the phaeton with a highly distracted, freshly washed face, paying no attention to that fact that his widowed mother was shouting after him from the open front door:

—Lipe, I beg you: take your thick overcoat . . . What's the matter with you, Lipe? . . . Take your overcoat.

---

*A light four-wheeled open carriage with one or two seats facing forward, drawn by a pair of horses.

Returning to his farm, Velvl felt deeply upset, and finally decided:

—From now on he'd seldom go into town . . . very, very seldom . . .

1.3

And he did indeed seldom go into town, very, very seldom.

He even told one of the brokers, who proposed some buyers for the rest of the grain:

—It might be more appropriate for these merchants to come down here, to me . . . It's perfectly all right; I never turn anyone out of my house.

As he made this remark, he was convinced that the broker would repeat what he'd said in the home of his former fiancée's father; that in the end merchants from the town would politely and respectfully start calling on him here, as politely and respectfully as they called on the Gentile landowners around him.

Every day he went calmly and in quiet expectation to the low-roofed sheds in which he stored his grain before moving beyond, where large numbers of peasant men and women had spread out over his farthermost fields and were hurriedly digging out his beets. In the evenings he lay all alone on the sofa in his well-lit cottage thinking about himself, about the money he'd earned, and about the fact that there in the shtetl Mirele, wearing a warm autumn jacket, was now wandering through the chilly, darkened streets. He reminded himself of his six thousand rubles which, together with Mirele's three thousand, were still invested with the old Count of Kashperivke, and took pleasure from the new furniture with which he'd only recently fitted out his well-to-do cottage:

—All things considered, had he done well to have thrown away a whole three hundred rubles on this furniture, eh? Certainly, he'd done well.

Outside at such times everything around his brightly lit cottage was lifeless and silent. An unusually expansive star-studded sky spread out over the darkened village, always so early asleep, and only in the priest's enclosed courtyard did the vicious dogs go on baying as soon as night fell, making a fearful disturbance in response to the slightest noise whether close by or far off, or for no reason at all simply raising their snouts in the direction of the sleeping town to fill the chill autumnal night air with their bewildered howling.

Around eight o'clock the dogs would suddenly start barking even more angrily and ferociously as the heavy tread of a peasant made itself heard at the kitchen door. Then from his place on the sofa Velvl would raise his head, listen attentively, and start calling out in the direction of the open door:

—Aleksey, has something come in the post, Aleksey?

He knew quite well that there would be nothing more than a copy of *Birzhevye vedomosti,* the Russian stock exchange gazette, yet every evening he'd shout out the same words to his manservant because they pleased him and because they were frequently shouted out by the well-bred Gentile landowners with whom he had neighborly dealings.

Then for a long while, with the comfortable consciousness of being his own master, he'd settle himself expansively next to the blue-shaded lamp and attentively peruse every page of the outspread newspaper. Several times he'd read aloud those passages he didn't understand and unfailingly check the interest rate on annuities in the stock market listings. He already had a considerable amount of ready cash with which he could easily buy an annuity for himself and keep it locked up in his dresser as his landowning neighbors did. Besides, annuities of this kind were always to be found in the possession of the diminutive, perpetually jolly and perpetually busy Nokhem Tarabay, that same Nokhem Tarabay who lived eighteen versts* farther on at the prosperous sugar refinery where he ran his wealthy household in the style of a nobleman and sent his children to be educated somewhere in the huge, distant city. Meeting this Nokhem Tarabay at a gathering somewhere, he'd once even taken the opportunity to show him that he, Velvl Burnes, was by no means totally uninformed, and had felt able to ask him cheerfully and loudly:

—*Pani* Tarabay, how are the four percents doing this week? Last week, the paper reports, the four percents were virtually worthless.

*An imperial Russian unit of distance approximately equal to one kilometer or two-thirds of a mile.

At the time, Tarabay had jokingly widened his enormous, lively eyes and gaped in feigned astonishment:

—Eh? . . . Was he really starting to talk about annuities already?

He stood for a while in seemingly open-mouthed incredulity and made no answer whatever.

This astonished expression meant something quite different, however. Not without reason did the broker who, in his horse and buggy, often called on Velvl tell him a short time later:

—On his life, a short while before Nokhem Tarabay had praised him, Velvl Burnes, to a large group of merchants.

The broker swore that, as he hoped for a fortunate and prosperous year, he'd heard Nokhem Tarabay himself say:

—Mark my words: Avrom-Moyshe Burnes is raising a jewel of a young man, I'm telling you: he has all the potential of a great landowner.

On one occasion this Nokhem Tarabay honored him with a visit. Driving past his farm, Tarabay turned his new phaeton into the courtyard and cheerfully inquired in Polish of Velvl's driver Aleksey:

—*Czy Pan Burnes w domu?* Is Pan Burnes at home?

This was about four o'clock in the afternoon.

From the window he noticed Tarabay springing down from his phaeton, was overcome with confusion, immediately opened the door of the front verandah which was normally kept locked, and with great respect led his visitor inside.

He had such sharp, lively little eyes, this diminutive millionaire who lived like a nobleman; he even noticed the brass plate affixed to the verandah door and praised his host as he entered his home:

—That's the way! . . . Absolutely the way! . . . I mean, why not? Why else are we living in the world?

This Nokhem had the habit of chattering a great deal about himself, about his extensive business affairs and his equally extensive house, of pointing a finger at his starched collar as he spoke and of repeatedly shooting his starched cuffs from under coat sleeves that were slightly too short.

All he really needed from Velvl's farm were some two or three hundred bales of straw for his oxen stables at the sugar refinery, but this merited only a mention in passing outside as he seated himself back in his phaeton. In the meanwhile Tarabay was able to chatter merrily away about his elder son who was working in a big bank somewhere, about his younger son who was studying at the polytechnic, and about his twenty-three-year-old daughter who was devoted to the village and her home and had delayed her education as a result of spending far too much time there:

—Recently, this daughter had told him:

"She wanted to travel to Odessa."

So he'd answered:

"Go to Odessa, then."

And three weeks later she'd returned from Odessa with the proof in black and white to inform him:

"You see, Father, I've passed the examinations in six grades."

And for quite some time after that, a great many odd thoughts about both Tarabay's daughter and his former fiancée filled the dull mind of this twenty-seven-year-old bachelor, Velvl. It seemed to him that this daughter's achievement in passing her examinations in six grades had some connection with him and with the fact that Mirele had returned their betrothal contract and was now keeping regular company with the crippled student Lipkis; that all of this mortified and humiliated him, that he couldn't permit it to continue and was obliged to put a stop to it.

And then something happened to him that actually shouldn't have happened.

He began fraternizing with the village schoolmaster, a Gentile who came daily to tutor the priest's too long unmarried daughters,* finally invited him over, and began secretly taking lessons from him.

On one occasion he even remarked to this Gentile:

—These fractions are a clever thing . . . really, a very clever thing to study.

And the Gentile schoolmaster went off and mockingly made this remark known everywhere.

---

*The Russian Orthodox Church permits some categories of its priests to marry.

As a result, the priest's daughters almost choked with laughter every time they saw Velvl passing their front verandah. And in town one day Mirele stopped his sisters to ask sarcastically:

—Apparently your Velvl is planning to enter university—is this true?

1.4

He met Nokhem Tarabay once more.

This was at the sugar refinery, where he was collecting what he was owed for the sugar beets that had been ordered from him.

With the deference of a loyal and bashful pupil, he stood before Tarabay listening to him prattle on cheerfully about how he'd recently met Velvl's former fiancée in town and had conducted a polite conversation with her.

Before he left, he'd embraced her in the aristocratic manner there in her father's house, had addressed her in Polish as *jaśniewielmożna panna*, "most distinguished young lady," and had whispered a secret to her about Velvl:

—He, Tarabay, had a match for her . . . an uncommonly fine match.

And he screwed up one of his eyes, gave Velvl a knowing wink, and laid his hand on his shoulder:

—Velvl wasn't to worry about a thing but was simply to trust Tarabay.

And Tarabay added an oath as well:

—He wished he might have as many happy years for himself as Velvl would have with so fine a wife as Mirele.

At the time he'd been immensely grateful to that shrewd, cheerful Tarabay, and smiling to himself had thought about him with great esteem as he traveled home.

—That's a clever man . . . That's a true man of the world.

For nearly two successive weeks afterward he was excited and happy, overeager to offer tea to the broker from town who called on him; he even made an unnecessary trip to the stables, where he cheerfully repeated to his driver:

—We ought to get you a new cap, Aleksey . . . Please remind me about this when we're next in the provincial capital . . .

It was good to lie on his bed all evening thinking about a time when Mirele's autumn jacket would at last be hanging in the entrance hall, and to imagine how, lying here on this same bed, he would answer Mirele's question:

—Why not? He didn't stint her use of the buggy, did he? If she wanted to go into town, she had only to order the buggy harnessed up and go whenever she pleased.

He was waiting for something, beside himself with impatience trying to guess how Tarabay would keep his promise.

—Well, Tarabay would come to town shortly . . . He'd certainly have to come down soon in connection with his business affairs and then he'd call on the man who should've been Velvl's father-in-law.

But days passed, and there was no sign of Tarabay's phaeton in town.

Mirele was as solicitous for the crippled student as for a blood brother, even meddled in his affairs, and pleaded his case behind his back:

—What was the point of it? Was there any viable future for him in staying tied to his mother's apron strings, teaching Torah to the girls of the town?

There was no news in town apart from nasty rumors that started spreading about the old Count of Kashperivke who was already living abroad with his son-in-law:

—The Count was heading for bankruptcy, no question, and Kashperivke would be sequestrated by the bank.

In response to these rumors, Velvl's mother sent him frequent notes in which she cursed his former fiancée and her father and continually complained:

—Six thousand rubles . . . this was no triviality! Six thousand rubles, in these days!

And more:

—To this very day the promissory notes were still made out in Reb Gedalye Hurvits's name and the Count recognized no one but him as an interested party.

Without being fully aware of it, he once again began sleeping away many of the brief, chilly days of late autumn, filling the air of his silent furnished cottage with the sound of his heavy, despondent snoring, starting awake every now and then and reminding himself:

—He was going through a very difficult time . . . and nothing would come of having thought continually about Mirele . . . And above all . . . above all, he'd been a fool to squander so much money on new furniture and new horses.

A while later here in town an unusually warm Sunday afternoon drew to a close. The slanting sun steeped straw roofs and leafless trees in red gold, and peasants in black sackcloth coats standing near the shop attached to an isolated Jewish house took enormous childlike delight in this red glow, felt tremendously pleased with themselves at the thought of all the grain they'd stored up for the winter season, and smiled at one another:

—It's time to pack bundles of straw against the walls of the houses to keep out the cold, eh?

That was when a messenger from his father arrived with the Count's promissory notes, woke him from sleep, and imparted some oddly disquieting information:

—The old Count had arrived in Kashperivke in the dead of night, and the man who was to have been his father-in-law . . . more than likely the man who was to have been his father-in-law had rushed over there in his britzka* very early that morning.

Half-asleep, he hurried off to Kashperivke in his own buggy, encountered the old Count alone in the bare manor house from which even the furniture had been packed away, and had all his promissory notes, made out in the name of Gedalye Hurvits, paid out in full. The old Count was even under the impression that Gedalye Hurvits himself had sent him here to cash in these notes of hand and consequently asked him to inform his principal:

—He was paying out six thousand rubles now and the remaining three thousand . . . He didn't have the balance at the moment, so he'd have to remit it from abroad.

Velvl understood from this that the three thousand rubles belonging to the man who should've been his father-in-law were lost for good, felt

---

*A Polish-Russian open carriage with a folding hood in which passengers can recline on long trips.

that he was now doing something contemptible, yet nodded his head at the Count:

—Good, good . . . he'd inform him accordingly.

Only at nightfall, climbing the first hill on the road home from Kashperivke in his buggy, did he recognize in the distance the britzka of the man who should've been his father-in-law with the Gentile lad who was its driver. He felt his heart pounding violently as he quickly instructed his own driver to turn left into a very narrow side road. He was alarmed, could hardly believe what he was doing, and for the first time gave a thought to the man who should've been his father-in-law:

—Did this mean that he'd spent the whole day from very early that morning on his own in the little wood? . . . Was he only now making his way to the Count of Kashperivke?

For some reason, from the narrow side road he kept glancing at the britzka of the man who should've been his father-in-law and saw:

As usual, the lank, emaciated horses were badly harnessed: the traces on the right-hand animal were too short, forcing it to keep leaping forward; the harness breechings on the left-hand horse with its blind, bulging eye were too loose, so that beast was forced to pull not with its chest but with its back. And up above, with his arms folded, sat Reb Gedalye Hurvits himself, his expression preoccupied, his head with its sharply pointed nose and gold-rimmed spectacles thrust a little upward, and his dark, forked beard blown to left and right by the wind.

Velvl felt profoundly distressed and shocked and wondered:

—Did this mean that the engagement was over? . . . Irrevocably over? . . .

The next day he rose very early and ordered his buggy harnessed up.

Outdoors it was cloudy and cool, and a late autumn shower dripped down intermittently, starting, stopping, and starting all over again.

All the way into town he was visibly angry and distressed, thought about Nokhem Tarabay's proud, unpleasantly sullen daughter whom he'd once seen in the provincial capital, and came to a decision:

—Nokhem Tarabay's daughter wouldn't want him—she definitely wouldn't want him.

The night before, thinking about Mirele, he'd made up his mind:

—He'd go over to the man who should've been his father-in-law and pay him his share of the money.

This decision pleased him so much that he was even keen to know what other people would say about it, above all, what Nokhem Tarabay would say about it . . .

But while he was still in the passage as he entered his father's house, he could hear Reb Gedalye Hurvits's appointed arbitrator yelling heatedly from his father's little study, and the way his father kept interrupting him with the softly-spoken argument of an unlettered man:

—What if things had happened the other way around?

He stood there for a while listening to the arguments.

Mentally he turned over the same question yet again:

—Did this mean that the betrothal was really over, that this was the end of everything?

And for some reason, instead of going into the little study he went into the dining room where his mother was reviling his former fiancée to visiting strangers. With a severe and displeased expression, he rebuked her angrily but politely:

—Hush! Just look at her!

2.1

Reb Gedalye Hurvits's business affairs plunged into ever greater confusion, and an ill-concealed disquiet troubled this preoccupied Torah scholar and his entire aristocratically reserved, well-to-do household.

With his worldly cousin, who was also his bookkeeper and closest intimate, Reb Gedalye now spent night after night conferring in secret. Both men stayed locked up all night deliberating in private, oblivious to the passing of the third watch,* at length threw back a shutter, opened a window, and noticed:

The dark beginning of the Elul day† approaching silently and sadly from the northeast corner of the sky, slowly but steadily drawing closer, mutely driving away the final moments of the pale, lingering night. All around, everything had now turned gray; cows still confined in the

---

*In the Jewish religious tradition, a single day is measured from sunset to sunset in eight equal watches, namely, every three hours. The night is divided into three watches, as indicated by the phrase "the middle watch" (Judges 7:19).

†Elul is the twelfth month of the Jewish civil year and the sixth month of the ecclesiastical year on the Hebrew calendar, usually corresponding to the months of August–September on the Gregorian calendar. It is a time of repentance in preparation for the High Holy Days of Rosh Hashanah and Yom Kippur.

courtyards of sleepy households lowed longingly for their penned-up calves and for the damp grass of the fields; and in various corners of the shtetl and the adjoining peasant village, cocks awakened for the third time. They crowed from close by and from farther off, one interrupting the other in haste to utter the first protracted blessing for the coming of day:

—Ku-ku-ri-ku-u!

His intimate, the considerate and deeply devoted bookkeeper, was still lost in thought, slowly tapping his nose with a finger while, as always, the perpetually preoccupied Reb Gedalye bombarded him with new, wide-ranging plans, continually leaning ever closer to his pondering adviser as though wanting to draw him over to his own side of his gold-rimmed spectacles and hurriedly demand of him:

—What do you think? Not so?

At this time, his soft Galician accent* was more than commonly evident in his speech, and when seated he'd throw the entire top half of his body forward whenever people called on him at home, as though someone had suddenly pressed an electric button concealed between his shoulder blades, abruptly compelling him to honor his guest with a bow and the sudden articulation of the few customary words:

—Please sit down, dear sir!

The entire household was afraid of some undefined menace, terrified that it might burst into the house at any moment; this state of fear lasted until well into the winter when for entirely specious reasons these business affairs became even more tangled, and disturbing rumors spread over virtually the entire district:

A rumor involving Reb Gedalye Hurvits's long-standing enemy in the provincial capital, who'd laid an accusation against him in a bank there.

A rumor involving the old director of the same bank, previously a consistently good friend to Hurvits, who personally served notice that all should be strictly on their guard and no longer extend a single kopeck's credit to him.

---

*Since Reb Gedalye was born and raised in Galicia, he is a follower of the Hasidic *rebbes* of Sadagura and Husiatyn.

Far too often at this time Reb Gedalye would hurry off to the provincial capital in his own buggy.

For the most part he traveled there on Sunday, almost always returning just before the lighting of the Sabbath candles the following Friday evening when he'd rush into the house in great haste and notice:

His wife, Gitele, wearing her black silk jacket, the ritual wig* she reserved for the Sabbath, and her diamond earrings, already seated near the silver candlesticks and the covered Sabbath loaves arranged on the dining room table which was now spread with its fresh white cloth, examining her red, freshly scrubbed fingernails and waiting for the first little fire of Friday evening to be kindled in the window of the rabbi's house in the row of whitewashed dwellings on the opposite side of the street.

At such times, as had become habitual, Reb Gedalye was extremely busy and preoccupied, gulping tea from a saucer at this table, unaware that the peak of his silk skullcap was slightly askew. Between one gulp and another, he rapidly responded to Gitele's inquiries:

—He'd hurried off to see that member of the board whose opinion, according to what the director had told him, carried most weight when decisions were reached . . .

—From that board member he'd hurried back to the director . . . To all intents and purposes he'd now persuaded both of them . . .

—Now there remained only the third member, an old general, and the fourth, a Polish nobleman . . . With God's help he'd win their support this coming week . . . There was no doubt he'd win it.

By no means downhearted, he had great confidence; despite his anxiety, he'd nevertheless remembered to bring presents home, and once he even made a witty remark about the new silk skullcap he'd brought back from the provincial capital. At the time, Gitele was deeply dissatisfied with this head covering:

—How could he pick out a skullcap for himself—she protested—without noticing that it fell down round his ears?†

*In strictly observant Ashkenazi communities, women crop their hair close when they marry and wear a ritual wig, known in Yiddish as a *sheytl*, to observe the requirements of Jewish law regarding female modesty.
†In the Ashkenazi fashion of the nineteenth century, this kind of skullcap was very large, shaped more like a toque, and covered most of the head.

Nothing more than his strained, sharply etched nose seemed to smile in response.

—Did Gitele really believe that his head was in the provincial capital just then? At that time, his head had been at home.

And presently he threw on his Sabbath overcoat and rushed away to welcome the Sabbath at the old Sadagura prayer house* where for a while after the service a few observant, wealthy young men kept their places on either side of his reserved seat at the eastern wall, watched him with eyes filled with high regard and feline gratitude, and were prepared at any moment to wish him all the joys of the World to Come because he'd behaved honorably and in good time had repaid what he owed them.

Of course they were well disposed toward him, these few observant, wealthy young men in their silk capotes, but because their money was so precious to them, and because they felt so guilty at having been afraid to trust Hurvits, now, walking home, they were mournfully silent and often, quite suddenly and apropos of nothing, remarked to one or another:

—After all, he's a decent man, Reb Gedalye, eh? Altogether a thoroughly decent man.

Meanwhile there was great curiosity in town to know how it would end:

*Before World War I the small town of Sadagura, eighteen kilometers north of the city of Czernowitz and two kilometers from the town of Ruzhin, was located in Bukovina (Galicia) and was thus part of the Austro-Hungarian Empire. Its Hasidic dynasty was founded by Rabbi Yisroel Friedman of Ruzhin (1796–1850), who settled in Sadagura in 1842 and established a luxurious court there. His six sons all subsequently founded Hasidic dynasties of their own: the youngest of them, Dovid-Moyshe and Mordkhe-Shrage, moved respectively to Chortkov and Husiatyn in Galicia, where they perpetuated their father's aristocratic manners and his fashionably elegant way of life. From all over Eastern Europe, thousands of Jews made pilgrimages to the court at Sadagura, which was distinguished as much by worldly as by spiritual riches. In contrast with other Hasidic leaders who lived in poverty and isolation, the *rebbe* of Sadagura claimed descent from the royal line of King David, conducted his court regally, and insisted that God be served with all the splendors of the world.

Would Reb Gedalye manage to extricate himself from his difficulties or not?

At this time, widespread interest was taken in the matter, which was frequently discussed.

The only person unwilling to discuss it was Mirele, his only child, that delicately brought up slender creature who, during that period, either through love for her father or love for herself, would often leave the house and stay out all day.

She was now unduly pensive and volatile, behaving with excessive harshness even toward the crippled student Lipkis, who on her account had not attended his courses at the university that year and limpingly followed her around everywhere. Walking by his side for hours on end, she was quite capable of forgetting that he was still alive, and would unexpectedly turn to stare at him with so strange an expression of astonishment it seemed as though she were unable to believe what she saw and could not understand it:

—Just look! Lipkis was still walking by her side! And she'd imagined that he'd gone home long ago.

When she did deign to notice him, she couldn't stop herself from hurting him with a sharp remark:

—Lipkis, why do your moustaches grow so oddly? They never grow so oddly on anyone else.

Or:

—Generally speaking, you're not bad looking, Lipkis, but when one studies you closely, you look fearfully like a Japanese.

At such times he felt inordinately ill at ease and was unable to respond. He could think of no reason why she kept silent, and many times decided that it was needful to say something encouraging to her about her father's situation and the brouhaha that had erupted in their home. Once he finally began to stammer:

—To be sure, he understood very well that unhappiness didn't derive primarily from money, and yet . . . He didn't know why, but every time he'd called on them recently and seen her father there, a tragedy seemed to be taking place around him.

Without so much as glancing at him, Mirele silently fixed her blue eyes on the sunset in the distance, and remarked with cold indifference:

—Well, lend him twelve thousand rubles and he'll free himself from his difficulties.

And with sorrow in her blue eyes she went on staring silently ahead, to the place where the sun was setting.

How odd: this delicately brought up creature even knew exactly how much her father needed to save himself. Quite possibly she knew also that had she not broken off her engagement to Velvl Burnes, his father, Avrom-Moyshe, would readily have supplied this sum. Quite possibly she'd given this matter much thought, which was why she could now say, so easily and simply:

—Well, lend him twelve thousand rubles and he'll free himself from his difficulties.

These words abruptly reminded the crippled student Lipkis of his widowed mother whom he and his elder brother supported, and of the old overcoat that she'd carried out after him that time when, traveling to the provincial capital with Mirele, he'd hastily hobbled out to the conveyance in which she was waiting for him.

At the time it seemed that Mirel, seated on the phaeton, had smiled and glanced aside.

Why had she glanced aside then? Was it because at that moment her former fiancé had come driving up from town in his buggy? Or merely because every Sabbath Lipkis's mother used that same old overcoat to wrap around her *tsholnt** in the oven?

In reality, though, this spoiled and self-centered young woman was incapable of thinking seriously about anyone who lived outside the confines of a soul like her own, shrunken by the solipsism inevitable in an only child.

Lipkis began to understand this clearly only some time later and subsequently even reproached her for it in the many letters he failed to send her.

—He wondered—he protested in one of these unsent letters—

Tsholnt is an Eastern European (Ashkenazi) Jewish stew simmered inside an oven at a low temperature. Because kindling fire on the Sabbath is forbidden, the stew is left in a preheated oven for as long as twenty-four hours before being served as the hot meal on the Sabbath.

whether her egoistic little heart was even capable of empathizing with the predicament of her own hard-pressed father, distracted by misfortune as he was, whom she, an adult woman, had felt no embarrassment in kissing before a room full of people?

The moderately cold air froze into unhearing silence, and the first snows settled over the dispirited shtetl and over the vacant, wintry district all around.

Unable any longer to endure her father's house even for a single minute, Mirel wandered aimlessly about the surrounding windswept fields as long as the short periods of daylight lasted, leaving her footprints and those of Lipkis behind everywhere. At such times they looked odd in the chill, distant air between the dirty skies and the snow-white earth, two people wandering in silence across the vast encircling fields and rarely speaking to each other. The silence of bereavement was all around them, from a solitary peasant hut under a white-blanketed roof right down to a frozen stream somewhere in a nearby valley; dozing here and there in scattered corners of the horizon, those whitened coppices that had buried themselves deep in the snow appeared pristine and unfamiliar from where they stood, deceiving the eye of anyone who might on a rare occasion pass through on a swiftly moving sleigh:

—Look! The little oak coppices should be there, shouldn't they?

No one noticed that by then she was on familiar terms with Lipkis and had started addressing him by his first name.

—Normally—Mirel remarked to him on one occasion, meandering aimlessly over these windswept fields—she had not the remotest feeling of love for him, but at times, for no reason, she felt pleased that he was walking by her side. Could Lipkis understand this or not?

And biting her lower lip, she began filliping his nose to help him understand, in this way forcing him to start grinning foolishly.

The sorrow in her blue eyes intensified, and from time to time it would gaze out with a melancholy glint; then she'd stare pensively into the partially blurred winter distance for a long, long time, and unpredictably pose bizarre questions:

—Lipkis, can you hear the way the world keeps silent?

Lipkis felt that he ought to say something about this silent world, made drawn-out preparations to do so in his throat and with his shoulders, and finally began:

—Yes, it would hardly be inappropriate if the two of them were to set off across these fields and never turn back again.

Paying not the slightest attention to what he said, she continued to stare straight ahead into the partially blurred distance, musingly developing her own thoughts:

—Could he imagine how alien and insignificant everything seemed to her now?

And a short while later, more of the same:

—If the whole of this frozen world, with herself in the middle of it, were now to be overturned, she wouldn't even utter a cry of fright.

But at other times she was possessed of a strange joy linked to a wild longing for life; on these occasions nothing could persuade her to return home and she went on at length about her father's creditors both local and distant who called on them daily, created an uproar, and banged on the table:

—These people were so disgusting . . . Her father was certainly to blame for having squandered their money, but this didn't automatically give them the right to barge through their home at will, shouting for help and accusing him of robbery so loudly that they could be heard ten streets away.

Once, on an ordinary misty day, a religiously observant, scholarly, and extremely naïve young man, an unadventurous stay-at-home with a little black beard and a pale, sickly, jaundiced complexion, came to their house from some neighboring shtetl. For a long time he sat silently in their dining room, waiting in a state of shock. Several times their relative, the worldly and devoted bookkeeper, loudly repeated the same thing to him, as though speaking to the deaf:

—Reb Gedalye was currently abroad, visiting his sister who owned her own village there; that's where he was now.

And the young man with the jaundiced complexion, still in a state of shock, went on asking in his soft, hoarse, feeble voice:

—Does this mean that the money Reb Gedalye owes me is lost? . . . Truly lost?

He appeared utterly devastated, this young man with the jaundiced complexion, and apparently regarded it as impossible to return home and go on living:

On that occasion Mirel ate no midday meal but spent an entire winter's day dragging herself about outdoors with Lipkis.

—He could well imagine how hungry she was—she repeatedly remarked to Lipkis—but that stunned young man was still sitting in their house. He looked so unhappy that she couldn't bear to look at him.

She kept sending Lipkis in to check whether the young man had left, impatiently waited for his return not far from the house, and then called out to him from a distance:

—Well? What? Is he still sitting there?

Night fell, and lamps were lighted in the town's houses. Lamps were also lighted in their house and at length, with her face red and frozen, she came indoors and without taking off her winter outdoor garments began comforting the young man with the jaundiced complexion:

—He could be certain: she'd do everything in her power to ensure that his two thousand rubles were returned to him.

Afterward she even accompanied him outside to his sleigh, expressed concern that his legs would be cold, and with her own hands helped him wrap them in sacking.

—He should tie this end of the sacking under himself . . . And he shouldn't hesitate to pull up his fur collar . . . like that.

For a long time afterward she followed his sleigh with her eyes, completely forgetting about herself and her hunger:

—Did he have any conception of how unhappy this man was?—she inquired pensively of Lipkis.

Lipkis was deeply troubled by the fact that he hadn't attended a single one of his lectures all that day, and felt decidedly odd, as though he were strictly observant and had suddenly recalled as night fell that he hadn't donned prayer shawl and phylacteries* earlier. More than usual

---

*Phylacteries, known in Hebrew as *tefilin,* comprise two boxes containing biblical verses and the leather straps attached to them. An essential part of the Orthodox morning prayer service, they are donned every day, except Sabbaths and festivals, by observant Jewish men above the age of thirteen.

he was infuriated and resentful, totally out of patience, and very nearly lost his temper over the thought:

—Would she ever go indoors or not?

But she continued to gaze pensively in the direction in which the sleigh carrying the young man was disappearing into the farthest end of the town, and was unable to forget his jaundiced complexion:

—He's so unhappy—she repeated quietly to herself.—Obviously no one's ever loved him, and now his small capital's been reduced by more than two thousand rubles.

2.2

From abroad, meanwhile, new letters kept arriving from Reb Gedalye.

Wholly preoccupied, he was unable to relax at his sister's, and he wanted to return as soon as possible to the tumult of his trading affairs and begged for mercy, as though from bandits:

—They'd taken and buried him alive.

Both his wife Gitele and his devoted relative the bookkeeper replied, taking trouble to set his mind at rest:

—Everything was sorting itself out, thank God. Little by little they were coming to terms with his creditors; because of good sleigh roads, the income from the Kashperivke woods had greatly improved; the bank had extended credit for three thousand rubles on the Count's note of hand; and Mirele, long might she live, was well, all praise to God. The stock of winter wheat in the Ternov mill was still registered in the name of the landowner, and the price of flour was rising daily. With God's help, Reb Gedalye would soon be able to return home; meanwhile, his wishes were being carried out and both the *Kuzari* and the first volume of Abravanel's commentaries were being sent to him by post.*

---

*The *Kuzari*, by the medieval Jewish philosopher and poet of Spain, Judah ha-Levi (c. 1075–1141), is a defense of revealed religion in the form of a dialogue between the pagan king of the Khazars and a Jew who has been invited to instruct him in the tenets of Judaism. Isaac ben Judah Abravanel (1437–1508), a medieval statesman, financier, philosopher, and exegete, took the social and political issues of his time into consideration in his commentaries on the Bible.

Meanwhile, for days at a time all was hushed and serene indoors; often all that could be heard was the bookkeeper scratching his pen over the accounts in the study, and the regular ticking of the pendulum on the great wall clock in the dining room as it counted off the minutes of the short, darkly overcast winter's day.

For days at a time no one now called at the house apart from one or another tardy creditor and Libke, the rabbi's young wife, a tall, freckled, half-masculine redhead who regarded herself and her husband as Reb Gedalye's closest friends and who always wore a half smile to irritate her enemies.

With needlework in hand, she could sit for hours here in the dining room next to the polite and uncommunicative Gitele, and with merciless slowness relate details of her husband's communal affairs:

—She argued with him, with her Avreml: What's it to you that the town doesn't want the assistant rabbi Shloyme's son as their ritual slaughterer?

She smiled far too much every time Lipkis inquired after Mirele in the hallway, while Gitele examined her fingernails far too closely whenever the rabbi's wife scratched her ritual wig with a blunt knitting needle and was plainly eager to ask her:

—Long life to you, but are you really not bothered at all that this fellow—to say nothing worse about him—keeps creeping into your house?

In the same silence that filled the unheated salon Mirele lay in her own room, did not so much as glance at Lipkis as he came in and didn't even change her position to acknowledge him. With sorrow in her blue eyes, she stared for a morosely long time into the corner of the ceiling directly opposite and found herself totally under the influence of the brand-new book that lay open beside her.

—Did he think—she merely asked him—that she'd ever fall in love with anyone again?

This question immediately filled Lipkis with profound regret that he'd come at all, so he went over to the window and angrily took to staring out into the winter landscape. He was even prepared to answer her question by assuring her that she'd never fall in love, and was on the point of beginning, venomously:

—Generally speaking . . . we really ought to examine the true meaning of this phrase, "fall in love."

But Mirel was already standing next to the furious young man in a frivolously lighthearted mood, gently pulling his hair:

—You're such a fool, such a fool—she whispered softly into his ear through childishly clenched teeth.

Soon she started putting on her outdoor winter garments and swearing all manner of oaths:

—If that red-haired dummy—she meant the rabbi's wife—didn't clear out of the dining room soon, she'd rip the winter seals off one of the windows and leap outside with him.

Short, damp days followed in quick succession, driving the shtetl ever deeper into winter. Neither indoors nor outdoors offered anything to awaken interest, stirring instead the same indifferent discontent toward everything around, so that one might as well stop every overgrown girl who occasionally strolled down the main street in smartly dressed self-importance, vent one's frustration on her, and rebuke her in the voice of an older, deeply discontented woman:

—Why are you so choosy, you? . . . Why don't you get married? Why?

For vast distances all around, the treasures of wind were imprisoned in the gray mists hanging in the air; they grew heavier and heavier, spreading over the frozen, snow-covered earth that grew dirtier from day to day. The skies were hidden, the horizon erased. The people had no sight of them and the shtetl had no need of them. Like great beasts, houses hunkered down ponderously under their heavy, snow-covered roofs and dozed in an unending reverie.

It seemed:

These houses had ears, hidden, highly attentive ears, continually listening to the great silence that bore down on everything around both from close by and from far away.

It seemed:

They were ready, in response to the slightest, most remote rustle from the fields, to spring up and in great rage and haste rush to confront it, like those starving dogs that race forward to challenge some alien intruder of their own species, an unwelcome guest.

Smoke puffed from the chimney of one of the houses, but instead of rising up into the sky it sank downward, feebly described circles in the air, and finally spread itself over the snow.

In the empty marketplace, several people with nothing to do stood around a sleigh that had brought reeds to sell as fuel. They mocked the stubborn peasant with his exorbitant prices and exasperated him with their sharp-tongued witticisms. And the shopkeepers, muffled up in winter clothing and lounging in boredom at the entranceways of their shops, watched all this from a distance, took pleasure in it, and laughed.

The marketplace was filled with vacancy, and only on the small square in front of the house of Avrom-Moyshe Burnes, the man who would've been Mirele's father-in-law, stood five or six expensive sleighs, fully harnessed and waiting for their owners who had business indoors. These sleighs were attended by their energetic, fur-clad drivers who, having nothing else to do, examined one another's horses and passed judgment on them:

—Just look at this one—it'll go blind in its left eye.

—And what about that one? . . . Even at rest it can't put weight on its hind leg.

And the horses stood where they were and did what came naturally to them; from time to time they shook themselves, trying to throw off the congealed sweat while numerous small bells tinkled on their necks, telling the outside world everything that was taking place within the house:

—Rich landowners were visiting, arranging loans for themselves in the smoke-filled study.

—Worldly merchants were there, speculators who weren't afraid to make purchases a year in advance, and the spacious, half-lit entrance hall was packed with estate stewards and couriers prepared at any moment to appear before their departing employers, ready to receive their instructions and drive out in all directions.

Whenever he had occasion to pass this house with Mirele, Lipkis did not feel entirely comfortable.

He tried in every possible way to forget about it, and to this end had even made strenuous efforts to fix his mind on serious thoughts:

—In two years' time he'd complete his studies in the faculty of medicine . . .

As though out of spite, however, Mirele insisted on staring at this house every time they passed and refused to leave him in peace:

—Could he explain it? Why on earth had they painted the outer shutters blue? That was so garish to look at.[*]

Or:

—All of them: Avrom-Moyshe Burnes, Brokhe and Feyge, her former fiancé's sisters . . . they were all such refined people . . . she'd once loved them very much. Even now she sometimes had a strong desire to see them.

Lipkis was outraged and could no longer restrain himself:

—He had absolutely no idea to whom she was referring in such exalted terms.

—And anyway, creatures were generally divided into only two categories: human beings and animals.

Thus, the next question followed logically:

—If these pigs were human beings, then what was he, Lipkis? . . .

Mirele turned to him with a strange look:

—*Milostivi gosudar,* most gracious sir, would you be so kind as to keep your philosophical speculations in check until tomorrow?

After this, he did not speak again the whole way, walked beside her in great anger, and tormented himself:

—What was there to say? . . . If every serious thought he had seemed foolish to her . . .

She didn't turn to look at him, even after they'd left the long main street behind and had stopped on the deserted, snow-covered promenade outside the town.

Gazing somewhere along the road that even a short distance ahead

---

[*]The choice of blue as a color for the newly painted shutters of this house is another of Bergelson's satiric comments on the attempts of Avrom-Moyshe Burnes to acculturate himself and his family, of a piece with the university student he hires to tutor his children in secular subjects. It was customary in Ukraine for Gentiles to paint their shutters and window frames blue; the normative color for Jews was brown.

disappeared into the mist and led to the farm of her former fiancé, she merely remarked, softly and pensively:

—Listen, Lipkis, if I were as nasty as you, I'd certainly strangle myself with my own hands.

And she stood like that for a long time, unable to tear her mournful eyes from the road.

Was she waiting for that speck, the sleigh that had pulled out of the distant mist and was making its way along the road in this direction, and was she curious to know who was seated in it?

Or perhaps at that moment she was simply dispirited and overcome by the vanity of all things and was unwilling to leave this deserted, snow-covered place?

Yet in town, several women still continued to maintain that her heart still yearned for her former fiancé, that handsome young man who had the patience to pass the long winter months on his productive but now fallow farm, and that there was nothing more to it:

—She'd always been pampered at home, and couldn't bring herself to marry such an ordinary young man.

Often the two of them, Mirel and Lipkis, wandered for long distances over the snow-covered fields, looked behind them, and noticed:

Far in the distance, the entire shtetl had sunk down into the valley between the two bare mountains, and had left no trace of itself in the misty air.

Lipkis was delighted that he was all alone with her here in the wintry silence of the deserted fields, that the uncommunicative Gitele was nowhere near him, and that Libke, the rabbi's young wife, wasn't scratching her wig with the blunt end of a knitting needle thinking about him. For sheer joy, clever philosophical thoughts even came flooding into his mind one after another, and he was ready at any moment to pose such clever questions as, for example:

—He couldn't begin to understand why human beings had built houses for themselves instead of wandering about in couples over this huge frozen world?

But Mirel looked sad and abstracted, and was quite capable of regarding every one of his thoughts as foolishness, so he thought better of speaking and walked on in silence at her side. They skirted the knoll with its heavily wooded copse and crossed the low, narrow wooden bridge under which, from the time of the first frosts, a silent frozen brook had lain in repose as though passing a long, wintry Sabbath. From there they ascended the easy incline of another hill and finally reached the level railway lines bordered by telegraph poles that stretched out into the distance like a long black stripe and divided the snowy whiteness of the fields in two. At this place every day three long passenger trains crept out of the distant horizon in the east, carried their great noisy clamor swiftly past as they disappeared into the misty remoteness of the west, and left behind in the surrounding silence of the fields the mournful echo of many unhappy tales begun but not concluded:

A tale of a beautiful young wife who'd deceived her husband for a long time and from somewhere near here had finally fled abroad with her lover.

A tale of a devout and observant Jew who passed through here, desecrating the Sabbath with his rabbi's permission, hastening to the great distant city so he might bend over the body of his dead son and rend his garments in mourning.

Slowly and impotently, in the air close by and farther off, these unfinished little tales floated about, lost themselves in the distant sleeping wood, and faded yearningly away. As they went, the silence all around deepened, and everything began gazing in the direction from which the train had emerged and into which it had disappeared, gazed for a long, long time, until from one of those mist-shrouded routes a new wisp of black smoke appeared and a long new train began rapidly snaking its way down.

Then Mirel snatched off Lipkis's student cap, set it on the hood that swathed her own head, and positioned herself close to the railway lines to await this long train.

—Among a whole trainload of passengers—she added quietly and dejectedly—there'll certainly be at least one unhappy person looking very disheartened who won't move from the window all journey long and will press his brow to the cold windowpane.

And if she did indeed catch sight of someone with that kind of unhappy expression at the window of one of the carriages, she bowed for a long time, waved the cap, and monotonously and mockingly repeated several times:

—We're also unhappy . . . also unhappy . . . also unhappy . . .

On one occasion, returning from the railway line to the shtetl and emerging on to the snow-covered, deserted promenade, Mirele recognized her former fiancé's sleigh in the distance, and stopped to wait for him.

Lipkis gave her a very odd look, as though he wanted to murder her, and she blushed deeply and even raised her voice at him:

—Why was he looking at her so strangely?

And this was only because she didn't want him to notice that her mood of desolation had unpredictably evaporated. She even added, in Russian:

— *Ty glupyi*—You're a fool.

And before long, with joyful abandon, she began throwing snowballs at him, hurling them and laughing, leaping about and laughing, once again snatching up whole handfuls of snow, throwing them and laughing again, finally forcing him to limp some distance away from her, hunch himself up, and cover his scowling face with both hands.

The conveyance with its new black horses drew nearer, so hiding her hands behind her back, filled as they were with snowballs, and smiling a little, she looked into her former fiancé's face with wide-open, inquiring eyes.

Clad in a wide, aristocratic sheepskin coat the outside of which was covered in blond fur, he sat deep within his highly polished sleigh, from time to time saying a few words to the driver in a manner appropriate to a landowner.

In truth he failed to look round the whole time either at her or at Lipkis, and for a long while, as though turned to stone, she stood where she was, following his sleigh with her eyes and watching it disappear with him among the first houses of the shtetl.

—He's grown handsomer—she observed quietly, as though to herself, and was soon lost in thought.

Only when they neared the shtetl did she grow a little more cheerful, acquire a strangely triumphant expression, and add:

—And his beard, Lipkis . . . he's shaved off his beard, after all.

Lipkis was furious and said nothing. He felt oddly bitter at heart, and never stopped thinking angrily:

—Who could believe the kind of rubbish this woman forced him to get involved with? . . . What possible difference could it make to him whether or not this oaf shaved his beard?

Mirel too kept silent all the way back, once again sank into deep melancholy and despondent pensiveness, and stared down at her slow steps with eyes too wide.

Suddenly she stopped and asked, without raising her bowed head:

—Didn't Lipkis feel the same as she did? . . . People were all far too old and far too clever to go on living. Perhaps now was the time for them all to die out, and for new ones to be born in their place.

With wistful sorrow in her blue eyes she stared vaguely ahead in the direction of the mist-covered fields for a while longer, unexpectedly twisted her lips into a grimace, and glanced round at Lipkis.

—It makes no difference now . . . —she indicated the deep darkness all around—so they'd better go straight from here to drink tea with the midwife Schatz.

Apparently she was also more than a little depressed, and in such a mood evidently had no desire to return home and pass the entire evening alone there.

In silence they crossed the left side of the deserted promenade on the outskirts of the shtetl and followed the well-worn, snow-covered footpath that led diagonally across to the peasant houses at the farthest end of the town, to those same peasant houses that encircled the northwestern corner of the town where they stood like sentries protecting it from the night and from the vacant fields that opened up immediately behind their unseeing rear walls.

Night had fallen, and in the pale gloom the snow dazzled the eye too greatly. Far, far away in the village a great many dogs met the approaching darkness with suspicious barking and recounted fearful primordial tales about the vast surrounding vacancy of fields:

—The Angel of Death lurks in the darkness over there . . . Death awaits whomsoever dares leave the shtetl to come here at nightfall.

Now, through the darkness, the last peasant cottage came into view, the semidetached dwelling in the left half of which, for the past two years, the Lithuanian midwife Schatz had dwelt peaceably with her peasant landlady. From the yellow ochre–smeared wall at the rear, her sole illuminated window now shed a ruddy glow deep, deep into the vast expanse of fields, glanced out at the sledges sliding silently home to bed from somewhere far away, and awakened in them lingering, cheerless, weary thoughts:

—There are certainly many unhappy people, all troubled and discontented. But as for living . . . in one way or another one can still go on living in a deserted and distant corner of a village, all alone and out of sight, smiling ironically, as the twenty-seven-year-old Lithuanian midwife Schatz did behind this window's ruddy glow.

2.3

In a long, dark wool peignoir fastened with two blue ribbons tied diagonally in a broad bow above her breast, the midwife Schatz lay on her bed smoking a cigarette and thinking about something with an ironical smile.

She was always smoking a cigarette and thinking about something with an ironical smile, the midwife Schatz. At the little table that held the lamp sat the short pharmacist's assistant* Safyan, his normally pale face drained of even more color, staring with great resentment into the flame of the lamp with his bulging, colorless eyes.

Under the table his knee twitched nervously. Not long before, with great seriousness, he'd voiced an opinion he held:

—Whenever he saw a woman smoking, his first thought was that here was an individual dependent on liquor.

Even for a moment the midwife Schatz ought to have given some thought to what he'd said and made some reply. But all she did was to listen attentively to the courtyard where the dog was harassing someone, rise from the bed and, without removing the cigarette from her

---

*In the tsarist empire, fully qualified pharmacists were among those categories of Jews permitted to live outside the Pale of Settlement, together with merchants of the first guild, exceptionally talented craftsmen, and university students.

lips, smile at Mirel and Lipkis who were coming in. So why did he need to sit there with his knee twitching under the table?

He actually rose from the chair wanting to take his leave, but Mirel had already cast an astonished glance first at the midwife and then at him, delayed taking off her overcoat, and from a distance demanded of him:

—What was he doing here? Was he really so afraid of the priest's son-in-law, the pharmacist?

So he, the neurotic, stayed on a little longer and, still feeling insulted, was obliged to listen to the way the midwife Schatz, without looking at him and blowing her cigarette smoke toward the low ceiling, joked with Mirele about her own life:

—To tell the truth, it wasn't only her present guests who said so . . . All of her acquaintances who called on her looked around and remarked that she certainly lived well. But she knew this far better than anyone else. What more was there to say? She regarded herself as supremely fortunate . . .

Each time Mirel paid some attention to the pharmacist's assistant Safyan on the other side of the room, the midwife, seated on the bed, moved the whole of her bulky frame closer to Lipkis and, staring at the wall, nudged him in the ribs with her elbow:

—Lipkis! . . . Too bad for you, Lipkis!

In this way, clearly, she was hinting that she knew everything that was going on between him and Mirele, chuckling inwardly and soundlessly as she did so. The infuriated Lipkis almost burst with vexation and finally bellowed:

—Who gave you the right? . . . How dare you pry into my most intimate feelings?

In response, the young pharmacist's assistant Safyan found his knee starting to twitch even more violently under the table, so that he finally announced nervously:

—He had to leave . . . Eventually he'd have to go back to the pharmacy, after all.

And off he went, alone with his nervous, bulging eyes. It seemed as though the slightest movement of a finger near those eyes would instantly make them pop from their sockets.

Of him the midwife Schatz remarked:

—A foolish young man . . . all in all, a foolish young man.

And she immediately forgot about him and went on talking about herself:

—Earlier that week, at the sickbed of someone she knew, she'd met the extremely busy Dr. Kraszewski and told him: I'll marry you, doctor, if you'll come with me now to one of my poor women in childbed.

Such was the nature of this bulky young woman with her smoothly combed hair and mobile, cheerful features: she could tell ironic stories about herself for hours without ever touching on her innermost life by so much as a single word. She'd probably inherited this disposition from her Lithuanian kin, so that, looking at her and thinking about this unknown family, what came hazily to mind was her eighty-two-year-old grandmother, a diminutive old woman as scrawny as a bird who'd come on a visit the previous summer and spent two successive months living in this room.

For long hot days on end, this little old creature lay propped up high on the pillows of the bed with her eyes shut, expiring from afar, like some harried and exhausted foreign parrot which, no longer able to endure the longing for its old home, constantly dreamed about the distant country across the seas where it had been born. It seemed as though she dozed for weeks in one long birdlike reverie, heard nothing of what took place around her, and didn't even notice the young people from the shtetl who called on her granddaughter and discussed a variety of interests. Some of them were even certain that the old woman was deaf and senile and hadn't spoken for a great many years.

On one occasion, however, a number of young people had been sitting here, theorizing at great length about themselves and their lives, and had then fallen silent for some time. Quite suddenly, all were greatly startled and clutched at their hearts in alarm.

Behind them, the little old woman had opened her sunken mouth, and her hollow voice could be heard across the entire room, a lethargic, plaintive voice materializing from some distant, crumbling ruin:

—Daughter of my daughter! Whoever talks less about herself talks less foolishness.

How odd that even now this little old woman also wanted to crack jokes. Her daughter's daughter, the midwife Schatz, was neither surprised nor incredulous. Smiling broadly, she'd merely plumped up the pillows behind the little old woman, and still smiling, had yelled into her ear:

—I remember, *bobenyu*,* I remember.

The midwife chattered on without cessation all evening, telling many anecdotes about herself and one of her uncles, an observant, good-natured Jew:

This uncle would regularly call on her and say:

—Really, Malkele? Will you really never get married? A pity . . . a great pity.

And Mirel sat on a chair opposite her, heard without listening, thinking about herself and the promenade on which she'd wandered about that evening, and lingered on here for an inordinately long time recalling only a hushed, unhappy tale that had been hers from childhood on:

—She'd grown up as an only child in the house of Reb Gedalye Hurvits . . . Some undefined longing had filled her, so at the age of seventeen she'd betrothed herself to Velvl Burnes . . . This hadn't been enough—so she'd taken herself off to the provincial capital to pursue her studies like everyone else . . . But this hadn't helped either, so she'd returned home and, as she imagined, had fallen in love with Nosn Heler here in the shtetl . . . But this too had proved insufficient, and she continued to believe that her future life ought to be entirely different. Once she'd told Nosn openly: "Nothing would come of this; he might as well leave the shtetl." She'd broken off her engagement and returned the betrothal contract . . . Now she was free once more, and was again filled with vague, undefined longings . . . so she wandered aimlessly about the shtetl for days on end, with Lipkis limping after her . . . And at present she was sitting with the midwife Schatz who for almost two years past had been living in her rented cottage at the farthest end of the peasant village.

No exceptional misfortune, it seemed, had marked either her life or

---

*Yiddish affectionate diminutive of the word *bobe*, "grandmother."

the life of the midwife Schatz, but then no exceptional happiness had distinguished their lives either, which was why she reflected with such sadness about herself, and about the undefined formative years that the midwife had left behind together with her anonymous family somewhere in Lithuania, and something in her wanted to say:

—Do you know what, Schatz? You're a strange person. Are you aware of this, Schatz? In the end you'll be laid in your grave, still with an ironic smile on your lips.

But now the midwife Schatz had rolled herself another cigarette at her box of tissue papers. Lighting it from the lamp, she cast a sidelong glance at the infuriated Lipkis, and smiled with the air of a prankster wanting to make peace:

—Everyone's odd, in one way or another.

It seemed as though she were preparing to talk about someone or other whose whole life was odd. Quite possibly she'd now talk about her acquaintance, the sturdy and solitary young Hebrew writer Herz, who took himself off every summer to a quiet Swiss village and every winter went back to the little Lithuanian shtetl where a granite tombstone had long since been erected at community expense over the grave of his deceased grandfather, the rabbi.

Yet there was good reason to suspect that the midwife had been thwarted in love, particularly for this young man, who now believed in nothing; that something unpleasant had occurred between them two years before as a result of which the midwife had unwillingly been forced to leave her shtetl and move to this bleak end of the village.

Mirel drew her chair closer to the bed on which the midwife had comfortably settled herself, while Lipkis's mind was still preoccupied with his ongoing everyday problems:

—Every day his mother nagged him to have a half-dozen sets of fresh underwear made ... Given all his expenses, in the end he wouldn't have enough to get to the city next winter.

By the time this thought had ceased to bedevil him, Mirel, her eyes alive with interest, was leaning intently toward the midwife and listening with great absorption to every word that came slowly from her mouth in a cloud of cigarette smoke.

—So Mirel wanted to know whether Herz corresponded with her?

Firstly, he was far too clever for that sort of thing and disliked doing foolish things, and secondly . . .

Drawing so deeply on her cigarette that its glowing tip illuminated her face, she exhaled the smoke from her mouth, adding with a grimace of aggrieved incredulity:

—One might think that she really missed not receiving letters from him . . .

Lipkis pulled a mocking face:

—Quite true: evidently the midwife never missed what she'd never had and would never have.

This was seemingly the way in which he wanted to pay her back for her earlier remark: "Too bad for you, Lipkis! Too bad for you!" but he restrained himself, glanced at her agitated features with hostility, and held his peace.

This single illuminated room in the midwife's cottage was remarkably quiet. Since it was evidently very late, the silence itself seemed audible. Through the calm of deep night that lingered in all the dimly lit corners, the only thing that could be heard was the way Lipkis leaned his head against the bedstead, and the dying fall of the carefully considered words about her acquaintance that the midwife Schatz tossed into the stillness:

—Two years ago he'd poked fun at himself and told her: To write during the day was a disgrace to him personally as well as to the entire Jewish population of the shtetl who had no need of it, so he wrote only at night, when people were asleep. At night, he said, everyone's sense of shame was diminished. And then he'd smiled and held his peace. Nothing else was left to him, he said, except this smiling silence.

The wandering shadow of this homeless young man seemed to hover in the very air of the room, creating the strong impression that somewhere in a nearby corner behind them he himself was standing at his full sturdy, somewhat stooped height. With blond, freshly barbered hair and equally fair, close-cut mustache and sideburns, he was placidly glancing in this direction with smiling eyes, listening to what the midwife Schatz was saying about him:

This winter, too, this rootless wanderer was doubtless drifting about in that tiny, desolate Lithuanian shtetl, passing his days rambling for great distances over the snow-covered fields.

Mirel broodingly called to mind her own situation every time the midwife related that he never spoke with any intellectuals over there, and even kept his distance from ordinary townsfolk. But if somewhere far, far away from the shtetl he encountered a peasant striding along somewhere, he'd stop and engage in a lengthy conversation with him.

—From what village did he come? Did he have a wife and children? And whose was the land he tilled: his own or a stranger's?

Then Mirel looked at the midwife again, listening as she disclosed more of the same:

—There, Herz would say, between the silent, craggy mountains and the tranquil lakes of Switzerland, the conviction grew in him that human beings would soon cease their hurly-burly and would encounter life and death alike with the same smile.

—He certainly regarded life with dread—she added in passing—yet this didn't prevent him from composing one of his loveliest pieces there in Switzerland.

Embarrassed to look directly at Mirele and Lipkis, the midwife turned her head away.

With shining eyes that flickered on the brink of a smile, she stared up into the topmost reaches of the wall opposite and slowly and quietly began reciting from memory this little piece of his:

"And I, the exiled vagabond, wandering thus all alone over the earth for years on end, less and less frequently encountered a human settlement anywhere, and in time I have forgotten how to compute the difference between weekday and Sabbath. One by one I have cast away the objects in the heavy pack I bore on my shoulders and have told myself:

Neither I nor anyone else has need of these things. Why then should I carry them with me and bow my back under their weight?

And when nothing remained in the sack full of holes on my shoulders, it too I cast aside and began my self-examination.

I am still comparatively young, I reflected, power and might sleep within me, yet dare I hope that I might yet again have need of myself?

And forgetting that which I had left behind me, I began slowly striding forward.

I reflected:

There is value in investigating what goes on there, in that region of the world which lies beyond the horizon. And perhaps . . . perhaps I might yet arrive somewhere.

And once, as dusk was falling, I did indeed arrive in a dead city, and there I found the doors of all the houses open.

In that dead city the dusk was neither of winter nor of summer, and I was not cold, and no fear overcame me. I went from house to house and saw that everywhere on the beds, stiff in the rigor of death, lay bodies clutching stones tightly in their fists. Before their deaths they had, it seemed, desired to hurl these stones at someone.

In a corner of one house I saw only a single, slender woman and, glancing at her, was transfixed. Darkly graceful, of lifeless pale complexion, clad in a long black robe, she stood leaning against the wall, staring into the distance with exhausted ebony eyes and had evidently already forgotten that she constantly clutched to her breast a child's waxen doll.

—You have come so late, she murmured to me with quiet indifference.—We have been waiting for you so long here, and now look: they are all dead.

I made no response, because in her eyes there already burned that fire that burns in the eyes of all who are deranged, and she continued to direct my attention to the doll that lay at her breast and said:

—Do you know what is here? It is a mistake that has been covered up.

And even as she sank down in death on the bed that stood beside her, quietly, extraordinarily quietly, she completed her thought:

—And overall . . . overall—it was—nothing more than a mistake that has been covered up.

Then I left the house and went to sit at the gate of the city.

Where then shall I go from hence? I murmured to myself. Rather let me sit here in the gateway forever and remain a guardian over this dead city.

And thus have I been sitting for so long at the gate of this city, into which no one enters and from which no one leaves.

Everything I once knew I have now forgotten, and in this mind of mine no more than a single thought remains:

All, all have long since died, and I alone am alive, and no longer await anyone.

And when I look about me once more, and feel the power and might that sleep in me, I no longer even sigh, but simply think:

I am the guardian of a dead city."

The midwife fell silent.

Mirel suddenly rose from her place, intending to take Lipkis and go home, but as the mood evoked by the tale still lingered with her, she stood sadly and silently where she was, still thinking of the dead city and of the midwife's expression which had undergone so strange an alteration as she was reciting.

Because the midwife had wanted to look her age, like someone wise and experienced, all the frenzy of her hidden love for this young man had leapt out on her . . . While she'd been reciting, there had been certain moments when her expression had seemed as foolish as the look on the face of an idiot.

And again the mood of the tale affected her. She stared at the window panes to which the blackness of the night beyond clung fast, and her ears no longer heard the quiet whispering of her own lips:

—This person whom the midwife called Herz . . . he seemed to go on living against his will and to go on writing against his will . . . How did the midwife put it: was there anything left for him except to go mad?

But now the midwife Schatz once more busied herself at the box of tissue papers where she rolled herself a fresh cigarette.

—He's as healthy as a peasant—she responded from over there.— He can endure everything in silence.

God alone knew why she also felt obliged to add cruelly:

—It makes no matter; the devil won't grab him there.

After Mirel had left, she was interested to look back into the room from outside and to see:

In absolutely no hurry to go to bed, the midwife Schatz had not even extinguished the lamp. Cross-legged like a man, with the burning cigarette in her mouth, she went on sitting motionless on the bed, staring out into the vacancy of her room.

Being well past midnight, no lamps were burning anywhere.

Deep, deep down toward the distant night-shrouded horizon beyond the snow-covered fields, only the oak trees in the copses spread out in long, black single file, and it seemed as though they too wanted to doze off but could not, that they were disturbed by the far-reaching ruddy glow from the midwife Schatz's illuminated window, and were continually jerked awake by yet another stray breeze that came rushing hither between the young trees, spreading among them the nocturnal melancholy of a misfortune newly born elsewhere.

Mirel continued to see before her the midwife Schatz, remembered the tale of the dead city, and fretted despondently:

—Now she'd undoubtedly dream all night about the dead city with its madwoman clad in black . . . all night.

But passing the slumbering house of her former in-laws with its blue outer shutters tightly closed, she noticed their aged night watchman there, and stopped to speak with him:

—Oh, Zakhar! Why did he never call on them, Zakhar?

Swept off his feet with joy, old Zakhar stood bareheaded before her:

—Oh, oh, oh! How many times hadn't he driven the *barishniya,* the young mistress, home at night? How many notes hadn't he brought her during the muddy season? . . . And now, now they'd told him in the kitchen that she was no longer betrothed . . . Was this really true, what they'd told him in the kitchen?

And she smiled and yelled into his ear:

—It's true, Zakhar, quite true.

She asked far too many questions about the members of the Burnes household, was evidently eager to find out whether her former fiancé currently spent the nights in town, but felt unable to inquire, either because Lipkis was standing at her side or simply because the aged Zakhar was quite capable of reporting whatever she asked to those indoors.

Lipkis was delighted when she finally broke off and turned away, though even he felt that the question he now asked was superfluous:

—He was curious to know one thing: what interest could she possibly have in passing a full half hour chatting to that old peasant?

But she made him no answer, stopped once more, reminded herself that the night watchman had to be given a tip so he could buy tea, and demanded a whole ruble from Lipkis for this purpose. In an instant he was again overwhelmed with anger, and snatching the silver coin from his pocket regarded her with fury:

—Unbelievable how plainly and crudely she demanded money from him! She took it by right, as though from a husband.

2.4

In Reb Gedalye Hurvits's house, preparations were being made to receive someone.

The imported rose-colored drapes were once again hung at all the windows, the chilly salon was heated daily, and the velvet runners were spread over all the floors. The whole house appeared to have invested commonplace weekdays with an air of festive sanctity, and seemed aware of nothing but the rumors about Mirel that spread through the entire shtetl:

—She was probably about to become engaged again, this time to Yankev-Yoysef Zaydenovski's refined son, in fact, that Yankev-Yosl Zaydenovski who stemmed from the nearby village of Shukey-Gora, who'd lived for the past ten years in a suburb of the distant metropolis where he owned his own distillery, and who still to this day exercised a great deal of influence locally because of his extensive oxen stables.

Lipkis was furious every time someone asked him about these rumors, and would reply angrily:

—How on earth should he know?

—And anyway . . . why was he, of all people, being asked about all this?

At that time he rarely encountered Mirel, so as though to spite someone, he behaved with unusual arrogance and self-importance, pretending not to know that all the rumors had been provoked by nothing more than an unpretentious out-of town matchmaker who'd stopped for a few days at the home of Avrom-Moyshe Burnes and had there complained:

—Of what benefit was it that Zaydenovski had a good-natured unmarried son? During the previous summer, Mirel had stayed in the same inn as he somewhere in the provincial capital, had stopped to chat with him a few times in the corridor and, it would seem, had completely turned his head.

But day after day passed and still no one arrived at Reb Gedalye's house. Mirele merely grew paler and more silent, and soon it seemed that she knew nothing and heard nothing, that it was all one to her whether she was praised or abused in town, with the result that she was impervious to the effect of such ill-considered, self-indulgent actions as stopping her former fiancé's sisters in the middle of the street, complaining that they never visited her, and protesting with the air of a social outcast on whom everyone turned their backs:

—In any event . . . she was certainly no worse than the photographer Rozenboym's wife to whom they ran twice a day.

After this encounter, Avrom-Moyshe Burnes's daughters stared at each other, and followed her with amazement in their eyes:

—Can you understand her?—the elder sister asked the younger.

And by herself Mirel continued on her way up through the shtetl. At the pharmacy, situated among the last of the Jewish-owned houses, she stopped in the middle of the road and looked around. No one was about except a ragged little urchin going into town; the pharmacy's glass door with its little bell was covered from within by a red half-curtain. She beckoned the boy over and asked him to call the pharmacist's assistant Safyan out to her. Embarrassed, the lad did as he was asked, and she stood waiting by herself until Safyan had finished what he was doing, had put on his coat, and had come out with his bulging, colorless eyes. Meanwhile some men returning to town in a hired peasant sleigh glanced at her in astonishment and began smiling oddly at one another. Pretending not to notice their smiles, with an earnest demeanor she remarked to the pharmacist's assistant Safyan:

—Earlier she'd wanted to ask him to escort her to the midwife Schatz. But now . . . now she had no desire to visit the midwife Schatz. Did he have time to walk with her a little way out of town?

In response to this question, the pharmacist's assistant Safyan was obliged to stretch his neck, swallow convulsively, and do up the topmost button of his winter overcoat:

—Did he have time? Actually, he was . . . He could, actually, walk a little way.

And, tense and agitated, he walked on her left without ever glancing at her, fixed his big bulging eyes on the mist that was spreading outward from the shtetl and, as malign chance would have it, found nothing to say and was silent. Since a peculiar heaviness made itself felt in his silence, Mirel glanced at him from time to time and finally asked him:

—She believed that Safyan was descended from an ancient family . . . She'd been told this not long before, if she remembered correctly.

And a short while later, again on the same subject:

—Her father was also descended from an ancient family that had settled in Germany and had for a long time intermarried among its members so that now, apparently, it was degenerating with age. This was possibly why she sometimes felt such purposelessness and was fit for nothing.

Walking across the snow-covered promenade, they were slowly approaching their destination. The agitated pharmacist's assistant unconsciously began fingering a letter of some kind in his overcoat pocket and, without looking round at her, asked in a tense, trembling voice:

—Of course this was none of his business, and she wasn't obliged to answer him . . . He merely wanted to ask why she didn't prepare herself for some public examinations and so equip herself for some kind of cultivated profession. He'd heard that she was only twenty-two years old.

And for some reason Mirel stopped and began looking down at where she'd dug into the snow with the tip of one of her galoshes:

—Yes, many people had already asked her the same question.

The misty gray air all around was still; in the vicinity, not even black ravens flew past now, and no living soul appeared in this wintry desolation. Mirel gave something like a sigh, glanced slowly and pensively to one side, and equally slowly and pensively began relating how one wintry Friday evening their maid had complained to her:

—How would she be able to survive until eleven o'clock without any sunflower seeds to chew? She'd go mad here.

A short time after that, strolling in the provincial capital, she'd over-heard a young woman student complaining to a friend:

—Dear God! She had absolutely nothing to read at home. She'd lose her mind sitting there all alone.

Only now did she turn to look at Safyan, walked on with him, and asked:

—Do you understand, Safyan? One person needs sunflower seeds and another person needs a book to drive it away, but it's exactly the same desolation. Do you understand?

The pharmacist's assistant Safyan's bulging, colorless eyes widened even more and one side of his nose began twitching from nervous en-thusiasm for abstract speculation.

—*Delo v tom*—here's the thing—Mirel had just confused two quite discrete ideas . . .

But Mirel interrupted him to point out some footprints in the snow:

—Did he recognize them, these male footprints? She and Lipkis had wandered about in the same place here not long before.

Did she simply wish to cut him short with this remark? Or did she actually want him to repeat it to Lipkis later on and so awaken in him a chagrined yearning for these footprints in the snow?

For a long, long time afterward she wandered about over the snow-covered fields with Safyan, continually asking him whether he found it pleasant to walk with her, and whether his employer, the priest's son-in-law, would be angry with him.

She returned to the shtetl with him when it had already begun to grow dark outside and the enveloping mists had started descending ever closer to the snow, thickening as night drew on. She stopped in front of her house in order to thank him once more:

—She was deeply gratified that he found it as pleasant to be with her as she with him . . . After all, she'd taken up so much of his time.

But on the threshold of a store situated in the row of houses oppo-site, a smiling relative of her former fiancé's mother appeared, called the attention of someone there to Mirel and Safyan and, it seemed, took pleasure in doing so:

—She's found another fish to fry, thank God.

So Mirel deliberately turned round to the departing Safyan once more and shouted out loudly after him:

—If he wished, she'd call him out of the pharmacy tomorrow as well.

Turning toward him yet again, she shouted out even more loudly:

—She'd call for him at the pharmacy at the same time as today.

Afterward, the whole evening in her isolated room was vacuous: vacuous because of the few hours she'd spent strolling about with the pharmacist's assistant Safyan, vacuous because of her former fiancé's relative, and vacuous because in the dining room a disgruntled Gitele was seated on the sofa listening in uncommunicative silence to the chatter of the rabbi's young wife, examining her fingernails with a little smile, and never for a moment forgetting about Mirel, in respect of whom she'd been implementing a policy of obdurate silence for the past two weeks, and because of whom the long-awaited guest still hadn't arrived, that guest for whose sake the drapes had been hung up, the velvet runners spread out, and the chilly salon heated.

Unable to remain calmly in her room, Mirele donned her jacket and coat again, swathed her head in her scarf, and paused for a moment in the dining room to observe to her mother:

—The salon doesn't need to be heated any longer, it seems to me; it makes no difference . . . and on the whole, I think it's high time to clear away all this festive decor.

On the sofa, the uncommunicative Gitele made not the slightest move, not even turning to glance at her daughter. Only an inflexibly stubborn smile played around her tight mouth as she remarked, coldly and quietly, looking away toward the big window above and behind the rabbi's wife:

—Whom does it bother that the house is festively decorated?

Provoked, Mirel left the house and disappeared alone for the rest of the evening. Meeting their relative the bookkeeper not far from the house, she stopped him to comment:

—Could he explain what kind of oddity her mother was?

And more:

—Essentially, her mother went on smiling without speaking as though to spite someone . . . Presumably, one was supposed to think that she actually had a great deal to say and kept silent only because she was too clever.

This pattern subsequently repeated itself for several days in succession: without a word to anyone she left home in the early evening and returned well past midnight, by which time the lamps had been extinguished all over the shtetl, and her own home was sunk in deep and heavy sleep. Where she disappeared to, no one could guess.

After all, for the past five days the midwife Schatz had been away in a neighboring village at the bedside of a landowner's wife who was in labor, and a huge padlock hung on the door of her cottage at the remotest end of the shtetl.

Once, coming into town on the landowner's cart to make some purchase at the pharmacy, the midwife Schatz drove up to their house and inquired for Mirel. Gitele flushed a little and replied quietly:

—Mirel's gone visiting . . . She's undoubtedly gone off to Royzenboym the photographer's wife.

But when the midwife Schatz called there, she found no one except the two sisters of Mirel's former fiancé, who were sitting in a small room with a low ceiling and a bright red floor filled with flower pots and the smell of Gentile cooking, listening to Royzenboym the photographer's wife playing a guitar.

—Hasn't Mirel been here?—she asked, coming into the room.

At which the sisters smiled oddly and exchanged glances, and the photographer Royzenboym's wife raised her head from her guitar and answered in astonishment:

—When did Mirel Hurvits ever come here?

What a totally Christian appearance this Royzenboym woman had! Not without reason was the whole shtetl alive with rumors that before she'd married the photographer Royzenboym she'd lived with an officer somewhere in a big town.

On one of these evenings, when, as always, Mirel was not at home, an unfamiliar hired conveyance stopped in the darkness next to Reb Gedalye Hurvits's house, and an out-of-town Jew of average height muffled up in furs alighted from it and made his way into the illuminated hallway, where he stood smiling and twinkling his little eyes:

—He'd been sent here . . . sent here from Yankev-Yosl Zaydenovski.

Gitele and their young relative the bookkeeper received him, saw him slowly disencumber himself of his fur overcoat and his sheepskin undercoat, and watched as, equally slowly, he hung them both up on the coat rack. Then they sat with him at the dining room table, listening to him relate in a deliberate and leisurely manner:

—He was, to be sure, no professional matchmaker . . . and, thank God, he had no need to depend on that kind of work for his livelihood . . .

He ran a warehouse of sacks in a large shtetl near the metropolis, and was a close, long-standing friend of Yankev-Yosl and his household.

He had a substantial graying beard and, curving right down to his mouth, a long nose under the skin of which stretched a network of blue-brown veins; he looked oddly respectable in his long, black frock coat, and his small gray eyes never stopped twinkling with great urbanity.

—He'd been sent here, to be sure . . . sent by Yankev-Yosl Zaydenovski.

The lamp hanging from the ceiling in Reb Gedalye Hurvits's dining room burned late into that night.

At length Gitele retired to her bedroom and lay down to sleep. Someone prepared a fresh bed in Reb Gedalye's study for this emissary who was their guest, and also went to bed. Only then did their out-of-town visitor draw from his bag Lippert's *Kulturgeschichte** in its Hebrew translation and sit down at the dining room table, apologetically explaining to the departing bookkeeper as he did so:

—He'd once owned a Jewish bookshop . . . From that time on he'd retained the habit of reading late into the night.

The relative took his leave and went home to bed. The maid locked

*Kulturgeschichte der Menschheit in ihrem organischen Aufbau [The Evolution of Culture] was published in 1886–87 by the Czech historian Julius Lippert (1839–1909). Its Hebrew translation was published in three volumes in Warsaw between 1894 and 1908.

the front door behind him and soon began snoring loudly in the unoc-cupied pantry. And the guest went on sitting over his book at the table, drawing the hanging lamp on its pulley farther and farther down to-ward him. When Mirel's knocking finally made itself heard from one of the outer shutters farthest away, he rose from his book and went to open the door for her, poking out his head with its twinkling gray, kindly eyes and, overcome with peculiar sensitivity and confusion like an embarrassed child, began stammering:

—Hm . . . A pleasure . . . A pleasure.

As soon as she saw this unknown face thrust out at her, Mirel trem-bled all over, and instantly and violently drew back, clutching at her beating heart:

—Oh! . . . How frightening this was!

Coming into the house, she kept edging ever farther away from him as though afraid he'd make a move toward her.

Clad as she was from head to foot in black, her figure appeared more slender and lissome than usual, and she emanated a barely perceptible fragrance all around her, all of which so agitated the out-of-town Jew that he found himself unable to stop smiling and stammering:

—Hmm . . . hm . . . frightened? How could this be? A pleasure . . . a great pleasure.

His childlike sensitivity and the fact that he decorously refrained from offering her his hand* made him appear thoroughly respectable, yet for a long time afterward she was unable to compose herself, wait-ing until he'd lain down to sleep before going to wake the soundly snor-ing servant girl:

—Who was this person?

—At any rate, at least she knew he certainly wasn't a thief.

And the stranger, their guest, could still hear her voice as he lay in his bed, and either from good nature or from tension smiled to himself in embarrassment:

—A thief? How could this be? . . . A good child . . . A very good child.

---

*Observant Orthodox Jewish men do not touch women in public, least of all women who are strangers to them.

The emissary lingered on in the house for several days, and every morning when Mirel awoke she heard them slowly drinking tea with milk in the dining room opposite the quiet salon, and knew there was no one there except the stranger who was assuring both the genteelly uncommunicative Gitele and her devoted relative, the bookkeeper:

—To be sure, they naturally want Mirele wholeheartedly . . . What a question . . .

—The young man himself, Shmulik, to be sure, desires it . . . and Yankev-Yosl himself . . . and Mindel, his wife.

And what else?

—They ask no money of you, not even a promise of money . . . They specifically bade him say so.

Hearing all this as she lay in bed, Mirele was revolted to her very soul. And the quiet, truncated conversation continued to reach her from the dining room:

—And as people, he was obliged to say, the Zaydenovskis were un- usually highly regarded . . . genial . . .

—And the young man himself . . . a fine young man . . . truly, a very fine young man.

The emissary eventually left and began sending frequent letters and urgent telegrams which Gitele and that tall young man, their devoted bookkeeper, eagerly perused. Gitele did so with the wordlessly ven- omous resentment of a woman obdurately determined not to speak, and the bookkeeper, standing silently next to her, wore a deeply fur- rowed brow, lifted his nose and snorted far too pensively, delaying his intention to discuss this with Mirele so long that one day she herself stopped him outside the house to say:

—Would he please be so good as to inform her mother: she could rest assured that nothing would come of this . . .

She was greatly agitated when she told him this, yet a few days later, after she'd taken herself off to the provincial capital on the spur of the moment, someone from the city came down and spread new rumors about her over the whole shtetl:

—Yes, she'd been seen walking out with Shmuel Zaydenovski.

She'd been seen in the Ukrainian theater with him and near the prison on the outskirts of the city as well.

Whether in traveling to the provincial capital Mirel had known she'd meet him there, or whether, even as far as Gitele and the bookkeeper knew, their meeting had been accidental and unplanned, no one could say.

A few days later, she returned pale and cheerless from the provincial capital. It was about two o'clock in the afternoon, and in the dining room the white cloth laid for lunch was still spread on the round table. Gitele still sat in her usual place opposite her relative the bookkeeper, picking her teeth with a matchstick. Passing through, Mirele spoke not a single word to anyone and for perhaps fully half an hour shut herself in her isolated room. During all that time, Gitele kept urging her relative the bookkeeper:

—Why couldn't he just go into to her room and ask her? She couldn't begin to understand why not . . .

But the preoccupied young bookkeeper was in no hurry, furrowed his brow, raised his nose and snorted. In her room, meanwhile, Mirel changed, put on her black jacket and scarf and started making her way out into the street. Only then did he rise from his chair, follow her out into the hallway, and stop her there:

—Yes, he wanted to ask her . . . He wanted . . .

He instantly received an answer, one displeased and peculiarly harsh:

—She'd already told him once that nothing would come of this.

For a time he hovered in the hallway, uncertain of whether or not to go back into the house, while with dispassionate cheerlessness she calmly descended the steps of the verandah and made her way slowly up into the shtetl somewhere. The dark melancholy day was in the grip of the light yielding frost that follows a sunny fair. The dirty snow was slippery underfoot, and Gentile pigs and Jewish cows thrust their snouts into such muddily filthy straw as lay scattered about. Here and there, swathed in furs and tightly bundled up, young wives stood near the doors of the small flour shops they ran, following her with curious glances:

—Is it true what they say—that Mirel's about to become a bride?

She turned left into the back street at the very end of the town, entered Lipkis's home through the front door and inquired:

—Isn't Lipkis at home?

His widowed mother saw her out with great respect, repeating several times:

—He's teaching somewhere at the moment . . . He's giving lessons to his pupils somewhere.

Leaving, she took herself off along the well-worn footpath that led out of the shtetl to the home of the midwife Schatz, found a lock hanging on the door there, and learned from her Gentile neighbor:

—She'd been called out to a woman in childbirth in Kashperivke yesterday evening.

Deeply depressed, Mirel returned to town, paused in front of the pharmacy but, appearing to think better of it, walked on, passing close by the house of her former fiancé's father with its unusual blue shutters; stealing a glance in that direction she saw:

Not a single conveyance was stationed in front of the verandah and no one was to be seen there. Only a tall farmer, a *szlachticz*[*] who'd apparently sought a small loan with which to cover the costs of the coming summer's work, left the house empty-handed, sighed very deeply, pulled the flaps of his fur hat down over his ears and reflected that as it made no difference now where he ended up, he might as well take himself off wherever his eyes might lead him.

She wandered about aimlessly until it began to grow dark outside and an even darker night began to descend on the shtetl. Not far from her father's house she met her former fiancé's eighteen-year-old cousin on his way to take tea with his uncle, and in a despondently quiet monotone she complained to him:

—Did he have any explanation for the blank emptiness that had started taking hold of everything here in town? . . . There was simply no one here with whom to exchange a word.

---

[*]A member of the *szlachta,* or Polish nobility.

2.5

Virtually every day thereafter she stood outside next to the house and saw:

With the approach of the midwinter festival of Christmas, the mild frosts grew more severe, and for long gray days on end the dirty, frozen, snow-covered district faced that depressingly murky region toward which the searing wind blew ever more strongly. From that direction, the town awaited yet another ill-starred, drifting snowstorm, hearing the violent sorrow with which the bare languishing trees all around creaked in expectation of it:

—Eventually this new snowstorm must break loose . . . it must . . .

In various corners of the town, warmly clad children returned one by one to heder* after their lunch. They walked slowly and sluggishly, stopping every now and then with their backs to the wind to muse:

—The blind night'll come . . . It'll definitely come very soon.

Every now and then, along the road that led hither from the dismal murkiness of the fields, a new out-of-town sleigh would arrive, bringing someone else for the festive season, perhaps a lightly dressed and severely chilled telegraph clerk who'd arrived in these parts very early by train. In the teeth of the burning wind, the sleigh swept him farther and farther onward, wordlessly making him fine promises:

—Soon, very soon: there'll be a cheerfully warm and brightly lit cottage, a home . . . there'll be a friendly smile from peasant parents and a long, dark village night—it's the festive season.

A local Jew who remained arrogant despite being unemployed and having come down in the world approached Mirel slowly, his back stooped. With his arms folded into his sleeves, he stopped, looked into the distance with a sigh, and slowly began telling about his young daughter, a former friend of Mirel's, who was now in her third year of study in Paris:

---

*The heder was the traditional religious elementary school where boys between the ages of three and fourteen were taught Torah and Talmud. The heder differed from the Talmud Torah in being a private institution run by the local rabbi or another religious functionary in his own home. The parents of boys attending the heder were expected to pay for their sons' tuition.

—From there she wrote home to say that she'd not be returning any time soon, this daughter of his . . . She'd not come back until she'd completed her studies.

The man looked broodingly into the distance along the road that led to that substantial, distant village with its sugar refinery where the perpetually jolly and perpetually busy Nokhem Tarabay ran his wealthy household in the style of a nobleman, and even more slowly began relating that this Nokhem Tarabay's children had all arrived in the village for the Gentile festive season.

—His younger son, the student at the polytechnic, was already there in the village, as well as his older son, a student at the science-oriented high school . . . and another young polytechnic student, a friend of his son's, so they say.

Great longing could be heard in the voice of this Jew who'd come down in the world, and he spoke of these two newly arrived polytechnic students with as much tenderness as though both were nothing less than bridegrooms for his pampered daughter who was now in her third year of study in Paris. When he'd finally grown bored with standing here and had wandered away to impart the same information to someone else, Mirel stood near the house for a long time, thinking about herself and about the days that were slipping by:

—Her life dragged by in such a banal fashion . . . It had been banal right up until this midwinter festive season and it would go on and on being banal.

Far, far away, a mere speck on the horizon, an image of the unknown village with its sugar refinery rose in her mind's eye, and her yearning heart was drawn in powerless silence to those two young, fresh-faced polytechnic students who were now probably taking a stroll after their long afternoon nap. An image also rose of the big city from which they'd come down only the day before, and the thought occurred:

—Before this Gentile festival, they'd finished some task in the big city . . . and returning there, they'd prepare themselves to start another.

—And she, Mirel, what had she accomplished up until this midwinter festive season?

She'd been in the provincial capital and for a few days had dragged herself about with a tall, wealthy young man named Shmulik Zayden-ovski; the whole shtetl knew about this by now—and nothing would come of it.

Having grown bored with standing outdoors, she went back into the house, lay down on the bed in her room, and thought coldly and indifferently about this young bachelor:

He was a tall young man in a high-crowned beaver hat and a new skunk fur overcoat* who ought to be married, and had a youthful father with business interests worth half a million. Strolling about the bustling streets of the provincial capital, he'd stopped on meeting his former Hebrew teacher and told him quietly and with sham earnestness how greatly he admired the work of some Yiddish writer or other and how good the big-city cantors were:

—Both he and the Hebrew teacher had melodious voices and had once accompanied cantors together.

Rich Jews, merchants who'd once known his father, looked at him from the opposite side of the pavement in front of the stock exchange, forgot their business affairs for a moment, reflected on the enormous dowries they'd bestow on their grown-up daughters, and spoke about Shmulik, and about his father whom they'd known long before:

—A very fine young man, this Shmulik Zaydenovski, they say.

But Shmulik himself had made the acquaintance of Mirel Hurvits, and would hear no word about other matches.

And why did she please this rich young bachelor so greatly?

He was now undoubtedly gliding swiftly onward somewhere far, far away, toward the quiet end of a suburb in the distant provincial capital, gliding swiftly onward by himself in his very own sleigh which had been sent out to meet him at the train, longing for Mirel, and thinking about what his parents would soon inquisitively begin demanding of him:

—How do you like Mirel Hurvits?

—And all in all, was she beautiful, this Mirel Hurvits?

She thought long about him, and about many other young men whom she knew, remembered the distant village and Tarabay's house

*In the early 1900s, skunk fur was among the most popular and costly of pelts from which coats were made.

there, where as a child she'd sought shelter from a summer storm with her father, and thought of Tarabay's son, the polytechnic student, and of his friend, their guest. Suddenly she paled in agitation, and with her heart pounding rapidly, she recalled Nosn Heler, that charming young bachelor with the fresh, oblong face and the barely visible whiskers who'd completed his studies at the science-oriented school and had twice failed the university entrance examination. A year before, solely on her account, he'd spent the entire spring here in the shtetl, awakening romantic longings in young women to whom he'd never addressed a single word.

During the quiet spring evenings she'd sat with him on the steep hill outside the town center, leaning her head against his shoulder, and listening sadly to him repeating the same thing he'd said the day before and the day before that:

—If she'd break off her engagement to her fiancé Velvl Burnes, he'd complete his studies at the polytechnic, become an engineer in a distant factory, and live with Mirel in an ivy-covered cottage there.

But once, in the late twilight of a spring evening, Mirel vividly pictured herself two years after her marriage to Heler, totally alone, having finished her late afternoon tea, lying on a sofa in that ivy-covered cottage near a factory and thinking indifferently and without the slightest desire in her heart:

—He . . . Nosn . . . he'd come home to bed from the factory so often on previous occasions . . . He'll definitely come home tonight as well.

And during that same twilight she searched all over the shtetl for Heler, eventually found him, and told him:

—Nothing would come of this, so Heler . . . Heler could leave the shtetl that very day.

After that, Heler had spent the whole summer with an uncle in the sugar refinery, had strolled all over the village with Nokhem Tarabay's children, and wanting to take his revenge on Mirel, had gone round saying:

—He certainly wasn't the first with whom Mirel had exchanged kisses.

Tarabay's wife and daughter soon got to hear of this, and over in the shtetl someone broadcast it all over the neighborhood.

One Saturday night, not far from the midwife Schatz's cottage, she encountered three apprentice tailors out for a stroll, made way for them, and heard them making ugly jokes in coarse language about her and Nosn Heler.

—He's a fool—one of them commented about her new fiancé.—He doesn't understand that it's better to have one percent in a good business than a full hundred percent in a bad one.

The day after that, when it was overcast and chilly outdoors and she was on her way to the provincial capital with her fiancé for no reason but to spite someone, she instructed the driver to make a detour to the village where the sugar refinery stood and where Nosn Heler was still idling away his time and, again to spite someone, she stopped in front of Nokhem Tarabay's house and sent the driver in to borrow a felt coat for Velvl:

—They'd left home so lightly clothed—she instructed the driver to say—that she was afraid Velvl might catch a chill, God forbid.

Subsequently she dreamed all night about Nokhem Tarabay's house in the village and his family's out-of-town guest, the polytechnic student, about whom their neighbor, the Jew who'd come down in the world, had told her the day before. Somewhere in the pale darkness she was climbing the bare hill outside the town with this student, smiling at him, and hearing him say:

—She, Mirel, had once had a fiancé; he'd seen him here. What a fool of a fiancé she'd once had!

When she awoke, she couldn't remember what he looked like, this visiting polytechnic student. She dozed off again with a vaguely troubling yearning in her heart and her hands pressed to her breast, started awake once more with the remembrance of another vague dream in which this polytechnic student closely resembled Nosn Heler, and was unable to tell for which of them her heart longed.

Later, on a beautiful day of freshly fallen snow when, to honor the Gentile festival, the sun had triumphed over the frost, moisture started trickling drop by drop from the blank white roofs and intensified the heart's longing. With red sashes round their long white fur coats, the Gentile village girls stood around in the marketplace merrily cracking sunflower seeds and laughing at the village lads who were staging mock fights for their benefit. There, in front of the town's only grocery store at the entrance to the marketplace, Tarabay's elegantly decorated sleigh stood waiting for his children who were greedily consuming all the chocolate in the shop.

A housewife coming out into the marketplace from inside the store carrying a sack of flour pressed to her belly stopped not far from Reb Gedalye's house to remark:

—They're such handsome boys, Tarabay's children, and his daughter, too . . . The daughter's very attractive as well.

Returning to the house with a large bottle of kerosene, the maid also paused next to Mirel on the steps of the verandah to report what she'd seen and heard in the shop.

—Their guest, the polytechnic student, had told the shopkeeper: "In your shtetl there's a *barishniya*[*] named Mirel Hurvits who loves milk chocolate, so for her sake you must stock chocolate."

The maid went indoors and soon forgot what she'd seen and heard. But Mirel remained standing on the steps of the verandah for a long time, unable to tear her gaze away from the store and the elegantly decorated sleigh in front of it. At length Tarabay's children emerged, paused to view the shtetl, and took great pleasure in the antics of the schoolboy from the scientific-oriented school who'd caught a kid in the middle of the marketplace. He twisted the animal's tail, demanding to know how the letters M and E written together were pronounced, and thus forced the kid to respond with a bleating cry of pain:

—Me-eh-eh-eh . . . me-eh-eh-eh . . .

Eventually they seated themselves in their vehicle and, setting off for home past Reb Gedalye's house, all of them, except the girl, stared at Mirel. Tarabay's son murmured something in the ear of his polytechnic student friend, who had a shrewd, eager, licentious face, in response to which he turned his head going past, grinned too obviously, and stared intently into Mirel's face with the same lustfully voracious eyes with which one stared into the face of an unaccompanied big-city whore:

[*]Russian for "young lady."

—So that's her?

Obviously:

He'd just been told about her and Heler.

And more:

Looking at her, lewd thoughts passed though the mind of this polytechnic student with his lecherous, grinning face.

For some reason his lascivious glance aroused in her an unspoken, lustful excitement that intermixed prurient thoughts with deep inner dejection. The lustful arousal disappeared with the departing sleigh, but the dejection remained, grew stronger, and yielded to an innermost sense of emptiness and regret. All at once she appeared small and demeaned in her own eyes and, wanting to shake off this feeling, for some reason reminded herself of that suburb in the distant metropolis and of him, of Shmulik Zaydenovski himself, remained standing alone near the house for a long while, and reflected:

—At least this Shmulik Zaydenovski looked like a European, and there was no disgrace in appearing in public with him . . . In any case, there in the provincial capital, everyone admired him . . .

2.6

Rumors circulated in town about Velvl Burnes:

He was making an excellent marriage, Velvl: he was marrying a beautiful young woman, it was said, a brunette who'd completed her studies at a *gymnasium** in the provincial capital and who'd remarked of him to someone else not long before:

—All in all, he's a thoroughly decent young man, that Velvl Burnes; he certainly stood higher in her estimation than all those of her acquaintances who'd graduated from high schools, and she certainly found no fault whatever in him that his first fiancée had rejected him.

Mirel rarely appeared in public at that time, and no one knew what she was thinking. Only once did she comment on these rumors to the midwife Schatz:

*In tsarist Russia—and still in Eastern Europe today—a *gymnasium* is a secondary school that stresses academic over vocational education.

—Quite possibly this young woman who's completed her studies at the *gymnasium* is no fool . . .

Regardless of the fact that the midwife was extremely displeased with this conversation and interrupted her, she went on:

—Be that as it may . . . she found it insulting and painful, and didn't want Velvl to get married.

Some time after that, a bleak, depressing Thursday thick with frost descended on the shtetl, and here and there, on the houses of the very poor, the weekly burden of earning a living lay very heavy:

—Prepare for the Sabbath, eh? Is it really time to prepare for the Sabbath again?

Jews without gainful employment stood around the shops in the marketplace chatting about the lavish soirée being held that evening at Tarabay's house in the village:

––Why not? Is there anything Tarabay can't afford?

And farther over, at that end of town which bordered on the peasant cottages, Mirel, warmly dressed and unhappy, was seated in Reb Gedalye's rickety sleigh drawn by his emaciated horses on her way to this party at Tarabay's home, and in her depression she bade the Gentile lad who was driving her make a detour to the midwife Schatz's remote cottage.

She was thrown into still greater despondency by the lock she found on the midwife's door, stood there crestfallen for a while, and finally left in the care of her peasant neighbor the invitation Tarabay had sent the midwife, adding a few words of her own:

—She was to come there immediately, not for the sake of Tarabay who recommended her professional services to all the neighboring landowners, but for her sake, for Mirel.

She paused there a little longer, reconsidering whether or not to go:

—This was really a foolish journey to an equally foolish evening at Tarabay's. She'd certainly do better to turn back and go home.

Afterward she was intensely downcast and depressed for the entire twenty-four versts of the trip, gazed at the vacant fields all around over which the cold, heavily overcast skies lowered with late winter desolation, and felt even more disheartened and diminished from the fact that far, far behind her, moving swiftly along the road to Tarabay's home, were the two expensive sleighs of those who were once to have been her in-laws, filling the silence of the fields with the jingle of their bells. She thought:

—The midwife Schatz . . . If only the midwife Schatz would come as well.

Half an hour later, these two fast-moving sleighs had caught up and drawn level to the left and right of her. Their silence was peculiarly disdainful, these people in these elaborately decorated sleighs moving so rapidly to the left and right of her. She glanced at them as though through a dream and noticed:

With a strained and distant expression on his face, her former fiancé sat in one of these elaborately decorated conveyances, and from the other his warmly clad sisters shouted out across her:

—Velvl! Did you bring it with you?

They shouted calmly and busily across her, as though across an inanimate object, received a mere shake of his head in reply, and swiftly left her behind.

Only when these two sleighs had sped swiftly into the distance and begun to grow smaller against the horizon did she rouse herself from her half-dozing state and notice:

The little Gentile lad who was driving her had been standing up the whole time, ceaselessly whipping the emaciated horses which were striving forward with their last strength, and was apparently trying to overtake those long-vanished other sleighs. She instantly leapt up from her seat and grabbed his shoulders:

—What a wretched madman he was! How long had he been whipping these worn-out beasts?

Ashamed of himself, the little Gentile pulled the exhausted animals to a halt, crept down from the sleigh in great embarrassment, and worked next to one of them for perhaps a full half hour, tying together a halter that had snapped.

Humbly and dejectedly she sat in the sleigh moralizing at him:

—She, Mirel, would be perfectly content if both these pitiful horses were to die on the same night, but as long as they were still struggling for life in this world, one ought to fear God and not whip them.

She arrived in the village just as night had fallen, when lamps had already been lit in all the wealthy Gentile houses, and when the harsh indifference of the glance that these illuminated houses cast on her unfamiliar sleigh intensified from moment to moment:

—The local Gentiles here were peaceable and rich—these houses wished to make clear.—Apart from their land, the local Gentiles here also had a prosperous sugar refinery close by which provided for them abundantly all winter.

By now the gloom of dusk lay on the village's long paved road that, in company with an entire plateau of rustic roofs, rose higher and higher up the gradual incline of the hill and ended where the sky's rim was a wash of intense red up into which the refinery's giant chimney poked like a festive exclamation point. Extraordinarily slowly, the weary horses dragged their way up this residentially developed hill, their heads continually bowed to the ground. And the surrounding houses with their alien appearance awakened a very particular kind of disquiet, the mournful Friday evening disquiet of an observant Jew who'd been delayed in returning home in time to welcome the Sabbath, who in the sanctified twilight was still lugging himself and his wagon through the deep mud on the country roads, hauling himself onward slowly and calling to mind:

There in the brightly lit synagogue in his shtetl, observant Jews were already swaying in prayer, swaying together in unison as they fullthroatedly followed the cantor's lead:

—Give thanks unto the Lord for He is good, for His mercy endureth forever . . .

With brightly illuminated, new-fangled windows, Nokhem Tarabay's big house occupied the full breadth of the farthest alley in the village, wordlessly communicating its master's patently obvious rhetorical question:

—I don't understand: if God is good and one earns well and enjoys good health, why shouldn't one live in worldly comfort and ease? Why should one live worse than the Gentile landowners?

The semicircular courtyard in which her weary conveyance stopped, the open verandah, the high, white-painted front door with its nickel name-plate, all were spotless and neat.

When she finally rang the bell at this front door, the short, perpetually cheerful Nokhem Tarabay, bareheaded and wearing a little black frock coat, immediately ran out to receive her, bowing with his little feet pressed elegantly together.

—*Jaśniewielmożna Panna* Hurvits has delayed her arrival by fully two hours.

Continually tugging his shirt cuffs from under his coat sleeves, he went on chattering to her in the brightly lit entrance hall while a smartly dressed maid helped her off with her outdoor things:

—The invitation explicitly stated that all guests were to arrive at four o'clock, and now she'd see for herself: his pocket watch was always accurate, and at present it showed exactly six, which even for Mirel wasn't very polite. But she might be certain: he'd always been a good friend to her and to Reb Gedalye, and he wouldn't be so much as a single minute late for her wedding.

In the entrance hall, which overflowed with coats of all kinds, she adjusted her hair in front of the huge mirror, glanced at her face and her décolletage, and forced herself to smile at Tarabay who was standing behind her:

—He might certainly believe her: it wasn't her fault . . .

But even in the first brightly lit room into which, having taken her arm, Tarabay led her, she was suddenly aware of the alluring power of her graceful figure in its close-fitting cream wool gown. Her gratified heart abruptly swelled with intoxicating pride.

—She'd actually done well to arrive only now . . . uncommonly well . . .

She seated herself in one of the low chairs of a suite in a corner of the room opposite Tarabay's shrewd, truculent wife, felt many of the guests' glances turn to her, and smilingly answered all their questions:

—Yes . . . Her mother was a stay-at-home; she'd always been a stay-at-home.

From time to time she stole a glance into the crowded depths of the room and saw:

Heads bent together, glanced sideways at her, and whispered to each other as they did so:

—Who? . . . Mirel Hurvits? . . . From which shtetl?

Among two such bent heads, seated on a sofa next to the locked French doors, were her former fiancé's two sisters, whose noses were already pinched in superior disapproval, as though someone were preparing at any moment to approach and remind them:

—Only ten years before, their father had been a pauper.

Despite being completely drunk, one of the guests, a heavy-set Pole with a boorish, unshaven face, remembered openly to flatter Tarabay, through whose good offices he'd not long before obtained employment at the sugar refinery. Barely able to stand on his feet, he stopped every guest, whether known or unknown to him, endlessly to repeat the single witticism Tarabay had uttered, almost shaking himself to bits with mirth and drunken enthusiasm as he did so:

—*A to szelma, ten Pan Tarabay . . . szelma . . .**

One of those guests from the sugar refinery who'd buried themselves in whist by the light of the candles on the little baize table, suddenly rose rapidly from his chair with the cards in his hand and just as rapidly shouted out to all the young people who'd crowded together in the adjoining room:

—Champagne later! . . . Champagne at exactly midnight!

And next to Mirel, as though next to the daughter of an old and valued friend, Nechama Tarabay went on sitting, scrutinizing her with her disingenuous black eyes before which even the smooth-tongued Tarabay quailed, and trying hard to engage her in worldly conversation:

—Recently she'd tried to reason with Gitele, her mother: since you take the train so rarely to the provincial capital, why don't you travel second class? . . . For Heaven's sake, how much more expensive is second class? Sixty kopecks, perhaps?

And more:

—Why on earth should one go on living in utter boredom there in that desolate shtetl? Here in this village . . . here, there's a sugar refinery . . . there are people here, one can have a social life . . . there are at least business opportunities here . . .

All the while, at the crowded table in the center of the overcrowded

---

*Polish: "Oh, he's a sly one, that Mr. Tarabay . . . sly as a fox . . ."

room, her former fiancé sat with his back to her, not knowing what to do with his hands. Every time she deliberately raised her demanding, high-pitched voice from where she was seated, he fiddled gratuitously with the back of his collar and stared too intently into the face of a tall young merchant who kept jumping up from his chair and arguing with great intensity:

—Quiet! Hadn't he begged Reb Nokhem a year ago to sow as many sugar beets as possible?

Standing a little farther on, at the very end of the room, all in deeply cut white evening waistcoats, were a few young men from the sugar refinery who knew everything that had passed between Mirel and Nosn Heler the previous summer and as a result stared at her décolletage and smiling face with drunken, lecherous eyes and whispered prurient remarks about her:

—How's that for a pretty piece of female, eh?

Someone called Nechama Tarabay away for a confidential chat, and Mirel was left alone here on the suite's low chair while the young men from the sugar refinery continued to stare at her. Casting an oddly distracted glance at her own slender figure, she rose and wandered off to a side room where she found, wearing a short, housewifely apron with hands clasped and one foot in front of her, Tarabay's daughter Tanya, no longer as young as she'd have liked to be, with her head tilted a little to one side, hoping in this way to suggest, by looking at no one and quietly clucking her tongue:

—She'd not expected this whole get-together, and she'd no intention of taking any part in it.

When someone in this room addressed Mirel by name, her heart pounded, but this was only a simple, religiously observant young wife from their shtetl, who wore a headkerchief, still lived in the home and at the expense of her father, the ritual slaughterer, and was related to Tarabay through her husband:

—What had she wanted to ask? She believed Mirel had come here in her own sleigh, and she, this young wife, now felt quite unwell here. Perhaps she might soon be able to ride home with Mirel?

Meanwhile, a tall young man was now standing beside Tanya Tarabay, trying to convince her that living in big cities had great advantages and listening courteously as she maintained her own contrary opinion:

—At the end of last summer she'd been in Odessa to write the qualifying matriculation examinations . . . She'd felt so unwell there . . . She could hardly wait to escape from the place.

Suddenly the young folk from the adjoining room rushed in all together in hot pursuit of Tarabay's younger son, the student at the science-oriented school, seized him, and boisterously dragged him back to where they'd come from:

—Why didn't he want to recite? What harm would it do him to recite something?

Someone totally unknown to her approached Mirel and began complaining about the science student:

—Only a few weeks before he'd recited magnificently—at a soirée in the metropolis he'd declaimed splendidly.

But by now Mirel was extremely put out by the fact that her former fiancé's newly arrived parents had settled themselves in the salon. She stood on her own with her back pressed against the wall, raised her melancholy face a little higher and saw:

Sitting with Nechama Tarabay at a nearby table laden with newly laid-out refreshments was the obese woman who was to have been her mother-in-law, breathing heavily like a fat goose on the run and complaining, between gasps and groans, about her asthma:

—It makes life a torment . . . an absolute torment . . .

A little farther to Mirel's right, cheerful little Tarabay popped up in front of the chair in which her former fiancé's big-boned father was seated and tried to bring a smile to the studiedly grave face of this unlettered parvenu who'd only recently acquired a veneer of refinement:

—What need is there for so much concern, Reb Avrom-Moyshe? Surely the children are all provided with marriage portions by now, thank God? . . . So one marries them off and waits for the grandchildren, eh?

Then Tarabay rushed away for a while to see out an important guest, and with a cigarette in his mouth, Avrom-Moyshe Burnes, this dark-haired, studiedly genteel ignoramus, made his way over to Tarabay's elder son, the student at the polytechnic, and began repeating to him a newly minted bon mot of his own:

—He'd only just this moment posed a riddle . . . He'd posed this riddle to his father only a moment ago.

Of average height, with simian forehead and nostrils pinched in arrogant disdain, this student had been silently sneering at everything for some time now; all in all, he intensely disliked both his own parents and their assembled guests. And now this studiedly genteel ignoramus Burnes was pestering him with his silly riddle:

—What exactly is the difference between the Count of Kashperivke and Vasil, his lackey?

Mirel took several steps toward the open, brightly lit dining room and, in low spirits, with her cheek pressed against the door, she stopped and saw:

Yet again the unusually long table was being laid, and plates were clattered together so often and so cheerfully that a few of those assembled had their appetites whetted anew. Some of the young people were drifting about there, while others gathered in small groups, and the newly arrived midwife Schatz, her face freshly colored by the cold outside, stood opposite the visiting polytechnic student smoking one of his cigarettes and smiling:

—She knew them . . . She knew them intimately, these dissolute polytechnic students who liked nothing better than chasing after girls.

Slowly and in an oddly despondent frame of mind, Mirel went up to the midwife, embraced her and, like a small child, pressed her whole body closely against her, her voice trembling:

—The midwife Schatz could hardly imagine how grateful she was to her for having come now! She, Mirel, would explain the cause of this gratitude another time.

Wine was drunk from a variety of sealed bottles which had earlier been carefully passed from hand to hand with smilingly appreciative comments on the information conveyed on their labels and lead foils.

Drinking went on uninterruptedly, both during the meal and afterward when plates were being cleared from the unusually long, damask-covered table, and Tarabay's cousin Notte, a remarkably tall, robust grain merchant, was already drunk, red-faced, and sweating. Every now and then he'd place full new bottles on the table, and chant portentous announcements in a loud, raucous voice, in imitation of the traditional manner of auctioning off the honor of carrying a Torah scroll round the synagogue during the festival of Simchas Torah:*

—This one is presented by Uncle Nokhem in the name of his eldest son, Boris, who works in a bank in Łodz, and will, God willing, soon become the di—rec—tor!

—This one is presented by Auntie Nechamka for her eldest daughter, Tanya, who passed her matriculation examination before Suk—kot.

Through the haze of smoke from a multitude of cigarette butts, the lamps flickered and burned dimly.

The confused murmur of thirty drunken voices filled the room and hung in the air, rendering barely audible the occasional yell that accompanied two bottles clinked together, and the burly grain merchant with his long, flapping arms continued to strain his voice, driving genteel, worldly people to grimace in distaste:

—This one is presented by Uncle Nokhem in honor of his younger son, Isak, who will, God willing, in two years' time qualify as an en—gin—ee—er.

Seated at this noisy table, Mirel experienced something wholly unforeseen:

The family's guest, the polytechnic student with the licentious grinning face who didn't look in the slightest sober, was exchanging salacious winks about her with one of the young men in deep-cut evening waistcoats:

—Might one risk it, d'you think, eh?

---

*Simchas Torah (Hebrew, meaning "rejoicing of the Torah") is one of the happiest days in the Jewish liturgical year, when the annual cycle of public Torah readings is completed with the last section of Deuteronomy and begun again with the first section of Genesis. During both morning and evening services all the scrolls in each synagogue's possession are removed and carried around the synagogue in a series of seven circuits with much singing and dancing. This honor of carrying a Torah scroll is often auctioned to raise funds.

With the crude grin of a village peasant, he seated himself on one of the unoccupied chairs beside her at the very moment at which, with a gravely sorrowful expression, she was glancing indifferently at the row of people opposite. He stole a nastily lascivious sidelong glance at her décolletage and with equally nasty lasciviousness coughed into the fist which he grinningly brought up to his mouth:

—Nosn Heler's a very fine fellow and good-looking as well, eh?

He started telling her something about how that idler Nosn Heler had failed the matriculation examinations for which they'd prepared together; about the fact that Nosn Heler's recently deceased parents had left him no more than five or six thousand rubles as his inheritance, and about how Heler, that frivolous, good-looking loafer, was now drifting about without employment in the metropolis and was considering accepting one of the two marriage proposals that had been suggested to him.

—Fifteen thousand rubles—he related—that's the kind of dowry he's been offered.

All this time, Mirel did not once turn to look at him, pretended not to hear, and with gravely sorrowful eyes continued to glance indifferently at the row of people opposite.

Suddenly she became aware that this half-drunken lout was moving his chair closer and closer to her under the table, was slowly placing his foot on hers, and was equally slowly starting to press that foot down.

Instantly flustered and burningly red, she sprang up from her seat with a cry:

—*Ne smeete!* Don't you dare!

An overwhelming feeling of anger and insult threw her entire being into turmoil. Her confused mind was filled with disconnected thoughts, her heart pounded too rapidly, and she took too much pleasure from the infinite disgust with which she finally shouted:

—You sot!

At this cry, people rose hastily from the table. Her former fiancé's family, casting glances at her, started whispering among themselves, and on the other side of the table the ironically smiling midwife began chatting to someone. But all this was a matter of unconcern to Mirel, who was unable to focus her mind on it.

With her back pressed closely to the wall, she stood alone at the very end of the deserted salon and slowly surrendered to an awareness of her own fall from grace:

—It really wasn't worthwhile . . . This whole stupid evening had probably not been worthwhile.

Some thought absorbed her entire attention as she stood with her back pressed closely to the wall, looking down with sorrowful, pensive eyes at a distant yellow stain on the floor:

—At bottom, this evening wasn't actually the central, overriding concern . . .

For some time now she'd felt the slow, painful demise of her vapid, commonplace, self-absorbed life. She felt it as she wandered idly about with Lipkis, and she felt it also in thinking for hours at a stretch about that wealthy young man named Shmulik Zaydenovski.

Meanwhile the full drunken uproar had carried through from the dining room to the salon. Creatures the worse for liquor with red, sweaty faces were all clamoring at the same time, demanding something as they surrounded the piano that stood in the opposite corner of the salon, shoving each other and yelling for Tanya Tarabay:

—It's all right! . . . It's all right!

—She won't be able to get out of it!

The drunken tumult slowly died away until it was finally choked in company with the hoarse, huckster's bellowing of Tarabay's cousin, the grain merchant:

—Quiet! Quiet! The *barishniya* Tanya will play something in honor of the guests.

In the silence that suddenly ensued, an expectant pause was followed by the first hushed, haunting tones of Beethoven's Piano Sonata no. 1, which made their way in quietly and modestly, embarrassed by the crude buffoonery that had preceded them and smiling about it with childlike naïveté to those gentle bass chords with which they had been intimately acquainted for so long:

—How did those bass chords feel now? Didn't they somehow feel oddly disgusted by all these persons who were listening?

Now no one ventured to break this haunting silence, and only from the opposite corner, near the door, the drunken elderly Pole, unable to hold his tongue, was pestering someone else, still openly flattering the shrewd Tarabay, almost shaking himself to bits with drunken enthusiasm:

—*A to szelma, ten Pan Tarabay . . . szelma . . .*

Then, crashing abruptly across this stillness, came the voice of the woman who should have been Mirel's mother-in-law:

—Look here! Wherever can Reb Nokhem have got to?

This gross woman stood alone in the middle of the salon, busily and distractedly peering about for a glimpse of Tarabay:

—She needed Reb Nokhem so urgently.

From among the dense crowd surrounding the piano, Mirel's former fiancé went over to her and led her politely over to a side of the room:

—Hush! Just look at her . . . You'll see Reb Nokhem a little later on.

At length Mirel left the salon and made her way despondently through the adjacent darkness to the dining room. She needed to find someone there:

—Yes, she needed to find the midwife Schatz there.

But entering another darkened room nearby, she saw her former fiancé and his parents gathered around Nokhem Tarabay near the door and instantly drew back. His father was explaining something to Tarabay:

—He's left the matter in my hands . . . He's said to me: take the dowry and deposit it where you wish.

And with her voice choked with tears, his wife supported him:

—Let Reb Nokhem be spared to a long life, and let the dowry be deposited with him . . . She no longer wanted to deposit money with Gentile landowners . . . She'd been punished once already.

Mirel retreated through the salon to the dining room, found the midwife there in an unusually jovial, half-tipsy state, and was deeply offended by the smell of wine on her breath:

—Well? Didn't the midwife Schatz ever intend to go home?

They donned their overcoats and, seated in Reb Gedalye's old sleigh, traveled home, moving out of the sleeping village into the surrounding night at a regular pace.

As he drove, the little Gentile lad wept quietly and with foolish simple-mindedness, complaining about the burly, smartly uniformed coachmen who'd playfully shoved him from one to another in the kitchen and the stable, and from all sides had kept rapping him on the head with their knuckles.

The tipsy midwife Schatz, on the other hand, went on laughing and chattering immoderately.

Mirel sat beside her in deep despondency. She glanced across to where the lamps of the sugar refinery patiently guarded its brickwork depots, feeling the emptiness of the days that had passed together with the emptiness of those that would start stretching out from tomorrow:

—Is this the end, then? . . . The end of everything? . . .

When Mirel eventually drove up to their house in the shtetl, knocked softly on the shutters of the kitchen window, and went quietly indoors, Gitele heard her crossing the dining room on tiptoe and in a very sleepy voice called out to her from her bedroom:

—There's a telegram on the table . . . a telegram from your father.

Mirel went over to the table, turned up the lamp and opened it:

—Reb Gedalye was returning home . . . He'd be back tomorrow afternoon.

For some reason she did not go to her own room, but with the telegram in her hand sat down on the sofa and, for the first time in a long while, thought about Reb Gedalye.

—At present she didn't love even him, her own father . . .

She felt only great compassion for his neglected illness, which doctors had continually been urging him to deal with, and for his unfortunate and muddled business affairs.

—It was said that he'd already made a mess of so much money, both his own and what had come to him by marriage . . . he was probably facing massive bankruptcy . . . But she, Mirel . . . she was unhappy herself, and quite unfit for any kind of work.

—She was quite unable to help him in any way.

Pale light was already seeping through the cracks in her shutters when she finally undressed in her own room and retired to bed. Somewhere far away, in the strained silence of this Friday dawn over the sleeping shtetl, the jingling bells on Avrom-Moyshe Burnes's sleighs, returning and offloading their passengers, spread the deflated mood of in-laws returning from a wedding. And for some reason, at this early hour in the house here, Gitele was already up and dressed, and by the light of the lamp had started pacing about the dining room.

This was very odd:

In unyielding silence this elderly, taciturn, stubborn creature had always loved her preoccupied husband and yearned for him. Now, evidently, she was greatly excited that he was coming back, had passed a restless night, and by pacing about, was hoping to shorten the time remaining until his return.

2.7

For the whole of that Sabbath, Reb Gedalye Hurvits had every reason to be content with his home. On Saturday night he peered cheerfully over his gold-rimmed spectacles at neighborhood acquaintances and former partners who'd called to see him, and even in his distracted frame of mind he shared a witty remark with them:

—Yes, while he was abroad they'd taken him for a young bachelor . . . they'd even wanted to arrange marriages for him over there.

In reality, while he'd been abroad he'd lost a great deal of weight, acquired the shadowed complexion of the terminally ill, and had brought back with him many bottles of medicine, a small nickel vaporizer, and the diagnosis of a dangerous, progressive illness. The bottles stood in a tedious row on the windowsill of his study as a silent reminder of the indifference of the foreign professors:

—Do I know? . . . Do these doctors really place any value on human beings?

About the diagnosis, the well respected local *feldsher*,* normally grimly uncommunicative, remarked among some of his convalescent patients:

---

*A *feldsher* was a rudimentary health-care professional who provided many medical services in tsarist Russia, mainly in rural areas. The word *feldsher* derives from the German term *Feldscher,* meaning "field doctor," which described medieval barber-surgeons attached to the Russian army as far back as the seventeenth century.

—Obviously Reb Gedalye has cancer. What else?

In Reb Gedalye's presence, people genuinely felt awkward and said too little for too long. Surreptitiously, they spat to one side every time someone mentioned his disease by name[*] and mused:

—He's still a young man, Reb Gedalye; I mean, after all, he's only fifty.

But Reb Gedalye continued to pay no attention to any of this. Preoccupied as he was, he wanted once more to take control of his unfortunate business affairs, and spent several successive evenings drawing up balance sheets in his study with his relative the bookkeeper.

Every time he broke off his work there late at night and went out into the well-lit dining room in company with his bookkeeper, his face was anxious and his red eyes troubled as he agitatedly gnawed one of his knuckles and kept interrupting his own thoughts:

—Well, it's certainly bad . . . There's nothing to discuss.

And later still, in his bedroom, he would linger unusually long over the recitation of the prayer before retiring, paying no attention to the reproaches that Gitele, already in her nightgown, heaped on him from her bed, but then always hurriedly and distractedly asking her:

—Eh? What did you say?

By this time Gitele had already mentioned her jewelry and diamond earrings far too often, had far too often tried to persuade Reb Gedalye that it would be sensible for her to take them with her on a trip to her rich great-uncle in a distant shtetl, and had far too often complained venomously against their relative the bookkeeper:

—But she'd told him . . . She'd continually warned him that he was projecting too substantial a balance, that's what he was doing.

Little by little the chaos of impending bankruptcy began breaking loose again, and once more awakened in Mirel a sense of disgust coupled with a detestation of the house and the strangers who created such uproar within it. From day to day, the conviction grew stronger in her:

—The chaos of bankruptcy . . . Surely there'll soon be an end to it?

---

[*]In the belief that this would ward off the evil eye and protect them from contracting the same disease.

Misfortune, it seemed, was about to overwhelm all the members of their household, the Jewish agents who worked in the Kashperivke woods and in the Tarnov mill, the bookkeeper, and even their cook, that overgrown girl who was now in the eighth year of her service with them.

But to Mirel herself all this was a matter of indifference, and at bottom . . .

At bottom, all this would leave her neither better nor worse.

For hours on end she lay in her room with this thought, took it with her when she called on the midwife Schatz, and brought it back with her a short while later, when, without glancing at the numerous creditors and their delegated arbitrators who choked the dining room with the smoke of their cigarettes, she shut herself up in her own room where she began turning it over in her mind yet again:

—The chaos of bankruptcy . . . Surely there'll soon be an end to it?

In the house, many sleepless, agonized nights filled with frantic searches for advice dragged by. No one but Mirel undressed or had any thought of rest at that time. Every now and then she'd start awake in her darkened room and become aware that everyone else was still awake; that, apart from the bookkeeper and Avreml the rabbi, the local solicitor was also present; that they were conferring furtively together, carefully whispering so that neither she nor the maid who slept in the pantry should hear; and that the solicitor's advice was clearly audible:

—The chief concern was to pay the interest on the Kashperivke woods and the Tarnov mill by the due date, because as soon as the title deeds were legally transferred, there'd be no force in any of the bank's threats.

Wearily and with the ease of a sick person she dozed off in the darkness and saw in her dreams a multitude of furious strangers who filled the house to overflowing, felt a little afraid again, started awake, and yet again heard the solicitor giving his advice:

—For her part, Gitele must transfer everything to the bookkeeper's name—what don't you understand about this? The chief concern is to have a third party in this matter.

Once more she dozed off, and in her light sleep she heard Gitele continually urging Reb Gedalye:

—Gedalye, go to bed, Gedalye . . . You're not well enough to be sitting up, Gedalye.

But Reb Gedalye paid no attention, and again sat up until dawn. As a result he looked very ill and under his gold-rimmed spectacles his sharp nose looked as ashen as that of a corpse.

One day during the week before Purim he came into Mirel's room with this ashen nose, stopped not far from her bed with his face toward the window, and there distractedly began fiddling with the knick-knacks on the tulle-covered dressing table.

Eventually he began complaining to her about Gitele and the bookkeeper:

—During all that time he'd begged them in his letters: for God's sake, don't touch Mirele's five thousand rubles . . . He'd pleaded with them as though pleading with robbers.

But at the very moment she'd turned her face a little toward him wanting to ask him something, the stubborn, embittered Gitele began repeatedly calling to him from the dining room:

—Gedalye? Please come here, Gedalye.

—Gedalye? I want to tell you something, Gedalye.

Since this obdurate, unfeeling summons was maddening, he eventually went back, displeased and a little irritated, but for some reason before he left he promised Mirel, who'd stayed in bed from early morning on with a headache and a heightened temperature:

—He'd come back to see her . . . In half an hour he'd come back to her room.

That day some new blow, some new misfortune, was expected in the house, so the maid was deliberately sent out for several hours, a paroxysm of stifled fear held constant sway, and in anxious haste all the family silver in the salon's old glass-fronted cabinet was carried off for safekeeping somewhere. Finally, Reb Gedalye permitted the stubborn Gitele to make the trip to her great-uncle in his distant shtetl. Even from Mirel's room she could continually be heard, driving Reb Gedalye out of his senses with her importunity and forcing him uncharacteristically to raise his voice:

—Well, well . . . What was she making such a commotion for? She'd
go in the end . . . She'd go there with the agent of the Kashperivke woods.

But everything happening around her made little impression on
Mirel.

In the debility of her illness she experienced another bizarre, feverish dream in which late at night Lipkis was telling Libke the rabbi's
wife that for three consecutive weeks typhus had left him hovering between life and death, that he'd called now to see not Mirel but her,
Libke; and at the very moment he was speaking, her former fiancé,
Velvl Burnes, was standing not far from her bed in deep despondency,
looking not at her but respectfully down at the floor while he tried to explain himself:

—He wasn't at fault for coming to her. She certainly ought to pardon
him. He'd recently married that dark-haired young woman and had
simply come by for no particular reason.

When she'd at length roused herself from this restless doze, the window panes looked like black ink. The ambience of deep night hovered
over the lamp burning in a distant corner of the room, and there
seemed to be no living soul in the entire lifeless, deserted house. Only
some time later, from far away in the entrance hall, did she hear footsteps come running swiftly into the house from outside and just as
swiftly go running out again with a slam of the door and a loud, hurried
shout:

—The shawl! . . . Gitele's forgotten to take her thick shawl . . .

At that moment, apparently, everyone had gone out to see Gitele off
on her journey to her great-uncle in his distant shtetl; by the light of the
lamp that had been carried out, they stood about in the courtyard
watching her seat herself next to the agent of the Kashperivke wood in
the ready-harnessed family sleigh.

Now Mirel remembered:

Something had taken place in the house earlier . . . She didn't want
to think about what would happen to her the next day . . . And that
morning . . . . That morning, it seemed, someone had sat there and related:

—Velvl Burnes was shortly to marry that dark-haired girl . . . even
now serving-maids were doubtless crushing almonds and cinnamon

for pastries, and it was said that soon after the wedding the young couple would go abroad somewhere.

—Abroad?

She lay in bed, her eyes huge and suffused with mourning as though at that very moment she could see the dark, distant night with the long express train that was bearing the young couple toward the border. She stared into the burning lamp and thought:

—It wasn't so very bad, perhaps, to travel abroad as a couple through the darkness of night . . . But for her, Mirel, this was now totally impossible, and at bottom, this wasn't actually the central, overriding concern . . . There was no point in thinking about this now. She felt unwell, and that five thousand rubles of hers . . . and her future life, ah! . . . She might as well curl up into a ball and go to sleep . . . to sleep . . .

And how long she slept!

Throughout the night, the solitary tread of Reb Gedalye's nervous pacing rarely died away in the dining room. Pouring boiling water from the samovar, he even drank his tea alone there, and for some reason he tried several times to open the door of her room. But in her semiconscious state she was floating about somewhere in a darkling world of chaos, forgetful of the distress she endured daily. Only toward the hour of the third watch, lying in bed, did she tremblingly awaken, notice narrow, barely blue streaks of night peering into her room through the cracks in the shutters, and see Reb Gedalye sitting on her bed apologizing:

—He was afraid he'd woken her . . . He'd been unable to restrain himself and had woken her.

He felt wretched, but with no understanding of how to speak of this with Mirel, he sat for a long time here on the bed and once again began complaining about Gitele and the bookkeeper:

—He'd pleaded with them as though pleading with robbers: he hadn't wanted to go abroad . . . He should never have dared to leave home . . .

Abruptly she turned to face him and asked:

—Father, how much money do you have left?

Immediately she saw Reb Gedalye shrug his shoulders, hunch himself up in a peculiar way like a small child about to be smacked, and begin gesticulating:

—Nothing . . . not a kopeck.

—Nothing? . . .

For no discernible reason she repeated this after him, and for no discernible reason her heart began pounding. Previously there'd been something she'd wanted to understand and couldn't, and subsequently she wanted nothing at all, stared at him with unblinking, somewhat astonished eyes, and couldn't understand why he was still sitting next to her on the bed.

Now she had nothing more to ask him . . . now she knew everything. She was afraid to think about anything, and felt it essential, absolutely essential to fall asleep again. So immediately after Reb Gedalye's departure she turned her face to the wall with her eyes tight shut, buried her head more deeply in the pillow, pressed her folded arms more closely to her breast, and called Nosn Heler's face to mind:

—Like that . . . just like that . . . Now she was falling asleep again.

The next day she awoke with a ready though undeveloped plan, and she lay in bed for some time in a state of semiconsciousness and attempted to grasp this plan:

—Once, it seemed to her, she'd had an opportunity to leave this house . . . wait . . . What opportunity had this been?

Reb Gedalye had already returned from the Sadagura study house with his prayer shawl and phylacteries, and with Gitele absent, felt very lonely in the empty house. He found Mirel standing all alone in her room, and once again distractedly began fiddling with the knick-knacks on her dressing table.

He said:

—The bailiff . . . It's possible that the bailiff might call here today . . . It's not yet certain, but in any case . . . in any case, she needn't be alarmed.

—Ah, the bailiff? . . . Very well.

She responded quietly and without looking round at him, and almost immediately took her jacket and black scarf and left the house.

—Where would she go now? It made no difference.

The main thing was that she could no longer stay in that house, and for a few days . . .

—For a few days she could even live with the midwife Schatz.

And for a few days she did indeed live with the midwife Schatz. For the most part she lay cheerlessly in bed, her eyes filled with intense sorrow, staring down in silence at something on the earthen floor. And sometimes, lying in bed without raising her eyes from the floor, she began speaking to the midwife with the quiet, slow enunciation of a mourner:

—She'd spent all twenty-three years of her life in that house.

She regretted neither the house nor the years . . . What else could she have done with those years? And the house . . .

—People born in such houses cannot laugh, just as she, Mirel, cannot.

On one occasion the midwife was obliged to slip into town to attend a woman in childbirth and was delayed for some hours. Remembering that she'd left Mirel, she hurried back home, and saw on her return:

With her hands behind her head, Mirel lay in bed in exactly the same place in which she'd left her. She was still staring up at something on the ceiling, and suddenly began articulating some of the thoughts that had absorbed her in the time that had passed:

—Such people as she, Mirel . . . either they became cabaret singers or they took their own lives.

Such talk made the midwife uneasy. Bustling about with household chores, she began gathering up all the small handkerchiefs:

—What did Mirel think? Might she be pardoned for mentioning it, but it would certainly not be out of place if the midwife were now to wash these handkerchiefs herself.

But Mirel, paying no attention to this remark, continued to pursue her own line of thought:

—But she was of no use for cabaret work, since she could neither sing nor laugh.

—And in order to commit suicide . . .

Lying in bed, she flung her slender, supple body so far back that all the blood rushed to her face; exposing her arms to the shoulders, she slowly examined them from all sides and equally slowly began caressing them.

—Such beautiful arms . . . She felt so sorry for them every time she thought of suicide.

At this, the midwife suddenly remembered that she'd forgotten to buy a box of sardines in town. She abandoned the soaking handker-chiefs and once again dashed off:

—How thoughtless she'd become lately! . . . Mirel would simply starve to death, living with her!

In her rush into town, she found time to pop in to see the pharma-cist's assistant Safyan for a moment to pick up a new, recently pub-lished book for Mirel to read. But Mirel was wholly indifferent to it, took it up apathetically, and from where she lay in bed read the opening two sentences aloud in a monotone. Almost at once she let the book fall from her seemingly nerveless hands, and with curious despondency began yet again staring at the window as she spoke:

—All these writers love starting their books with the sorrow-filled springtime of someone's youth and so intensify everyone else's sor-row.

And after a pause, and a sigh, more in the same vein:

—When one's heart was light, one forgave them and read them. But when one found oneself in so depressed a mood as hers now was, every phrase seemed like an unrelenting fly that settled on one's nose and persistently irritated one with the reminder: "But you feel awful . . . aw-ful . . . . awful . . ."

One evening, though, the midwife took up the small, ancient copy of *Dicta sapientium*[*] that an elderly Catholic noblewoman had given her as a gift not long before, sat down with it on the bed next to Mirel, and began reading a chapter from the yellowed, tear-stained pages, trans-lating and explaining one sentence after another:

—*Omnis felicitas mendacium est*[†] . . .

The two young women suddenly seemed like mourners, and it looked as though they were drawing comfort from reading to each

---

[*]This book's full title is *Dicta septem sapientium Graeciae* (*Sayings of the Seven Sages of Greece*), a collection of moral aphorisms from the classical world compiled in Latin by Desiderius Erasmus of Rotterdam (1466–1536). For centuries it was immensely popular as a source book for easily digested moral precepts. An English translation with commentary by Thomas Berthelet was published as early as 1525, during Eras-mus's lifetime.

[†]Latin: "All happiness is false."

other from the Book of Job: there were, if one reflected, greater sorrows to be found elsewhere in the world.

Nevertheless, this reading made the illuminated room a little more cheerful and lifted the mood of depression for a time. With a smile, the midwife Schatz even rolled herself a cigarette at the box of tissue papers, returned to smoke it sitting next to Mirel on the bed, and recalled her acquaintance, the writer:

—He'd told her once: Nowadays, happiness is only to be found among traveling salesmen. This would be deplorable if it didn't have its own consolation: such people were always so busy playing cards that they were unaware of it.

And both kept silent for a while, taking their revenge on these traveling salesmen:

—They weren't even aware of their good fortune.

Mirel even smiled at this:

—*Eto khorosho*. That's good.

But her smile was oddly feeble, too akin to the grimace that sometimes precedes tears.

2.8

In town, meanwhile, the fact that she was living with the midwife Schatz kept tongues wagging ceaselessly. In Avrom-Moyshe Burnes's house, excessive pleasure was taken from this, and every recently arrived guest who might have something new to tell was joyfully accosted:

—Well, what's happening? What else had he discovered?

In his own house, Reb Gedalye was profoundly vexed, and continually consulted his relative the bookkeeper about it:

—He'd be quite frank with him: he could hardly wait for Gitele to return. Gitele was the only person who was capable of sorting this out . . . not so?

And he rushed about all over the house in a highly agitated state of panic, continually pushing his gold-rimmed spectacles back and forth over his nose:

—Who could say? Perhaps it would be best to send Gitele a telegram asking her to return home as quickly as possible?

But very soon the Fast of Esther[*] came round on a beautiful, sunny day. The air was redolent with the warmth of winter's end, and the frost was so limited and insubstantial that it could barely keep whole the blank white surface of snow on the surrounding fields, frolicking over it in the sunshine with myriad silver and diamond sparks.

During the course of the day a sleigh arrived at the home of the midwife Schatz, bringing her a letter from the wife of a landowner in the village:

—Her advice was sought, and if she wasn't busy, she was asked to come.

Covertly, the midwife was all for sending the sleigh back empty and to this end had even written a letter to the landowner's wife. But Mirel suddenly became aware of this and responded very firmly:

—No . . . The midwife was to go there at once.

And when the midwife began arguing, Mirel's face grew pale with anger and for some reason she set about washing up the dirty saucers and glasses.

—If the midwife didn't go, she'd get dressed and leave immediately.

In this silent washing up of crockery there was a clear hint that, as an only child, she was accustomed to getting her own way and was fully capable of doing what she threatened and going off somewhere else; all this apart, there was something very singular in watching her at this work.

Half an hour later, the sleigh bearing the midwife Schatz was gliding over the snow in a southwesterly direction far, far outside the shtetl, and Mirel was lying in calm despondency on the bed. In a quiet monotone, she invited the pharmacist's assistant Safyan, who'd only just come in, to be seated, and just as quietly responded to his inquiries:

—The midwife certainly wouldn't return before evening.

As usual, the pharmacist's assistant Safyan was nervous, earnest, and dour. With his bulging, colorless eyes he looked not at her but somewhere into a corner of the room, evidently thought ill of the mid-

---

[*]The Fast of Esther is observed on the thirteenth day of the Hebrew month of Adar (generally corresponding to the secular month of March), a day before the festival of Purim, which is celebrated annually on the fourteenth day of Adar.

wife, and was silent. After his departure, a heavy emptiness remained behind in the room. The silence intensified. Near the window outside, two Gentile girls in boots could be heard running about, chasing each other and laughing, laughing and chasing each other.

Lost in thought, Mirel at length sat up on the bed and stared wearily at the rectangular patch of sunlight playing slowly in the middle of the floor.

Quite suddenly she dressed herself, locked the midwife's half of the cottage, and went outside. Since it was about half past three in the afternoon, the sun was still shining in the southwest, and in its sea of light the insubstantial frost still frolicked with myriad silver and diamond sparks. The big girls in their boots were still running about, chasing each other and laughing, laughing and chasing each other. Mirel turned left and walked slowly down toward the shtetl, from time to time looking to either side of her.

The weather was so fresh and mild. Somewhere far away, in a great, noisy city, a young mother had for the first time surely sent her three-year-old child out for a walk with the governess and the child had returned home enchanted, with its little cheeks bright red, with a fresh and smiling little face, and with a single strange new word:

—Mama, *vyesna! vyesna!* . . . Spring! Spring!

And here in the shtetl, next to the synagogue which stood a little farther down from the pharmacy, some Jews of various ages stood in a little huddle; patiently waiting for the Torah reading during the afternoon service that would signal the end of their fast,* they were delightedly watching some urchins throwing snowballs at each other.

Noticing her, these men forgot about the urchins for a while. They knew:

—She, Mirel Hurvits, had left her father's house and was living over there . . . She was living with the midwife Schatz.

Slowly and wearily she walked farther down into the shtetl. In front

---

*The Fast of Esther is observed from daybreak until the appearance of the stars at night. While according to Jewish law the fast must continue until nightfall, people who feel unable to fast the whole day try to fast at least until after the afternoon service.

of the house with the blue shutters that belonged to the man who should have been her father-in-law she lingered a little and saw:

Her former fiancé's sleigh stood before the verandah and the front door, and through the back door, which led into the kitchen, the scent of freshly baked sugar pastries regularly wafted out together with the steady pounding of a few restless brass pestles, bringing to mind an approaching and long-awaited wedding:

—The groom's a refined and reserved young man . . . and the bride is worthy of him . . . worthy . . . worthy . . .

And strangely enough:

All this awakened no sense of yearning in Mirel, and aroused no fear for her future life.

With cold, vaguely formed resolution she neared her father's house, and with the same icily unemotional determination she went inside. The empty rooms were all in semidarkness, and there was no one about who might notice her. Slim and sorrowful, she lingered at the door, and it occurred to her that she didn't live as other people lived but wandered all alone along the periphery of life, in the World of Chaos;[*] that from childhood on she'd been stumbling about there in a long restless dream that had no beginning and no end:

Now, it seemed, she'd come to some decision and would take some action, yet perhaps she'd come to no decision and would take no action. All alone she'd merely continue to stumble about as in an eternal dream of chaos and would never arrive at any destination.

And now she stood once again in the very house in which she'd stood so many times before, wandering slowly from one room to another. As in times gone by, the gloom of twilight held sway, intensified, and was transmuted into haze. But in times gone by there had been people here, and now there were none. The doors between one room and another stood open; here and there a dark emptiness yawned in those corners where before one or another piece of familiar soft furniture had always stood. Mirel could see no one. No one stopped her, no one was made happier by her arrival. Something, it seemed, was too

---

[*]According to Jewish lore, this is the place to which erring souls are exiled.

late here, had already ended. But the people? What had become of all the people?

Suddenly she noticed Reb Gedalye all alone in the semidarkness of the study. Her constricted heart was powerfully drawn to him, and she put entirely out of mind her vaguely defined resolution. Hunched over and markedly shrunken, he sat there with his back toward her, his head thrown oddly forward and his mouth open, gasping like a fish before the medicinal steam he was pumping from the nickel vaporizer he'd brought back with him from abroad. In the deepening gloom of late twilight, the little machine burned before him with a blue-green flame, a turquoise light that barely illuminated his face, wet with countless drops of sweat and condensed steam.

He stopped pumping steam and extinguished the vaporizer. Slowly he wiped his face with a handkerchief, still not sensing her presence behind him. But she was shattered. Choked with tears, she moved slowly over toward him filled with compassion for a father who'd been transformed into a helpless child.

—What had become of him!

A little while later she stood at the window with him. She wiped his face, kissed his brow, and noticed the way he kept turning weakly away from her toward the window with the whole of his hunched body trembling, sobbing quietly to himself as though fearful that he might drool:

—Wh -wh - wh - ff - ff - ff—why've I deserved this? Ff - ff - ff—In my old age—ff - ff - ff . . .

He calmed himself a little when the maid returned from town and lit lamps in both the study and the dining room. Then Mirel went out into the dining room where she found the bookkeeper and looking straight at him, paused to say:

—What did he think: if a telegram were sent to Zaydenovski immediately, could the betrothal party still be held that Saturday night? Yes? Then she'd ask him to attend to that telegram at once.

—But if he would wait a moment . . . She thought she'd wanted to tell him something else but had forgotten . . . No, no . . . She'd remembered now. He could go off and attend to the telegram . . . She'd remembered now . . . The key . . . She still had the key to the midwife's locked cottage; she'd have to take it back directly herself.

An hour and a half later, when she returned home, she found the house brightly illuminated. Reb Gedalye was still hearing the Book of Esther read in the Sadagura prayer house, and in the dining room, next to the table with its fresh white cloth and burning candles, stood Gitele, newly arrived, her face aflame with color. Perhaps still thinking about what she'd brought back with her from her rich great-uncle, she was listening as a pious Hasid, wearing his prayer girdle,[*] was reading the Book of Esther to her:

—In those days while Mordecai sat in the king's gate . . . [†]

She stopped Mirel with a gesture, wanting to ask her something, but afraid to speak out and interrupt the reading she pointed instead to a scrap of scribbled paper lying on the table.

—Well— . . . this . . . well . . . See if Zaydenovski's address is correct.

And for some reason, reading over the address, Mirel made her no reply. She went off to her own room and in the darkness lay down on her bed.

What followed was impossible to believe:

In town someone swore later that the very same evening, when the midwife returned home she found Velvl Burnes's sleigh waiting next to her darkened house. Velvl Burnes himself stood there bareheaded in the moonlight for perhaps ten minutes and could barely speak for agitation:

—He'd thought he might see Mirel here—he said.—He wanted . . . he wanted to tell her something . . . But actually . . . Actually, he hoped the midwife Schatz would pardon him.

Two days later, a thirty-five-year-old bachelor stopped his sleigh outside Reb Gedalye's house and inquired from Avreml the rabbi, whom he encountered coming out:

—Does Reb Gedalye's daughter, Mirel Hurvits, live here?

The rabbi glanced questioningly at him and at his huge sergeant-

---

[*]Before prayer, every Hasid ties around his waist a black sash or girdle made of silk or wool, known in Yiddish as a *gartl,* symbolically to separate the heart and mind from the lower part of the body.

[†]Esther 2:21.

major's mustache, followed him into the entrance hall, and watched as he took off his sheepskin coat and warmed his ice-cold nose and whiskers. The rabbi assumed that this was some new emissary from Zaydenovski who'd come in connection with the betrothal contract and the marriage. Subsequently this thirty-five-year-old bachelor, who was Nosn Heler's uncle and who worked in the sugar refinery, sat on interminably in the salon with Mirel and, in the big-city manner, bored her until nightfall. He spoke Russian badly, like a dentist,* saying "s" instead of "sh" and relating that his nephew, Nosn Heler, still asked after her, Mirel, in every one of his letters:

—In every letter he begged to be informed of how she was.

Because this old bachelor wasn't overly intelligent, because no rational person was capable of paying this foolish, small-town social call, Mirel found it frightfully tedious to sit here in the salon with him, and she was irritated both by his tales about Nosn Heler and by the suspicious glances with which Gitele continually kept hovering in the doorway. She wrapped herself in her shawl and kept wishing for him to go, and when he finally did leave, she found the whole house as intolerable as the betrothal party that was being prepared there, the whole of her future life, and Gitele's questions:

—What did he want, that young man?

In agitated anger she responded:

—Let her mother quickly get a rider to saddle up and gallop after him to ask what he wanted.

She went off to her room, undressed, and retired to bed very early that evening. Several days yet remained before the betrothal party: something might yet happen before then, and even now she had absolutely no obligation to think about him, that wealthy young man

---

*Before World War I the profession of dentist—for which Bergelson himself tried to study in his youth—was highly popular among Jews in the tsarist empire. It occupied an intermediate position between that of a fully qualified physician and the lower rank of *feldsher* or medical aide. Here Bergelson is satirizing the attempts of upwardly mobile Jews to assimilate into Russian society by adopting the Russian language.

named Shmulik Zaydenovski, or about the unpleasant new experiences awaiting her.

Before she fell asleep, a thought of Heler unexpectedly flashed into her mind, and the whole night thereafter she dreamed of his oblong face which made him look like a Romanian. Around ten o'clock at night he was wandering alone somewhere in the great city, that provincial capital in which he lived, was on his way to visit a friend who lived at the opposite end of town, and all the way there could think of nothing but his friend's warm, well-lighted room.

There one could sit for a long time with a glass of tea and pensively and with great longing relate:

—In a little shtetl somewhere far, far away lived a young woman named Mirel Hurvits. She once loved me, this Mirel Hurvits . . . she once loved me very deeply.

She recalled his features all the next wintry day, recalled them vaguely and with shadowy fondness, and drew the thought close to her heart. But in the house the approaching betrothal party made itself increasingly strongly felt. In her bedroom the noise of tables being moved about in the adjacent rooms, of someone complaining and calculating could all be heard:

—What do you think? We'll really have problems if there are more than three in the Zaydenovskis' party.

So she no longer had any desire to hold Nosn Heler's features in her mind's eye and made every effort to dwell on the fact that Shmulik Zaydenovski looked like a European:

—She'd thought of this once before . . . Walking out with him in the provincial capital she'd thought of it.

2.9

Together with the bridegroom, their eldest child, they arrived on Friday afternoon, the middle-aged parents who lived at the quiet end of a suburb in the distant metropolis, bringing with them a refined, barely concealed smile of inward self-satisfaction and the bridegroom's seven-year-old little sister, their late-born youngest daughter. This smile later became seductive: it appeared even on the faces of total strangers from the town, making the Zaydenovskis appear deeply good-natured, and compelling everyone to reach the same conclusion:

—These people, these prospective in-laws, loved each other very much . . . Years before they'd even made pilgrimages to Sadagura together, and to this very day they loved each other even more than the newly betrothed couple.

Like an adult, the seven-year-old little girl changed her dresses far too frequently, and clambered onto her mother's chair too often every time her parents told the story of how she'd contradicted an elderly general in the second-class railway carriage they'd occupied.

—Since her older daughter—the mother-in-law-to-be related—was completing her schooling at the *gymnasium* this year; she was obliged to study and had no time to spare, but they'd brought this one, their youngest, so she could enjoy herself a little.

Looking deeply into the child's face, her mother blinked her little black eyes rapidly like some short-sighted night bird and, peering with menacing suspicion at a black spot on the child's nose, demanded in her hoarse voice:

—How d'you like the bride? Have you seen her yet?

Sitting in polite silence opposite, Gitele scrutinized her:

She was a tall, scrawny, somewhat worn woman with a dull, saturnine complexion on the elongated face of a well-to-do bourgeoise, a small, very dull mind, and extraordinarily big hands and feet. The huge heirloom hairpin in her chestnut-colored horsehair wig bore a diamond and was evidently valuable, but since she herself had no conversation, she went on smiling excessively in self-satisfaction and began the same account from the very beginning every time:

—Well, as soon as the telegram arrived, just as the Purim feast was about to begin, in fact . . . and as always there were some fifteen people at our feast . . . well then he, Yankev-Yosl that is, gave the instruction immediately, of course: Wine! Bring up the wine! (He'd laid down wine in the cellar in the very year Shmulik was born.) Well, you can imagine . . .

A little farther away, at an open volume that lay on the little bookshelf, stood the slim, twenty-four-year-old bridegroom in company with the family's intimate, the bookkeeper. He was in awe of the florid Hebrew style of the bookkeeper's two letters which had reached him at home, regarded him as a *maskil*,[*] and therefore spoke loudly about Ahad Ha'am[†] to show that he too was an educated man:

—Do you understand? Ahad Ha'am is quite capable of publishing nothing for a whole year.

He wore a still-youthful reddish-blond beard, which, freshly trimmed and bypassing his ears, merged with the chestnut-brown hair on his head and stretched round his face like a taut leather strap. Yet he closely resembled his thickset, powerful father, that brisk, cheerful, dark individual of medium height and middle age with his huge, intensely black untrimmed beard and sharp, lacquer-black eyes. When tea was served, this cheerful soon-to-be relative by marriage openly and generously embraced Reb Gedalye, barely restrained himself from kissing him, and perhaps compensated for this by abruptly bellowing across to Gitele in his rich baritone:

—My dear mother of the bride! You'll soon see the quality of the six sponge cakes we've brought you for the party.

Preparations for attending evening prayers to welcome the Sabbath were made.

By now, meanwhile, seated between the mothers of the bridal couple was Libke the rabbi's wife with her visiting mother-in-law, a woman with a homely face who'd lost her front teeth in early youth and wore a silk kerchief on her head. This woman was at a loss about what to do with her rough, work-worn hands, and was anxious to hide one of her thumbs which had for many years a useless sixth finger growing from it. Next to the groom's father, Avreml the rabbi was smiling and twisting one of his curly earlocks. He took pleasure from the fact that in honor of the Sabbath the groom's father wore a black silk surtout,[‡]

---

[*]Here a Hebrew scholar with a love of secular learning and culture.

[†]Ahad Ha'am, pen name of Asher Ginsburg (1856–1927), was born in Skvira, near Kiev in the Ukraine, and became a central figure in the movement for cultural Zionism. Initially enthusiastic about Ahad Ha'am's ideals, in time Bergelson and his circle came to reject what they regarded as the narrowness of his "cultural nationalism."

[‡]A surtout is a long, single-breasted lightweight coat. The fact that this one is shortened denotes its wearer's gradual move away from Jewish tradition toward a more modern, Westernized style of dress.

albeit somewhat shortened, and from the fact that well-to-do observant Jews were still to be found in the world. In consequence, he shyly and quietly expressed an opinion in passing:

—In the study-house, the worshipers would almost certainly desire Reb Yankev-Yosl to favor them by leading the prayers . . . They almost certainly still vividly recalled the way he'd led the prayers during the High Holy Days in Sadagura.

And smoking the last cigarette of Friday afternoon, the worldly relative-to-be assumed an expression of seeming reluctance:

—Who? Was he to lead the congregation in prayer? God forbid!

He wanted to be begged.

Suddenly all in the room rose from their places. The father-in-law-to-be forgot completely about the rabbi and from a distance began bowing in a worldly manner to Mirel who, clad in a long gray silk gown, made her appearance here in the dining room for the first time. Her blue eyes smiled at her newly arrived prospective in-laws, but her freshly washed face was pale with exhaustion and looked somewhat older than it really was. To the eye of a stranger she seemed to be no artless girl, but an unusually passionate young wife who'd been living for three or four years with a husband whom she loved to distraction and to whom she unreservedly gave herself with great devotion; that because of this her refined face appeared so weary and pale with exhaustion, despite the fact that she'd only just spent a long time refreshing it with ice-cold water and applying all manner of lotions.

The prospective father-in-law paid no attention to what she smilingly said to him with her newly freshened blue eyes. He half-turned to Reb Gedalye:

—What? Time for prayers? Yes, he was ready.

And when he turned to face her again, she'd already forgotten about him. She stood at the window opposite Shmulik and smiled at him with the same newly freshened blue eyes:

—After he'd left the provincial capital, she'd been there once on another occasion and she'd wandered through the deserted streets all alone. When had this been? She'd remember in a moment.

But already thinking about something else, she was wholly unable to recall, suddenly hurried off to her own room again where she once more did something to her pale face, then returned to the dining room and suggested to Shmulik, who hadn't gone to prayers for her sake:

—Did he perhaps feel like putting on his skunk fur overcoat and taking a walk through the shtetl with her?

In various places afterward, girls in shawls dawdling in front of their fathers' houses saw them both strolling through the shtetl, leaving the main street and making their way to the back alleys with their illuminated study-houses where the Sabbath was being welcomed. All around these study-houses, crooked windows sealed with clay displayed the little flames of their Sabbath candles to the late evening air. At one such window, two young women, shortly to be brides, who'd gone to visit their neighbor, stood with their hostess watching Mirel and her husband-to-be, wanted very much to catch a glimpse of Shmulik's face and couldn't. And quite by chance, a young wife who was standing outside saw Mirel stopping with her husband-to-be in front of the clay-caulked door of Lipkis's house and pointing it out to him:

—A very close friend of hers lived here; his name was Lipkis and he was a student. But he was very poor and walked with a limp.

On Sabbath morning, the town learned that Reb Gedalye's relative by marriage would lead the congregation in prayer. By the time of the Additional Service,* the Husiatyn study-house† was packed with householders from both prayer houses as well as from the big artisan's synagogue. Listening to the way this relative by marriage unhurriedly ended one series of blessings and moved equally unhurriedly on to an-

---

*Musaf is the "additional service" in the Jewish liturgy, recited on Sabbath and on festivals in commemoration of the additional sacrifices formerly offered in the Temple of Jerusalem (Numbers 28, 29).

†Like Reb Gedalye, all those who attend services here originate from, or have ties with, the Hasidim of Galicia. Husiatyn, today a town in western Ukraine, is located on the west bank of the Zbruch River, which formed the boundary between the Austro-Hungarian and Russian Empires before World War I. The Hasidic population of the town grew sharply after Rabbi Mordkhe Shrage-Feyvish Friedman (1835–1894), the youngest son of Rabbi Yisroel Friedman of Ruzhin, established his court there in 1865. Rabbi Mordkhe was succeeded by his son Rabbi Yisroel Friedman (1858–1949), who led the Hasidim in Husiatyn until 1912.

other, those in the backmost rows stood on tiptoe to get a better view, but owing to the height of the central reading desk could see no more than the tip of the gold-embroidered collar on his prayer shawl, and reflected on the good fortune of this middle-aged, big-city magnate: there at the eastern wall his son, the bridegroom, was standing next to Reb Gedalye, while he himself led the prayers in a strong, pleasant voice:

—He led the prayers like the very best cantors.

The fatigue induced by the lengthy service hung in the air over the heads of the congregation. High above, the brick walls of the study-house oozed moisture; curtained off, the Holy Ark looked down from the eastern wall in hallowed Sabbath weariness; and the face of the beadle, who kept banging on the desk before every prayer in order to intensify the silence, gleamed from the height of the central reading desk.

They left the study-house late, around one o'clock, and hurried home, feeling weak from the gnawing pangs of hunger.* For the rest of the day, the entire shtetl lived as though in a Sabbath dream, remembering the in-laws-to-be and the bridegroom who were staying with Reb Gedalye, and the betrothal party that would be held that evening.

Warmly dressed young women certainly felt excessively festive this winter Sabbath and spent far too long parading up and down the long street onto which the front windows of Reb Gedalye's house looked out. Only some way off, near the beginning of the marketplace, the big house with the blue shutters belonging to Avrom-Moyshe Burnes, the father of Mirel's former fiancé, stood strangely isolated and abandoned. Every joyful melody that the Husiatyn Hasidim sang in Reb Gedalye's house caused it distress. No one entered it and no one left it throughout that entire Sabbath, and it gazed out as though rigorously banned from all social contact. Velvl Burnes himself was assuredly not there but was spending the day somewhere or other on his farm. Nevertheless, it was now common knowledge in town that he was breaking off with his second fiancée, and that what he himself went round

---

*This is because, according to Jewish law, eating a full meal is not permitted before the recitation of the morning service.

telling everyone—that his wedding had been postponed until the Sabbath of Consolation*—was merely to save face.

That Saturday night, Reb Gedalye Hurvits's house was brightly lit and filled to overflowing with many wealthy guests, both local and from out of town. In the entrance hall, several of Reb Gedalye's shockingly impoverished agents derived great pleasure from these guests, were delighted that their employer still had good friends, and after each new arrival, cheerily cadged a smoke off one another:

—What d'you say about that one, eh? . . . Also not a pauper, eh? Give us a cigar.

There was a crush around the big circular table that stretched from the hallway to the widely opened doors of the well-lighted salon. At its head, between the parents of bride and groom, his face freshened from the cold outside, sat the perpetually cheerful Nokhem Tarabay. He'd only just arrived in his own sleigh and had no hesitation in personally telling the groom's father, Yankev-Yosl, that he wished Reb Gedalye well and had therefore come to his daughter's betrothal party, even on a Saturday night. He'd been on the road until ten o'clock, had even taken a wrong turn somewhere in the dark behind a sleeping village, but had made his way here despite it all. Now he made a boisterous commotion with his merry hand-clapping, his nimble capering about, and the fatuous questions with which he continually attempted to animate the oddly morose Reb Gedalye:

—How else? He couldn't understand: how could he not be present when Reb Gedalye was celebrating his child's betrothal?

All day Reb Gedalye had been deeply unhappy and depressed, registering nothing of what was said to him. Sitting without speaking on the left of the groom's father, his bowed head filled with the negative thoughts of one who'd come down in the world, he was fully aware that all these guests had assembled here not for the sake of Gedalye the

*The Sabbath of Consolation is the first Sabbath after Tisha B'Av, the fast of the ninth of the month of Av (July), which commemorates the Destruction of the Temple in Jerusalem. It derives its name from the reading from the Prophets for that day, Isaiah 40:1–26.

bankrupt, but for the sake of his relative by marriage, the rich Yankev-Yosl who was worth half a million and flaunted his wealth in the grand manner; that this arrogant, hearty relation-to-be knew this and therefore paid Reb Gedalye no attention. And for their part, the guests pitied Reb Gedalye, and left him in peace.

By now he'd even grown a little afraid of Gitele, who suddenly came up to ask him for his keys. Hunched over, he struggled to his feet in disoriented confusion, groping fumblingly in one pocket after another.

From some distance away, Mirel noticed this. Her heart went out to him in great compassion, and she came up.

—Here they are, your keys . . . they're in your top pocket.

His sorrowful expression broke her heart. She'd always believed that her father was strong and would do whatever was necessary to retain his dignity and his self-respect. And now for the first time she saw him impotent, looking truly wretched at his ruin and loss of status. Sadly and in submissive silence she sat beside Gitele and the groom's mother, listening to that myopic dullard trying to avoid speaking ill of their cousin Ida Shpolianski who also lived in the provincial capital, where she deceived her husband. Starting to report that on one occasion she herself had seen Ida at the theater in company with an officer and a tag-along polytechnic student, the groom's mother caught herself and tried to gloss over it:

—But then Ida was a well-known person, and her husband Abram was undoubtedly a fine young man. He did business with the provincial administration and was away from home for months at a time. But their home . . . their home, it's said, is run on modern lines . . . free, very free . . .

Around the substantial, well-supplied tables with their gleaming candelabra, ritually observant guests who'd risen to wash their hands and recite the appropriate blessing before eating had resumed their places. There, after the recitation of the blessing over bread, they were soon beaming with post-Sabbath contentment, drinking toasts and chatting, clinking their glasses together, then drinking and chatting some more. The conversation flowed from sixty eating and drinking mouths simultaneously, but none of this prevented Mirel from feeling as isolated as she'd felt before when she thought of the great provincial capital where she'd live with Shmulik in three or four rooms, and imagined the streets she'd once visited there as a child with Reb Gedalye.

—There one summer evening they'd stroll out somewhere as a couple, would walk slowly and have nothing to say to each other, would return home and again have nothing to speak about there.

No great happiness would derive either from this evening stroll or from that return home. Yet she, Mirel Hurvits . . .

—What could she possibly do with herself now?

The half-drunk tumult intensified. Shouts of various kinds continually stifled the table hymns other people were trying to start, and the groom's boisterous father, Yankev-Yosl, drank so much and with such doggedness that it seemed as though he were determined to drown the thought that his son's marriage was allying him to a pauper who'd recently gone bankrupt and now hadn't a kopeck to his name. He persistently banged the table with his powerful fist, bottles fell over and spilled their contents, the ceiling lamp trembled and dimmed, yet he went on banging, never once turning to glance at Reb Gedalye, and yelling out to Avreml the rabbi:

—Reb Avreml! Rabbi! I want you to drink! . . . I want you keep pace in drinking with me!

Mirel still sat in silence at the opposite end of the room. Every now and then it seemed that the cause of all this uproar was not she but some other Mirel who was perfectly content with this betrothal party, and she, the real Mirel, was observing it all as an outsider wholly unconnected with it. And when she roused herself from such moments, she went on believing that there was still considerable doubt about whether she would ever marry this Shmulik who was sitting at the head of the table and to whom all were drinking toasts, and that consequently it was foolish not only for everyone to be rejoicing at this betrothal party as though it were some truly important event, but also for her to have swathed herself in this new gray silk dress and to be sitting here among this foolish company like some sort of chrysalis in a cocoon. Only a few hours earlier, in the mirror in her bedroom, she'd glanced at her own bare arms and her long, tightly laced corset, and had been overcome with a strong desire to have at her side that very

Nosn Heler whom she'd previously sent packing. But this desire, too, was nothing more than foolishness, because once before she'd openly told Heler:

—Well, good—she'd marry him. And then what would she do?

And what of Mirel Hurvits herself?

—To all appearances she was now an adult and she felt as unhappy as only a deeply serious person could feel, yet she still remained wholly unaccountable even to herself, and from time to time such foolish thoughts still crept into her head.

She was fully roused from her reveries by the drunken tumult round the circular table, filled with wild outcries, by blessings chanted in the cantorial manner, and by heedlessly interrupted table hymns. For several minutes now, someone over there had been mulishly shouting out her name.

Having made some sort of wager with Nokhem Tarabay, her half-drunk prospective father-in-law Yankev-Yosl had been banging on the table with a glass, broken it, snatched up another, and had started banging again:

—Mirel! Come here! Come here, I'm telling you!

This shouting roused disgusted resentment in her. Making no response, she turned her back on it and saw:

Among a crowd of people listening intently, Shmulik stood in the middle of the room with a foolish expression on his face, singing an extract from the liturgy of the High Holy Days and gesticulating like a cantor.

Earlier she'd longed for him to be absent from the house at this time so that she wouldn't be obliged to see him, but now despondent indifference had deepened within her, and she found herself without desire of any kind. For a while she stared at him from a distance, and was astonished at herself:

—What could she possibly have wanted him for, this young man? . . . And taken all in all, what would she do with him all the rest of her days?

Abruptly she left her place at the end of the dining room, went off to her own room, undressed very quickly, and just as quickly lay down in her bed and extinguished the lamp.

Several times after that Gitele knocked on her door, and finally burst in, greatly agitated:

—It's quite simply scandalous! . . . Who does things like this? It's quite simply appalling.

And lying in bed in a state of complete indifference, Mirel replied in some irritation:

—Who told her that this was appalling?

She wanted to fall asleep but was unable to do so because the drunken uproar in the house went on for a long time; only now were tables and chairs carried out of the dining room, and dancing started there in earnest. For a long time she tossed and turned in her bed and was angry with herself:

—In any case, nothing would come of this. It would never lead to any wedding, and she, Mirel . . . she wasn't obliged to think of him, of this young man in the dining room who was singing an extract from the liturgy for the High Holy Days and gesticulating like a cantor.

2.10

The prospective in-laws spent one more sleepless night here, secretively discussing matters with Reb Gedalye and Gitele.

This went on from Sunday night until Monday morning, and no one in the house went to bed. Around four o'clock in the morning, Mirel was summoned to the dining room as well.

They peered up at her from the low chairs on which they'd been sitting the whole time, and the prospective in-laws inquired of her:

—Well, how did she like the idea of fixing the date of the wedding for the Sabbath after Shavuot?

Mirel stood opposite in silence. There was still a long time before the Sabbath after Shavuot, she thought; until then, much mischief could be made to disrupt these marriage plans. She wanted the prospective in-laws to leave the house taking Shmulik with them as soon as possible, so she replied:

—Good, let it be the Sabbath after Shavuot.

Afterward she slept through the entire misty, muddily mild morning, slept through the thorough cleaning of the dirty, deserted house after the early departure of the prospective in-laws, and long after that, when order, cleanliness, and silence reigned in all the rooms once more and Reb Gedalye and his bookkeeper had hurried off to the provincial capital to which they'd been summoned by a telegram from the Count of Kashperivke's son-in-law, who'd just arrived from abroad.

Only once did her eyes open on the vacant air of her room. Unwilling to remember what had happened to her, she promptly shut them and dozed off again:

—In any case . . . what was there to think about?

There was nothing any longer:

—If only she could sleep away all the years that were left to her, and forget about the accounting she needed to make of her life.

In this regard she'd once heard a story:

A story about an exhausted soldier who'd completed his term of military service and, in the middle of winter, returned to his parents' home in a small shtetl; there he immediately lay down to sleep and slept through the entire winter. He awoke only in the warm days before Passover and saw himself lying outdoors among the bedding that had been carried out to air in the sunshine; somewhere nearby, matzo was being baked, and indoors windows were being washed and walls scrubbed down.

When she opened her eyes on the vacant air of her room for a second time, it was around four o'clock in the afternoon. Silence reigned in the adjacent rooms, and somewhere far away, near the kitchen, Gitele, who'd wakened from a long sleep, could be heard yawning loudly, someone was telling Libke the rabbi's wife about the favorable impression the prospective in-laws had made here in the shtetl, and then everyone was chattering on, all at the same time, commenting on the unexpected celebration now taking place in the peasant village at the home of the midwife Schatz:

—This was the second day that her acquaintance, the Hebrew poet, had been staying with her; because of his arrival, Poliye, who'd taught in the village the year before, was leaving her present post and returning for Passover very early; and Shabad, the local Hebrew teacher, had already gone there twice, hoping to meet the midwife's guest, but had missed him on both occasions.

Everything from the betrothal party to settling the wedding date and the abrupt departure of the prospective in-laws now seemed so far in the past that it all appeared well behind her. It seemed scarcely credible that all this had taken place very early that same morning. She had a fleeting image of how the train carrying Shmulik and her prospective in-laws was being borne far, far away through those familiar stations that passed on mute greetings from the distant provincial capital. Extraordinary, the way matters had transpired: that she'd actually been engaged to marry Shmulik, that the whole shtetl knew this, and that on the very next Sabbath her prospective in-laws would make a special *Kiddush*[*] in their home where her name would be mentioned when the toasts were proposed.

Rising from her bed, she remembered that she had something to do: she had to write a letter to Shmulik in the provincial capital, giving him clearly to understand that nothing would come of the betrothal. But she felt so at peace, and such a pleasant languor overcame her at the thought that Shmulik was no longer here in the house. Yawning, she soon returned to her bed, reflecting that the chief menace had now passed, and that there was ample time in which to annul the engagement contract.

—There was still quite enough time before the Sabbath after Shavuot.

That evening Gitele came to her in her room, holding out a letter:

—It came in the post, addressed to her, to Mirele.

The letter was from Nosn Heler, and began with those words, it seemed to her, with which so many letters had already begun:

—He understood that she, Mirel, was now a bride.

---

[*]*Kiddush* (Hebrew, "sanctification") is a blessing recited over wine to sanctify the Sabbath or a Jewish festival. By extension, the term *Kiddush* may also refer to a reception of wine, cake, soft drinks, and buffet items following the Sabbath morning services at the synagogue. Often a *Kiddush* is hosted by a family celebrating a bar-mitzvah, a wedding, or—as in this case—an engagement.

From its very first words the letter disgusted her, so she put it down next to her, and then tried reading it again:

—She'd been made to listen to a great deal of slander about him, Heler.

Having no patience to go on, however, she laid it down again and never finished reading it.

Subsequently the letter was left lying open on the chair next to her bed, and once, coming in from outside, she noticed:

Gitele suddenly jerk away from her bed and quickly leave the room—and the letter . . . the letter lay no longer on the chair as it had before, but a little farther away, on the floor. She could have sworn that the prying Gitele had read it.

Later Gitele certainly spent far too much time furtively discussing this with Reb Gedalye who'd arrived home one night.

—She'd read the letter herself, and he continued to address her in the familiar manner of close acquaintances.

Unwilling to hear anything of this, Reb Gedalye was annoyed with Gitele:

—He didn't know what she was bothering him with all this for— what for? . . . She was imagining all kinds of ridiculous things!

He was now wholly preoccupied with, and devoting all his time to, the plan that had been proposed to him by the Count's son-in-law, who'd come down from abroad and redeemed Kashperivke from the bank:

—For a mere eight thousand rubles he was prepared to take Reb Gedalye on as a partner in the ownership of the big wood, would entrust its management to him, and would charge him the price paid by merchants in the provincial capital. Perhaps in this way, Reb Gedalye might be saved financially . . .

But Gitele still refused to leave him in peace:

—He was apparently under the impression that he'd settled everything with this daughter of his . . . Well, let him judge for himself: she was now saying that she wouldn't travel to the provincial capital to have her wedding clothes made. Under no circumstances, she said, would she travel there.

One Sabbath two weeks before Passover a fresh spring breeze sprang up.

The snowdrifts that poked up here and there amid the mud dried out and turned gray, and there was no clarity about what festival the church bells were ringing to honor just before sunset.

Wrapped in her mother's black shawl, Avrom-Moyshe Burnes's reclusive daughter stood for hours on the verandah in front of her father's house watching the peasants making their way from their village at one end of the town to the church at the other end. They walked slowly, keeping close to the Jewish houses in the long main street, seeking well-worn pathways and keeping their feet dry.

Meanwhile the yawning emptiness of approaching summer made itself increasingly felt everywhere. Constantly restless in the deserted pharmacy, the assistant Safyan set off on a walk through the shtetl, but kept stopping with the desire to turn back. Eventually he met Avrom-Moyshe Burnes's daughter, and kept her company in a stroll over the freshly trodden pathways to the peasant cottages, avoided looking at her, yet spoke as ponderously as though he were addressing an intellectual.

—Lipkis—he said maliciously—is no longer here; eventually he came to his senses and went back to serious study in the metropolis. And Mirel Hurvits . . . Mirel has now been in the provincial capital for over a week, having her wedding clothes made. *Kak eto shmeshno*—it's so ridiculous.

Avrom-Moyshe Burnes's daughter felt uncomfortable walking with him, and made no reply. She knew—wrinkling up her nose in distaste behind his back—and the whole town remarked on it, that he was in love with the midwife at whose home her acquaintance, the Hebrew poet, was spending a few days.

But he continued to stare neurotically somewhere far in front of him and went on pursuing the same subject:

—Whom did Mirel think she was fooling: herself or the whole town?

Suddenly they saw a tall, broad-shouldered young man striding in their direction from the peasant cottages. They stopped and stared at him from a distance:

He looked like a young, well-to-do doctor who'd only recently completed his university studies but hadn't yet started to practice.

Quite evidently this was the midwife's guest, and it was impossible to surmise where he was going now.

Mirel, after all, hadn't been at home for over a week. And on the outskirts of the town, which he was now approaching, there was no one to be seen, apart from a small group of Jews waiting outdoors for the Sabbath afternoon service to begin. He glanced at them from some way off, and they glanced back at him. All were silent, but when he'd passed, the men, their faces wreathed in smiles, followed his retreating figure with their eyes and started talking about him:

—What does he write, you say?

—Leaflets.

—Well, and why not? For my part, let him go on writing.

2.11

Just before sunset on an altogether dry, somewhat chilly day, Mirel unexpectedly returned from the provincial capital and found her father's house in the disorder that always attended preparations for Passover. All the furniture had been moved from its accustomed place to one central location and covered with sheets. Gitele was negotiating their pay with the old house painter who'd whitewashed the ceilings, and with the two peasant women who'd spent the whole day washing the windows and the doors, and she'd engaged these two women to come on the following day as well. At home, meanwhile, there was news:

Very early that morning Reb Gedalye had returned from the capital, where he'd succeeded in entering into partnership with the Count's son-in-law to run the extensive Kashperivke woods. Several times that day he'd told Gitele about this auspicious new business venture, and now, because of it, he'd closeted himself with the bookkeeper in his study, where the cleansing had been completed. There his confidant sat at the desk deep in thought and Reb Gedalye paced up and down next to him in his fur-lined slippers, repeatedly stopping with his back to the unheated stove to peer over the tops of his gold-rimmed glasses at his bookkeeper:

—Not so? A fortune could be made from the profits of these woods. And more:

—Could he imagine how much raw material could be extracted from the three hundred *desyatins** in the center!

Because Reb Gedalye had succeeded in calming the household and bringing his affairs back into order, because he was now wholly engrossed in these affairs and thought about nothing else, Mirel grew steadily convinced that being engaged to be married and suffering because of it served no purpose for anyone here in the house, that everyone cared about this as little as she herself had cared about it some few weeks before, and that the wedding clothes she'd just ordered in the provincial capital were thus all as superfluous as the fact that she'd traveled there at all and lingered on for a full eight days:

—She hadn't needed this contrived trip to the capital; from the very beginning she ought to have said that the betrothal party was foolish and that there would never be a wedding.

The bookkeeper was no longer in the study, where a lamp had now been lit. All alone in the silence there, Reb Gedalye sat at the desk, poring over the balance sheets of his new woods, and she was still pacing about in her own room, which now seemed oddly unfamiliar after the eight days she'd spent away from home. Unable either to lie down or to sit at the little table, she thought about what she would soon do:

—She'd go to Reb Gedalye in his study and tell him: "Of course no one needs this foolish betrothal any longer. The wedding will never take place no matter what, so let there be an end to it."

She thought about this for a long time, pacing about in her room, and finally went to see Reb Gedalye in his study. She even had her opening words prepared:

—I need to speak to you about something.

But there, in Reb Gedalye's study, something overcame her and she unexpectedly found it difficult to utter another word. At first Reb Geda-

---

*A *desyatin* is an old imperial Russian unit of land measurement equivalent to 2.7 acres. The area under discussion here is therefore about 800 acres.

lye did not look round at her, clumsily manipulating the beads on the abacus and repeating the sums aloud. When he did finally interrupt his work and turn to face her, she was suddenly struck by the tranquility that had returned to him in the last few days. Now the continuation of this tranquility depended solely on her. It could last no longer than a few minutes more. All that was needed was for her to utter a few words and he would again be profoundly miserable, frozen in his seat like a mourner who'd suffered yet another blow.

For a while she stood opposite, looking at him. And then, not responding to his question, she left the study and went back through the disarranged rooms. She postponed the matter for a while, was angry at someone, and consoled herself:

—The wedding will never take place, no matter what. The engagement contract will certainly be annulled very soon.

That evening, she sat among familiar guests in the midwife Schatz's well-lighted cottage, and there, for the first time, she felt alone and alien.

Apart from the teacher Poliye and the midwife herself, also present was the Hebrew teacher Isak Shabad, as swarthy as a Gypsy, and Esther Finkel, the daughter of that local Jew who remained arrogant despite being unemployed and having come down in the world. She was a tall young woman with a long, sad face, who was now in her third year of study in Paris.

Burdened with a wife, the Hebrew teacher had for a long time enjoyed no social contact with anyone apart from his young pupils and, worn out after a full day's work, he seemed to be quietly dozing to one side; this was the third time he'd waited for the midwife's guest, the Hebrew poet, who'd left the house well before sundown and was expected back at any moment.

The young women paid him no attention. All three of them sat disconsolately next to Mirel on the little sofa next to the unheated stove, and all of them ignored her. None of them wanted to insult her, but on the other hand none of them had anything to say to her.

Esther Finkel spoke of the profession for which the Parisian university would qualify her in eight months' time:

—In general, she could hope that one way or another she'd push on through life, and as for happiness . . . in Paris one grew out of the habit of thinking about excessive happiness.

Esther Finkel's last words seemed to have some connection with Mirel. No one knew for certain exactly how, but the all-pervasive silence around the burning lamp evoked memories of some quiet, lonely event, one that had taken place on a Saturday evening two weeks before when the prospective groom and in-laws had been guests in Reb Gedalye's house and the Husiatyn Hasidim had sung table hymns in the twilight during the third meal of the Sabbath.* At that time, these three young women had been strolling abreast in the fiery sunset outside the shtetl. Each was oppressed by a yearning sorrow, but together they'd all come to the same decision about Mirel:

—A young woman who was now capable of finding herself at sundown in a house where Hasidim were singing table hymns around a fiancé whom she'd met through a matchmaker . . . Basically, what could possibly be worth thinking about such a person?

The midwife's guest, the Hebrew poet Herz, returned only around nine o'clock that evening. In his dark blue suit he sat at the head of the table looking down at his glass of tea. Smiling in concert with his expression was the green glint in his small, deeply set eyes, and this smile revealed something about him:

—You see, I'm a particularly clever person and believe very little in sentimentality and even less in my own talent. But now you see me at the very moment at which I've done something foolish: in the course of making a trip abroad, I've come down to visit a perfectly commonplace young woman who interests me perhaps even less than you do.

Because of his arrival, the silence in the room grew heavy and oppressive. The young women kept silent, and as a result appeared more serious and refined than they actually were. Esther Finkel had already risen to her feet, donned her overcoat, and made preparations to go

---

*Three festive meals are eaten every Sabbath: on Friday night, Saturday midday, and early Saturday evening. After the ceremony of *Havdalah,* which ritually marks the separation of the Sabbath from the working week, a fourth meal or snack commemorates what is called *melava-malkah* (Hebrew, "escorting the queen").

home. Yesterday the midwife had informed her that Herz strongly disliked female university students, so now she was furious at leaving, especially as she recalled:

—In Paris she was personally acquainted with some of the Yiddish and Russian poets there, and none of them was as arrogant as this tall fellow with his short, fair hair.

Meanwhile the Hebrew teacher had suddenly grown excessively alert and voluble, holding forth in what he took to be a serious discussion, and expressed himself wholly unable to comprehend:

—Why should Herz be so indifferent to his own poems, many of which had been published in various anthologies?

Since Herz paid absolutely no attention to what he said, the Hebrew teacher was rendered pitiable, something he himself was quite unaware of as he went on arguing instead that what he was saying was literal truth:

—He could bring some ten or fifteen boys from his Talmud Torah[*] here tomorrow, all of whom could recite by heart Herz's poem, "On the Approach of Dawn."

Herz rose to his full height from behind the table and began pacing about the room. The twinkling green glint in his eyes had vanished. Now he wanted to do something entirely different and couldn't because Shabad and Mirel, neither of whom interested him, were still in the room. He started whispering in the midwife's ear, asking her to rid him of Shabad who was boring him. Then Mirel reacted: something seemed to irk her, and she rose abruptly, cutting the teacher short:

—Would Shabad be willing to see her home soon?

As things turned out, in the end it was not the teacher Shabad but the midwife's guest Herz who accompanied her home, and he had nothing to say to her. In the darkness enveloping the shtetl as it awaited the coming of Passover, the air was chilly and silent so that the last words

---

[*]The Talmud Torah was a tuition-free elementary school maintained by the Jewish community for the poorest children. It was generally better organized and employed more-efficient, better-qualified teachers than the traditional heder because it was supervised by the leaders of the community.

Shabad had addressed to Mirel went on reverberating too loudly in her ears:

—Take her fiancé, for instance . . . Her fiancé, it's said, knew Hebrew very well.

The darkness erased both the long, well-worn pathway and Mirel's lissome figure, at which Herz continually stole glances: the figure of a well-to-do young woman who was engaged to be married, who was tightly sheathed in a black autumn overcoat, said nothing, avoided glancing at him, and bore within her the secret of her unknown, solitary life.

Eventually he asked:

—It would seem that she was very shortly to be married?

Then the congeries of Mirel's despondency deepened, and depressing thoughts began filling her mind:

—The wedding . . . It's still uncertain . . . on the whole, there's still some doubt . . .

With no wish to articulate these words she did not look round at him, but he repeated his question. Resentment suddenly flared up in her; provoked, she responded somewhat truculently:

—She wanted to ask something of him . . . He could surely do her this small kindness and keep quiet for a little while; there wasn't much farther to go now before they reached the first of the town's houses, so very soon she'd no longer be afraid to walk on alone.

Now his curiosity about her was aroused, and once again the green glint twinkled in his eyes. He accompanied her much farther than the first of the town's houses, right up to the verandah of her father's house, in fact. But she no longer so much as glanced at him, and disappeared through the open gates of the verandah without even bidding him good night.

The following morning, returning from the post office at the opposite end of the town, Mirel met Herz walking there alone. His face now seemed to her as familiar as if she'd known him a long time. He stood at the side of the road, staring at a humble dwelling in which matzos were being baked and listening to the bustle that came from within.

When he caught sight of her, his eyes began smiling. He approached her and said:

—He'd thought about her the night before, and spoken of her at length with the midwife—the fact that she'd bidden him be silent the night before pleased him.

For a while she stood facing him, looking him over. The way he spoke created the impression that he was someone who unquestionably knew much more than others about people and about life; that, at least, was the way he regarded himself, and he wrote books about it. Only it never occurred to him to talk about that to her, this young woman engaged to be married whom he'd met here in the shtetl. That was why he spoke to her so superficially and always with a flippant remark. Intensely conscious of the effect of her sorrowful blue eyes, he forced a smile and repeated:

—He meant it seriously: the fact that she'd bidden him be silent the night before pleased him.

As she walked slowly along at his side, it occurred to her that making their way down to the marketplace now was he, Herz, whose poems boys from the Talmud Torah were trained to repeat by rote, and she, Mirel Hurvits, Shmulik Zaydenovski's fiancée, about whom the teacher Shabad had openly remarked before Herz:

—Take her fiancé, for instance . . . Her fiancé, it's said, knew Hebrew very well.

She had no wish for him to feel superior to her, and it irritated her that he reiterated his question of the night before and continued to speak in the same flippant tone. For a while she said nothing and heard him apologize:

—He'd certainly meant nothing with his question of the night before . . .

She brusquely interrupted what he was saying and began telling him that here in the shtetl was a pharmacist named Safyan.

—He was fond of belles lettres, this Safyan; he'd also read Herz's little story about "The Dead City" and had remarked that the image of the doll was too superficial and crude, and entirely lacked poetry.

By now they were standing near the verandah of Reb Gedalye's house. Herz turned rapidly to look at her. His face turned very red and he began smiling in embarrassment:

—Listen to that!—he began, wanting with the same smile to resume his frivolous banter.

But she'd already stretched out her hand to him in parting and, without a backward glance, had mounted the steps of her father's verandah.

A little Gentile boy from the town later brought her a note signed jointly by the midwife and by Herz, inviting her to tea. She sent the boy away without any reply and spent the whole day at home. That evening, returning alone from the local haberdashery store where she'd failed to find the merchandise she needed, she noticed that far, far in the distance one entire area of the sky was reddening above the roofs of the peasant cottages and that approaching along the road that stretched into the shtetl from beneath that ruddy glow were the midwife and Herz. Unwilling to think about them, she lay for a long time alone in her room, turning over in her mind the engagement contract she had to break:

—How would she be able to annul this contract before Passover?

A little while later, however, the midwife came into her room to ask:

—Wouldn't Mirel consider going for a little walk?

The midwife smiled far too much, either because Herz was waiting outside for her or because he'd nagged her almost to death to go in and fetch Mirel. Because Mirel responded coldly that she had no wish to come, the midwife felt awkward, lingered on a little while, and started prattling about herself and about Herz who'd suddenly remembered Mirel when he'd awakened from his afternoon nap and had remarked smilingly about her:

—He longed for her company . . . What did they call her? Yes, he longed for the company of "the provincial tragedy."

Mirel paled; astounded, she stared at the midwife without replying, but later, when Schatz was no longer with her, she thought for a long time about that Hebrew poet Herz, and his remark about her still echoed in her ears:

—A "provincial tragedy."

She couldn't tell where the barb of this insult, and the resentment she felt at it, really lay: whether in the fact that Herz couldn't be bothered to remember her name or in the phrase itself that he'd coined about her:

—"A provincial tragedy."

She thought that both he and his remark were of no concern to her, wished to shake both off, and decided in regard to Herz:

—Whatever the case, the whole incident was ridiculous. And she, Mirel . . . She had other matters on her mind and would certainly never see him again.

The next morning, however, Herz spent far too much time wandering all over the shtetl, and several times passed very close to Reb Gedalye Hurvits's verandah. Through the window, Mirel noticed the way he turned his head in the direction of the house every time he went by and couldn't understand why he did this. Once, indeed, she even shrugged her shoulders and mused:

—What could he possibly want?

That night, though, she wrapped herself in her shawl and, seemingly for no specific reason, went out on to the verandah. Noticing her from a distance, he approached, looking serious:

—He absolutely had to say a few words to her. Nothing more than a few words. Would she put on her coat and walk with him a little while?

Feeling even as she did so that to do as he asked was foolish, she went inside, put on her coat and set out with him across the shtetl.

—This sort of thing was more appropriate for a seventeen-year-old schoolgirl than for her, Mirel, who had other things on her mind.

For a while they walked through the shtetl in this way, were silent, and avoided looking at each other. In the end, turning her infuriated face toward him, she was the first to start speaking:

—"A provincial tragedy"—that was how he'd described her yesterday, apparently.

Herz reddened in embarrassment, but the green glint in his eyes began twinkling again. His voice took on the same frivolously bantering tone as the day before:

—But Mirel needed to understand what he meant by that . . .

Mirel turned pale and stared at him: no, this person was poisoned with the same taste for ridicule as the midwife and her aged grandmother. He had to be kept firmly in check, otherwise he was quite capable of mocking himself all day for the sake of mocking someone else for a single moment.

--—He, Herz himself . . . he too was nothing more than "a provincial tragedy."

She no longer wished to hear what he had to say and interrupted him:

—Listen! What's your name? Are you willing to make the acquaintance of your critic?

And no longer looking round at him, she began calling to the pharmacist's assistant Safyan whom she saw in the distance.

On Sunday afternoon, a day before the eve of Passover, because of the domestic upheaval occasioned by the imminence of the festival Mirel left the house and wandered about for several hours somewhere far outside the shtetl. At dusk, when she returned home, she was informed:

—Herz had sat in her room for two hours waiting for her.

A note from him lay on her dressing table:

—He was leaving that day. A pity he'd missed her and been unable to wait any longer. If he were ever to return to the shtetl here, it would be exclusively for her sake, for Mirel.

Underneath he'd scribbled his address.

So he'd concluded even this little note with a piece of banter—banter that was ambiguous and might perhaps resolve itself into a truth.

—If he were ever to return to the shtetl here, it would be exclusively for her sake, for Mirel.

No longer thinking about what she was doing, she put on her outdoor clothes again, went off to the midwife Schatz and stopped in front of her front door which was padlocked from the outside.

—Did this mean that Herz had already left, then?

In the darkness of early evening she walked home by herself, oppressed by the emptiness of the approaching days so soon to start dragging by again:

—Did this mean that Herz had already left, then?

And after this, there was no longer anyone in the shtetl with whom to exchange a word, and the night during which the ritual search for leaven had traditionally to take place enfolded the dimly lit houses.[*] And she remembered Herz, whose train was already carrying him off in the direction of the border somewhere:

—If he were still here . . . if she were to meet him now, for instance, returning home . . .

Such a meeting certainly wouldn't have pleased her, but then perhaps her loneliness wouldn't have been so great either. Herz was perfectly capable of understanding her and so of lightening her burden somewhat. But this was absolutely unimportant to him, and he'd made a flippant remark about her:

—He'd called her "a provincial tragedy."

The whole business was probably childish, but was distressing all the same: he was capable of understanding her but hadn't wanted to do so and had joked instead:

—She needed to understand what he meant by that . . .

For a time she lay alone in her darkened room thinking this through. At length she rose, lit the lamp, and sat down to write him a letter:

—"The provincial tragedy" disliked people who did nothing but joke. Throw aside this frivolous banter for a while and listen: in eight weeks' time I am to be married.

The house was chilly and quiet because the windows had been left open all day, and tethered next to a shop outside, someone's saddle horse whinnied. Several of the adjacent rooms, cleansed for Passover, were kept in darkness so that no one might accidentally carry any

---

[*]The Torah (Exodus 12:15–20) prohibits the eating or possessing of any bread, leaven, leavening agent, or any food containing such, from the day before Passover until the end of the eighth day of the festival. All leaven, down to the smallest particle, must be removed from every observant Jewish household. The night before Passover, therefore, immediately after sunset, the head of every Jewish household begins the ceremony of "the search for leaven." Equipped with a candle, a feather which acts as a broom, and a wooden spoon into which the crumbs of bread are scooped, the head of the house goes from room to room reciting the appropriate blessing.

leaven into them. Reb Gedalye, with candle in hand, could be heard visiting each of these rooms in turn to make the ritual search for leaven, stopping after the recitation of the prescribed blessing to say something to Gitele in Hebrew about a feather duster and bread crumbs. Farther off in the dining room, the stove was being heated for some reason, and across the silent house its inner little cast-iron door could be heard thumping as it was sucked rapidly backward and forward over the flame:

—Pakh-pakh-pakh . . . pakh-pakh-pakh . . .

Pen in hand, Mirel paused for thought, staring into the lamp flame:

—Quite possibly she'd have no strength left to fight off this marriage.

She'd have no more strength, not because she needed this marriage, and not because someone else needed it, but because all of it was a matter of indifference to her, and she felt strong aversion every time she thought about canceling this second engagement contract.

And yet from time to time, because she still felt such a great yearning for love, she lay on her bed and reflected:

—While she was lying here alone on the margins of life, other people were living fully. From a distance she saw the way they lived.

For a long time now, it seemed, they'd known that love wasn't the most essential concern in life. Everyone knew this, but no one ever said so. But then where was the most essential concern in life? Did life perhaps offer some hidden corner where a few words about it might be heard?

When she'd finished writing, it was about ten o'clock at night. She took up the letter, read it through again, paced across her room once or twice, stopped for a second time at her desk, took up the letter once more and pensively ripped it into tiny pieces:

—What a foolish letter! And of what importance was Herz to her that she should write to him?

Distractedly, she noticed on the dressing table several letters that had come from Shmulik while she'd been away from home. There were four thick packets, all addressed to her. She opened one and saw:

The first half had been written in Hebrew and the second half in Yiddish; it began with the florid Hebrew phrase, "Beloved of my soul" and ended with two blank, dotted lines.

Resealing the letter, she left it on the dressing table and went off to the dining room. There she found the bookkeeper sitting at the table, and in the presence of Reb Gedalye and Gitele she said quite openly:

—What had she wanted to ask of him? Several letters from Shmulik had come for her. Would he be so good as to write to Shmulik in reply: she, Mirel, disliked writing letters, and on the whole . . . on the whole, she begged him not to send her so many packets in future.

2.12

For the last two days of Passover, Shmulik came down.

He arrived suddenly, virtually uninvited, attended services in the Sadagura prayer house with Reb Gedalye, and felt relaxed and at home in the house, like a newly minted son-in-law in the first month of being supported by his wife's father.[*]

In the shtetl he was regarded as a fine young man. Women smartly dressed in honor of the holy days discussed him:

—He's so good-natured . . . He's totally without malice.

Mirel, however, did not even find him sexually attractive, and already regarded him with apathy and indifference. His big face had grown more familiar and sallower in color than before, his small, soft, evenly trimmed beard redder, his mustache scantier and longer, and his fleshy nose made uglier by the fact that it broadened out stupidly around the nostrils and had retained from childhood a barely noticeable but ineradicable sniff.

It was soon evident that he spoke Russian badly, yet insisted on speaking it to the midwife Schatz; that he enjoyed taking naps during the day; and was fond of telling long, tedious worldly stories that made his listeners break into cold sweats.

In the salon on one occasion he was recounting one such long-winded story yet again to the midwife when he suddenly noticed a barely concealed smile flit across her face, lost the thread of what he

---

[*]It was formerly the custom in Orthodox Jewish families for the engagement contract to include a specified number of months after the marriage during which the young couple would live at the expense of the bride's father.

was saying, and didn't know how to end his narrative. Sitting to one side, Mirel was revolted by him, by his shallow, one-dimensional soul, and by the rambling, wearisome tale he was now repeating for the second time. Unwilling to go on listening to it, she began inquiring about Herz from the midwife:

—What did the midwife think? Would Herz really never come back here?

But hearing this name, well known in literary circles, Shmulik joined in the conversation:

—Ah, yes: he'd read his books; he even knew his cousin, a rabbi who'd lost his faith.

Mirel was incensed by his participation. She wanted to tell him that he was lying, that he hadn't understood a word of what he'd read, but she restrained herself, went over to the window and, filled with suppressed rage, stood there until she'd calmed herself.

She thought:

—Velvl Burnes—he was certainly more ignorant than Shmulik, yet all the same . . . he certainly didn't inspire the same disgust.

A few days later, when Shmulik was dogging her footsteps on a walk through the shtetl, she saw Velvl's buggy waiting in front of Avrom-Moyshe Burnes's house. She stopped, and without looking at Shmulik, remarked:

—Was her former fiancé really back in the shtetl at present? If his parents weren't so repellent, she'd call on him with great pleasure.

This was extremely exasperating.

Nothing of her remark made the slightest impression on Shmulik—so insipid was he, possessed of such a cold, one-dimensional soul. Sniffing slightly, he soon went on explaining that he and Mirel wouldn't be living with his father in the big old house, but in the smaller, newly completed wing at the end of the orchard, the front windows of which overlooked the quiet street of the suburb.

Chatting on in this way, he felt completely at ease with her and took her arm. Without looking at him, however, she disengaged herself, drawing back a little with an expression of displeasure on her face.

—She disliked being taken by the arm . . . She'd always disliked it and had told him so several times.

The whole way back she was silent and refused to look at him.

At home she reminded herself that Shmulik would certainly be leaving very soon, and immediately felt lighter in both mind and heart. A while later she stood in the early evening darkness that filled her room, peering through the shadowy window and thinking about this:

—Reb Gedalye, too, would undoubtedly soon go off for weeks on end to the new Kashperivke woods.

The tranquility that had reigned before Passover would return to the house, and she, Mirel . . .

—Soon she'd be able to live here alone once more . . . whatever else, alone at least.

From dawn onward on a truly hot summer morning, the glowing heat of the scorching, newly risen sun had shimmered before the open windows at the front of the house, heating both panes and frames and playing along floors and walls.

In Reb Gedalye's house, everyone had risen earlier than usual to prepare Shmulik for his journey. In her darkened bedroom, Mirel caught the sound of people drinking tea with milk in the dining room, of Gitele asking Shmulik where she should pack the butter pastries which had been prepared for him, of the arrival of Avreml the rabbi who'd popped in before morning prayers and was loudly remarking about Shmulik:

—Even if he were to leave at noon, he'd still get to the train in time.

In the courtyard the britzka* was being washed, oats were being fed to the horses, and a driver was engaged to take Reb Gedalye to the Kashperivke woods immediately after Shmulik's departure.

When Mirel rose, it was already late, around ten o'clock. One side of the house was already trapped in the short shade that came with deepening morning, while a light, barely perceptible breeze made its way into the house through the open windows and tugged feebly at the long drapes.

Mirel drank her tea at the table in the dining room around which sat

*A britzka is a Polish-Russian open carriage with a folding hood and space in which passengers can recline when taking a long journey.

Reb Gedalye and Avreml the rabbi. Still wearing his phylacteries, Shmulik pottered about for a long time. He recalled that during the last two days Mirel hadn't spoken a single word to him and so was feeling upset and insulted, and he looked down at his own feet treading over the floor. He stole a sideways glance at her no more than once, only to see that she was looking not at him but at the dignified German mechanic who was present, and heard Reb Gedalye say to the bookkeeper:

—He insists that the sawing machinery is better set up near the small ravine, over there . . . eighty-six *desyatins* into the woods.

A while later, without his phylacteries, Shmulik went to see Mirel in her room. There he found her alone at the open window.

Standing with her back to him, she did not turn around, and he was overwhelmed with desolation. His face grew sallower by the minute; he was waiting for something.

Abruptly Mirel turned to face him, taking the last two days as an illustration:

—He could expect to have very many such days from her . . . He'd be unhappy with her for the rest of his life.

What else was there to say? She didn't love him and couldn't marry him . . . She'd no idea what need he had of her. He could certainly still make a good match for himself. She didn't know very clearly what kind of wife he wanted, but here in the shtetl were Burnes's two daughters, for example:

—He'd be better off marrying either of them than marrying her.

After an inordinately long pause, when she turned back to face him there were tears in his eyes. Two teardrops overflowed and ran slowly down the sides of his nose, and feeling them, his nose responded to their damp creep with a quiet sniff.

Mirel suddenly felt free and at ease, and a thought about his weeping flashed into her mind:

—This means he's resigned himself to what's unavoidable . . .

A short while later she threw on her black scarf, left the room and from the doorway glanced back at him for the last time:

—This meant that they'd go their separate ways . . . She wished him everything of the best, and wanted to ask only one last thing of him: not to make any kind of disturbance here in the house, but until he left to go on behaving as though they were still betrothed. She begged him not to mention this to anyone here at present. Her parents need be informed of it only later when he, Shmulik, was no longer staying with them . . . Personally she esteemed him as a decent person, and had every confidence that for her sake he would do as she asked.

Unobserved by the rest of the household, she hurried outside through the kitchen door and went off to the midwife Schatz.

There she waited with great impatience until the time for boarding the train had passed, lying on the bed in the midwife's home and thinking:

—Now there was finally an end to it . . . At last she was rid of Shmulik, and of the engagement contract that had bound her to him.

2.13

When Mirel returned home from the midwife's it was around three o'-clock in the afternoon. Next to the houses, short dark shadows lay everywhere, prolonging the tedium of the hot, boring day throughout the entire shtetl.

Deep quiet and peace lay all around Reb Gedalye Hurvits's house. Behind, a pig dozed in the muddy ditch where the kitchen slops were thrown, and the gate on the front verandah was locked from within, as was the custom on the Sabbath. Apparently everyone inside was taking an afternoon nap.

Mirel entered the courtyard and looked around. The britzka that always stood in its covered port was no longer there. The stable, too, was empty and locked.

—This could mean only that the britzka had already taken Shmulik to the station; that Reb Gedalye, too, had by now gone off to the Kash-perivke woods; and that no one but Gitele was indoors. Now Mirel was filled with longing to enter that quiet house in which no one was to be found.

In the coolness of her room she'd lie in the same place for a long time, and there in the silence she'd think about herself, about the fact that she was free again, and about the possibility that something of significance might yet happen in her life.

But as soon as she reached the dining room she realized her mistake and instantly forgot everything she'd been thinking a moment before.

The house was full of secrets and alarmed disquiet, all of which had been hidden from the town and from people who were in the habit of calling.

From behind closed doors she was summoned to the salon where everyone was seated around the weeping, despondent figure of Shmulik, urging him far too often to drink up a glass of tea that had long grown cold. The aim was to persuade her, in front of Shmulik, to change her mind, and a few tactful questions had already been prepared for her. But she refused to go in. She locked herself up in her own room feeling intensely oppressed and unwell and reflected:

—She'd actually been foolish and childishly naïve . . . How could she possibly have imagined that everything could be ended so quickly and easily? . . .

For a long time discussions went on behind the closed doors of the salon from which Shmulik seldom emerged.

Avreml the rabbi was drawn into the heart of these deliberations, the bookkeeper was not permitted to leave the house, and that good friend of the Zaydenovski family who'd been sent here the previous winter was summoned by telegram.

That evening Reb Gedalye came into Mirel's room and demanded to know:

—What did she want? Could she actually say what she wanted?

Her expression serious and set, Mirel responded coldly and angrily:

—She wanted nothing . . . She wanted to be left in peace.

As he turned back to the door leading into the salon, Reb Gedalye remarked quietly, as though afraid that someone might overhear:

—He wants to send for his parents . . . It simply disgraces us in the eyes of the town.

And more:

—Perhaps she imagined that his business affairs had begun to prosper again? Perhaps she imagined that the fifty percent share he held in the Kashperivke woods would give him more than just enough to pay off his debts and then to live frugally and without anxiety for a few years?

He stood there a while longer, pondering the last words he would speak:

—He was obliged to tell her once again: they, he and Gitele, washed their hands of responsibility for her . . . She could do whatever she thought best.

All was clear: they, her parents, had done everything they could for her. Now they were insisting she become her own mistress and were saying:

—Do as you please.

After Reb Gedalye had left, the situation weighed on her even more heavily than before, and she began to fear her approaching isolation:

—Reb Gedalye and Gitele would bear witness to her never-ending lonely life; they'd never speak of it, but they'd think: "Well, what could they do about it?"

In her dreams that night she saw the angry faces of Shmulik's parents who were spending hours packing up here in the house, refusing to speak a word to anyone. Suddenly, as dawn broke, she found herself at a window watching her parents' buggy driving away. Seated in it were Avrom-Moyshe Burnes and his wife, with Shmulik hunched over between them. His head was bowed, his shoulders shook with suppressed sobbing, and Avrom-Moyshe Burnes and his wife were poking the little Gentile boy who was their driver, urging him to drive ever faster to the railway station.

When she awoke, unusually early, her first thought was that Shmulik's parents were not yet here in the house. As the effects of the oppressive nightmare began to leave her, she lay in bed thinking that there was still time for her to retract . . . that she could reconsider and decide to marry Shmulik—not for ever, but temporarily, for a while.

Mirel made her peace with her fiancé, and the wedding was again fixed for the Sabbath after Shavuot.

There was much talk about the two brand-new clauses that Mirel had insisted her fiancé insert into her betrothal contract:

—He shouldn't expect to live with her as a husband lives with a wife.

—And she . . . she retained the right to leave him and his house for good whenever she chose.

What further explanations were needed?

Even at this late stage, Shmulik Zaydenovski could without doubt still make the happiest of marriages with someone else. If he'd determined to live the rest of his life with Mirel as though every day were Yom Kippur,[*] it could only be because he was no less besotted with her than Velvl Burnes had been. But in and of itself the story was extremely intriguing and interesting, and gave ample reason for townsfolk to crowd at windows and doors to watch this couple strolling down the main street—a couple that intended to live not as husband and wife but in some bizarrely different way, as no couple in a shtetl had ever lived before.

For some reason Shmulik now came to seem like some kind of holy man to everyone. As before, he continued to tell long, boring stories to his acquaintances, but now his voice was lowered as though he'd come down in the world, his expression was mournful, and he gave the impression of someone who was fasting. People felt compassion for him, and deplored his luck:

—Just imagine: it's heartbreaking for him as well . . . He's also been gravely misled, and no mistake.

And strolling through the shtetl, Mirel continued to behave so harshly toward him that he dared not even take her arm.

On one occasion, in the middle of the street, she totally ignored him for perhaps half an hour as she stopped to speak with Brokhe, the shoemaker's wife, who'd been her wet nurse for six months when she was an infant.

—Yes—she remarked very seriously to this Brokhe—your house is falling down. You must definitely rebuild it this summer.

All around, people stood on their verandahs gaping in amazement:

—Did you ever! Is this a way to behave when one goes out walking with a fiancé?

*Conjugal relations are among the many quotidian activities prohibited on the Day of Atonement.

Moreover she insisted that Brokhe's husband come to measure Shmulik for a pair of shoes, and shouted out loudly after his wife:

—It's perfectly all right! Your husband's a good craftsman. He certainly doesn't stitch leather any worse than the shoemakers in the big cities.

2.14

In the end Shmulik stayed on in the shtetl for fully eight days. He constantly looked downcast and postponed his return from day to day.

When he'd finally left, the wedding's rapid approach began to be keenly felt in the house, and in the kitchen the oven fire burned day and night. There half a dozen women and more bustled about with their arms wet and bared to the elbows, peeling almonds, beating eggs, pounding cinnamon—all under the supervision of a hoarse caterer from out of town, a woman in blue-tinted spectacles who, like a good Jewish widow, spoke little but expeditiously did much.

As before, Reb Gedalye spent weeks away in the Kashperivke woods.

Meanwhile Gitele's needy out-of-town relative had taken charge of the domestic economy, and the front rooms were crowded with a considerable number of women's tailors who'd come down from the provincial capital with Mirel's half-completed clothes and were finishing the work here in the house.

In town, people still refused to believe that Mirel was truly going to be married, and the subject was still discussed in Avrom-Moyshe Burnes's dining room:

—Wait and hope. With God's help she'll still return the engagement contract to Zaydenovski as well.

For some time now, neither the midwife Schatz nor the pharmacist's assistant Safyan had called at Reb Gedalye's house. They went strolling down to the shtetl together every day, grew ever more estranged from Mirel, and no longer found anything of interest in her.

—What could possibly be interesting about her? Had they never seen a young woman about to be married before?

And Mirel, it appeared, was fully aware that she'd recently come down a great deal in the world; was aware of it when she stood all afternoon in the stillness of a room bestrewn with linen; was aware of it when she gathered all this linen together and bent down to pack it into the open trousseau chest. All around her the wedding preparations went steadily forward, and from time to time through the stillness in the cool rooms could be heard the grating rasp of the large tailoring scissors. As he sat bowed over his sewing machine rapidly pumping its treadle with his foot, one of the young tailors' assistants attempted to break this silence. Wholly unexpectedly, he suddenly burst into full-throated song:

> O my beloved!
> On a distant road
> I take my way.

Later, the solitary rattle of the rapidly stitching machine was all that could be heard—heard at length, hoarsely and angrily, until it was finally silenced. In the opposite corner, a second machine was preparing to start stitching, while through the open window a mild breeze from the town pressed its way in, blew gently on a curtain high, very high up near the ceiling, and called attention to the fact that in the late April weather outdoors the skies were somewhat overcast and that far, far away in the peasants' little orchards the fruit trees had been in bloom for some time.

Mirel was summoned to the salon for a fitting. There some ten tailors' apprentices, suddenly forgetting their upraised needles, stared with idiotic popping eyes at her bare shoulders and arms. And in the newly basted dress she stood before the mirror and remembered:

—She, Mirel, had once been someone and had a very strong aversion to something . . . and now she was nothing and had come down in the world and had absolutely no idea what would become of her in the future, and yet—absurdly enough—she went on fitting these wedding clothes of hers.

Abruptly she grew agitated and annoyed and pushed aside the tailor who'd been begging her to stand straight.

—What kind of excuses was he trying to make, this tailor? The entire shoulder puckered up, and the dress as a whole was ruined.

One afternoon, one of the young seamstresses from the provincial capital was standing on Reb Gedalye Hurvits's verandah pressing a new silk dress. She repeatedly picked up the hot pressing iron, sprayed the garment with water from her mouth, and heard one sewing machine pick up the rhythm of stitching from another indoors. Far, far away, near the town bridge to the east, the regular beats of the blacksmith's hammer died slowly away one after the other, and the shtetl fell silent. Suddenly from the same end of town came the jingling of some out-of-town bridle bells, and an unknown hired chaise drew steadily closer. Sitting up in it was a tall, unfamiliar young man who, in driving by, did not let Reb Gedalye's house out of his sight for a moment. The young woman briefly forgot about the dress she was pressing, followed the chaise with her eyes as far as the farthest peasant orchards, and composed herself:

—Probably a stranger . . . probably someone just passing through.

A little while later, however, someone calmly came to the house and reported, quietly and phlegmatically:

—Word has it that the guest she'd entertained before Passover had come to visit the midwife again.

At the time, with her face hot and flushed Mirel was standing in front of the mirror with her shoulders bare, trying on another dress.

—Who?—her eyes suddenly opened wide in astonishment—Who do they say has arrived?

Before she'd received any answer, she'd completely forgotten about the master tailor who was kneeling beside her, pinning her garment from all sides. She rapidly stripped off the unfitted dress and snatched up her everyday jacket.

The tailor, vexed beyond endurance, turned to face the two apprentices who were now left with nothing to do because they'd been working on this dress, and wiped his sweating brow.

—Can you believe Mirel's caprices! . . . He'd known them for a long time by now, but this time he'd been certain that they'd finish their work by Tuesday evening and would be able to return home very early on Friday.

But Mirel's lips were trembling as her fingers buttoned up the little collar of her jacket:

—What did he want of her, this tailor? She'd absolutely no idea what he wanted of her.

Rushing from the salon, she began anticipating the arrival of some visitor with great impatience. Every time the outer door banged, she would dash from her bedroom to the dining room and agitatedly send the maid to look in the entrance hall:

—Well? Who? Who's come in?

By nightfall her mood was downcast and her face forlorn and weary.

No one had come to call on her.

Wrapped in her summer shawl, she sat alone on the steps of the verandah watching the way the setting sun here and there reddened the tops of the thatched roofs. Scheduled to take place somewhere else through that night was the watch that traditionally preceded a circumcision,[*] so from the marketplace a magnum of wine was being carried there. The liquid splashed about inside the demijohn, gleamed in the light of the setting sun, and appeared too clear and red, evoking an image of the house in which this watch was to be held: the laid tables, the shining faces of the Jews who'd sit round them and drink toasts to life. And it evoked also an image of a semidetached peasant cottage situated far beyond the town limits that would be illuminated until very late that night, in which the midwife would be sitting with Herz and with the pharmacist's assistant Safyan. And even while discussing all manner of subjects, all of them would know what had been written in the letter which she, Mirel, had posted off immediately after Passover. Though not one of them would speak a word about it, each would privately reflect:

—What was there to say about it? . . . A foolish story about a letter . . . Really, a very foolish story about a letter that Mirel had written . . .

Very early the next morning the midwife got hold of a borrowed horse and buggy and drove herself at great speed across the shtetl.

---

[*]Throughout the night before the ritual circumcision of a Jewish male child, the father devotes himself to Torah study and recites prescribed passages from the Zohar. Children are also invited to the home of the newborn where they recite prayers, say psalms, and partake of a small meal which includes chickpeas.

Women saw her at sunrise as they were herding their cows out to pasture.

Soon it was common knowledge:

There'd been drinking all night in the midwife's little cottage at the end of town. Those taking a full part had been Herz, the midwife herself, her landlady's son who'd just completed his term of military service, and some teacher or other from a nearby shtetl, a shabby thirty-eight-year-old fellow in a blue peasant blouse who'd once had rabbinical ordination and the daughter of a ritual slaughterer for a wife, but was now in love with a prosperous shopkeeper's daughter not yet seventeen years of age.

Having drunk too much, Herz had been infuriated that they were trying to discuss Mirel with him, and had said, half in mockery and half in earnest:

—He couldn't understand what they wanted. She was nothing more than a transitional point in human development, and nothing would come of her. Still, she was a good-looking girl.

During the course of the day, all this was discussed in Reb Gedalye's house. Someone described the odd impression the midwife had made as she rushed headlong across town in the horse and buggy. Someone else mockingly inquired:

—Please tell us, how old might she be, that midwife?

Searching for something under the mound of linen and clothing around her, Mirel heard this, stopped rummaging for a moment, and fixed a piercing glance on the person speaking.

At dusk she bumped into the midwife in the street. Each young woman stared at the other for a while, had nothing to say, and felt that she hated the other.

Mirel said:

—She'd heard that Herz had come down.

And the midwife smiled maliciously like a tailor's daughter taking revenge on someone.

—Yes—she said—he's been here since Sunday.

A pause.

—Will he be staying long?

—A few days.

Another pause.

—Did the midwife know why Herz hadn't replied to her, Mirel's, letter?

Then the midwife's smile grew as spiteful and her laughter as unnatural and poisonous as though Mirel had attempted but failed to snatch something away from her.

—She had no idea why Mirel persisted in running after Herz. He certainly had a great deal more to think about than Mirel and her little letters.

And Mirel stood opposite her, staring her in the face.

She returned home more hurriedly than usual, without being aware of it. In the entrance hall the master tailor said something to her which she didn't hear. Then she lay for a long time in her room without any consciousness of doing so.

Suddenly she sprang up, rapidly buttoned on her summer overcoat and without glancing at the master tailor who again attempted to stop her she strode rapidly up to the midwife Schatz's cottage at the end of the town.

When she turned to go back home it was already about ten o'clock at night. With her face aflame she went into her room and stood stock-still there; anxious to remember something, she began interrogating one of the young seamstresses:

—Did the girl perhaps remember what she, Mirel, had been meaning to do that afternoon?

She then went across to the big room farthest away where, with the lamps turned down, the exhausted tailors were dozing in their seats after their day's work. There she demanded a fitting of the unfinished dress they'd been obliged to put aside because of her earlier conduct, and expressed extreme dissatisfaction with the master tailor who wanted to return alone to the capital the next day. Her face grew very red as she adjusted her corset in front of the mirror and insisted:

—They were leaving for the wedding the following Monday, and she'd trust no one but the master tailor—not even to pack up the clothes.

She required there to be as much fuss as possible around her in the house; she even hurried off to Reb Gedalye in his study, brought him with her, and compelled him on the spot to repeat her own words to the tailors:

—If the tailors were to start working at night as well, they'd get paid more.

2.15

All too soon Friday arrived, a beautiful day on which the tailors' sewing machines finally ceased rattling. Curtains now hung on all the windows, and in great haste the house was tidied for the last time.

This was the Sabbath eve immediately preceding the wedding.[*]

At about three in the afternoon outside Reb Gedalye's house stood two large peasant wagons to which the tailors were hurriedly tying their sewing machines and dressmakers' dummies. While they were busy, the preoccupied Reb Gedalye himself arrived from the great Kashperivke woods, smiling cheerfully at all the shtetl. Climbing down from his buggy, he displayed great largesse, demonstrating to the tailors here on the freshly washed steps of his own verandah that he was still in a position to pay handsomely for his daughter's trousseau. His face shone with happiness, and, setting off immediately for the bathhouse in his still-harnessed buggy, he did not forget to stop and pick up Avreml the rabbi on the way there.

People stood about in the marketplace watching the tailors clamber hastily into the wagons and whip their horses into a gallop down the road toward the provincial capital, smiling good-naturedly at their efforts:

—Those tailors will gallop off into the Sabbath, so they will.

—They'll definitely be whipping their way into the Sabbath for a good few hours.

---

[*]A week prior to the marriage ceremony—during which the bride and groom do not see each other—on the Saturday evening following what is known in Yiddish as *shabes forshpil* ("prelude Sabbath"), the bride's family arranges a party to wish her a long life blessed with many children. On the same day, the groom is called up to the reading of the Torah, after which the congregation showers him with nuts and sweets, symbolic of the same wishes.

Afterward great silence reigned both in the shtetl and in Reb Geda-lye's tidy house.

Rose-colored curtains hung at the windows, velvet runners lay on the floors, all yearning for an absent joy.

A runner lay stretched out to its full length on the spotless floor of the salon, deeply envious of some other runner lying somewhere far away in some other house, one that had also been neatly tidied in honor of an imminent wedding.

—In that other house, the bride is happy—this runner seemed to be thinking.

The long curtain at the window stirred ever so slightly, seemingly ready to add sadly:

—She loves the bridegroom, that bride in the other house.

And Mirel still stood in front of the small mirror in her room, dressing very plainly, as on every other Sabbath.

Silence filled the surrounding rooms; a longing for the life of an only child that was now on the verge of expiring made itself felt, and there was not the slightest desire to think about Shmulik, who, in a suburb of the distant metropolis, was preparing himself for the same wedding as she. In any case, the whole of this marriage was nothing more than a charade, temporary and provisional. More than at any other time she was convinced of this, now on this Sabbath of the week preceding the wedding ceremony; she felt as she felt on every day of every week of every year; and as though this were any ordinary Friday, she even went out to buy something at the pharmacy.

Walking alone along the street that led into the shtetl, she reflected that she was lonely, was somehow stubbornly inured to this loneliness, and needed no one now, no one at all; from time to time she still brooded that her life lacked some central, overriding purpose, but a moment later she no longer believed either in herself or in this supposedly overriding purpose, looked at life around her, and realized that no one believed.

And suddenly she flushed and remembered that she'd written the selfsame words in the letter to which Herz hadn't replied. Hurrying up the steps of the pharmacy, she was deeply vexed at herself.

—What a ridiculous letter . . . Who needed a letter like that?

A little while later, when she emerged from the pharmacy, the distant flame-red sun hung low on the western horizon like a great golden coin, and standing alone on the outskirts of the shtetl, poised to receive the Sabbath was Herz. As always, the green glint twinkled in his small, deeply set eyes as, bending forward, he looked attentively at those Jews who'd just returned from the bathhouse and were standing about here and there next to their widely opened front doors preparing to welcome the Sabbath in the synagogue. With his face wholly steeped in the glow of the setting sun, he appeared to be made of gold. Noticing Mirel, he took several steps toward her and directed her attention to the shtetl:

—She ought to look closely. This was truly a Sabbath sky; there on the western mountain even the green fields all around looked as though they were welcoming the Sabbath.

Glancing mechanically in that direction, Mirel saw nothing but a weary peasant still plowing his fields as twilight drew on. A great band of plowed earth stretched across the entire face of the verdant mountain, encircling it as though with a broad black belt. Uncertain of whether or not Herz's words were ironic, she stared at him with startled, astonished eyes:

—She'd no idea what someone like him wanted of her, and found it impossible to understand him rationally.

His eyes twinkling even more ironically, he shrewdly appraised her as he asked, apparently for no reason other than in jest:

—Had she ever thought about Jews?

Something deep within Mirel seethed in anger. Pale with vexation, she did not look at him, kept her lips tightly compressed and breathed heavily and overmuch.

—Who'd sent for him?

Something made her think of the note he'd left in her room before he'd gone away the first time. "If he were ever to return to the shtetl here, it would be exclusively for her sake, for Mirel." This was why the oddly cold and distant attitude he now adopted toward her, as well as the fact that he'd been talking about her behind her back in the midwife's home, made her feel so deeply and powerfully insulted. No, there'd been something far worse than a frivolous joke in that note.

Accompanying her back down through the shtetl, he said:

—A few days previously he'd seen her father here . . .

But she immediately interrupted him:

—There were people who felt compelled to insult others with every word they uttered. The only good thing they could do was to be silent . . . She, Mirel, had asked him to do this once before.

And no longer even glancing round at her abashed escort, she stopped to speak with a woman approaching from the opposite direction to whom Reb Gedalye had only a few days previously paid the last installment of what he'd owed her, including the interest, and had forgotten to take back his notes of hand. The woman's smiling, good-natured face beamed under the brightly colored silk scarf she wore only on Sabbath as she spoke with deep respect of Reb Gedalye:

—How could one esteem Reb Gedalye's integrity highly enough? Hadn't she said earlier that he'd never take what didn't belong to him, God forbid, and that he'd never owe anyone a single kopeck?

And Herz, who was still standing there, afterward accompanied her right to her front door.

—Listen—he said, his face red with embarrassment yet wanting to conduct a worldly conversation with her—he knew young women who became particularly attractive at the very moment they were about to be married . . .

Unwilling to hear more, she stretched out her hand to him in parting.

—He'd have to excuse her; she had to go inside.

For some reason, he added:

—He thought she might be free at present; the midwife would return home only very late that night . . . He'd noticed an exceptionally pretty spot beyond the town's orchards.

But leaving him standing there on his own, she went into the house and then into her own room. There, only a short while later, she felt drawn to him, wanted to see him again and had something to say to him, even though he'd gone back alone to the midwife's cottage. Among the many thoughts that crowded her mind, a few kept thrusting to the fore and repeating themselves:

—On Monday she was traveling out to be married . . . Herz was alone in the house from which the midwife was absent.

Later she stood for a long time outside on the verandah, waiting until it had grown completely dark, until Jews started returning from prayers and Reb Gedalye, in his silk capote with a cheerful smile on his shining face, came up the stairs and repeated twice:

—A blessed Sabbath! A blessed Sabbath!

On Sunday morning, Herz wandered round the shtetl once again and on his own eventually called at Reb Gedalye Hurvits's house.

Odd:

At the time, some five or six local Jews, all well known to each other, were seated round the table in the dining room in company with Avreml the rabbi, drinking to Reb Gedalye's good health:

—May God grant that you travel safely and return safely.

—To life! God grant you success and blessing!

From the adjacent rooms came the sound of baskets being packed and crates nailed down, of Gitele's out-of-town relative jangling her keys and shouting to someone outside through the open window:

—Come at noon tomorrow; by half past twelve we'll already have left.

Quite unexpectedly the door opened to admit Herz, a tall, robust young man whom none of the company present knew, who was asking for Mirel.

Those around the table stared at him; so did Reb Gedalye, raising his pointed nose with his gold-rimmed spectacles, clearly under the impression that this was some kind of traveling musician who'd come to the shtetl to play at quite another wedding and had blundered into the wrong house.

At that point, Herz began smiling at Mirel who'd heard his voice in the salon and, greatly startled, now appeared in the doorway.

For half an hour they spoke together behind the locked door of the salon. When they emerged, Mirel's face was burning with indignation. She avoided looking at him, and he walked calmly in front of her, smiling to himself.

They stopped on the steps of the verandah to make way for some of the visitors who'd already taken their leave of Reb Gedalye.

Mirel glanced up at the blue summer sky over the shtetl, and said coldly, to spite Herz:

—She was so pleased that the last few days had been so fine and clear. The day of her wedding would certainly be just as beautiful as well.

And he merely smiled more obviously, nodded his head, and made his way slowly back to the cottages on the outskirts of town.

In town, report circulated that on Monday, a few hours before her scheduled departure, Mirel had walked all round the shtetl on her way to the midwife Schatz, had found no one there, and had learned from Schatz's peasant landlady:

—Herz had gone abroad the evening before and wouldn't return.

Very early that morning, both master and mistress left Burnes's house for the provincial capital.

Later that day, when Reb Gedalye's house was deserted and locked up, someone called on Burnes's children to assure them that the local tailors, who hadn't been entrusted with the preparation of Mirel trousseau, had written an anonymous letter about Herz and Mirel to Shmulik's parents, a letter that would unfailingly reach them on the Sabbath immediately preceding the wedding ceremony.

There was excessive jollity round the tea table in Avrom-Moyshe Burnes's dining room, where the photographer Rozenboym's wife sat with her guitar while the children made far too much noise at play in the adjacent rooms. These little ones were finally allowed to run on ahead when everyone went for a walk across the shtetl. Now that there was no one living in Reb Gedalye's house, the air seemed far less confining.

Walking past this locked house, however, everyone suddenly felt strangely cheerless at the sight of its bolted outer shutters and its inner abandonment. In broad daylight the watchman, a peasant in a fur coat, sat on the steps of the verandah guarding its close-fastened front door. And the house itself wordlessly related something about those who'd gone away and about the enormous reception room at a distant railway station where Mirel's marriage would be solemnized the next day.

An image formed in the minds of passersby:

There in that distant, paved little shtetl on the other side of the railway tracks, the same quiet summer afternoon was passing in the same way as here; there musicians were playing at the celebratory lunch given by the groom's family, and Mirel, preparing to make her way there, was attiring herself in her new silk gown with its ample train.

When someone in the walking party proposed that they turn back and go instead to the little oak coppice, everyone did so indolently, without any real motivation. From a distance Burnes's younger daughter suddenly caught sight of the buggy that had only just drawn up before their front door. Without the slightest understanding of the situation, she yelled out:

—Just look, it's Velvl's buggy! . . . Velvl's come!

All the others in the walking party knew full well why for the last month and a half Velvl hadn't come to the shtetl even once.

On her own, the elder daughter quickly made her way there, entered the dining room and saw:

In his light dust coat, with his head bowed, Velvl was standing by himself looking down at the outstretched finger with which he was idly rotating the water left behind on the oilcloth after tea.

Thinking of him and of Mirel, the young woman stupidly called out:

—Just look—Velvl! . . .

She wanted to convey her joy at his arrival, but he made no reply and did not raise his head.

For a while all was silent. His sister felt awkward. She went over to one of the windows, drew back the curtain, and for a long while stared out disconsolately. Finally she turned to face him once again:

—Velvl—she asked—will you be spending the night here?

Only then did he cease rotating the water with his finger, hid both his hands in the side pockets of his dust coat and, without looking at her, queried:

—Eh? . . . What? . . . No, he was going back home.

And almost immediately he went outside and seated himself once more in his buggy.

The walking party heard him instruct the driver:

—Back home . . . Back to the farm.

Everyone in the street stood staring idly after him:

The horse and the well-sprung buggy sped swiftly back between the last houses on the outskirts of the town, and high up in the vehicle and slightly bowed, Velvl sat with his back to the shtetl and did not turn round even once.

3.1

—Shmulik, go away!

Shmulik stood over her with his mouth half-open, chuckling and picking his teeth after his meal. Fully harnessed and waiting for him outside was his own britzka, which would take fully three hours to carry him to his father's distillery.

He eventually moved away from the sofa on which Mirel was lying, sucked something from between his teeth, abstractedly spitting the debris from his mouth as he passed through the doorway, and lied to her:

—Friday, Mirele, Friday.

On Friday he'd return early from the distillery. He'd be in town and would find out why the big grandfather clock hadn't been sent.

His lie was superfluous; it awakened not interest but disgust in her. She had no desire even to look at him. Every inch of his neglected figure, including his reddish beard which he'd not trimmed for two weeks now, called to mind that a month previously she'd given herself to him with neither passion nor will; that Shmulik had now received from her everything he needed, and had therefore grown calmer, shabbier, and more repulsive. The day before had been the Sabbath, and in his white shirtsleeves he'd spent the whole afternoon sleeping on the low sofa in his small, square study. Just before sunset, one of his mother's young relatives had woken him with tickling, and he'd rolled himself into a ball and begged this youth:

—Don't . . . Stop tickling . . . I'm an old man already.

And Mirel had imagined that she'd married in jest and had stipulated a clause in her engagement contract:

—He should have no expectation of living with her as a husband lived with a wife.

Many young brides-to-be who had no idea of what they wanted imagined, as she had done, that they were marrying in jest, merely for the time being, and had stipulated the very same clause in their contracts with their luckless bridegrooms.

At long last the clatter of Shmulik's departing britzka was heard, and the fact that he'd be away for a whole week lightened the atmosphere somewhat. Later, though, gloomy silence pervaded all four of their newly furnished rooms, while from the kitchen came the sound of dishes being rapidly washed up. Plates clashed against other plates with a plaintive muffled rattle, as though being knocked about caused them pain.

For no particular reason she went out to her large half-cultivated, half-withered garden, stopped, and looked around:

By now everything there was yellow, parched, and redolent of late summer; plucked cherry trees stretched all the way down from her small wing to her father-in-law's huge whitewashed house, whispering secrets to one another about the melancholy skies and the chill onset of the month of Elul. And in the farthest corner of the orchard into which the glass conservatory of her father-in-law's house jutted out, her mother-in-law poked her head out of an opened window and yelled:

—Mirele! That half pound of tea . . . You borrowed a half pound of tea—why haven't you remembered to return it?

This immensely rich woman was not concerned about the half pound of tea itself; she was annoyed by Mirel's nonchalance and wanted to teach her a lesson:

—A young wife ought to bear in mind once and for all: what one borrows, one must remember to return.

Mirel made no reply. She detested her mother-in-law. She turned back to the front entrance of her own wing where she sat down on the verandah steps.

A well-rested coachman on a hansom cab was driving slowly off toward the long chain bridge that led to the provincial capital with its many streets and its half-million bustling inhabitants who filled day and night with the din of their weekday tumult. From where she sat, she followed the cab driver with her eyes:

—What might she be able to start doing now?

Far, far away, on the paved road at the other end of the deserted suburb, someone else's moving cab rattled along, but this noise sounded not like that of churning wheels but of a dry, disembodied voice that kept on repeating:

—Tomorrow will be just the same . . . The next day will be just the same . . .

Directly opposite, an old cock scrabbled its way up the dilapidated stone wall that enclosed the deserted courtyard of the church and opened its beak:

—Ku-ku-ri-ku-uu.

And then silence. Nothing. Filled with penitential thoughts,* all the houses around this sandy end of the suburb, grand and mean alike, seemed to have breathed their last. People were nowhere in evidence, and an incident that had taken place at the beginning of summer, two months before, came to mind:

Reb Gedalye and Gitele had been here. They'd spent the noisy Sabbath immediately preceding the marriage ceremony, traditionally known as "the joyful Sabbath," here in her father-in-law's house. Feeling ill at ease and isolated because they'd married into the family of people wealthier than they, and having nothing of their own with which to impress or assert themselves, they'd kept calling each other aside to whisper secrets together. Later they'd sat like outsiders among the many affluent guests from the city who'd come to celebrate the concluding meal of the Sabbath† here in her and Shmulik's newly fur-

---

*As this is the month of Elul, the houses too seem figuratively to be observing the period of penitential prayers in preparation for the coming High Holy Days.

†Known by the Hebrew phrase as *melave-malkah,* "escorting the queen," this final

nished wing and they'd left without fuss, with the hidden distress of es-tranged relatives who'd come down in the world.

Now they were infinitely remote from here, with their sense of infe-riority, with all the desolation of their little shtetl, and with their veran-dah, the door to which was always kept locked. If they did ever come to mind, it was exclusively as people who slept during the day, whose rooms were perpetually silent, and whose walls stretched up in bore-dom and mused: "Mirele's been married off by now, married off by now."

Now she'd given herself to Shmulik, and went often into the city to visit her cousin Ida Shpolianski, an enormously rich, licentious woman-about-town who deceived her frequently absent husband. As Mirel had often passed the time right in the center of the provincial capital, it was not long before she'd encountered Nosn Heler, who was attempting to publish a penny newspaper here in the metropolis. On one occasion, returning home from visiting Ida late at night, she'd been walking down the central avenue when she recognized him from be-hind for the first time. In a broadly cut new autumn cloak, he was standing at a deserted intersection next to the tall upright of an electric lamp about to be extinguished, speaking to a respectable elderly Chris-tian about his long-planned penny newspaper:

—*Ponimayete*—you understand—but the first number must appear no later than the fifteenth.

Overcome with confusion, she was not fully conscious of what she was doing until she was close enough to recognize his oblong, olive-skinned, youthful face with its freshly shaven cheeks and whiskers that appeared intensely dark, like those of a Romanian.

—At last—he said excitedly, standing opposite her—at last they'd met each other again.

For a short while her heart pounded rapidly. What he'd said was plainly ridiculous, and made her think:

—He's no cleverer than he was before, this Nosn.

---

meal—held after the ritual conclusion of the Sabbath—is prolonged late into the night, especially among Hasidim, so as to extend the beauty and holiness of the Sabbath, metaphorically personified in the Jewish tradition as a queen.

But all around him the fragrance of the air called to mind those spring evenings in her shtetl two years before and the damp grass of the green hill near the peasant cottages on which they'd sat until late into the night.

In her sleep she dreamed that she was two years younger and was in love with Nosn. And in the early mornings thereafter she was drawn to the bustling city center and beyond, to that quiet, leafy street where Nosn was supposed to wait for her at the start of every evening.

During the day she reflected that she was foolish to be so drawn to him. She sat on the steps of the verandah, gazed out at her deserted end of the suburb, and mused that she herself had once despised this feeling and had sent this fellow Nosn packing. At that time she'd wanted something else, but now her life was empty and she'd given herself to Shmulik and had parted forever from Reb Gedalye and Gitele.

As twilight drew on, her sense of desolation intensified. Her reason and emotions seemed to be clouded with the burden of the day that had passed, and recollection came that somewhere people were happy. At almost the same time, the automatic gate to the left at the end of the iron fence that surrounded her father-in-law's house seemed regularly to clang behind Shmulik's very smartly dressed younger sister Rikl as she went out. She was a tall nineteen-year-old who'd completed her studies at the *gymnasium* only the previous summer, looked older than she actually was, imparted around herself an attitude of either weariness or apathy, and who with huge hat and coiffure—both angled to one side—seemed to have been manufactured according to big-city fashion. She stopped laboriously next to Mirel as though she were too tightly laced into her long corset and new big-city suit and explained that she was just about to take a streetcar into town:

—Was Mirel sure that she didn't need anything from town?

Looking her up and down, Mirel evaluated her:

Tall and slender, she had a dark, lackluster face with dark, lackluster eyes to match, kept silent for the most part, and would hear no word about the matches that were proposed for her. She gave the impression of never saying anything clever only because she was too tired to do so. In reality, however, her mind, like her mother's, was too dull and thoughts were rarely born there. But the suspicion persisted that in town this young woman had somehow been made aware of Mirel's meetings with Heler and would expose them in her mother's house one of these days.

In response to this last thought, Mirel's heart pounded and seemed to die away within her. Having watched Rikl disappearing into the distance, she went inside and spent a long time dressing in her bedroom. She then walked over to that side of the suburb where the clanging of newly arrived streetcars could always be heard, seated herself in one that was already brightly lit, and traveled over the long iron bridge that led into the city.

With no moon visible, the late summer evening was silent and dark, its skies brilliant with stars. Below the bridge, placid, dimly illuminated boats glided here and there over the broad surface of the powerfully flowing river, stopped, whistled, drew back, and passed on mute greetings from those of their passengers who'd traveled down to the provincial capital during the day:

—Well, well, well! . . . They've all had a good afternoon nap, these people, so by now they must certainly be in the theater, in their clubs, or in the city parks.

On the hillside directly ahead twinkled the brightly illuminated city, its myriad fires, dense and sparse alike, glittering through the darkness as it flung out the clamor of its early evening tumult. Every time the streetcar stopped, this commotion made itself heard like the croaking of thousands of river frogs, calling to mind the distant, quiet street somewhere along which Nosn Heler was waiting.

This streetcar, its lights burning well before they were necessary, was always packed with people sitting politely and silently in their places. Through this silence, each attempted to suggest that he or she noticed no one else, yet each emerged as a comical figure who gave the impression of being nothing but a capricious being that had only just woken up in a bad mood.

For the most part Mirel hadn't the faintest interest in any of these creatures, but somewhere behind her there always happened to be a couple of prominent suburban householders who leaned in toward each other and fell into whispered discussion about her:

—Isn't that Yankev-Yosl Zaydenovski's daughter-in-law?

At home they'd heard that Zaydenovski's daughter-in-law was one of those women to whom young men were strongly attracted, so they wanted to see her with their own eyes and with a particular motive as well:

—The whole world says so; surely it's worth learning what the world finds so fascinating?

On one occasion, an officer who was sitting opposite with his wife stared at her for a long time. He was apparently reminded of his first love and had begun to believe that he'd made a mistake in marrying the woman he had. Mirel was instinctively aware of his gaze and in glancing back at him she opened huge, sorrowful eyes that gazed out, deep and blue, from under the dark lashes of her abiding grief and told of how frustrated her own life had been. Both the officer and Mirel blushed, and, suddenly oppressed by the unyielding corset that stiffly encased her sides, she rose from her place and went to stand on the streetcar's small open platform.

When she finally alighted where the city's broad, tumultuous central avenue began, the brilliant white fires of the electric streetlamps had already started blazing everywhere, merging with the glow of the pale twilight and flowing into one festive surge of light. Far, far away in the depths of this arrow-straight road, this festival was apparently being celebrated. From a distance it resembled a candle-lit wedding procession that was drawing near, approaching from some enchanted, turbulent kingdom accompanied by the beating of innumerable unwieldy, deep-toned drums.

Encountering each other on the broad sidewalk opposite were elegantly dressed young men who stared boldly into women's faces, expensively clad young wives who longed to deceive their husbands but didn't know how, and crowds of precocious students of both sexes who always looked preoccupied and, finding themselves on one avenue, were continually under the impression that they were missing something on another.

The sidewalk was abruptly intersected by the quiet street with its long central island of trees on which her cousin Ida Shpolianski lived, but she walked straight on. Approaching from the opposite side were still many people festively attired in black evening dress, all of whom were unknown to her. But then the street began to grow quieter, fewer people made their appearance, and she'd already turned left into another hushed, leafy lane.

This lane was already far quieter, even more dense with foliage, and the fourth was illuminated only by simple, dimly burning gas lamps, next to one of which Nosn Heler had been awaiting her coming for some time and from which he now strode impatiently toward her.

Thinking she wouldn't come, he'd barely been able to compose himself. Now he was afraid that she might be cold and was pleased that she permitted him to throw his broadly cut autumn cloak over both their shoulders. Under this cloak, the hand with which he encircled her waist, the waist of Shmulik Zaydenovski's young wife, had even started trembling. Her hair, he said, smelled not of perfume but of a scent all its own, the scent that wholly enveloped this fastidious only child.

After all, he remembered her from her little shtetl.

And she kept silent, bearing in mind that whatever drew her to him and led her to wander about aimlessly in his company wouldn't last long.

She glanced at two obviously wealthy young women approaching from the opposite direction. Both had evidently been born in the big city and knew what a handsome young bachelor signified; they stared at Heler and smiled, walked on for several paces, turned their heads to look behind them, and smiled again. Mirel, however, paid no attention to Heler's self-absorbed chatter about his penny newspaper, reflecting that she had no use for all this aimless wandering about with him:

For them, for these two young women born in the big city, this might perhaps represent something significant, but for her, Mirel Hurvits . . .

She herself had sent this fellow Nosn packing once before.

Something else was missing from her life; even as a girl she'd started to develop some awareness of what this might be, but now she'd grown confused in this tumultuous provincial capital to which she'd recently relocated. But this confusion would soon pass . . .

Assuredly, it would soon pass.

3.2

From day to day, the Nosn Heler she'd known two years earlier revealed more and more of himself. He was still light-minded, and as always his shallowness called to mind a big-city high school student who'd been expelled.

Mirel wasn't in the least interested in all his chatter about wanting to break off the engagement he'd contracted here in the metropolis four months before to a rich but sickly young woman who was an orphan.

But one evening he importunately began demanding that she should divorce Shmulik and marry him, Nosn Heler, who would make a great financial success of his penny newspaper and was respected here in the provincial capital.

She found this repugnant, and he complained that she wasn't listening to what he was saying, but was thinking of something else:

—No one made him feel as small and foolish as Mirel did.

Making him no answer, she merely gave him an odd look and stopped coming to meet him in the quiet, leafy lane in the evenings.

From then on she once again passed days on end in utter boredom on the steps of her enclosed verandah, reflecting that of late she'd demeaned herself and dared not permit this to continue:

—After all, even as a girl she'd chosen a course of action for herself, and had only married Shmulik provisionally, for the time being.

She had to do something to free herself from her present situation, but didn't know what.

This was intensely oppressive emotionally.

Moreover, the days themselves dragged by, gloomy, autumnal, and cheerless: every afternoon, overcast skies silently lowered over the deserted, sandy outskirts of the suburb, and every evening the passage of visitors, marked by the regular clang of the iron gate in her mother-in-law's fence, sharpened awareness that something had to be done:

—Wait . . . Careful analysis and consideration were called for: what further needed to be done by a young woman who'd grown up as an only child in the home of Reb Gedalye Hurvits, who'd already acquired some glimmering of understanding, and who'd married only in jest and for the time being?

One Sabbath she received a letter from Heler declaring that he loved her and that his life without her was desolate; that on the previous Tuesday his fiancée, who'd been made aware of this, had without his knowledge taken herself off to her brother in Łodz and there demanded that new matchmakers be sent for; that this day was the Sabbath and during all the time that Mirel's husband would be at home and the two of them would be entertaining guests, he himself would be wandering about all alone along the quiet lane as he did on every other evening because his home was repugnant to him, and while he was suffering unendurable torment, he would think:

—Perhaps . . . Perhaps she might feel drawn to him after all, and would come?

Unread, the letter drifted about next to her as she lay on the sofa face up, with her hands beneath her head.

Her whole encounter with Heler—a young man with no parents and no siblings, who for the past two years had been kicking his heels in a rented room in the center of the city—now seemed to her excessively wearisome and foolish. She visualized him tediously whiling away his time on that quiet, distant lane next to its only Jewish shop, now shut for the Sabbath; understood how he found everything there soul-deadening, and how dreary he found the rented room in which he couldn't endure to spend much time. And she was astonished at herself:

—She, who was Mirel Hurvits . . . What had she needed them for, these trips she'd taken into town to see him day after day?

That Sabbath Shmulik yet again spent the whole afternoon in his white shirtsleeves sleeping in his small study, and yet again, just before sunset, one of his mother's young relatives awakened him there by tickling him.

—Shmulik! . . . Open your eyes . . . The distillery's on fire, Shmulik!

Mirel couldn't abide them, these smiling young relatives, and never addressed a single word to them. Passing the open study door she avoided so much as glancing inside. But now, with his eyes open, Shmulik lay on the sofa in there. He stretched the whole of his sleepy body and smiled at her gently and good-naturedly:

—Mirele, will you come across to Father's, Mirele?

Without looking round at him, she immediately strode into the dining room. A few Sabbaths before, in response to the same question, she'd retorted: "He'd find his own way there without her." He wasn't too much of a child to remember this answer and to stop pestering her.

Later, after Shmulik and his father had gone off to Sabbath afternoon prayers, from the dining room she suddenly heard the sharp ring of the new doorbell and the rapid entry of someone making equally rapid inquiries about Shmulik:

—Not here? When will he be back? Has he gone to his father for the last meal of the Sabbath?

This was Shmulik's cousin, Big Montchik.* In honor of the Sabbath he was wearing a brand-new gray suit and brand-new patent-leather shoes to match. All in all, with the distracted expression of a busy merchant and the energetic frame of a big-city wheeler-dealer, he was in haste to return to the center of the bustling metropolis from which he'd only just come down, as though waiting for him there was not some dishonestly acquired little profit but some entirely new and important debauchery. Indeed, his huge black preoccupied eyes now gleamed even more than usual. Yet for quite some time he sat bareheaded next to Mirel, behaved toward her as though with a newly acquired relative with whom he wished to be on comfortably familiar terms, and told lengthy stories about himself and Shmulik, about the Lithuanian *melamed*† with whom they'd studied in Uncle Yankev-Yosl's house when they were children, and about the doves they used to breed in those days, in the very wing in which Mirel and Shmulik now lived.

Once they had as many as ten pairs of doves at one time, so they took a male from one pair and a female from another, locked them up in the small room that was now Shmulik's study, and had waited to see what would come of it. Could Mirel believe that? Such scamps as they were! And he, Montchik, wasn't yet ten years old at the time.

To be sure, the notion of locking up an unpaired male and female in

---

*The name Montchik is a Russian diminutive of Monia, which is in turn a diminutive of Solomon.

†A *melamed* was a Hebrew teacher who instructed the smallest children—boys between the ages of three and four—in basic knowledge of the Pentateuch.

the same room had been his, Montchik's—he'd proposed it, and Shmulik had carried it out. Clearly this was the reason he exuded the air of one well versed in the sins of the big city. And many such sins, it would seem, still lay before him, which explained why he was so powerful, so energetic, and so preoccupied.

Mirel barely heard what he was telling her. Lying on the sofa, she stared at him with enormous eyes and thought that in all her life she'd never before encountered a character like this. Once, during the first days of her arrival, he'd bumped into her in the very middle of the city's noisiest street and had accompanied her for several blocks. That was when she'd seen for herself that he had a great many acquaintances, both Christian and Jewish, that he was on familiar terms with virtually all of them, and that he shouted after some of them:

—Come and see me this evening; I need you.

—Be sure to be at home at eleven o'clock, d'you hear? At exactly eleven o'clock.

In her mother-in-law's house they thought the world of this preoccupied young man. Every time he snatched a moment to come down from town to visit them, they surrounded him and peppered him with questions:

—Montchik, why didn't you come last Sabbath?

—Montchik, Auntie Pearl's sent you a gift from Warsaw—have you seen it?

—Montchik, will you come to the distillery with us on Sunday?

For some reason, all the Zaydenovskis were excessively fond of him, and since none of them ever remembered that they'd often described him in the same terms to every new member of the family, they'd all start simultaneously repeating that he was very clever, very shrewd, and had been possessed of remarkable intelligence from childhood on, and that he knew a great deal, a very great deal, even though at the age of eighteen he'd abandoned his studies at the commercial school and with his clever head had manipulated his way into some kind of prosperous merchant partnership of which he was still to this day the principal. In the metropolis he had by now acquired a reputation, considerable credit, and a wide acquaintance, and people often sought business advice from him. When he'd run out of things to say here, and, holding his hat in his hand, was ready to take his leave, he suddenly remembered one of these seekers after advice, and delayed his departure a while longer:

—This very week a young man who'd come to seek his advice mentioned that he was an acquaintance of Mirel's; he was good-looking, this young man, very good-looking indeed; he looked like a Romanian. Wait, what was his surname? . . . Hel . . . Hel . . . Heler, yes, Heler. He wanted to publish a penny newspaper in Russian here, but all told he had a capital of only three thousand rubles. Well! . . . It wouldn't work; it wasn't a viable business proposition.

Mirel's heart immediately started pounding and almost died within her.

Montchik might've mentioned this encounter in passing, simply by chance. But then again, he might've had some intention in doing so . . . He might've been sent by her mother-in-law.

For quite some time after Montchik had left, she lay where she was, so calm and detached that she surprised even herself. But quite suddenly she began to resent the fact that Heler moved in the same circles as her husband's relatives and spoke of her, Mirel. She no longer wanted to think about him and, seemingly in anger, rapidly began dressing in order to go that quiet lane on which he was waiting for her:

—No . . . This had to come to an immediate end; she was disgusted by the whole sorry tale. He'd have to stop building hopes about her, Mirel.

As always Nosn Heler was waiting for her next to the closed post office located on the quiet lane, tensely overwrought and afraid that she wouldn't come. Every now and then he screwed up his eyes and gazed intently toward the farthest end of the street on which the distant low-hanging sun still blazed down, inflaming the yellowing leaves on the surrounding trees and the roofs on the nearby houses. From time to time some gilded person emblazoned with red-gold sunshine approached from that direction—but it wasn't Mirel. When he did finally catch sight of her coming toward him, he failed to recognize her and didn't believe that it could really be she. He remembered that he ought to tell her something about himself, about the unendurable days he'd lived through, about the fact that he could no longer go on in this way. He was strongly attracted to her slender figure and to her face; he wanted to weep.

But coming up to her, he noticed that her expression was sad, severe, and estranged, and he instantly forgot what he wanted to tell her. For a while they stood opposite each other without speaking. While his head was bowed, Mirel glanced at him but said nothing. He heard her draw a long, quiet breath and slowly start walking. He, too, gave a sigh of sorts and followed her. Clearly, she'd come to him for the last time. His whole body trembled. Had he attempted to speak, his teeth might have chattered in his mouth. He looked not at her but opposite, at the closed post office. Its roof still glowed in the last of the sunshine; a missing pane from one of its windows had been patched from within by a sheet of blue paper. Only now did he look at Mirel again, noticing that in the last few days she'd grown very haggard and that there were dark shadows under her eyes; she'd almost certainly locked herself away indoors all that time, and had been tormented by thoughts wholly unrelated to him, Heler. Since this pained him, he said:

—What else could be expected? He was nothing to her, after all . . .

Mirel made no reply.

They turned left and walked downhill following the wide, crooked street with the cobblestones, which were bigger here than elsewhere to control the rush of water during the rainy season. Presently they reached the end of this winding road, which marked also the city's farthest extremity, and at this terminal point they sat down on a bench opposite the many windows of an elongated, one-storied foundry. The red fire of the distant setting sun was reflected in its electrically illuminated windowpanes, and, to the right, the high green hills and the clay pits that prevented any further extension of the city steeped themselves in it. There on a knoll near a deserted windmill a tethered horse grazed on the reddened grass, and a Gentile boy in white canvas trousers stood on its crest gazing down at the city. All at once Nosn, sensing that he was growing more agitated from moment to moment, began speaking well before his mind knew what words it wanted his mouth to utter:

—He knew . . . One thing he knew for certain. He actually wanted to ask her . . .

Mirel stared at him in astonishment, not knowing what he wanted.

He was still unable to gather the thread of his thoughts. Fancying that Mirel was looking at him as though he were a babbling idiot, he grew even more agitated; he was overcome with a powerful resentment against her that helped him to pull himself together and quite unexpectedly to say what he wanted without fully anticipating it himself.

—This was what he wanted to know: did Mirel love him? She couldn't deny it. So he asked only one thing of her: why didn't she want to divorce her husband and marry him, Heler?

Mirel heard him out, shrugged her shoulders, and glanced down at the lines she'd scratched out on the ground with the tip of her parasol:

—Well, and afterward, after the wedding . . . ?

—Afterward?

Heler did not understand what she meant by this.

—Afterward they'd go abroad . . . afterward . . .

Mirel again shrugged her shoulders and rose from the bench.

Heler wanted to make some other affirmation, but she anticipated what he was going to say. She found it distasteful to listen and stopped him coldly:

—She disliked talking too much.

But Heler was now beside himself:

—How on earth had she managed to live for four whole months with her foolish husband? He was ridiculed in town . . . People openly laughed in his face . . .

He stopped talking only because Mirel turned to face him with an expression of even greater alienation from him; he regarded it sadly and a shudder seemed to pass though him.

She responded:

—She'd asked him several times not to speak of her husband and to leave him in peace . . . Her husband was a good man . . . At least he harmed no one.

She was annoyed at herself. It seemed to her that a great many young wives had spoken the selfsame words about their foolish husbands to the young men with whom they wandered the quiet streets.

—All events he, Heler, wasn't someone for whom it was worth changing her opinion of her husband.

She had no wish to think about these words, the last she'd spoken in anger before parting from him. Without looking back, she tried hard to put him out of her mind. Walking on at a brisk, regular pace, she wore her customary sorrowful expression as she tried to shake off her agitation and clarify her thoughts:

—Now she'd broken with him, with Heler. And now . . . Wait . . . She had to break with someone else, it seemed to her . . . Yes. With them, with the Zaydenovskis. She had to bring all that to an end very quickly.

Now she had to get home and put this task in hand.

3.3

Late in the evening, after several more hours of aimless wandering, she returned to her little house on the outskirts of the suburb. From its unlighted windows a wave of desolation suddenly swept over her, and she no longer had any desire to ring for the sleeping maid and pass through its darkened rooms. Across the way, festively illuminated this Sabbath evening, the windows of her father-in-law's big house looked out over the shadowy orchard. She was overcome by an urge to call in, to observe things again in order to convince herself once more of the truth of what she was thinking:

—She derived absolutely no benefit from not yet having left Zaydenovski's house.

In the end she did go in, and sat for long time desperately bored in the dining room without taking off the jacket she'd worn in the street and without speaking a word to anyone.

As always, virtually the entire extended family had gathered here on this Sabbath evening. They sat on chairs both old and new ranged round the long, spread table and next to the big sideboard, stood in groups beside the glass-fronted heritage chest fitted high up on the wall, or lolled about on the huge, wide sofa over which the room's sole embroidered picture hung low.

Young and old alike, all these relatives loved Shmulik, regarded him as exceptionally good and tenderhearted, and played games with him as though he were a clever child. All of them knew that Mirel was beautiful and refined, yet none was completely satisfied with her and kept her at a distance, repeatedly remarking among themselves that she wasn't the one for whom both they and Shmulik had waited these last few years, and continually recalling a very rich local girl, Ita Moreynes, who to this day continued to pine for Shmulik.

—It's remarkable that only the other day old Moreynes himself specifically said that he'd intended to settle twenty thousand rubles on Shmulik.

Among the relatives that evening was the somewhat disaffected former university student Miriam, tall, handsome, and big-boned, who had a past as a canny, confirmed revolutionary. As recently as eighteen months earlier she'd married a party comrade, the engineer Lyuba-shits, had a child with him, and immediately after her first lying-in had started putting on weight, smiling excessively, and once more calling regularly at Uncle Yankev-Yoysef's house. Like all the others, she too said that she'd never been indifferent to Shmulik, smiled at him far too warmly, and kept on remarking on one of his good-natured idiosyn-crasies:

—Three weeks before she'd bumped into Shmulik at the main rail-way station and had introduced him there to his relative, Naum Kluger. Naum was traveling from Kharkov, where only this year he'd just qualified as a doctor . . .

This particular idiosyncrasy sprang from the fact that good-natured Shmulik was as naïve as a child. This was the first time he'd met this young doctor, a relative whom he'd never so much as seen in his life be-fore, yet he was immediately on familiar terms with him and in all se-riousness insisted:

—Naum, come and spend the Sabbath with me, please do, Naum! Have your ticket stamped to show that you've interrupted your forward journey, Naum!

From the master's study, with one of the master's cigarettes in his mouth, now emerged a middle-aged man, a tall, partially observant matchmaker wearing a surtout too wide for him, a narrow oblong beard, and an expression of Sabbath contentment on his face; he had a predilection for making himself appear more idiotic than he really was. At the big table he caught a few words of the conversation being con-ducted there and instantly began loudly asserting:

—What? Women students? Might all his prayers for a good year be answered as surely as all of them were practically dying to get married. At first they pretended to deny this and mocked the idea, but as soon as they saw a serious possibility developing, they stopped laughing and burned with eagerness instead . . . as true as he was a Jew.

These remarks were directed at Shmulik's sister Rikl. On the other side, with a shawl over her shoulders, Mirel's mother-in-law sat at the head of the table stupidly blinking her eyes. A little earlier, before Mirel's arrival, she'd been murmuring complaints in the ear of the former student Miriam:

—But the whole business was troubling . . . She went to town every day, that Mirel, so why shouldn't she sometimes ask Shmulik to go with her?

Now she'd told an elderly woman about two young female students who'd rented a room in town from Uncle Ezriel-Meir's daughter:

—Uncle Ezriel-Meir's daughter says that very often a male student calls on these girls late in the evening and stays overnight.

A little farther on, in the middle of the large room, stood the master's youngest brother, Sholem Zaydenovski, a perpetually discontented young man with a saturnine complexion and the appearance of an overgrown yeshiva student who'd only recently shortened both his earlocks and his surtout. He stood there completely alone, regarding the company carefully and patiently as though he were not part of it, and maintaining a supercilious silence. After the death of his fanatically observant parents not long before, he'd found himself to be nothing more than a partially agnostic, venomous freethinker, had married for the sake of her dowry a lanky young woman no longer in the first bloom of youth whom he'd rejected for three consecutive years, had moved with her to a nearby shtetl which was home to a wonder-working rabbi, and had there been forced to open a warehouse that sold planks. Toward money he now felt a deep antipathy coupled with a shopkeeper's pathological love for it that was his genetic inheritance, believed that no one was as capable of making it as he was, and for this reason held an uncommonly negative opinion of Jewish youth:

—Our people are quite incapable of producing any healthy types.

From the outset he'd behaved badly and with hostility toward Mirel, as though he could never bring himself to forgive her for marrying his brother's foolish son, Shmulik. Not once the whole evening did he look at her, though her beautiful, sad face and troubled blue eyes excited him; at length he went over to young Lyubashits, the student, who was seated not far from Mirel and commented to him in a tone suggesting that he was speaking of an incident that had lately taken place before his very eyes on one or another of the city's bustling streets:

—Yes . . . from childhood on these young people grow up among us thinking: I will be a prince . . . somewhere there's a princess waiting for me . . .

Montchik arrived from town. He came in late, preoccupied, with the appearance of someone who'd dropped down from an extraterrestrial world. Some kind of profitable piece of business had only just slipped out of his hands, so his mind was still in town, brooding over ways and means to save this little money-spinner, while his glazed eyes stared vacantly into the lamp. At first he was wholly unconscious of the way his young female relatives were giggling and jostling each other behind his back, how every now and then one or another of them furtively tugged at his jacket or pushed orange peel down the back of his collar. When he did finally turn round, they were all laughing loudly at him, and only the former student Miriam Lyubashits made any effort to keep a straight face as she joked:

—Shame on you, Montchik! . . . I've been asking you a question for the past half hour . . . What's wrong? Why don't you answer me?

Only then did Montchik remember that he was hungry, and start thinking back in puzzlement:

—Just a moment: he certainly hadn't yet drunk any tea this evening. But what about this afternoon? . . . What could this mean? He hadn't the faintest recollection of whether or not he'd eaten lunch that day.

They laughed at him again as they brought him something to eat. Without sitting down, he absently snatched a few bites and once more lost himself in thought, taking a glass of tea off its saucer and carrying it with him as he paced across the room.

At the head of the table they were still talking about "female students." Someone had overheard the cynical way the two young women who rented a room from Uncle Ezriel-Meir's daughter had spoken about the student who spent the night with them after he'd left them very early one morning. The mother-in-law grimaced in disgust and spat loudly, but a frisson of lust passed over the men, and they started exchanging prurient stories. Someone took Shmulik aside and began furtively describing a petite, highly passionate newlywed, a student, who'd left her husband, a traveling salesman, in Kursk, and had fallen pregnant by another man here in town. Totally oblivious of the people who filled the spacious dining room Shmulik, his face burning as he listened to this story, could be heard asking loudly:

—Really? Here? In town?

Meanwhile the dark passageway between the study and the dining room was now filled with the resounding bass of the powerful, dark-haired master of the house, still vigorous in his middle years:

—Have the horse harnessed immediately, Borukh! You still have an hour and a quarter before the train leaves.

In the dining room, silence suddenly fell. When his virile figure appeared in the doorway, everyone looked respectfully in his direction and saw him lay his hand on Montchik's shoulder with a smiling wink:

—You're making a big noise in the world, eh?

No one knew whether this remark was spoken in jest or in earnest. As always, Zaydenovski's eyes gleamed as though he'd only just varnished them, and his whole bearing wordlessly repeated what everyone had long known but what he'd never openly said of himself:

—Worth half a million . . . not bad, eh? With a reputation throughout the entire district . . . And not just anybody . . . no, no—one of the Zaydenovskis!

From across the table where she still sat with her coat on, Mirel looked at him. This man, who loved cracking jokes, who to this day traveled to Sadagura for Yom Kippur, and whose vanity demanded that every one of the lengthy third meals he served before the conclusion of every Sabbath be attended by at least ten male guests, seemed to her at times to be nothing more than a common libertine in respectable clothing. There was reason to believe that, his observant Jewish practices notwithstanding, he was often covertly unfaithful to his wife and behaved licentiously, otherwise it was impossible to understand why every now and then he quite suddenly humbled his proud, stubborn nature and treated even his own little children with gentle timidity.

At last he noticed her, his first daughter-in-law, approached her with a smile and an ingratiating move, and began joking with her in a tone suggesting that only he was privy to the deep secret that she was absolutely no wife to his son:

—Ah . . . Mirele . . . how are you getting on with running a household?

All looked in that direction, smiled, and kept silent. Only the former student Miriam Lyubashits, who'd deliberately obscured herself behind someone's back, quietly responded for Mirel with a witticism, to which no one paid any attention, in an attempt to attract Uncle Yankev-Yosl's attention to herself.

There was general laughter at the father-in-law's facetious notions:

—Could Mirel imagine what would happen if she were suddenly to dismiss her cook and were then unable to engage another one?

—After all, a *zabastovke,* a workers' strike, of cooks, for example, was certainly conceivable.

The only one who didn't laugh was the father-in-law's arrogant, deeply malicious brother, Sholem. Hugely puffed up with his own self-importance, with a contemptuous conviction that all these people around him were wholly incapable of understanding either his penetrating intellect or the reason for his hatred of people, he stood to one side, isolated from everyone else, and said nothing. With his head at a slight angle and his right hand thrust between the buttons of his tightly fastened surtout, he fixed his eyes malevolently on Mirel as though regarding her from a great height. Among the whole company assembled here, he alone regarded his older brother as a vain and commonplace social climber, but knew that no one here except himself would understand this and consequently had no wish to speak about it. He lowered his head still further, thrust out his broad shiny chin on which hair rarely grew, began arrogantly pacing about the room, and made not the slightest reply, even to the former student Miriam, who regarded him as a skinflint and who had been pursuing him for several minutes with the same tedious question:

—Sholem, when do you say we should come to visit you?

The father-in-law was no longer in the room. The rest of the company had reverted to behaving with too much jollity and lack of restraint, and Mirel still sat at the table in her overcoat. All at once she became conscious of Sholem Zaydenovski's glance resting on her yet again, and quite unexpectedly, even to herself, she sprang to her feet.

Taking leave of no one in the house, she made her way home alone and was still unable to calm herself:

—No, she'd eventually have to tell this yeshiva student that he was a great blockhead or some other word to the same effect.

Even after she'd undressed in her room and retired to bed she continued to feel thoroughly disconcerted:

—Now Sholem Zaydenovski's glances were beginning to affect her . . . and the overriding concern . . .

The overriding concern was that every day she felt something ought to be done, but didn't know what or how. Every day she thought she'd know what it was the next day, but the next day she failed again because she still found herself under the same roof as Shmulik, and was still his wife. Sooner or later she'd have to find some means of escape from this whole existence.

There was nothing more—

—Other people spent years looking for the same means of escape, and when they failed to find it, they eventually took their own lives, leaving behind half-foolish, half-perceptive notes.

Well after midnight, she fell into a light sleep. The house was very dark and quiet. Somewhere in the kitchen at the other end of the corridor the maid, who'd fallen into a deep sleep still fully dressed, began snoring loudly, and the cat began tumbling a cube of sugar over the floor, with the result that Mirel was unable to drift off into forgetfulness. The end of her last thought kept repeating itself in her drowsy mind:

—When they failed to find it, they eventually took their own lives, leaving behind half-foolish, half-perceptive notes.

She couldn't recall how long this restless dream lasted.

Half-asleep she suddenly felt a cold hand brush against her bare back. Her whole body shuddered and she opened her eyes.

The bedroom was brightly lit by the study lamp that had been carried in, and next to the bed, in his underwear, stood Shmulik, hunched over, trembling and smiling. He'd been aroused by the suggestive tales he'd been hearing all evening about the pregnant little newlywed from Kursk.

For a while Mirel stared at him in fright.

—What do you need here, Shmulik?

Very soon the reason he was standing here next to her bed became clear to her, and a flame of stubbornness and resentment instantly kindled in her eyes:

—Shmulik, take a pillow and lie down in the study at once.

A pause.

—Do you hear what I say, Shmulik?

Without moving, hunched over and half-naked, Shmulik still stood there, trembling and grinning foolishly. But now Mirel had the button of the electric bell in her hand and was ringing without pause for the snoring maid in the kitchen. The shrilling bell seemed set to shatter the whole house to smithereens before the maid's bare feet could be heard slapping over the floor. Then in discomfited embarrassment Shmulik took up a pillow and went off to his study. The maid carried the lamp out of the bedroom and extinguished it, and darkness and desolation once again descended on the house. Someone, it seemed, was weeping with suppressed sobs torn from the very depths of the heart. But for anyone who might have sat up in bed and listened attentively, all that could be heard was the cat tumbling the cube of sugar over the floor and the regular breathing of the snoring maid.

3.4

The next day Mirel rose late, at about eleven o'clock in the morning.

From the kitchen came the sound of rapid chopping, and in the courtyard the britzka that had conveyed Shmulik to the distillery as dawn was breaking had already been unharnessed. The father-in-law's most trusted servant, his coachman, spent a long time fussing over the returned britzka, shouted at Shmulik's little brother for getting under the horse's feet and at the mother-in-law's Gentile maid for throwing dirty kitchen water into the freshly swept courtyard. The mother-in-law herself stood there wondering why Shmulik had taken himself off to the distillery so early and inquiring after a letter from the yelling coachman. A short while later, when Mirel passed through the courtyard, no one was there. By then the quiet of the working week rested over all the locked stables, the coachman was sitting somewhere in the kitchen and for some reason only the unharnessed, well-sprung britzka, with its shaft still in place, stood in the middle of the freshly swept courtyard wordlessly calling to mind Shmulik, who'd gone away:

—The night before he'd stood next to her bed in his underwear and for a long time had been unwilling to move away . . . Now he was ashamed to look her in the face and would therefore be in no haste to return from the distillery.

Presently she returned to the dining room, wrapped herself in her shawl, and lay down on the sofa. So much heaviness and disgust on her soul left her feeling as though her heart had been snatched out and steeped in filth. From under the overcast skies outdoors a bleak new Sunday stared in, spreading its single tedious thought all around:

—A new week . . . a bleak week . . . a dreary week.

A dull ache gripped the back of her head all the way down her neck in consequence of the agitated, sleepless night she'd passed. The pain was weak and ill-defined, as with the onset of typhus, her eyelids drooped of their own accord, and in her drowsy, fuddled consciousness confused thoughts came and went, merging the sound of the chopper that echoed from the kitchen with reflections on her own lost life, the dull pain in the back of her head, and an awareness that she'd lie here on the sofa for a long, long time:

—She'd lie dozing here all day.

Drifting in and out of sleep on the sofa there, she started awake, noticed the table laid, rose, and attempted to eat something, but finding herself unable to do so, lay down and dozed off again, opening her eyes only toward sunset to see:

An ill wind had blown in a young man, a synagogue cantor who was passing through, a tall, thin fellow in a short, worn little surtout with a dirty paper collar and a tuning fork in his pouch. Speaking with a nasal drawl, he inquired after Shmulik as after an influential trustee of a synagogue:

—In general, did Madame know when the Master would return?

—*Ponimayete-li,* was it Madame's understanding that the Master would return for the Sabbath?

She felt not the slightest obligation to spend time being bored in his company, to inhale the stench of rotting salted fish that he diffused around himself, or to keep answering him in exactly the same way she'd answered him before:

—I don't know.

—No.

—I don't know.

Earlier, under his very eyes, she'd attempted to air the room and had opened all the windows in the hope that this hint would help. But since he still refused to budge, she finally left him on his own there, went outdoors, and seated herself on the steps of the verandah.

Slowly, very slowly, the darkness of early evening drew on, spreading silence over the scattered houses on the sandy outskirts of the suburb. By now there were no longer any passersby, and the air was utterly still. Somewhere far away, near the barn stacked with bales of straw situated opposite the church's large courtyard, a threshing machine worked on the priest's dried-out grain as night fell. To the left, between the father-in-law's trees where a little earlier a horde of relatives had appeared to see Sholem Zaydenovski on his way, the mother-in-law could be heard thrashing one of her little boys. The child could be heard struggling and screaming, and as she struck the blows the mother-in-law went on and on repeating in her hoarse, dull-witted voice:

—One dared not speak about a mother that way . . . One dared not speak about a mother that way . . . That wasn't the way to speak about a mother.

The screams of the weeping child evoked a clear picture of the way she was holding the boy bent over her knee and peering shortsightedly at the place she was beating. This prompted the thought that this tall, stupid woman was utterly without understanding, had no idea of how to treat children, and ruined them as a result; that in exactly the same way some fifteen or sixteen years before she'd thrashed Shmulik, the man who was currently her husband, and had yelled at him too, exactly as she was doing now:

—One dared not speak to a mother that way . . . One dared not speak to a mother that way . . .

For this reason, because there was now no doubt that Shmulik basically needed a wife who would thrash his children just as his mother had thrashed him, she suddenly felt relieved of a heavy burden, and her light heart was suddenly filled with the half-forgotten hope:

—Wait! . . . Nothing at all bound her to him, to Shmulik, or to this house, and she, Mirel . . . she could leave whenever she chose.

Now all she needed was to devise a plan.

An event that had taken place in the provincial capital some years before came to mind:

A stubborn, uncommunicative young wife, a daughter-in-law of the wealthy Dizhur family, had left her accustomed place early one morning, had spoken no word either to her husband or to her parents-in-law before her departure, and had never returned again.

This was soon known all over the city, and in well-to-do homes jokes were made:

—Never mind, she'll come back . . . With God's help, she'll show up for a meal one Sabbath or another.

But the young wife did not return, and to this day no trace of her could be found . . . No one knew what had become of her . . . But knowing this had now become an absolute necessity for her, Mirel . . . She'd work it out:

—Where might this young wife have got to?

Sending not the slightest information about himself, Shmulik stayed on at the distillery from which he was preparing to travel to Warsaw with the herd of oxen he'd acquired before Passover. In this connection, the overseer of the oxen stables, Reb Bunem, came to town. He was a short, stocky little man with a very red neck whose clothes were always greasy: he wore a long caftan in summer, and made it a habit never to forget what his employer had told him. He'd brought along a number of stable lanterns for repair, and purchased a great many short lengths of rope together with several pood[*] of rock salt for the oxen to lick on the road. Carrying in with him the smell of the distillery's fermenting mash, he also called at the house, found Mirel lying alone on the sofa, and delivered the message with which he'd been charged:

—The young master said to give him the ledger from before Pesach, that's what he said.

Mirel heard him out without making the slightest movement from her place, and sent him off to the kitchen.

There the maid, apparently under the impression that what was wanted was some sort of vessel used only for Passover preparations, stared at him wide-eyed:

—How was she supposed to know, since she hadn't been in service here before Passover? . . . He'd better ask the coachman Theodor in the courtyard.

The little man wandered up and down in the courtyard for so long that he was finally summoned to the old master in the big house who demanded to know:

—What? Hadn't the young mistress handed over the ledger yet?

With her shawl over her shoulders, the mother-in-law finally went over in person to Mirel's house, rummaged about among the books in the study closet until she found the one she was looking for, peered into it with her shortsighted eyes, and read over the first line, which was written in Hebrew, with the delivery of someone reading from the Women's Bible:[†]

—Statement of account for oxen purchased during the months of Shevat, Adar, and Nisan.[‡]

---

[*]In the Imperial Russian system of weights and measures, a pood was equivalent to 36.1 pounds, or 16.38 kilograms.

[†]The so-called Women's Bible, known in Yiddish as the *Taytsh-khumesh*, is a rendering in Yiddish of the Pentateuch. It is not a direct translation, but a paraphrase interspersed with passages from the great commentators and interwoven with homilies and legends that aimed to impart ethical instruction to women. Prepared by Rabbi Yitskhok ben Shimshon ha-Kohen (d. 1624), it was first published in Prague in 1608 and was in continual use until the mid-twentieth century.

[‡]These are all months of the Hebrew calendar, roughly corresponding to the secular months of February, March, and April.

—Here, take it—she said to the overseer in a deliberately loud voice, and left without turning to Mirel. Beside herself with indignation, she went back to her own house and began casting infuriated glances at her husband's study, where he was dealing with some businessmen. She restrained herself from speaking during the midday meal, waiting until Yankev-Yoysef went off to lie down in their bedroom, whereupon she sat down next to him near the bed and began whispering to him as quietly as though someone were strangling her:

—Do you understand? I mean, what kind of wife is she for Shmulik, for pity's sake?

—Yes, and all the things she does . . . And all her trips to that fine cousin of hers, God help us . . . And the fact that I have to run her house for her, and try to remember that her ceilings have to be repainted . . . What's the meaning of it? I even have to send out her chickens to be slaughtered.

The powerful, dark-haired master of the house, who had the crafty eyes of a thief, lay on the bed in his white shirtsleeves smoking his cigarette in silence, frequently glancing warily at the door as though afraid that someone was eavesdropping. He made her no reply. He'd apparently resolved long before that Shmulik had chosen badly and wished to bring all discussion about it to an end as soon as possible. But she, that shortsighted dolt, was still quite unable to calm herself, continually blinked her eyes and whisperingly came to a decision:

—Nothing makes any impression on her . . . It's clear enough what would've happened if she'd made her match with other people . . . But she's made it with us . . . And Shmulik's as peace-loving as a dove . . . So there's nothing to do . . . We have to grin and bear it! Keep quiet . . . as though we've seen nothing.

A few days later the mother-in-law went into Mirel's house with two house painters whom she'd engaged. Paying no attention to Mirel, who was lying on the sofa, she took the workmen from one room to another, pointing out the ceilings to them:

—D'you see? After the furniture's been moved out into the dining room, the ceiling in the study must be painted first; then the dining room furniture must be moved into the study and the dining room ceiling attended to.

Without turning round, the mother-in-law took herself off and the artisans immediately carried all the study furniture into the dining room and set to work.

Very soon the house began to stink of oil paint and a mixture of ochre and English lamp-black.* The disorder grew from day to day. The disarranged rooms were cleaned neither during the day nor at night while the house painters went on doing their jobs, slowly covering one ceiling after another.

They were by no means old men, these two Jewish workmen. They wore embroidered shirts under their paint-stained overalls, and the devil made sure that girls were still beguiled by them and by the work they did. All day the two of them stood on their makeshift scaffolding drawing lines with their rulers, applying paint with their brushes, deriving pleasure from their labor and whistling sad journeyman melodies to accompany it.

A while later, one of the painters had occasion to pass through the adjoining room to collect some necessary piece of equipment and noticed something. Returning to his work fairly excited, he looked round carefully to make sure no one but his companion was there, and asked him with a suggestive wink:

—The mistress of the house isn't bad-looking, eh?

He kept her in mind all the time he was seated on the high scaffolding, smoking cigarettes and sharing one of his schoolboy stories with his companion:

—When was this? . . . It must've been about eight years ago . . . At the time we were working in the administrative village† of Kloki and the master of the house had a young daughter-in-law, a sly, frisky little thing she was.

In the disarranged room next door, Mirel went on lying on the sofa in her wide, low-cut dressing-gown with its bell-shaped sleeves, wrapped herself in her thin shawl, and conjured up images of various places to which she might travel once she'd left this house:

---

*All of these are pigments formerly used in oil-based paint.

†One of the network of smaller units of local self-government through which tsarist Russia controlled each of its fifty provinces.

—Wherever that might be, nowhere could be worse than here.

All around her stood the beds, both wardrobes with their mirrored doors and the armchairs from the salon together with the huge washtub from which the sodden floor-rag hadn't been removed for days on end. Everything here resembled a bizarre Passover eve that had fallen in the middle of the month of Elul.* All that afternoon the surrounding air had been gloomy and overcast, the thoughts in her mind hazy and confused, and this day seemed to be taking place not in the present but five or six years earlier.

On top of all this came the episode with the book: the arrival in the post of Herz's new book in Hebrew which reeked of new paper, of fresh printers' ink, and of the unknown young man himself.

One day the postman had delivered it to the in-laws' house with the rest of the mail. Everyone there had clustered around it, as afraid as if it were a living thing. Someone noticed something in the firm masculine hand in which the address had been written:

—Just a minute ... Shmulik's name's been deliberately omitted from the address.

And more:

—What else could be expected? Didn't they all know well enough that, from girlhood on, young women like Mirel always had to have young male admirers?

Regarded by everyone as the surreptitiously discarded, living fruit of a sin Mirel and someone else had committed together, the book lay on the table for a long time without anyone knowing what to do with it:

—Shouldn't we send it to Mirel before Yankev-Yosl comes home?

When they did eventually send it to her, she became strangely agitated and confused. She dressed quickly and set off to the telegraph office but almost immediately turned back and sent her maid over to her mother-in-law's house with clear instructions:

—She was to ask for a letter over there, did she understand? A letter ought to have come, she was to say, together with the book.

---

*That is, six months after it normally occurs. Nisan is the month of Passover; Elul is the month of the High Holy Days.

From then on there was much putting of heads together at secret meetings in the mother-in-law's house.

—There was nothing else to be done. In the end they'd have to discuss this with Shmulik and convince him that this was no life for him.

All understood:

No one dared tell him outright that what had taken place between himself and Mirel that Saturday night was common knowledge; everyone understood this. Hence a suitably diplomatic intermediary was sought who could be sent to the distillery, and great reliance was placed on the advice of the former student Miriam:

—Perhaps Miriam's right . . . Perhaps the best person is young Lyubashits, the student?

One evening, just before sunset, the young student Lyubashits returned from the distillery covered with dust. He wore the smile of one who out of the goodness of his heart had discharged an errand that was improper for him, and he related, in the private room into which he was led:

—Yes, he'd discussed the matter with Shmulik there.

Almost all the adult members of the household, with the mother-in-law and the former student Miriam at their head, were gathered around. Care was taken to prevent eavesdropping, all the little children were chased away, and everyone hung on his every word:

—Was he saying that Shmulik's eyes had filled with tears when he recognized Lyubashits?

Like all members of his family, the young student Lyubashits was a tall, strapping, big-boned blond fellow. With his broad shoulders pressed against the safe, he looked tired from his journey. In sum, he was a bit of a poet, shaved closely in consequence of having published some of his verses in a student journal, was given to excessive theorizing about every subject under the sun, and had independent views about Tolstoy. But when he spoke about Shmulik, his face relaxed into the same childlike smile it took on when he was drunk, and it seemed as though soon, very soon, tears would gather in his own enormous blue eyes:

As soon as he'd recognized Lyubashits, Shmulik had apparently said:

—Just look—it's Shoylik!* What brings you here, Shoylik?

Shmulik appeared to believe that everyone already knew why he didn't come home and was embarrassed, even with Shoylik. But later, while they'd been strolling over the distillery and Lyubashits had mentioned Mirel's name, Shmulik had taken him by the arm and begun speaking so quietly and strangely that it wrung Lyubashits's heart:

—You understand, Shoylik?—he'd remarked—Mirel is a torment . . . Unquestionably a torment, but if she wants to, she can be good.

Then with tears in his eyes, Shmulik had fallen silent. Yes . . . and then he'd taken Lyubashits by the arm once more and said:

—Don't think there are many such Mirels in the world, Shoylik . . . It's only that she considers me a fool . . . A complete fool.

3.5

Shmulik did indeed not return home; he went straight from the distillery to Warsaw with the oxen.

Frequent telegrams from him arrived at the father-in-law's house reporting on the unusually lively state of the sizable market. Like an experienced merchant, he'd abruptly raised the price, decided to stay on with his oxen for a second week, and asked that the heaviest beasts from all their oxen stalls, both those in the vicinity and those farther away, be sent to him as soon as possible.

This matter was discussed several times a day in the father-in-law's study. Even the little children had been allowed to come in, and an opinion was jokingly sought even from the youngest, a freckle-faced six-year-old lad who reeked of the stables and whose little backside the mother-in-law frequently thrashed:

—What do you say, little rascal? Shall we send the oxen?

Everyone was genuinely in high spirits:

—No question—when God helps and the market is favorable, one can earn a fortune.

The mother-in-law devised a pretext on which to enter Mirel's little house, ostensibly to check that the ceilings weren't being painted too

*A Russianized diminutive of the Hebrew name Shoyl, Saul.

dark. She found Mirel lying on the sofa in the disarranged dining room, told her that Shmulik was in Warsaw and that a letter was presently being written to him:

—Yes, so what message should be added from her, from Mirel?

Mirel shrugged her shoulders with indifference.

—Nothing . . . She had nothing to write to him.

Since she was now standing with her face to the window, she didn't see the expression on her mother-in-law's face as the woman left the house. Instead, as Mirel returned to the sofa, the sense that this house was repulsive to her returned as well, together with the recollection that she ought to do something:

—She had to find a way of leaving this house.

Overcome with restlessness, she found herself unable to stay in one place. For several successive days she kept going into town, wandering about on her own for long periods of time, and finally, as evening drew on, making her way to the quiet street with its long central island of trees where her cousin Ida Shpolianski lived. She felt she ought to tell Ida, who paid no attention to the derisive rumors that were circulating about her in town:

—Listen, Ida, you've certainly thrown off all conventional restraints, but what would you say were you to be told: Mirel's cast Shmulik off and no longer wishes to live with him?

As it happened, most evenings Ida was never to be found in her luxurious home, but was freely and openly taking her pleasure somewhere with the young, enormously wealthy officer whom Mirel had once met here at sundown, and neither of the two housemaids knew where she'd gone or when she'd be back.

All five rooms were dark and quiet. Almost everywhere lay large new carpets on which fashionable soft furniture was arranged throughout, and all of it seemed pensive, as though possessed of many secrets about the mistress of the house, that well-known woman about town who was unfaithful to her husband while he was earning huge sums of money in the distant provinces of the Russian empire; about the fact that he, the master of the house, would eventually be made aware of this, and this home would be destroyed.

After some hours of waiting and lazing about on the silk chaise longue in Ida's bedroom, she finally left her cousin's apartment feeling like some kind of vagabond idler. She returned home thinking that, alone in this huge provincial capital, she was superfluous and forlorn; that all the people she encountered were following specific goals and purposes. Whatever they did was what they had to do. And she, Mirel . . . she began recalling everything she'd done in her life and everything that had resulted from it:

—Nothing would've been lost if she'd been left lying in her bed from the day of her birth and hadn't moved from that day to this.

Finally she stopped going into town entirely.

For days on end she stayed indoors wearing the same dirty, unbuttoned, rust-colored dressing gown with an oversized pair of men's slippers on her feet. She donned these garments as soon as she rose from bed at eleven o'clock in the morning, neglected to wash her face or comb her hair, lay down on the sofa in the dining room, and went on tormenting herself with the same old thought:

—If she were truly unable to find some means by which to escape from her present life, then everything was lost . . . Whatever might be, remaining here in the Zaydenovskis' home was out of the question for her and couldn't go on much longer.

After the incident respecting her letter to Shmulik, her mother-in-law had totally stopped speaking to her. Once she'd come in with her Gentile maidservant and set her to washing the windows and doors and cleaning the rooms with Mirel's housemaid. Blinking her eyes, she spoke not to Mirel but to the two servants:

—What's going on here? It's now almost four months since the walls were even wiped down.

She instructed them to air all the bedclothes out in the garden, and sent in a floor polisher from town, making quite sure that he moved the beds and the chests of drawers when he shined the bedroom floor. In the third of the rooms, she even lifted her skirt and grimaced, looking down at a very dirty corner of the floor that she'd discovered. She could be heard spitting loudly in disgust, moving over to one side, pulling away one of the chairs, and instructing the floor polisher in Ukrainian:

—*Het' skriz' . . . het' skriz'*—everywhere, everywhere.

While all this was going on, Mirel never stirred from her place on the sofa. Everything around seemed unendurably detestable to her. Overcome by a strange desire to rend the garments at her breast and to keep on ripping them, she pressed both her hands tightly, very tightly over her face in silent anguish:

—What an unendurable debacle . . . To suffer from such intolerable helplessness . . . All she needed was a single plan, but such a plan seemed impossible to find.

In the mother-in-law's house, Shmulik was keenly expected. There they even knew exactly when and on what train he was due to arrive.

Montchik Zaydenovski's aid was quite suddenly enlisted when, preoccupied as always, he'd called in from town for a short while on a matter of business. He was ambushed as he emerged from Uncle Yankev-Yosl's study and was dragged off to a private room:

—Montchik, a great misfortune's befallen Shmulik! Why are we putting off dealing with it, Montchik? . . . Who else do we rely on?

Montchik glanced absently at the women who'd surrounded him and called to mind the number of people who'd been left waiting for him in the corridor outside his office.

Some six or seven individuals had probably been obliged to hang around for him there . . . He still had appointments in two banks . . . And they, his aunt and Miriam Lyubashits, were saying that Shmulik was greatly to be pitied . . . Come to think of it he, Montchik himself, had originally thought that this marriage had been a misalliance from the start . . . Eh? What was his aunt saying? . . . Certainly . . . He was of the same opinion:

—He, Montchik, had a duty to do something about this.

In great haste he returned to his business affairs, but he came back later and, after ringing sharply at the door, rushed into Shmulik's wing of the house.

There he found Mirel in her disheveled dressing gown and men's slippers lying on the sofa, and absentmindedly noticed:

Everything in the immaculately clean rooms was tidy and silent in anticipation of Shmulik's arrival; even the table in the dining room was spread with a festive blue cloth. But none of this was of any concern to Mirel, who was lying listlessly on the sofa; as a result thoughts turned more to the wife than to the husband, and a strange air of desolation emanated from the newly waxed floors and the carefully arranged chairs.

For a long time he sat opposite her at the table pretending to notice nothing and speaking at length about his business affairs, about his mother, his sister, and his younger brother, all of whom he supported and with whom he'd lived from the time his father had died leaving his affairs in chaos:

—His sister—he related—was only two years younger than he, dark as a Gypsy, who virtually from the day of her birth had chattered on and on like an old-fashioned flour mill. For a year after completing her studies at high school she'd stayed quietly at home, grown bored, and spoken ill of women students. Only now, during the past winter, had she started to convince herself that she had a voice and had begun taking singing lessons with a teacher.

Without interest, Mirel stared into his mobile, preoccupied face and waited. With every passing moment it became ever more obvious that he'd been sent here from her mother-in-law's house. The only surprise was that he didn't immediately start asking:

—Yes, well, what exactly did she think of Shmulik? What did she imagine could be the outcome of such a life?

But snatching distracted glances at her every now and then, he went on retailing stories of various kinds, giving the impression at times that he had no other motive in doing so than to lift her despondent spirits for a while:

—He, Montchik, certainly didn't regard himself as musically gifted, but he literally couldn't endure his sister's voice, some kind of rasping shriek produced not in the chest but somewhere in the throat and nose. When he begged her not to sing while he was at home, she felt deeply insulted, wept, and complained about him to his acquaintances: a true brother, she said, ought to support and sympathize with her, but he—not content with lacking any sympathy for her, he also wanted to destroy her life's most treasured ideal.

Every now and then he stopped, looked at her in his preoccupied fashion, and seemed to be thinking of something else. Then he suddenly fell silent entirely, dropped his eyes, and began smoothing the blue tablecloth. The silence grew oppressive, filled with yearning. From the kitchen could be heard the voice of the mother-in-law, inquiring from the maid whether clean slips had been put on the pillows, the sound of her tread as she went into the bedroom with her own servant girl and rummaged about in the closet for a long time, searching for the key to the linen chest, and finally the sound of her bustle as she helped her servant girl pull on the pillowslips, left the room, and returned home without a backward glance at anyone.

Still lost in thought, Montchik ultimately took his leave of Mirel and returned to his uncle Yankev-Yosl in the big house. In the entrance hall he failed to recognize some polite young man who offered him his hand in greeting, but went straight into the private room where he was beleaguered once more; he seemed lost in a dream as he fixed his black eyes on those around him in a radiant, wide-eyed stare:

—What on earth could they possibly have against Mirel? . . . He'd just spent almost an hour with her . . . To tell the truth, he didn't know who was suffering more, Mirel or Shmulik.

When the women stared at him in astonishment wanting to remonstrate with him, he paced distractedly about the room without noticing them, suddenly recalled something and again stopped before them with a raised finger:

—She's highly intelligent—he insisted, wagging this finger—she's shrewd, and she . . . he, Montchik, hadn't known any of this at first.

Mirel noticed him when, dreamily lost in thought, he was walking back to the streetcar stop and passed by near her window. Something suddenly occurred to her, so she rapped on the pane to attract his attention and prepared to start another conversation with him:

—Before anything else, Montchik needed to be quite clear: if he was now in haste to get home, there was no urgent need for them to chat.

Her face and eyes expressed a refusal to hear any excuses, however, and as he looked at her, Montchik, remembering that he did indeed have no time to spare, nevertheless responded courteously:

—What? In haste? God forbid . . . On the contrary.

He held her in great respect, and later accompanied her into town.

And when she suggested they meet again the next day, he again responded courteously and agreed. His head spun with the impression that she was continually thinking not about what she was saying but about something she deliberately wished to conceal; that he had to tell Shmulik, whom he loved, something about her, this most interesting and intelligent woman who was assuredly no mate for him. But after he'd seen her home and gone back to the streetcar stop alone, he forgot all these considerations and distractedly immersed himself in his everyday business concerns. In the closely packed, illuminated streetcar, the very same young man who'd given him his hand in his uncle Yankev-Yosl's entrance hall sat down next to him, and began discussing a business matter with which Montchik was thoroughly familiar, and Montchik stared at him wide-eyed and was angry at himself:

—To be sure, he, Montchik, met hundreds of merchants every single day, but why couldn't he recognize people any longer?

3.6

Late one evening a few days later, Mirel again traveled into town with Montchik and, walking down the central avenue with him, recognized Nosn Heler waiting for them at a deserted intersection in the distance. In his broadly cut autumn cloak he stood there on his own, looking unhappy and staring directly at Mirel.

In order to avoid encountering him, she immediately led the abstracted Montchik across the road to the sidewalk opposite and took him into an overcrowded, noisy café where from nightfall on the clatter of plates had been competing fiercely against the screeching tunes of the strident orchestra. But when she left the place at midnight with Montchik, the young man in the autumn cloak was still standing opposite the café and, as before, was staring directly at her. Recognizing him, she actually trembled and pressed herself close to Montchik as though in fear:

—Could Montchik understand why that man over there was staring so?

For a moment Montchik roused himself from his commercial cogitations but failed to understand her question. He glanced around abstractedly but noticed nothing. Walking at her side, he soon lost himself in thought over the molasses factory in Kuropoliye, which was doing badly and was about to be sold:

—The week before he'd succeeded in bringing together the Kuropoliye shareholders and the buyers . . . If their director weren't such a swine and bribe-taker, something positive might come out of all this the following week.

Suddenly he stopped and pressed two fingers to his frowning forehead:

—Just a moment . . . For the life of him, he couldn't remember whether or not he'd signed the telegram he'd sent to the director earlier that day!

He felt distinctly uneasy and glanced at Mirel with an expression of great pleading, as though he desperately needed her compassion:

—Mirel had to excuse him. He had to slip into the nearby telegraph office for a moment to make an inquiry.

Mirel led him to the telegraph office herself, and there roundly rebuked him for his unwillingness to leave her outside on her own:

—What was Montchik making a performance for? . . . He was to go into the telegraph office that instant. She'd find her way home without him.

All the time she was talking to Montchik, and subsequently when she was left alone on the deserted sidewalk looking around her, she was drawn to Nosn Heler. The man himself was still standing at the intersection following her with his eyes. He wanted nothing; he was simply unhappy—and he followed her with his eyes.

Suddenly she turned in the direction of the suburb in which she lived and swiftly seated herself in a droshky.[*]

She was annoyed at the sentiment that drew her to him, at herself for continuing to drift about in the Zaydenovskis' house, and at the fact that not a single useful thing had come from anything she'd ever done in her life.

---

[*]A droshky is a low four-wheeled, horse-drawn Russian hackney carriage in which passengers sit astride a narrow bench, their feet resting on bars near the ground.

—She needed some means of freeing herself from Shmulik and couldn't find it.

—She'd been wandering about all over town with Montchik for several days now and had been considering asking him about such means, yet this was totally uncalled for and stupid . . . Because Montchik . . . Montchik was Shmulik's near relation and loved him. And apart from that . . .

—What could he possibly tell her about this?

Unaware that she'd crossed the bridge leading to her suburb and had reached the farthermost street on which she lived, she suddenly noticed that all the windows of her house, except those of the bedroom, were brightly lit, boasting to the midnight darkness outdoors:

—We have guests, guests, guests.

Astonished, she peered in through these illuminated windows:

—Perhaps her father or her mother . . . She'd not written them a single letter since her marriage.

But while she was still in the passageway, after the maid had locked the front door behind her, she soon noticed that nothing untoward had occurred and that there were no guests: only Shmulik, after a month of tiring travel from Warsaw, had returned home. By coming back so oddly unannounced and somewhat self-consciously, he showed that he knew: no particular pleasure awaited him here.

His hair and beard had been newly and closely cut, as though the next day were the eve of Passover. The new light-colored suit he wore had been made in Warsaw; his new shoes squeaked. All in all, he looked as pristine, animated, and fresh as though he'd only just come from the bathhouse, as though during the time he'd spent in his distillery and in Warsaw he'd taken pains with himself and curbed many of his boyish mannerisms.

Mirel passed through the dining room without glancing at him, shaming him in the eyes of their oxen buyer, a grizzled, grimy old man who sat at the table with stick in hand and eyes inflamed and damaged, exuding the pungent stench of snuff and goat flesh. Mortified, Shmulik looked down and began chewing on a matchstick. Tears sprang to his eyes.

Mirel was now in the brightly lit salon, where she took off her jacket, not knowing why she hadn't gone directly from the dining room to her unlit bedroom. She tried without success to recall something but remembered only that Shmulik was next door. For some reason she started putting on her jacket again, but immediately removed it and once more passed straight through the dining room to her dark bedroom. There, without taking off her close-fitting silk blouse or tightly laced corset, she immediately lay down on the bed. Hiding her face in both her hands, she began preparing herself for what would soon take place:

—An end . . . Now an end must come . . .

Through the silence that reigned in all the surrounding rooms came the sounds of Shmulik pacing slowly across the dining room, the dirty oxen dealer expressing his pleasure at the few thousand rubles' profit that would now accrue to him as his small commission, and his continued amazement at the extraordinarily buoyant market Shmulik had found:

—The like of such a market, he might venture to say, hadn't been seen since Napoleon's time . . . Could Shmulik believe it? Seven rubles a pood! . . .

His diseased eyes watered under their inflamed lids. Oblivious of the tears running down his cheeks and in places into his grizzled, dirty, yellowing beard, he stuffed tobacco into his nose and raised his smiling face somewhat higher, like a blind man in a daydream. He was visualizing another such profitable market:

—So if Shmulik really wanted to go to Warsaw again straight after Sukkot,* the eighteen heifers from Popivke would have to be left in the Stolin stables . . . Also the seven from Yelizavet that were housed near the door . . . Yes, and the frisky one as well, the one with the big horns . . . Here was a funny thing: three of them had been there for nearly three and a half months but they hadn't put on any weight . . . He'd taken a feel of them there the other week . . . Yes . . . No weight to speak of . . . He disliked oxen like that.

The old man finally left, and Shmulik locked the door behind him.

---

*Sukkot, known in English as the Feast of Tabernacles, is a seven-day festival that follows five days after Yom Kippur and commemorates God's benevolence in providing for all the needs of the People of Israel during their forty years of wandering in the desert.

The silence was now total, as in the dead of night. All that could be heard was Shmulik pacing slowly across the dining room, the squeaking of his new shoes disclosing something about their owner's great heaviness of heart, about the fact that he was now thinking of Mirel lying in bed in her darkened room, that he loved her, wanted to go to her, but couldn't and didn't know how; that he felt unhappy, and that this unhappiness would never ever leave him:

—For example here he was, home after an absence of four weeks . . .

He'd earned a considerable sum of money . . . He was becoming a very wealthy man . . . He'd bought and brought home for Mirel blouses and other gifts, thinking they would please her . . . And his thoughts had taken him even further:

—When he returned home after having been away for six weeks, she'd start speaking to him again . . .

He was still chewing the matchstick, and there were still tears in his eyes:

—Mirel considered him a fool.

He saw her fresh, sweet-smelling face vividly before him. Now she was lying on her bed in the dark adjoining room with her eyes shut. Perhaps she was already asleep in there, or perhaps not. He knew:

Were he to approach her now, he'd have nothing to say. Yet he went in all the same, slowly, step by step, stopping every few moments, never raising his bowed head, always bearing in mind:

—Mirel considered him a fool.

He crossed the threshold of the darkened room and stopped. The glow from the lights in the dining room reached in here; on the bed opposite, her figure took shape, a slender, lissome figure tightly sheathed in its narrow black dress. Slowly, infinitely slowly, with his head bowed, he went up to her: first one step, then stopping, then another step. Now he saw her face: positioned a little downward, high on the pillow, eyelids shut. For a while he stood beside the bed, his own eyes downcast. Knowing that he ought to turn back, he nevertheless moved still closer, noticed her partially outstretched hand drooping over the side of the bed, and quietly took hold of it.

Quietly, very quietly, he stood holding her hand, and just as quietly began to weep.

She did not take her hand from his. He heard her speak. As though half-asleep, she sighed and said, softly and tonelessly:

—Why do you need me, Shmulik?

He sat down on the bed then, and began sobbing. He kissed her hand. Again and again he kissed her hand. She neither opened her eyes nor said anything. He moved closer and embraced her. Still she did not open her eyes and still she said nothing. And for a short while, farther away in the kitchen, the servant girl awoke from a deep sleep. Her bare feet slapping over the floor, she went from room to room extinguishing the lamps.

3.7

The day after Rosh Hashanah, when Shmulik had driven off to the distillery for a few hours, Mirel packed some things into her yellow leather valise and prepared to go home to her father.

She said not a word about this to anyone and stuck doggedly to her predetermined plan:

—Now everything was definitely coming to an end . . . She'd free herself of the Zaydenovskis.

The oppressive atmosphere of the Fast of Gedalye* hung heavy in her mother-in-law's dining room. In his expansive, self-congratulatory manner, the master of the house sat at the head of the table entertaining a female relative of some wealth who was passing through with her scholarly husband. She stayed too long and spoke too loudly with an unmistakably provincial inflection.

The conversation touched on Aunt Pearl in Warsaw who, according to Shmulik, had enjoyed a very good year; on Aunt Esther here in town whose situation in life, might she be spared the Evil Eye, was even

---

*The Fast of Gedalye, a minor fast day observed immediately after the second day of Rosh Hashanah, commemorates the assassination of the Babylonian-appointed official charged with administering that remnant of the Jewish population left in Judah following Nebuchadnezzar's destruction of the First Temple and the start of the Babylonian exile in 586 BCE. Gedalye's death, recounted in 2 Kings 25:25–26, deprived Judah of all trace of Jewish rule.

more comfortable now than it had been while her husband was still alive and who traveled abroad every summer; on the fact that Montchik, who supported her, had been born in the very year in which Uncle Ezriel-Meir had lost his first wife, and that, although he was now twenty-six years old and earned very well, Montchik was in no haste to marry and never spoke of it.

Suddenly a member of the household came in to whisper Mirel's secret plan into the mother-in-law's ear; she in turn whispered it immediately to her husband, staring challengingly into his face and blinking her eyes in a peculiar manner. For the last few days Shmulik had looked very happy. On the afternoon of the second day of Rosh Hashanah he'd been seen standing with Mirel in the sunshine on the steps of the verandah, and as a result the mother-in-law had had even gone so far as to canvass the opinion of Miriam Lyubashits:

—According to Miriam's sense of justice, which of them should now be the first to get back on speaking terms with the other, eh? Surely it behooved Mirele to make the first approach, eh?

With her shawl over her shoulders, the mother-in-law hurried over to Mirel's wing and there began warily to initiate a conversation, first with the servant girl and presently, even more warily, with Mirel herself:

—Are you going away for long, Mirele?

And more:

—Perhaps you'll wait until Shmulik gets back?

With an expression of grave inflexibility on her face, Mirel busied herself with her two pieces of luggage, began rapidly pulling on her overcoat, sent out for a droshky, and answered her mother-in-law's questions brusquely and to the point:

—She didn't know.

—She'd see.

—She couldn't wait.

Her mind was now so firmly set on carrying out her plan that she surprised even herself:

—She could've done this simple thing a month before, even two months before . . . What had she been thinking of all that time?

During the entire eighteen-hour train trip she felt as light and fresh as though all her past and present hopes depended exclusively upon this journey, as though from this moment on she were beginning to live anew, totally anew. She took excessive pleasure in standing for half hours on end at the clean, wide window of the second-class carriage looking out on unfamiliar cottages, on unknown fields and vistas adorned with orchards and coppices that rapidly revealed themselves to the speeding train and were just as rapidly left behind. At the same time, she recalled her own blue eyes, looking out with great sadness from under their long black lashes, and was alive to the fact that she, this tall, slender young woman clad in black, was now free and on her own among these travelers with their unfamiliar faces, all of whom gazed at her with intense curiosity each time she was obliged to pass by close to them, who made way for her with great respect yet dared not engage her in conversation. A blond man sitting opposite her, who'd been uninterruptedly devouring the pages of a book in German with keen interest, at length fixed his eyes on her for quite some time and then politely inquired:

—Hadn't he met her two years before in Italy?

At a large station where for a full half hour the dust-blanketed train stopped to draw breath, she attracted the prolonged attention of a tall, wealthy Christian, a hunter who carried a double-barreled shotgun slung over his shoulder. He hovered near the table at which she was breakfasting and finally sat down directly opposite her to drink his tea.

On the second day of her trip, in the buggy that was transporting her from her final stop, all this still came to mind together with vague, undefined thoughts about a new life and a sense that she'd done well to answer the probing of Shmulik and her mother-in-law with cold imprecision:

—She didn't know; she'd see.

But later that same day, around one o'clock in the afternoon when the unanticipated hired buggy drove up to the outskirts of the shtetl, a blast of bygone despair from the old, familiar melancholy houses struck her, and she was overwhelmed with the everyday desolation of her girlhood, as though she'd never left this place and hadn't returned to it now.

The entire insignificant, poverty-stricken little shtetl with all its old, familiar, impoverished, and scattered houses seemed to have been frozen into a single never-ending, all-pervasive thought:

—There was no way to reverse the misfortune . . . And there was no one on whom to build any hope . . .

And there, a little farther down, already peering out from behind the marketplace was her father's house with its verandah; as always, the house stood there in sorrowful loneliness, still telling everyone who passed its façade:

—She's has been married off now, has Mirel . . . She's over there now, in a suburb of the metropolis, is Mirel . . .

No one came to see her, and no one rejoiced at her arrival. No changes had taken place in the house. Gitele had merely started wearing every day the ritual wig she'd previously kept only for Sabbaths, and her jewelry was still missing. When she first caught sight of Mirel, she rose slowly, very slowly, from her chair at the round table, flushed, and barely smiled:

—Just look—she said with quiet diffidence—it's Mirele . . .

For some reason she still clutched the top of the round table on which she leaned both her hands. Evidently she found very odd both Mirel's sudden and unexpected arrival and the fact that for the entire three and a half months during which Mirel had lived in the suburb of the metropolis, no one had heard a single word from her; Shmulik alone had added a formal greeting in Hebrew on her behalf in each of his letters.

—My dear wife Mirel, long may she live, sends you her regards.

Without thinking, it seemed, Gitele added:

—Mirele's looks hadn't improved at all.

And in a little while she took the compresses from the servant girl and went off to the bedroom to apply them to Reb Gedalye, who'd recently suffered a recurrence of the previous winter's illness.

Fully dressed, he lay there on one of the two old single wooden beds.[*] Without groaning, he held the tin compress close to his belly.

—I'm lying down now—he said to Mirel, smiling in some embarrassment—but earlier today I was walking about.

---

[*]Orthodox Jewish law forbids a married couple from sleeping in the same bed.

His face was yellow and he looked more ill than usual, while his smile no longer suited the sharpness of his nose.

For some reason, a glance at him prompted the thought that he wasn't fated to live much longer, that his voice had changed to resemble that of someone who'd already been summoned to heaven and been shown the severe judgment inscribed against his name in the Book of Life:

—Look here: you will die . . . When?—That's not for you to know.

At sundown, when his pain had abated, he rose from his bed and gave instructions for the buggy to be harnessed so he could ride out to the Kashperivke woods where he needed to be. Having donned his dust coat in readiness to leave, he went up to Mirel and, revolving something in his mind, stood for a little while before her with his head bowed.

Outdoors the harnessed buggy was already waiting for him, and Gitele was no longer in the room.

Quite possibly he was troubled by the thought that while he ought to give his visiting daughter some kind of gift, he no longer had the means to do so.

Suddenly he asked her:

—How was she getting along? He meant how was she getting along with Shmulik? He was surely not a bad husband . . .

But evidently he seemed to feel that this wasn't what he wanted to say to her and, overcome with embarrassment, he again bowed his head and lost himself briefly in thought before finally pulling himself together:

—Well! Let's get on our way.

For some reason, soon after his departure the taciturn Gitele slowly and quietly began speaking:

She related that the Kashperivke wood had turned out to be far from the bargain it was initially thought to be; that as they no longer had any work for him, Reb Gedalye's relative, their bookkeeper, had taken a position with some merchant partners in the provincial capital:

—Yes, well, he'd always been a capable, devoted, and considerate employee. Velvl Burnes specifically invited him to come and work for his father and offered him a salary of a thousand rubles a year . . . Gedalye and I urged him to take it . . . And Avreml the rabbi also told him he was mad not to accept . . . Well, he's a stubborn man and didn't want to.

After this confidence, they drank tea and had nothing more to talk about. Later Mirel stood for some time alone near the front door, gazing out at the shtetl.

As always, everything there was desolate and sunk in penitential dejection. In the late twilight the teacher Poliye, who'd taught there two years before, was on her way to visit the midwife Schatz who lived in the village, as were the pharmacist's assistant Safyan and the crippled student Lipkis . . . The shtetl was dark and cold and a gust of wind drove the dust from the marketplace. Velvl Burnes already knew that she'd arrived and had therefore driven off very early to spend the night on his farm. Only in the big Sadagura prayer house, which peered out through its illuminated windows from a side alley opposite, was there any sign of life: there Jews in penitential depression swayed in the traditional manner as they recited the evening prayers, shouting aloud in great sorrow after the cantor:

—A psalm of David!

Newly awakened from a refreshing afternoon nap, a stocky young man with coarse, unfamiliar features and the appearance of a would-be intellectual, evidently a new teacher at the Talmud Torah, passed close by in the gloom of the chill early evening. His powerful body shivered with cold and he had pleasure in thinking:

—There'd be light and warmth at his destination; a lamp would be burning on the table that held the welcoming glasses of tea, and there would be joking and laughter.

But to Mirel, everything appeared nugatory and stupid. It was stupid to have pinned her hopes on someone all the time she was traveling here. It was stupid that gathered together now in the midwife Schatz's Gentile-owned cottage were the very same people who'd gathered there two years before; stupid that they were presently talking about the very same things they'd talked about last year. All of them—the midwife, Poliye, Safyan, and Lipkis—all were discontented with their lives, but none of them did anything to reconstruct those lives. There were many such people in the world, and all of them were now coming together to pass the evening in illuminated houses in various towns and villages, and afterward all of them returned to their homes where they went on doing those things they'd done the day before, things that had been repugnant to many people before them.

And in the end . . . now in this chill twilight that was enfolding the whole world . . .

—In the end, there had to be others who were trying to do something different.

When she went back indoors, the hanging lamp on its pulley had long been lit in the dining room, and Libke the rabbi's wife had long been sitting there, smiling at the taciturn Gitele and making some worldly wise, married woman's remark about Mirel's condition:

—Is that so, indeed?

Disgusted and oppressed, Mirel went into what had formerly been her own room opposite the dark salon, stopped inside, and contemplated it by the light of the lamp she was carrying. Everything in there was so fusty: the tables uncovered, the air as chilly as though it were winter outdoors but the stove hadn't been heated for a whole month; in the empty closet hung one of the dresses she'd left behind with a short, shabby autumn jacket padded with cotton-wool. The bed wasn't made up, but loosely covered in such a way that the pillows and the featherbed poked out from under the blanket. And for some reason it seemed to her much easier to be eternally a homeless wanderer than ever to lie down in that bed again.

She found it difficult to remain in there. Returning to the dining room, she sat down at the table with her head in both hands, thought for a while, and then suddenly began inquiring about trains to the metropolis:

—Two trains used to go from here . . . She didn't know which one would be more sensible for her to take in order to return home the next day—the one in the morning or the one in the evening?

With a smile, Gitele posed an astonished question. The rabbi's wife added a remark. Mirel heard nothing; she was still staring straight ahead of her.

—So she'd be going back to the suburb of the metropolis the next day . . .

This journey of hers had been a total failure. She found it impossible to spend more time than was absolutely necessary here in this house. She had now to find some way to save her life entirely on her own. And if she were now returning to the suburb, it wouldn't be for long, in any event . . . she was only going back for a short while.

3.8

Two days later she returned to the suburb, late at night when everyone was already asleep. She looked unwell, as though she were recovering from an illness, spoke to no one, lay fully clothed on her bed, and did not leave the house for several days. Some books in Shmulik's study which she'd carried into her bedroom one by one were scattered around the bed on which she lay. Now she had nothing against Shmulik: he could make her neither better nor worse. She was simply firm in her determination to leave him as soon as possible. She could not endure his occasional lingering about in her room, however, never looked at him, and never replied if he spoke to her.

Shmulik knew that the doctors had despaired of her father's life; Avreml the rabbi had communicated this information to him in a letter. In her own house, his mother was dumbfounded and wholly unable to comprehend:

—How can this be? When a father is dangerously ill, how can a daughter not bring herself to spend at least a few days with him?

When he tried to speak to Mirel about this for the third time, she grew agitated and interrupted him:

—She didn't know . . . she didn't know . . .

Tears rose to Shmulik's eyes then, and he drifted over to the window in the dining room where he stood for some time, staring out with these tear-filled eyes at the overcast scene outdoors. He was deeply upset, and his mind was a blank. In this distracted state he went across to his father in the big house where something in his troubled expression excited comment, so his mother discreetly drew him aside:

—What's the matter, Shmulik? Is there something new wrong again?

But downhearted as he was, he assumed the expression of a grave and serious-minded adult and even frowned in displeasure:

—No, who says that? . . . No . . . Nothing . . .

He went directly to his father's study where three employees from different stables were discussing the possibilities of taking another drove of oxen to Warsaw. When his father sought his opinion, he had no idea what was being asked of him, and responded:

—Eh?

In the dining room of the mother-in-law's house one afternoon during the intermediate days of Sukkot* the family had gathered to drink tea round the long table, covered with its white cloth. Because of the festival, almost all their relatives from the city were present, all cheerful and deliberately blocking out every thought of Mirel. It occurred only to his mother that all was not well with Shmulik, but she was so dull-witted that she soon forgot about this and began foolishly blinking her eyes.

Also seated at the table was the former student Miriam Lyubashits, cradling in her arms a six-month-old baby, a blonde little girl with uncovered head, eyes like bits of blue glass, and a damp, pouting upper lip. Only fifteen minutes before, almost the entire household had been fussing round this infant. Every member in turn had snatched her up to dance round with her and lift her high up into the air, and the frightened child had stared at all this with her eyes like bits of blue glass, frequently whimpering. The mother-in-law had then taken the baby in her arms and, blinking her eyes, had started talking to her, whereupon the child had wrinkled up her little snub nose, poked out her little tongue, and begun smiling merrily. Everyone had been utterly charmed, and Miriam Lyubashits had announced:

—Do you all see? . . . She loves her auntie already.

Now silence had descended on the dining room. All the relatives had moved into the salon and the child lay in Miriam's arms. Dribbling, the little one raked her weak little fists over her mother's face, emitting a piercing yell that carried across the hushed room, as though her mother's face were a windowpane and the child were stubbornly determined to smash it. Turning her face to one side as though afraid of a

---

*During the intermediate weekdays of the Festival of Sukkot the usual restrictions that apply to Jewish holy days are relaxed but not entirely lifted.

blow from these little fists, the mother tried her best to answer her aunt's question:

—What's there to think about? Mirel certainly can't be regarded as a normal person.

Almost all the chairs around the table were unoccupied and the children were playing noisily in an adjoining room. The mother-in-law peered round to check that no one could overhear what she said, asked someone to shut the door that led into the passage, and moved closer to Miriam:

—Who can speak of "normal" now?

And the former student listened in silence to the mother-in-law's complaints and shared her opinion that there was no question of any normality here:

—Because, after all, take her, Miriam Lyubashits herself, for example. Dear Lord . . . here she was—she also lived with a husband!

Miriam rose, gave the baby to the elderly Gentile wet nurse, and set off home. All the way to the streetcar stop, the mother-in-law, who was accompanying her, expatiated on her complaints:

—And another thing: what does she want of Shmulik? Does she want a divorce? If she wants a divorce, let her say so . . .

Outdoors was cloudy and drizzling. Alone, Mirel stood in the window with a shawl over her head watching the two of them with sadness in her eyes.

Suddenly they stopped and saw:

Descending from the streetcar that had just arrived from the city was Montchik Zaydenovski. Preoccupied, carrying two large bundles of books under his arms, he passed by without noticing them. One book fell from under his left arm, and an unknown woman walking behind him shouted out loudly after him:

—Listen! . . . Excuse me! . . . You've dropped something!

But without turning round he strode rapidly on, straight to Mirel's wing of the house.

On her way back, the mother-in-law called in at the same wing and saw:

The house was quiet and drowsy and Big Montchik was no longer there. In his white shirtsleeves Shmulik was sleeping on the sofa in his study, and in the bedroom, with many books both old and new scattered all around her, Mirel was lying on the bed which hadn't been made since very early that morning.

From then on, the mother-in-law viewed Montchik with great disfavor and began harboring suspicions against him.

She found herself unable to look him straight in the face.

She had no idea how to share her suspicions with her family but if he had, broadly speaking, gone over to Mirel's side and had no desire to tell anyone what he discussed with her, she felt justified in accosting him as he came in on one occasion and asking him sarcastically:

—Perhaps he could explain to her what Mirel wanted from Shmulik? Word had it that he, Montchik, knew all Mirel's secrets.

Montchik stared at her with his huge round eyes and made no answer. He spent a short while in his uncle's study where he had money matters to discuss, left immediately to return home, stopped before the front door of Shmulik's wing without going in, and then made his way rapidly to the streetcar stop, thinking that he needed to discipline himself:

—What kind of conduct was this? People might justifiably think that he wanted to rob Shmulik of his wife.

He stopped coming down to the suburb.

3.9

Meanwhile, at sunset one ordinary weekday evening Shmulik returned from the stables at Libedin where, over two days, he'd made an inventory of the new oxen, and found Mirel's door locked from within.

For a while he stood there, knocking on the door, paused a little and then knocked again. No one inside responded. He began pacing across the dining room and the study, stopping every now and then to stare through the window at the overcast scene outdoors. He remembered that Mirel hadn't spoken to him for the past two weeks; that his underwear was now very dirty and that several days before he'd needed to get to the closet in Mirel's room; that the relationship between him and Mirel was worsening all the time; and that he was powerless and could find no solution for all these problems.

That night, walking round his house, he came to that part of the garden on which the windows of Mirel's room looked out. The place was sodden. An autumn shower, driven by a gust of wind, streamed down diagonally while the cherry trees shuddered, were soaked, and protested faintly against something. A row of old poplar trees standing at one end of the orchard all bowed their crowns in the same direction, gesturing despondently to the heavily overcast corner of the sky from which the wind was driving the clouds:

—From over there . . . That's where the misfortune's coming from.

The shutters of Mirel's room were fastened from within, but the glow of a burning lamp striking through their cracks indicated that she was still awake.

Shmulik returned to his study and lay down on the sofa, unable to sleep, not knowing what to do, scratching on the oilcloth next to him:

—His life was hopeless, it seemed . . . hopeless.

Eventually he dozed off in his clothes, waking with a start once, about one o'clock in the morning, when Mirel's room seemed flooded with light, and a second time very early, when the servant girl was still washing the floors and the first light of a new rainy, overcast day had started to peer through the windows.

Now Mirel's room was dark. She was sleeping.

He went outside, roused his coachman, bade him harness his britzka, and went off to the distillery.

Once arrived, however, he felt that he needed to be not here but there, in his own home. He could busy himself with nothing. His office was located among the ceaselessly boiling copper vats in the largest set of buildings where the heat was intense and the air pungent with the stench of malt, distilled alcohol, and scorched barley. Around two o'clock in the afternoon, the sun struck though the cloudy skies to reveal the frightful ugliness of everything in the distillery courtyard on which its sickly silvery light fell. Many wagons loaded with iron barrels, drawn up near the open cellar next to the stream that flowed past the distillery, were receiving bellowed instructions in Russian from the perpetually drunk, perpetually bad-tempered cellar-master:

—*Stoi!* Stop!

—*Podavay!* Give it here!

—Kuda poliez? Where the devil are you going?

From somewhere in the rear, from the valley behind the largest set of buildings, wafted the foul-smelling vapor of the fresh beer must that was being offloaded in the oxen stable, and the vats were being heated for the night shift.

Then Shmulik again ordered the britzka harnessed and drove back home.

Though it was not raining, the weather had turned cloudy and cold again. The sky was as gloomy as dusk, and the sodden fields all around reeked of damp, ploughed earth, of fresh horse manure, and of rotting pumpkins from a partially cultivated bed nearby. Both his big bay horses trotted along with confident energy, merrily bowing their heads and responding instantly to every sweep of the coachman's whip with either a contented forward bound or a healthy equine sneeze. The well-sprung britzka swayed as it effortlessly followed after them, and Shmulik sat deep within it, reflecting all the while that it was he, Shmulik Zaydenovski, who was traveling along in this way, he who already possessed his own capital of more than thirty thousand rubles, was no longer dependent on anyone, not on a single soul, not even on his own father, and was now hurrying home. There he had a wife who'd been lying locked up in her own room for nearly two weeks. Now he needed to go in and ask her:

—Mirel—he ought to ask her—do you perhaps find my presence oppressive? I can rent two or three rooms for you in the center of the city where you can live apart from me. Do you understand, Mirel? I demand nothing of you.

Thinking of these things, he took so much pity on himself that tears sprang to his eyes, yet it seemed to him that what he was about to say to her was beautiful and that he would please Mirel with it.

He wanted to get home all the more quickly.

As soon as he drove into his father's courtyard, however, he suddenly felt as bad as he had the previous restless night, and was starkly conscious of the burdensome, lonely hours that lay before him this day, the next day, and all the days thereafter . . . Outdoors it was already dark as the evening drew on. Inside his father's big house, almost all the windows that overlooked the courtyard were illuminated, whereas those of his own house were all dark. Light was visible only in the two windows of Mirel's room at the very end of the wing, but the shutters were bolted from within.

She was evidently still locked up in there.

Climbing down from the britzka, he remembered the dirty underclothing he was wearing and started making his way straight toward his home.

He was suddenly stopped, though, by his father's maid, who'd hurried over to him from the big house:

—He was being summoned—she shouted after him—he was being summoned to his father's study. They were insisting that he come in immediately.

—Immediately?

He couldn't understand what had suddenly possessed them over there, and went over, only to find his father's study hot and thick with cigarette smoke. Everything suggested that an earnest discussion about him and Mirel had been going on in there for hours.

At the desk opposite his father sat his mother, Miriam Lyubashits, and the younger Lyubashits, the student Shoylik, all of whom had the flushed faces of people who'd been airing their views and conferring together for a long time. As soon as Shmulik entered, the younger Lyubashits left the room. He was embarrassed, apparently, and went over to speak to Rikl in the dining room. Not looking at Shmulik as he came in, his father seemed afraid to meet his eyes, lowered his head, and lit a fresh cigarette. Miriam moved something along the desk top with a finger. Only his mother half-turned toward him, blinked her eyes a few times, and beckoned him closer to the table:

—Come over here, Shmulik . . .

One of Shmulik's temples started throbbing and he grimaced slightly, so unpleasant and difficult did he find the conversation that his mother initiated:

In bewilderment he heard her mention his name and Mirel's name. She was saying something about how she, his mother, had gone into Mirel's room and had started speaking to her, and how Mirel had immediately interrupted her and answered like a person who was certainly no longer in her right mind:

—I don't wish to speak—she'd said to her—I wish to remain silent.

And soon he heard the word "divorce" frequently repeated on his mother's lips.

Greatly troubled by the fact that his mother kept on repeating the word "divorce" so often, he even grew angry and mimicked her briefly:

—That's a fine thing: divorce, divorce . . . a very fine thing.

Recalling Mirel, who was now lying on her bed in her room, he muttered this angrily. He wanted to get home as quickly as possible and knock on her door. But his father suddenly raised his head and began saying the same things as his mother:

—What else but a divorce? Have you another alternative?

And Miriam Lyubashits rose from her place and supported his father:

—One can't live like that forever.

Also rising from her place, his mother added:

—There's never been anything like this since the world began. It's unheard of.

After a silence of some minutes, all three of them left him alone in the study. They had nothing more to say to him.

His mother went over to the younger Lyubashits, the student, in the dining room and whispered to him:

—Go into the study and tell him . . . He respects you, after all.

So the younger Lyubashits went into the study, spent a while scratching at the blue cloth over the desk, and finally said:

—The fact is, Mirel dislikes you . . . She disliked you even before the wedding. You see yourself that she doesn't want to live with you. How can you force her?

Shmulik stood with his back toward him and heard:

—The fact was, Mirel disliked him . . .

He had no idea where these words originated: whether they came directly from Mirel's own mouth, or were simply Lyubashits's conjecture. Nevertheless, if all of them, all the members of his family, understood this, and if Shoylik said that she disliked him, then this was certainly no fanciful notion . . . Shoylik wouldn't say something like that without good reason. And if Mirel truly did dislike him, he certainly couldn't force her to live with him.

Barely aware of what he was doing, he left Shoylik in the study and, hunched over, went into the dark nursery nearby. The window had been covered from inside with some kind of black cloth. All around, the youngest children were already fast asleep in their little beds against the walls, breathing steadily. He leaned his hunched back against the cloth-covered window and lost himself in thought:

—Then of course he'd divorce Mirel. And afterward she'd live somewhere with her father in the shtetl . . . And he, Shmulik . . . he'd be back here . . . all alone, he'd be here.

He'd certainly never marry again . . . Who could think of getting married now? . . . And now his life was truly hopeless . . . for good and all . . .

And, quite unexpectedly, here in this room, his heart contracted tightly with infinite pity for himself, and over there, in the dining room, all fell silent and heard him weeping aloud.

—Who's that?—his mother demanded in fright, listening intently and with a sinking heart to the sounds from the nursery.

Quiet prevailed, and someone's heart could be heard pounding. Suddenly someone else said loudly:

—It doesn't matter. Let him have a good cry.

Everyone looked round, astounded to discover that this remark had come from Shmulik's sister, Rikl.

She knew about everything that had taken place between Mirel and Nosn Heler. A male student of her acquaintance had told her.

Out of a great sense of propriety she'd kept this to herself the whole time, but now . . . now she felt able to relate that one evening she'd been walking along Nosn Heler's street in company with this student acquaintance of hers and had seen Mirel arriving from the suburb on her own, turning in the appropriate direction, and entering Nosn Heler's lodgings.

3.10

Shmulik locked himself up in a room alone and refused to come out.

Miriam Lyubashits pottered about in the dining room. For the past few days she'd stayed over with her child, continually wearing the grave expression of an experienced midwife whose expectant mother was going into labor in the adjoining room. About Shmulik she'd remarked:

—If he's truly made up his mind to divorce, why should we let him go back to Mirel?

And her comment carried so much weight that they did as she said and no longer allowed Shmulik to return home.

The whole of this huge house came to seem as agitated and preoccupied as though someone inside were desperately ill. The salon was disarranged, dirty, and filled with cigarette smoke since for nights on end people conferred there and ate at odd hours. From two o'clock in the afternoon until nightfall the table was laid in the dining room, and the youngest children went round with their stomachs as hollow as on fast days. The night was well advanced before anyone hastily sat these little ones down at the table and gave them something to eat, while the adults stayed closeted in the salon, in secretive whispered discussion with the family's good friend, the urbane Jew whom they'd once sent to call on Reb Gedalye Hurvits and bidden him say:

—They ask no money of you, the Zaydenovskis, not even a promise of money . . .

One night they'd summoned this family friend by telegram, and now they all sat round him, investing him with full authority:

—If Mirel wouldn't agree to a divorce, he was to tell her explicitly that provision could be made for her. They could pay her up to six thousand rubles for a divorce.

Shmulik was completely bewildered and took no part in this discussion. The whole of his past life seemed shrouded in a fog, like a dream, and he drifted ceaselessly about the salon hearing nothing that was said and thinking of his future life without Mirel: how every Sabbath he'd attend services in the synagogue where they wished to elect him to a trusteeship, how someone would point him out at the eastern wall:

—Sadly, that young man's a divorcé; his first wife didn't want him.

When at length everyone had risen from their seats and Shmulik was no longer present, Miriam Lyubashits went up very close to the urbane family friend and rapped him on the forehead with a knuckle:

—What poor understanding you have, Uncle!—she remarked, alluding to Mirel and Shmulik.—We've only got you to thank for making this match.

The urbane family friend felt so uncomfortable that he hunched his shoulders, pondered a moment, and began expostulating with his hands:

—How could this be? How could one know? She seemed a good child, Mirel . . . A very good child.

And when everyone had left the salon and only he remained behind, he wandered about alone and deep in thought, muttering to himself several times:

—How could this be? How could one know?

Around noon, the courteous family friend knocked on Mirel's door.

He felt very uncomfortable. In the dining room the barefooted servant girl had followed him all over and given him no peace:

—Listen, Uncle, take my advice and give up wanting to knock on her door—you'll get it in the neck if you do!

Entering Mirel's room, he stopped and made a dignified bow, took a few more steps forward, stopped and bowed again. Since he was dressed in a black frock coat, he had nowhere to put his hands, and his good-natured face wore a sheepish smile:

—I've come—he said, forcing a laugh at himself—I've come to talk matters over with you.

In her dressing gown and slippers Mirel lay on the bed. Annoyed that this little man had obliged her to open the door for him, she was unwilling to look at him. During the two weeks that she'd locked herself up in her room her face had grown haggard, and for the entire period, to spite both herself and someone else, she'd stopped speaking completely.

She strongly resented the fact that she was still being pestered and that emissaries were now being sent to her, so she raised herself a little and said to him:

—Please be so kind as to inform my mother-in-law that as soon as I have anything new to communicate, I'll lose no time in letting her know.

She thought the little man would leave at once, but instead he again began smiling sheepishly:

—Please understand, the heart of the matter is as follows . . .

Having broken into a sweat, he produced a handkerchief from somewhere, sat down on a nearby chair, and began wiping his brow back and forth:

—Yes, the whole affair is, as I'm sure you'll understand, not pleasant for me, not pleasant at all . . . But please understand: the family regards me as a good friend and holds me somewhat responsible . . . Well . . . So I must.

—That means . . . that's to say . . . . yes: among us Jews the usual way is, I say, that if a couple lives, God forbid, unhappily together, and they have no children . . . And here, for example, is my own daughter . . . yes, indeed . . . only a year ago she was divorced . . .

Now Mirel sat upright in bed. Her heart began pounding.

—Divorce?—she abruptly interrupted him—Fine, fine. Tell them, if you please, that's fine.

The little man was bewildered. He rose from his chair without fully believing what he'd heard:

—I'll go—he said distractedly—I'll go and tell them.

But he stopped in the doorway, considered for a moment, then turned back to her:

—They will provide for you, your mother-in-law and Shmulik . . . So indeed they'd instructed him to say . . .

But Mirel interrupted him again:

—Fine, fine . . .

After the little man had gone, she threw herself back on the bed. It seemed to her that nothing had happened, so she went back to the book she'd been reading before he'd come in.

This was a thick, well-bound volume dealing with women from the Middle Ages to more modern times but she found herself unable to read it all from beginning to end because it got on her nerves. As had become habitual with her, she dipped in here and there, skipping some bits and snatching at others, while part of her mind turned over what was taking place in her mother-in-law's house at that moment. Muddled up among the medieval castles and romantic heroines of love poems that filled her book were Miriam Lyubashits and her baby, her mother-in-law, Shmulik with his devastated expression, and the little man from out of town who'd only just been in her room and who'd left with the words:

—Does that mean divorce? . . . Yes, yes. He was going . . . He was on his way to tell them.

In the end she was obliged to put the book aside, lose herself in thought, and feel once more the powerful pounding of her heart as she sat upright in bed:

—Wait . . . She'd now go back to the life she'd led as a girl, before she was married . . .

A feeling of health and strength surged up in her. In company with the joyful pounding of her heart, this feeling grew stronger.

She uttered a little shriek, feeling the return of the Mirel she'd been two years before: all in all, she uttered only one little shriek, but with immense joy. She suddenly remembered the snow-covered fields on the outskirts of their shtetl, the snowballs she'd thrown a year before at the crippled student Lipkis, and she was suddenly overcome with the desire to wash in a great deal of fresh, ice-cold water.

Seeing the little man, the family's good friend, passing by in the courtyard, she instantly opened the window wide and called him over:

—She'd neglected to ask him one thing more. Would he be so good as to convey the following: would they please arrange the divorce as soon as possible, and without any unnecessary formalities?

Through the open window, the overcast skies and the mournful, sodden cherry trees peered in.

A long, late autumn downpour was in progress.

The servant girl seized the moment at which Mirel left her room to make up the untidy bed and replace the books and clothes that had been strewn about all this time. Now cold air and the damp autumn ripeness outdoors filled the room in which Mirel paced up and down in the tightly laced shoes and close-fitting black dress she'd made no effort to put on for fully two weeks past. A new calmness made itself felt in every one of her slow steps, in the youthful power that the tight-waisted jacket imparted to her swelling breast, and in the thoughts of her own newfound freedom that steadily came to dominate her mind:

—Something ought to be written down . . . Perhaps someone ought to be informed in writing about the divorce.

Looking for notepaper on the desk, she noticed the book Herz had sent her, the pages of which hadn't yet even been cut:

—Were she now, for instance, to send Herz a telegram, he'd come.

She didn't touch the book and moved away from the desk. That passing thought had been irrelevant and foolish . . . She, Mirel Hurvits, wasn't so petty as to be unable to keep more important thoughts in mind.

Subsequently unable to leave the house all day because of the endless downpour, she read the book about women through the ages until two o'clock in the morning. After she'd fallen asleep, she dreamed that the Middle Ages were a kind of twilight kingdom in which people all stood outdoors shouting something in unison at the moon, and where no one knew what anyone else wanted. She found herself walking alone across an open field somewhere, toward a church where a great many yelling people had congregated, demanding to know:

—Is a woman a human being or not?

But in the middle of the night she suddenly started awake and remembered that she was very shortly to be divorced from Shmulik. Once more her heart leapt in joy and in longing for the freedom of the future. Drifting off to sleep again, in her dreams she saw all around her a frighteningly dark night through which a bolt of lightning suddenly flashed; in that split second of white light, she recognized on the horizon the important new life she sought.

When she awoke again it was around ten o'clock in the morning, and everything that had happened the day before came back to her in a rush:

—Quite possibly the divorce could be arranged very quickly, perhaps even that very week.

For a while she lay in bed thinking of this.

She remembered her last dream which now seemed perfectly credible to her:

—Only one small thing was left, it seemed . . . All in all, there was only one small thing she still needed to grasp with both reason and emotion, and the central, overriding essence of her life, that which she'd been seeking for so long, from the time she'd been a child, would be clear to her.

3.11

That afternoon, the rain stopped pouring from the dirty brown clouds of the day before. The puce sallowness of twilight hung in the air, spreading silence around the wet, cheerfully sluiced-down houses and over the puddles that had formed on the sandy outskirts of the suburb.

Appearing out of nowhere, barefoot Gentile boys herded their white geese while at the top of his voice a young man, one of the householders of the suburb, was discussing the newly arrived little wagonload of furniture which had only just been delivered to his door:

—That little sideboard's a first-class piece of work; it's made of oak, that little sideboard is.

Mirel dressed and went off to town on foot across the chain bridge.

There she stopped in at the main post office and wrote a few words to Herz. She had a strong desire to tell someone—anyone—about her new situation, but to write to her parents at home was premature and futile.

Returning from the post office along the central avenue, she noticed Montchik coming out of a building in the distance:

—There's Montchik.

She slowed her pace and a faint smile flitted across her face.

All Montchik had left to do was to call in at one particular bank that stayed open until half past four. But this was hardly important! If he'd now had the good fortune to bump into Mirel, the bank and all his business affairs could go to the devil. He'd not seen Mirel for so long now, and it would give him great pleasure to stroll up and down the avenue with her. Mirel wasn't aware of what had taken place: he was no longer able to call on those in the suburb, not on his uncle and not on Shmulik . . . They'd simply become unendurable, those Zaydenovskis . . . No, wait . . . It was truly a great pleasure to have met her here . . . Only that morning, someone had approached him at the stock exchange to contribute to the Jewish National Fund.* Understandably, he, Montchik, hadn't wanted to do so . . . How could he contribute when he was unconditionally opposed to Zionism? But now he'd seek out the person who'd approached him and make a contribution, on his word of honor.

—He'd give him a full twenty-five rubles.

The normally preoccupied Montchik was greatly excited and very happy. His great black eyes gleamed and twinkled in sheer high spirits, and several times in his delight he so far forgot himself as to attempt to take her arm and squeeze her hand.

Looking at her with joyful, smiling eyes, he finally stood still:

—Could Mirel imagine how much pleasure he derived from having met her now?

For a little while he stood looking at her in this way. Then he doubled over on the spot and burst into loud laughter:

—Couldn't Mirel see how delighted he was?

Mirel walked slowly along with him, a faint smile flitting across her face. She knew that there, in the Zaydenovskis' home, they remained convinced to this day:

—Montchik was in love with her and wanted to alienate her from Shmulik.

But he, Montchik himself . . .

Though he might never express his feeling aloud, he was perhaps more devoted than all those of her former admirers who'd paid court to her, and was possibly her very best, true friend.

—You're a good boy, Montchik.

Suddenly she slowed her pace even more and said:

—Montchik, do you know that I'm divorcing Shmulik?

This didn't fully register with him. He stopped, assumed a grave expression, and fixed his huge eyes on her. A little earlier he'd wanted to ask her how she'd been during the time he'd not seen her, but some foolishness had entered his head and his mind wandered.

---

*The Jewish National Fund (JNF) was founded at the Fifth Zionist Congress in Basel in 1901 to buy and develop land for Jewish settlement in what was then Ottoman Palestine.

At first he assumed she was joking, but then he seemed to freeze, and his huge eyes were no longer fixed on Mirel but on some distant point ahead of him.

—No, wait . . . That's very strange . . . It's . . . God knows what it is.

Mirel was obliged to touch his hand and remind him that he'd been standing long enough in the middle of the sidewalk. He shrugged his shoulders, scratched the nape of his neck, chewed on his lower lip and again lost himself in thought:

—He was damned if he could even begin to imagine how all this had suddenly come about! Was Mirel really serious about this?

He walked alongside her, reflecting on the divorce and on the new situation in which Mirel was now beginning to find herself. Sadness had now overcome them both, and both recalled the words that Mirel had only just uttered:

—Can you imagine, Montchik? I still have absolutely no idea what'll become of me.

She didn't even know where she'd go when she left the house after the divorce. Quite possibly for the first week she wouldn't even have the wherewithal to see her through a day. But now she wasn't at all afraid. The world seemed so extensive to her now. The day before, after the divorce-broker had left, she'd given a shriek of joy only because she'd reminded herself that she could wash in an enormous amount of cold water.

—She'd find somewhere to go when she left the Zaydenovskis' house . . .

Her home in the shtetl . . . That home meant nothing to her now, and was merely a source of frustration. She had no attachment to her mother, and her father . . . it would be easier if she and her father lived apart from each other. They certainly couldn't help each other, in any case.

She was thinking a great deal about herself; she'd always been used to thinking a great deal about herself.

Not long ago she'd re-read one of Turgenev's books: a Russian girl could no longer cope with life around her, so she retreated to a convent and came to nothing.* But she, Mirel—she was no longer a girl, while

---

*The novella to which Mirel is referring is *A House of Gentlefolk* (*Dvorianskoe gnezdo*), by Ivan Turgenev (1818–1883), first published in 1859. Liza, the heroine of this

the concept of a convent was totally alien to her and seemed so silly. From childhood on she'd never been taught how to be religious. Since she could no longer cope with the state of affairs in which she found herself, she'd have to seek farther afield:

—She couldn't say whether or not she'd find anything, but go she would.

Having reached the start of the chain bridge, they stopped. Because of the Zaydenovskis, Montchik could go no farther into the suburb. A sad little fire burned in Mirel's dreamy eyes; deep, deep within the dream it burned, gazing out dreamily to some distant place diagonally across the broad, flowing river. Above the blue shadows under her eyes, her long black lashes seemed even longer and blacker than usual, investing with particular grace her alluring, perfectly straight mouth, which she now kept sternly shut. Suddenly that little fire flashed like lightning in her eyes:

—I have an acquaintance, a Hebrew poet, Montchik. For the most part he smiled a great deal, this acquaintance of hers, and generally held his peace, but once he'd said of her:

—Nothing would ever come of Mirel, he'd said. She was nothing more than a transitional point in human development, and nothing would come of her.

A smile of self-mockery kindled in her eyes, and she turned to glance at Montchik with it:

—I myself—this acquaintance of mine has said—am nothing, and will never get anywhere. The centrally overriding consideration, he says, are those who will come after me.

She wanted to part from him and cross the bridge alone, but Montchik, who was lost in thought, started as though awakening from sleep:

—Out of the question! He might be unable to call on the Zaydenovskis, but he could certainly accompany her to the other side of the bridge.

Afterward he was so confused that he couldn't remember when he'd

---

novella, retreats to a convent to escape the pressures of a world she cannot cope with.

recrossed the bridge and boarded a streetcar. When he paid the conductor his fare, a wallet stuffed with papers fell from his pocket. An old general sitting opposite him noticed his state of distraction, picked up the wallet and returned it to him, but he stared straight at the general with unseeing eyes and didn't even thank him. Such idiotic thoughts crept into his mind:

—No, this was certainly something that couldn't be, this possibility now so seemingly feasible, that he, Montchik, might ostensibly be able to marry Mirel. It was so absurd. And he had no idea how such a hopeless prospect could ever have occurred to him. Firstly, he could never imagine such happiness for himself . . . Mirel was something of an intellectual, after all . . . And secondly . . . What? Who? When? Did Mirel need him? Mirel needed something else . . . Wait . . . Perhaps that acquaintance of hers was right in saying that she was "a transitional point" . . . "a transitional point." But wait . . . Recently he, Montchik, had made so much money, and she, Mirel . . . . She'd soon be needy . . . How could it be otherwise?

—After all, it would simply be a pleasure if Mirel would consent to take as much as she needed from him . . . First of all, she needed to go abroad on her own . . . to Italy, for example. Winter was coming on . . . She'd definitely have to rest after the summer she'd just lived through. But wait: how could one tell her this? How could one possibly propose this to her?

By the time he'd shaken off all this confusion, the streetcar had carried him to another side of the city and farther than he needed to go. He finally got off and started walking back home. But soon he was overcome by confusion once more. Some elegantly dressed young man, a merchant, delighted to have met him here in the street, dismissed those of his companions in whose company he was on his way to pass the evening and began discussing business with him:

One contract here, another contract there.

Montchik stood opposite him, biting his thumb and looking down at the pavement in a daze. The elegant young man was under the impression that Montchik couldn't hear him over the incessant rattle of passing streetcars and droshkies, so he led him to the top end of a quiet street nearby and there began repeating everything from the beginning again. But Montchik stared at his interlocutor with glazed, staring eyes, finally took him by the arm, and made his position clear to him:

—Man alive! You can go on talking to me as much as you want, but I can't hear a single word you're saying . . . What can't you understand here? I'm dealing with a difficult personal matter at the moment and I'm simply not capable . . .

3.12

The Zaydenovskis postponed the divorce until the following Wednesday week and decided to relocate it to a town downriver[*] where they weren't well known.

This notion originated with Miriam Lyubashits, who once unexpectedly remarked:

—I don't understand why a huge fuss has to be made about this divorce here in the city.

Her aunt seized on her objection and took it off to her husband in his study:

—I beg you: Miriam's quite right, after all . . .

Of late, nothing generally got done in the house without Miriam's advice and approval. Her aid was even enlisted when Shmulik locked himself up in his room for a whole day and refused to allow any food to be brought in to him. Toward nightfall, someone remarked:

—Where's Miriam, for heaven's sake? Why shouldn't she go into Shmulik's room and see to it that he eats?

And Miriam went in to him, and he ate.

The younger Lyubashits, who wasn't directly involved in any of this, observed it all with great amusement. He held his sides as his substantial frame doubled up with laughter:

—Oh, Miriam, what's become of you?

---

[*]Every Jewish bill of divorcement must specify the name of the nearest river. Although Kiev, the provincial capital in which the Zaydenovskis live, is situated on the Dnieper River, in order to avoid publicity they decide to move Mirel's divorce proceedings out of town. The nearest downriver alternative with a strong Jewish presence is Cherkassy, some 120 miles south of Kiev.

Before her marriage, he recalled, she'd been a person of significance, and in political circles her name had continually cropped up in connection with even the most trivial activity. But now she'd been reduced to nothing more than a commonplace wet nurse. How could she possibly pretend otherwise? What great difference did it make whether she nursed her own child or someone else's?

Miriam was livid and glowered at him as if he'd gone mad.

—Can anyone understand this Shoylik?

Her baby started crying, so she took the child from Rikl who was holding her, glaring at the younger Lyubashits, her face flushed in fury. She was on the verge of saying something coarse to him, but her aunt heard the child's crying and suddenly came up:

—Listen, Miriam, have you done anything to soothe the little one's stomach?

Miriam immediately put Shoylik's idiocy out of her mind and began complaining to her aunt:

—She didn't know what to do and was at her wits' end. The child had been in distress all night and the warm compresses hadn't helped at all.

Little by little, its former tranquility returned to the house.

In the silence that prevailed in the hushed, tidied rooms, the adults once again started taking naps during the day, and the noisy children were now confined to their own distant nursery. Shmulik alone still failed to sleep through the night, suffered from migraines, and strongly resented his mother for continually coming in to take his temperature:

—Why was he continually being bothered with the thermometer? Why wasn't he left alone? He had no temperature.

That he looked worse from day to day, spoke to no one, and locked himself up in his room where he paced up and down for hours on end in his stocking feet, had all become familiar to the members of the household. But one night something wholly unexpected befell him and shocked them all just after they'd extinguished their lamps and retired to bed. From one room to another the sound of frantic shrieking ripped through the silent darkness:

—What's happened?

—Who's unwell?

—Get a lamp lit immediately!

Around the lamp that had been lit in Shmulik's room, there was a rushed jostling of women's bare shoulders, men's uncovered arms, and glaringly white drawers. Someone raised Shmulik's head, someone else sprinkled water on his face. He'd already slowly opened his eyes, staring bemusedly at the people who surrounded him and were informing one another:

—It's nothing, nothing . . . Shmulik suddenly felt unwell; he imagined he was going blind.

He soon dozed off, started awake, then dozed off again. The doors of his room were opened wide and the lamp was left burning, a chair was placed next to his bed with a peeled orange on it, and all returned to their night's rest. But some while later, Shmulik awoke once more and couldn't fall asleep again. He began pacing about his room.

This was about three o'clock in the morning. From all around came the sound of comfortable snoring. He strode back and forth, impatiently waiting for the dawn. When day came, he'd go in there, to Mirel's wing, and would tell her:

—Early on Wednesday morning—he'd tell her—they'd travel out for the divorce . . . Everything was over. He wished to ask only one thing of her: would she come in with him to take formal leave of his father and sit with him for a while, not more than fifteen minutes? . . . That quarter-hour would demonstrate that nothing untoward had occurred between them; that she'd simply come with him to visit his father.

He wanted Mirel to give him a passing thought at the end:

—Shmulik's changed completely . . . He's become a different person.

The next day he went across to their wing several times but found no one there except the servant girl. He waited until fires had been kindled for the evening and went across again. This time Mirel was in. She'd only just returned from town. A lamp was burning in her room, and in front of the open wardrobes stood the large trousseau chest in which the maid had been helping to pack her things all morning. She lay in bed facing the door and her features, still flushed from the chill outdoors, expressed both curiosity and astonishment as he entered. He took fright and looked down.

Later, in the same state of fright, he sat opposite her on the chair next to the bed and said something totally different from what he'd been preparing to say:

—He'd thought that perhaps . . . perhaps she might still go in to take her formal leave—that's what he'd thought.

He didn't look at her. Quite suddenly he felt her stroking his knee with her smooth, soft hand. He slowly raised his eyes and saw:

Still lying on the bed, she'd moved closer to him. Leaning on her elbows, her head in her hand, she looked directly into his eyes.

—Shmulik—she asked—have I done you harm?

Shmulik's heart pounded.

—Harm? No . . . Who says so?

Mirel was obliged to rise very early to finish packing what remained of her belongings. She had also to reserve a room in the quiet hotel opposite the Shpolianskis' apartment and leave instructions for her luggage to be sent on there. The boat that traveled downriver to the city where the divorce was to be finalized left at ten in the morning. The proceedings would take place between five and six that afternoon after which, to avoid traveling with the Zaydenovskis, she'd return by train and Montchik would meet her at the station. He'd promised. By that evening she'd undoubtedly be exhausted. Even now she felt a great weariness throughout her body. But was this any excuse? Now she felt some compassion for Shmulik, and had given him her word. She'd have to put on her shawl and spend a few minutes in the big house.

Her mother-in-law's maid, who opened the back door for her, started back, so stunned was she by Mirel's sudden entrance. Because of her arrival, the mood in the dining room suddenly tensed. The chair next to her mother-in-law was vacated for her, but no one dared start any conversation. Someone called aside the visiting out-of-town relative, a newly married young woman who was sitting at the table; Miriam Lyubashits began whispering in Rikl's ear and soon went out into another room with her; and Mirel, feeling oppressed, began to regret having come. She thought:

—She'd done her duty . . . Now she could go back.

But her mother-in-law suddenly started blinking and leaned closer to her. During the last few days, she'd not been able to rid herself of a suspicion of an exclusively female kind. Now she had to question Mirel about it.

At her first question, Mirel blushed violently. Without looking at her, she answered brusquely and irritably:

—No.

—I can't remember.

—For a long time.

Suddenly her mother-in-law, looking like an astounded small-town grandmother, straightened her entire foolish frame:

—Yes—her expression said—I'm content now.

She looked around, but there was no one here except Mirel. So she turned to her once again and said with loud incredulity:

—Mirele, you're pregnant, you know!

—What?

She thought her mother-in-law had taken leave of her senses. She was simply speaking like an idiot.

To spite her, she instantly rose from her place and demanded loudly:

—She didn't understand . . . And that apart, what had this to do with the divorce?

But all around her the tumult in the room was now so great that no one was listening to what she said. Someone called Shmulik in. Someone else hurried off to the study to give Yankev-Yosl the news. And Miriam Lyubashits was already standing in the doorway again. As soon as the mother-in-law had rapidly imparted some information to her, she looked across at Mirel and nodded her head:

—Of course; what a question!

3.13

That night, Mirel felt intensely nauseous and woke the servant girl twice. She made her take a note to Shmulik in which she wrote that she didn't love him and reminded him that even before their wedding she'd stipulated in a clause in their betrothal contract that she reserved the right to leave him at any time; that she still didn't believe she was pregnant but that in any case she couldn't have a child with him; that if she was indeed pregnant, he alone was responsible and a remedy for the pregnancy had to be sought.

Shmulik was persuaded to drive off to the distillery and wait there for a few days.

With everyone standing around him, his mother comforted him in a private room before he left:

—What was there to think about? Now the situation was very different. If Mirel were to bear a child, she'd become far more tractable.

For three whole days, Mirel suffered alone in her room, was conscious all that time of the place below her breast, felt intense aversion to it, and finally began calling on her mother-in-law in the big house once again.

On her way there, she kept reflecting that she ought to say something, and so put an end to something. But every time she went in, the will to speak deserted her, and her hatred toward that place below her breast intensified within her. Her patience was taxed by her mother-in-law's repeated "Sit, Mirele," by Miriam Lyubashits and her child, by the younger Lyubashits's ruddy face and tedious intellectualizing. As the disgust within her grew, it seemed to her that it had become a physical thing that could literally be seized; that she might all at once rip it from her, and would then grow light and wholesome once again.

Leaving her mother-in-law's house, she went into town, called twice at her cousin Ida Shpolianski's apartment but did not find her in, and returning home, lay down and tried hard to calm herself:

—Who could tell? Perhaps it was easier to do nothing, and let things take their course. Perhaps it was better to endure without complaining for the rest of her life . . . lying in bed like this . . . suffering in silence.

She didn't love Shmulik. She loved no one. Sometimes she felt drawn to Nosn Heler, but she didn't trust that feeling. And mothers loved their children, after all. Who could say? Perhaps she'd grow to love this child . . . She would be a mother.

For several days she suffered in silence without leaving the house, imagining how she would be a mother.

Some joker would certainly make fun of her as he had of Miriam Lyubashits:—What had become of her!—he'd say—She'd become nothing more than a wet nurse! But she'd take no notice and pretend not to hear. Bowed beneath her yoke she'd simply spend every minute following the child's every footstep and fearing only one thing:

—That, God forbid, the little one didn't fall.

Soon, though, a beautiful frosty Sunday dawned, and in its brilliant sunshine the intense whiteness of the snow dazzled the eyes for the first time that season, and all the shops were shut because of the Gentile holiday.

Many sleighs both privately owned and publicly hired sped over the frosty whiteness of the city. And the tale that the revitalized outdoors told the surrounding stillness of the fields was wholly composed of the weakened peal of distant bells and the merry sneezing of horses that a sleigh speeding past had here and there mislaid.

Mirel stood alone at the window. Her heart was void of resolution and her sorrow intense. Standing next to a coachman whose sleigh had just been vacated, she noticed, was a young couple keenly interested in both the sleigh and in its wet horse on which the new-fallen snow was slowly freezing. All three, the coachman and the young couple, laughed at the meager amount of small change that was all they could offer for a sleigh ride, and all three were delighted: the coachman from the little windfall that had come his way that day, and the couple from the first snowfall of the season and the fact that they were in love.

Slowly Mirel began dressing to leave the house on some outing. From the closet she unhurriedly drew out her karakul jacket,* paused, lost herself in thought, pulled on the jacket, and again fell into a reverie. She'd even gone to the door, but stopped there to examine her own narrow hand and the long fingers with which she'd grasped the handle. Recently her hands had grown very weak, and greenish-blue veins were now clearly visible under the deathly pale skin. For a while she stood there looking at her hand. Then quite suddenly she reconsidered, returned to her bedroom, undressed, and threw herself back into bed. Now everything was so disgusting and oppressive; now it was no

---

*A lamb's wool jacket made of the curly fleece of a breed of sheep named from the area around Kara Kul, a lake in central Asia, where it originated. The fleece resembles astrakhan but has a flatter, looser curl; it comes in black, brown or gray.

longer possible to endure the weakness and submissiveness of the last few days:

—What did they want of her? . . . Why did they want to make a mother of her? . . . She couldn't be a mother . . . She didn't want to bear a child . . .

That same day she spent some time with Ida from whom she learned that there were two obstetricians in town prepared to do "it."

—One was an old Christian: first he moralized for two hours, then he demanded nothing less than two hundred rubles for "it." The second was much younger and a Jew. He took no more than a hundred rubles, and word had it that he did the job equally well.

She went to consult the younger doctor, the Jew. Answering all his questions, she was conscious that he was insulting her through the way he looked at her, through his lewd thoughts, and through the tone in which he gave her to understand that although he undertook to do "it," he regarded her as a sinner and morally far below himself, and therefore he repeated remarks he'd already made:

—Perhaps she was still single and consequently didn't want any members of her family to find out about this? It was all the same to him. He merely wanted to explain that by doing the work here in his surgery he put himself at far greater risk of discovery, and therefore he required double the fee.

He added:

—In any case, we can wait for two weeks and try a few other methods that can do no harm.

She was cruelly cut by his use of the word "we." Abruptly interrupting him, she made him feel like a charlatan:

—Good, he'd be paid double.

Afterward she lay calmly by herself in the dining room counting the days that remained of these two weeks:

—When was the appointed day? . . . Yes, the Monday after the next Sabbath . . .

And now there was no one to confide in about herself, about the approaching danger that held no terror for her, and about that fact that her hopes for her future life were uncertain and slight. Yet her heart was still drawn to something, and various plans still drifted into her mind. She still thought about herself and about Nosn Heler's penny newspaper which had recently started appearing and had even found its way into Shmulik's study:

—Now there was even Nosn Heler . . . Even he had succeeded in accomplishing something.

Under the weight of his sufferings, Shmulik sat in his study with that very newspaper. Glancing into it like a mourner, he kept silent for hours at a time, thought constantly of Mirel, but dared not go in to speak with her. He looked like a man who was fasting intermittently. Most of the time he stayed in the distillery; when he returned home, he spent the night in his study, and rarely left it. When the younger Lyubashits, that incessantly chattering student, called on him on one occasion, he couldn't endure that fact that he, Lyubashits, was prattling on so heartily and loudly while Mirel was lying on the sofa in the adjoining room, and he stopped him after his first few words:

—Hush! . . . Quieter, please . . . What's making you so cheerful?

3.14

And the Monday came.

Around eleven o'clock in the morning, Shmulik arrived back from town on the streetcar and saw in the distance:

Wearing her karakul jacket, Mirel stood at the streetcar stop opposite one of the Gentile city messengers with whom she was sending a letter to someone, and the messenger nodded his head in its red cap as he listened to the identifying characteristics of the person into whose hands he was being instructed to deliver it.

For some reason, Shmulik returned to town. When he finally returned home at around three in the afternoon, Mirel still wasn't back. For a while he drifted about alone over there, then went out into the courtyard and ordered the britzka harnessed. When someone reported to his father in the big house that Shmulik was driving out to the distillery yet again, his mother felt decidedly uneasy. Going across to his wing to investigate, she found him ready and wearing the fur coat he used for traveling.

—Shmulik—she asked him—you got back from the distillery only yesterday?

Shmulik looked down.

—Tomorrow evening—he said—is Christmas Eve; the workmen all have to be paid before then.

And turning to face the window, he began waiting in silence for his harnessed britzka to leave the courtyard as quickly as possible.

The same day, when lamps were being kindled at nightfall in the dark houses of the suburb, a hired sleigh drawn by two horses drew up before the front door of Shmulik's wing and a Gentile city messenger, having helped Mirel descend, took her arm and assisted her into the house. Mirel was deathly pale and barely able to walk. With the help of the messenger in his red cap she dragged herself to her bedroom and had hardly strength enough to fall into her bed. The terrified servant girl, the only person left in charge of the house, wanted to raise the alarm and hurry off to seek help from the mother-in-law in the big house, but summoning what strength she had, Mirel stopped her and called her over to the bed:

—It wasn't necessary . . . It wasn't necessary . . . The girl was to take her purse and pay the messenger and not dare to speak a word of any of this to anyone.

Dozing in weakness and pain, her features somewhat contorted, she lay in bed with her eyes shut and passed a restless night, her thoughts jumbling together the numerous morbid events of the day through which she'd just passed. She remembered the hours of waiting in the doctor's reception room, the young woman in mourning who'd sat there silently, the agitated, small-town young wife who was continually scurrying about the room in terror, the foolish, embarrassed giggling of the unmarried young woman with the intelligent face who'd been escorted by an elderly Jewish midwife. All this seemed to merge with the frosty sunshine that peered in through the double-glazed windows, and all of it ceased to exist the very moment the door of the surgery closed behind her. Afterward something happened to Mirel outside. She was feeling as though her legs might give way beneath her and she might collapse at any moment, and her head was spinning when she recognized the

Gentile city messenger in the distance. But now everything was over. Outside, night had fallen, and she lay in her own bed, suffering a little pain but remembering only one thing:

—The danger of pregnancy had passed, but now a new danger lay before her. It was possible . . . highly possible that she would never get down off this bed . . .

Three days later, when Shmulik returned from the distillery in the morning, her face was aflame with fever for the second day in succession. Although her lips were dry, not a single bottle of medication was to be found in the whole room.

Mirel clutched his hand and begged that everything be kept secret:

—I had to do it, Shmulik. We'd both have been unhappy for ever otherwise.

Standing at her bedside with downcast head and an expression of utter desolation, he nevertheless nodded:

—Good . . . No one will know of this.

Of late, Shmulik had changed completely. That afternoon, when his mother called him aside in a private room and started saying something about Mirel, he was greatly offended and even responded in some anger:

—What did everyone want of Mirel? Everyone had some or other complaint against Mirel.

Subsequently he spent hours pacing over his house, thinking over the new plan he intended to propose to Mirel and about the possibility of traveling somewhere with her for a few days and starting a rumor that he'd divorced her.

—Come what may, he'd never marry again. He had no use for his life and for the huge sums of money he was earning—at least he'd know one thing: Mirel was settled somewhere and he was able to send her the means on which to live . . . He was also prepared to send her the bill of divorcement at a moment's notice, whenever she might need it.

Meanwhile at the elder Zaydenovski's house a great many telegrams addressed to Mirel kept arriving from somewhere. Each time Shmulik was summoned to the big house and secret conferences about these cables were held with him. Shmulik was scared, read every newly arrived telegram with a pounding heart, and finally rushed off in great haste on the express train. He returned a few days later with an ashen face and very red eyes. He'd apparently spent hours weeping somewhere. Mirel, her face haggard but no longer feverish, was sitting up in bed by then. Lost in thought, she stared through the window and asked him nothing. And fearful of something, he stood opposite her in a state of utter dejection with a carefully prepared lie ready to hand:

—I've been visiting Aunt Pearl, that's where I've been. Sadly, she's just lost a son.

That evening the tall young doctor with the light brown hair called at the house. He was anxious to keep a very low profile, this doctor, which was why he called at night, looked carefully around him like a thief as he went in at the front door, and stayed in Mirel's room no longer than few minutes.

—Everything is as it should be—he said.—Mirel could get up the next day.

He made haste to leave and was soon gone. Taking a lamp from his study, Shmulik saw him out as though he were a wonder-working rabbi, but the doctor, appraising him with a shrewd glance, bade him put the lamp down:

—She's got a proper blockhead for a husband—he thought, in regard to Mirel.—Evidently he's got very few brains.

Shmulik, however, was in a state of confusion and held ready a full twenty-five rubles so, snatching the banknotes with one hand the doctor placed his other hand on Shmulik's shoulder:

—You've a fine young wife—he flattered Shmulik hastily.—She's very strong . . . May the same be said of all Jews.

Only one small matter remained:

Shmulik had to be approached in his study, interrupted for a moment in going through his accounts, and abruptly told what had to be done:

—Shmulik, tomorrow we're going to the town downriver.

But Mirel herself was still very weak from her ordeal and Shmulik unexpectedly set off for Warsaw before dawn, leaving with the maid a letter for her in which he outlined his new plan. He'd stayed up all night preparing this letter, had rewritten and re-read it many times. Eventually he was satisfied with it, though as a result he'd been unable to fall asleep before he left. But Mirel had glanced through no more than the first few lines before she asked the maid in astonishment.

—What?

Then she replaced the letter in its envelope and returned it to the maid, all of which she did very slowly. On the whole she felt very composed, and after her illness she was more patient than usual. Steadily her strength returned, and she waited calmly for the second week when she'd feel completely well and Shmulik would return from Warsaw.

Every afternoon she put on her jacket and her black scarf. Since she was still too weak to go into town, she stood outside next to the steps leading up to her front door, unhurriedly pacing to and fro and awakening wishful thoughts in the well-to-do young businessmen passing by in their own or in hired droshkies on the road outside. All turned their heads toward her, unable to tear their eyes away, and at the same time all of them felt very odd, as though none of them had ever sinned before and she had for many years been the unknown bride of their dreams.

In her father-in-law's house, what she'd done during the past two weeks was already known. Her mother-in-law was often to be found closeted with her husband at all times of the working day, sitting opposite him, her face red with anger and her nostrils tightly pinched, beside herself with vexation and powerlessness:

—I'm telling you: such a despicable person is rarely to be found even among Gentiles.

And Mirel pottered about in her room, thought back to the pregnancy she'd escaped, and continued to have little faith in the new life that lay before her. With nothing else to do, she once more started going into town and disappearing there for whole evenings at a time. At first no one knew where she went and with whom she passed the time, but in due course she met one of her husband's relatives in the street on which Nosn Heler had his lodgings and in her mother-in-law's house this was discussed fully and frankly:

—What possible question could there be? That woman was despicable . . . She'd been in love with that young man before she was married, and now she spent evening after evening in his company.

During this period Shmulik returned from Warsaw, gave orders for his bed to be carried into the study, stopped going across to his father's house, and generally started living like a recluse. His quiet conduct and crestfallen demeanor bespoke something mute and stubborn and it seemed that even while he was pacing about in his room, he found himself somewhere far, far away across a distance of a hundred miles and more. Meeting him in town on one occasion, Ida Shpolianski asked him about the divorce and he answered her coldly and quietly:

—Who knows? . . . Quite possibly the whole situation might reverse itself.

Then Ida had summoned Mirel by telephone,* wandered through the quiet streets with her until nightfall, and reported this:

—Now you'll see . . . Now Shmulik won't grant you the divorce.

Exactly the same thing had happened with her Abram four years before. During all that time he'd been prepared to give her a divorce, but when matters came to a head, he'd left home for an entire month and informed her through his younger brother Ziame:†

—At present Ida doesn't need the divorce papers, but as soon as she finds she must have them, I'll provide them within two hours.

That evening, looking distressed and exhausted, Mirel called on Heler, lay on his sofa longer than was her custom, and was more than usually pensive. Clearly she'd been coming here not for Heler's sake but for the sake of his quiet room where she could calmly reflect on her future life. Here she rarely broke the silence, had her white kerchief spread over the pillow because Heler's pillowcase was far from clean, lay back, and repeated what she always said:

*The first telephone installations in Russia, introduced in the 1890s, were made by the American Bell System and were extremely expensive, which meant that only the richest private individuals—and only those living in cities—could afford them.
†Russian diminutive of the name Zinovii (Zalmen)

—She felt comfortable here in this room . . . She'd never felt as comfortable anywhere else.

The chief reason she felt so comfortable here, it seemed, was that Heler had finally come to his senses and no longer spoke to her about marriage.

She related:

—She wasn't in the slightest concerned about what Ida had just told her.

She had merely to speak the word and Shmulik would immediately grant her a divorce. There was nothing more.

A month and a half before, she'd known very clearly why she'd needed the divorce; now she lay thinking about every action she'd taken until now:

Everything she'd done up to this point hadn't come about through acts of her own will but as a result of curiosity and compassion.

She'd derived so little pleasure from her life that she might as well still be eighteen years old. But were she indeed still eighteen, no new step in life would lie before her, and nothing would be left for her but once more to feel compassion for her father and for herself, to marry Shmulik all over again, to divorce him, and to be left lying here thinking:

—Well, good: she'd divorced him. Now what would she do?

Heler thrust his hands into his trouser pockets and began pacing across the room, barely able to contain his pent-up indignation:

—He was nothing to her . . . She came here not for his sake but for the sake of his sofa and his quiet room in which she could calmly think about herself. He was convinced that no woman had ever behaved in this way toward a man.

He observed her as she donned her outdoor garments, as she made ready to leave, and as he accompanied her out. He respected her silent pensiveness.

Every evening afterward, in this quiet room suffused with the greenish light that seeped from under its lampshades, he continued to await her coming, longing for her as one longed for a wife with whom one had recently entered into a sanctified and long-awaited marriage. The very air here in his room was redolent of her. He was drawn to the place where she'd lain, to her sorrowful, remote expression, to the thought that on her account he'd once given up preparing for his university entrance examinations; that here in the city his former fiancée had by now hastily married some young jurist who was a widower; that his financial investment in his penny newspaper was going steadily downhill and that this was the common talk of the town:

—Only a miracle's keeping that penny paper going; it'll collapse very soon.

But all in all Mirel came to see him only once more, and then only for a few minutes. She'd been left oppressed and disconsolate after a highly unpleasant scene that had taken place a little earlier between her and her husband in regard to the divorce, and hadn't wanted to discuss it. All she did was to pace briefly through the room deep in thought.

She said nothing, did not remove her coat or her overshoes and found difficulty in swallowing, like someone who was fasting. Without looking round at him, she left almost immediately. When he made as though to accompany her, she bade him stay indoors, but he followed her outside nevertheless, pursued her to the next intersection, and said a few words to her that he himself didn't believe:

—Someone wanted to buy his penny newspaper and had offered him five thousand rubles . . . They'd be able to travel abroad . . . This might be sufficient until he could qualify as an engineer over there.

Again she did not look round at him, quickened her pace, and merely shrugged her shoulders. In the end he was left standing where he was, and from a distance saw her seat herself in a streetcar and return to the house she hated.

On a second occasion he met her in the street near the huge, luxurious house in which lived her husband's relative Montchik. She was walking with a dark-haired young woman who looked some five or six years older than she; apparently this was her cousin Ida Shpolianski. He stopped and doffed his hat. She noticed him but, as previously, looked at the young woman accompanying her, said something to her, and passed by very close to him. Wordlessly, her severe and unbending carriage revealed much about her, this unhappy only child: she truly could find no place for herself in this life, but she clung obstinately to some notion of her own and had compassion neither for herself nor for anyone else.

She turned at the next corner and disappeared with her companion. Still standing where she'd passed him, he sighed, replaced his hat, and strode on his way.

He was obliged to call on Montchik Zaydenovski, to feel uncomfortable in his company as one of her husband's relatives, and to ask him:

—Perhaps after all he might be able to find someone with money prepared to come into partnership with him on the penny newspaper? . . .

3.15

Montchik's desk was low, heavy, and wide. On it, apart from various ponderous objects, also stood photographs of his late father and of Mirel, each in its own leather frame, directly facing this young entrepreneur. From time to time, leaning his head on his hand, Montchik gazed at the latter, his eyes huge:

—Something's going on with Mirel . . .

Since the last time he'd met her in the street and escorted her over the chain bridge, a city messenger had brought him a letter in which she asked him to lend her two hundred rubles. Then the two hundred rubles had been returned to him together with a formal note in Hebrew from Shmulik:

—My dear kinsman, our teacher and master Montchik! Thanks and thanks again for the generous loan you made to my dear wife Mirele, long may she live.

As his younger eleven-year-old brother came in from the dining room, he greeted him warmly and loudly:

—Ah, Reb Liolia* . . . What does a Jew have to say for himself, Reb Liolia?

Like him, Liolia disliked the Gentile youths who called on his sister the singer, and like him could also not endure her shrieking. Montchik loved him because he was a tough, wiry boy with good understanding

*Liolia is a diminutive of the Russian name Izrail' (Yisroel).

who often exposed his sister's lies, and above all because he'd certainly make something of himself. He also loved him because Mirel had seen him once, had said that she liked him, and had caressed his head. Taking Liolia by the hand, he asked him a question, glancing sideways at Mirel's photograph, his mind still preoccupied with his earlier thought:

—Something's going on with Mirel . . .

About three o'clock one afternoon Montchik was sitting lost in thought at this desk, responding wearily to the parting greetings of the last of numerous clients who'd been coming and going in his office from early morning on.

His mind was numb, filled with the chaotic events he'd lived through the day before. There in the suburb, in his uncle Yankev-Yosl's house, the entire Zaydenovski family had been in total uproar, because for the second day in succession Mirel had been living in the hotel on the quiet street with its long central island of trees. At eleven o'clock at night his mother, Aunt Esther, had been summoned, frenzied information having been given her over the telephone about what was taking place in that overcrowded, panic-stricken house:

—Shmulik had disappeared . . . He'd not been seen since the evening of the day before . . . A search had been instituted for him . . . He'd been looked for everywhere in town. Eh? . . . In the distillery? Yes, in the distillery as well.

Lying undressed in bed, Montchik had waited for his mother until three in the morning. His head throbbed, and deep within himself he felt the full weight of the panic in the Zaydenovskis' house. He said nothing, but he had some idea of what was taking place there, and he knew that all his relatives over there suspected him, something that was ridiculous . . . Now he was quite unable to call there.

His mother returned about four in the morning. In his underwear he opened the door for her himself and then sat on her bed with her for a long time. All the while his distracted mind was racing wildly, but his mother took her time . . . By now she too apparently knew about the suspicion that had fallen on him as she very slowly imparted the melancholy tidings:

—Well, what more is there to say? . . . Shmulik's not there and they're all afraid that something's happened to him.

. . . . When that woman does the kind of thing she does:

Very soon after "that woman's" departure, Shmulik had posted a notice outside announcing that his house was to let and that he was selling his furniture; people said that he'd also left a letter addressed to his parents. Very likely they were too ashamed to make this letter public . . .

—Ida Shpolianski's brother-in-law reported that he'd seen Shmulik skulking near Kromowski's pharmacy the evening before. Now someone had read in the evening newspaper that a hanged body had been in the coppice around the hospital, and everyone had instantly rushed off to the morgue.

As dawn broke, Montchik dozed off and dreamed that he was living in the same hotel as Mirel, in the room adjacent to hers, and from the window noticed Shmulik wandering up and down on the sidewalk opposite.

Now, after a half-day's work, he was extremely tired and preoccupied. He remembered the foolishness of thinking, as he awoke that morning, that he had to call on Mirel at her hotel that very day, and that Mirel would be very pleased he'd come. He still had business in the banks and several people to see at the stock exchange, so he hastily locked his scattered papers in the safe and snatched up his overcoat. Outside his front door, however, he suddenly froze and turned deathly pale, as though he'd seen a wandering corpse: on the sidewalk opposite stood Shmulik, his dull features the color of clay. He was unwilling to say where he'd spent the past two nights, and had now come to Montchik to ask a favor:

—Two days before—he related—Mirel had left the house and had refused to take any money from him . . . He'd begged her but she'd refused and gone away . . . And now . . . Perhaps Montchik might be willing to call on her in her hotel and entreat her to take some money? . . .

3.16

Some weeks later, a tall young man in a black autumn cloak and a very broad-brimmed, foreign-looking hat left a house that rented furnished rooms on the central avenue and strolled slowly down to the chain bridge leading into the suburb. This was Herz, the midwife's acquaintance Herz.

For six consecutive weeks in the godforsaken shtetl in which he lived, he'd smiled at the letter in which Mirel pleaded with him to come, and now he'd finally done as she asked, seemingly in jest and on the spur of the moment. Around noon, when he awoke in his furnished room here in town, he suddenly reminded himself that he was still a bachelor; that he was now thirty-two years old, and that at times very few of the pieces he'd written pleased him; that here in this city Mirel, whom he'd thought of all the time he'd spent traveling down, had a husband, a home, and an entire family of relatives. And he'd been given his just deserts, after all . . . He fully deserved the self-mocking laughter that often broke from him as he was dressing.

Smiling good-humoredly, he'd wandered about the streets for a few days.

—What was he doing in this city?

Nothing in particular: since this was the first time in his life he'd been here, there was some value in admiring the architecture of the apartment buildings and the theater, in strolling down to the chain bridge, stopping near the Gentile lads who were chewing sunflower seeds, and observing, as they did, how the sheet ice on the wide river below had now split into chunks and was waiting in great silence for some message from afar.

On one occasion, however, he crossed the chain bridge and strolled farther into the suburb, smiling again over Mirel's letter which lay in his pocket.

The festival of Purim was approaching, and the bright day spun its warmth from pure sunshine and clear spring air. The wheels of rapidly passing droshkies clattered more noisily than normal over the newly exposed cobblestones, and toward dusk the sunshine dissolved into a rivulet of molten silver that flowed over both near and distant hills on the outskirts of the city.

—Most important for the coming spring were the bare patches of earth that were steadily being exposed through the melting snow.

On the branches of the trees lining the streets, birds lost themselves in twittering delirium as governesses led their charges home. The air was filled with the scent of light frost, of young women, and of the joy of small-town children who'd soon no longer be obliged to go to school in the dark.

Finding Shmulik's wing locked and empty, Herz stopped. A passerby directed him to the Zaydenovskis in the big house, so he went across, and in the entrance hall enquired for Mirel.

In the dining room, dough was being kneaded for Purim pastries and honey balls. All the members of the Zaydenovski household, including children and female relatives, were crowded round the long table, irritated by the small freckled lad who kept thrusting his hands into the warm honey-dough until someone shouted at him:

—Feh, you! . . . What are you licking your fingers for?

The maid was the first to receive Herz in the entrance hall. Not knowing how to answer him herself, she carried his inquiry into the dining room, and almost at once more than a dozen people rushed in, darkening the brightness of the little room as they inquisitively surrounded this unfamiliar young man whose features were ready at any moment to break into a smile.

Looking him over, one young woman was especially anxious to know who he was, so she called out the name of the hotel in which Mirel was staying:

—She was living in two rooms over there.

Someone else knew that all this time Mirel had been waiting there for someone who was supposed to join her here in the city. She made passing reference to Shmulik, who'd been to that hotel a few days earlier and had been wholly unable to gain access to her:

—Mirel was unwell in some way, it seemed . . . Apparently she'd been confined to her bed for some days now.

Suddenly, blinking her nearsighted eyes, the mother-in-law herself appeared on the threshold of the room:

—Sha! . . . What were they all standing about here for?

The unknown young man who was asking for Mirel was pointed out to her, so she went right up to him. For a while she peered at him with her eyes screwed up. Then she stretched out her hand to her little boy and very cautiously drew him away from this unfamiliar young man as though she were afraid the child might touch this stranger and so defile himself. She spat to one side the way superstitious folk spit when mentioning someone's dreadful illness, and forced herself to remark, with the mien of one who wanted absolutely nothing to do with this young man:

—Yes, well . . . She lives there . . . in the hotel . . . that's where she lives.

4.1

These events took place during the icy snowstorms between Christmas and the Gentile New Year.

His face red with cold, Velvl Burnes stood in his father's dining room. He'd only just arrived from his farm and was unable to grasp what was going on around him. Looking concerned, almost all the members of the household were clustered around a charity collector, listening to what he had to tell:

—Reb Gedalye's end was very near . . . The doctor from the provincial capital had declared that there was nothing more he could do. Reb Gedalye's sister had already arrived from abroad . . . And his daughter . . . Rumor had it that his daughter was ill herself . . . In all probability, in her father-in-law's house over there, the telegrams that were being sent almost hourly from over here were being kept from her.

All was quiet, and through the double-glazed windows the gray winter dusk peered silently in; it spread its fearful desolation into all the darkened corners of the room, and the huge black sideboard, already enveloped in it, stared out in wordless reproach at the melancholy faces of those around it:

—For two years in this very room you cursed Reb Gedalye . . . And now he's on his deathbed and the boys from the Talmud Torah are on their way to recite psalms in his name.

Someone called attention to these Talmud Torah boys outside and everyone besieged the window from which they saw:

Across the way, Reb Gedalye's house was brightly illuminated with lamps that had been lit very early, not to bring happiness but to mark the agony of death in all the rooms. And here, passing along the darkened street before the house, more than forty Talmud Torah boys in tattered sheepskin overcoats trudged knee-high through the deep snowdrifts following two of their teachers who were leading the way toward the Husyatin study house.

The local ritual slaughterer came in, the same pleasant, well-known functionary who'd once been sent as an arbitrator to Reb Gedalye when the engagement contract was returned. He reported:

—He'd just come from there . . . The will had only just been rewritten to allocate the profit of eighteen thousand rubles which the merchants of the provincial capital had paid for a share in the great Kashperivke woods. The remaining debts amounted to twelve thousand seven hundred, and thirteen hundred had been left to the town's general charity fund.

Looking sad, with his mind fixed on the affairs he was attending to, the ritual slaughterer seemed in some way sanctified and cut off from the mundane world, as though he'd just immersed himself in a ritual bath prior to undertaking some pious, God-fearing act.

Only Avrom-Moyshe Burnes stood near him, smoking a great many cigarettes, finally calling him into his study to seek his advice:

—What did he think? Perhaps it behooved him, Avrom-Moyshe, to call at Reb Gedalye's house now?

Velvl followed him to the study and listened in to what was being said. The ritual slaughterer frowned:

—What was there to think about? Of course it would be fitting.

Feeling much lighter in heart, Velvl stole quietly into the dark passage where the full-cut fur coat he used for traveling hung. He donned it stealthily and went quietly outdoors.

Following the side alleys, he made his way surreptitiously to Reb Gedalye's house, his legs sinking deeply into the newly fallen snow, the hem of his long, wide fur coat dragging behind him and leaving tracks wherever he went. In the aftermath of the snowstorm, silence prevailed everywhere. Everything, from the pallid, noiseless night to the few illuminated houses scattered here and there, appeared oddly expectant and mute, as in the pale obscurity of a dream. From one of these side alleys came the loud slamming of a door and a woman who'd emerged from her house yelled out to her neighbor:

—God could still help Reb Gedalye! . . . He'd certainly deserved help!

He noticed Reb Gedalye's relative, his former bookkeeper, who was making haste to return to Reb Gedalye's house from wherever he'd been. Velvl overtook him:

—A word, if I may . . . Is there any news? Not good, eh?

The bookkeeper stopped and sighed:

—What news can there be? Assuredly not good.

Reb Gedalye's relative wasn't at all surprised to find Velvl lingering in the vicinity here, and he responded as he would to any good friend of Reb Gedalye's. So Velvl went on to the house. A group of men was standing around one of Reb Gedalye's former couriers, listening to his description of Gitele, who'd been suffering from a severe headache for the past three days:

—Reb Gedalye's sister was sitting with her in the darkened bedroom; she wouldn't permit Gitele to leave her bed.

Avoiding this group, Velvl made his way around the back of the house and stopped outside the illuminated window of Mirel's room:

—Evidently this was where Reb Gedalye lay.

A little old man, a learned Jew who was now ill, afflicted with a severe cough and failing eyesight, came along the narrow alleyway that led from the Husyatin study house. Groaning, he stopped and, peering narrowly into Velvl's face with his diseased eyes, wheezingly inquired:

—Who's this? . . . Oh . . . Oh . . . Velvl?

The little old man complained bitterly about old age, about life, and about death. Velvl waited until he'd disappeared on to Reb Gedalye's verandah and then moved closer to the window. Now he could see everything that was taking place in the room. Imagination suggested that the air in there was heavy with the stench of medication, of sickness and approaching death, and it seemed as though all within was silent, unnaturally silent. At a little table on which a lamp burned under a blue shade sat the harassed local *feldsher*. Having gone without sleep for several nights, his features were strained as he stared straight ahead at the sickbed on which fell the blue-tinted glow of the shaded lamp. As though walking on eggshells, Avreml the rabbi, looking greatly distressed and agitated, wandered back and forth accompanied by his shadow: his right shoulder jutted upward while from his left the arm hung down oddly, as though paralyzed, almost completely hidden in his sleeve and twitching automatically. And there on the bed against the wall lay the sick man, seemingly lost in abstraction. Because of the leeches that had been applied after the doctor had left, his head had been shaved, making his earlocks and beard appear too big and black and his features too gaunt and shrunken. Every now and then his head moved slowly, very slowly from side to side. The people in the room drew closer to the bed. Standing on tiptoe outside, Velvl saw them doing what Reb Gedalye appeared to be asking of them and sat him up; undressing him, they clothed him afresh in a new, lustrously white shirt in which he looked sanctified and pure, as on the night of Yom Kippur after a fast of twenty-four hours. Slowly, very slowly, they lowered him back on to his pillows and bent closer to hear what he was saying. Someone brought Mirel's picture into the room and held it up behind Avreml the rabbi, but the rabbi made an angry gesture of dismissal:

—It's not necessary. It's not necessary.

Apparently Reb Gedalye had asked after his daughter.

Once more they bent down to hear what he was saying. Evidently it moved them greatly. His sister turned aside, suppressing her sobs and wiping her eyes. Suddenly Velvl noticed the *feldsher* whispering something into the rabbi's ear, and the rabbi shaking his head and leaving the room. He moved from the window to the verandah where he found a courier looking out for a buggy to drive him to the nearby village in search of more leeches. Taking the man by the sleeve, Velvl led him toward his father's house:

—Here's my buggy. It's harnessed and ready to go . . . Tell the driver to hurry.

Around midnight, commotion and shouting from outside filled the Burnes's dining room. Seated at the table, both the daughters of the house turned pale with shock: one clutched her heart and the other peered out through the double-glazed windows, noticed a number of people milling about in the pale gloom of night, and turned back to the table in fright:

—God help us! . . . Reb Gedalye's just passed away, it seems.

One of the two children who were sleeping fully dressed on the sofa started awake with a frightened wail; although the daughters were afraid to stay in the house on their own, Velvl swiftly threw on his fur coat and with a pounding heart rushed outside once more. This time he didn't steal round the back but went straight along the broad main street where lights were still burning in most of the houses. A number of Jews were standing in a huddle in the marketplace, all talking at the same time as though participating in the Blessing of the New Moon.[*] One of them shouted out:

—What about pallbearers?

—Have patience!

The entire shtetl was awake. People from all ends of the town kept going up into Reb Gedalye's house, and Velvl followed them, pushing his way from one overcrowded room to another. In the crush of the dining room, he recognized his tall father; sundered from everyone else, he was leaning against a cupboard and gloomily smoking a cigarette from his silver holder. The congestion at the entrance to the third room was very great: numerous candles were burning in there and much weeping could be heard. Velvl found himself shoved from all sides. Behind him, someone pointed out Reb Gedalye's son-in-law who'd only just arrived from the railway station. By the time Velvl had reminded himself that he need go no farther, it was too late and he found himself deep in the house, in the room with its numerous burning candles, and no one around him was shoving any longer. To his left, alongside Gitele and the sister from abroad, the newly arrived son-in-law was bent over

---

[*]In the Orthodox Jewish tradition, the monthly reappearance of the moon is recognized with praise to the Creator through a liturgical blessing recited in the open air, facing the moon, preferably in a prayer quorum of ten adult males.

the corpse, while opposite, his face contorted, was Avreml the rabbi, who looked at Velvl in a peculiar way. He wanted Velvl to be aware that he'd truly been a close friend of Reb Gedalye's, and that tears were now flowing from his rabbinical eyes.

As the gray dawn broke, the corpse was carried out on a bier so narrow and short it seemed to have been made for a child. Running with it on their shoulders, as though carrying something that ought to be hidden from sight as quickly as possible, were the rabbi and the rabbinical judge, both the shtetl's two ritual slaughterers, the son-in-law, and one other, an ordinary young man who used to buy two small wagonloads of flour every week from Reb Gedalye's mill. Someone drew Velvl closer to the bier and pushed the young man aside:

—Stand back, stand back, it's Velvl Burnes.

And Velvl put his shoulder beneath the burden and together with the son-in-law carried it a long, long distance, right to the cemetery. When he lowered the bier, he found himself greatly confused and dazed. Because he'd yielded place to him, the ordinary young man felt drawn to Velvl, approached him and said:

—He's light, Reb Gedalye, eh? Completely emaciated . . .

And Velvl stared at this young man, unable to recall his name or remember where he'd seen him.

4.2

Gitele and Reb Gedalye's sister observed the mandatory Seven Days of Mourning* in the house, and Avreml the rabbi arranged a prayer quorum twice a day† by calling in passers-by from the street. No one was allowed to evade this duty:

*Shivah (Hebrew "seven") is the name given to the week-long period of mourning mandated by Jewish law for first-degree relatives: father, mother, son, daughter, brother, sister, or spouse. To spare the mourners the strain of leaving the place where they are observing the Seven Days of Mourning, it is customary to gather a prayer quorum to recite the prescribed weekday services twice a day.
†The afternoon and evening services are customarily recited one after the other in the late afternoon.

—Never mind . . . Reb Gedalye deserved it and you owe it to him.

Doing as they were asked and joining the prayers, people noticed the stillness and emptiness of the house, and the way Gitele sat on the floor in the salon next to Reb Gedalye's sister, looked down at the boards, and was silent.

Reb Gedalye's sister wanted Gitele to return with her to her home abroad. When there was no one else in the house, seated on the floor next to Gitele she argued her case with their relative the bookkeeper and with Avreml the rabbi:

—After all, whom does Gitele have here? . . . I mean to say, why should she stay here all on her own?

—And for a little while . . . For a little while, at least, she could certainly come to stay with me.

Neither the rabbi nor the bookkeeper made any response, and the sister herself seemed scarcely to believe in the earnestness of her own tone. Gitele did not raise her head, the room was filled with silence, and the desolation that follows when everything has ended clung to the walls and ceiling, calling again to mind that Reb Gedalye was now dead and that Gitele had now no single place on earth.

A buyer was sought for Reb Gedalye's house, but none was found. The furniture was sold covertly, without Gitele's knowledge, and on the day of her departure, a carpenter was engaged to board up the windows from outside.

To bid her farewell came Avreml the rabbi, the former bookkeeper and his wife, Libke the rabbi's wife, and an elderly, querulous widow who used to collect a Sabbath loaf from Gitele every Friday to provide for a poor shoemaker burdened with a great many children. Now this widow kept sighing even more frequently than usual and for some reason went on and on about her elder daughter who'd died:

—She'd continually pleaded with the Master of the Universe: Dear Lord, what use is my daughter to you? Take me instead . . .

So heavily swathed in furs and scarves that her face was barely visible, Gitele seemed to have been turned to stone, neither speaking nor moving from where she sat. She was the last to leave the house, but at the very moment she wanted to seat herself in the sleigh, something overcame her. Her head jerked round and she seemed on the point of collapse. Attempts were made to support her and assist her into the sleigh but she refused to permit them, freed herself, ascended the steps of the verandah once more, and kissed the mezuzah.*

In town, word had it that Velvl Burnes had been at the railway station that day, that he'd gone up to Gitele and said to her:

—Be well.

And Gitele had risen from her bench in the second-class and replied:

—God might yet help him.

On the last warm Sabbath before Passover, some five local tailors' apprentices were walking along the freshly trodden pathway that led down into the shtetl. Pleased that the mud was drying and that the tranquility of Passover was approaching, they cracked jokes and from some distance away denied free passage to all the well-rested servant girls who passed.

Conceiving a liking for the verandah of Reb Gedalye's abandoned house, they sat down there to warm themselves in the sunshine, started indulging in horseplay, and unintentionally smashed a few panes of the front windows.

This was noticed by one of the town's householders, an elderly Jew who was passing on his way to afternoon prayers. He stopped and yelled at the apprentices:

—Get off the verandah, you hooligans! . . . The devil take the lot of you, have you no respect?

The apprentices did as they were bidden and left the verandah. The panes, however, remained smashed, and blindly called to mind the suburb of the distant metropolis and Reb Gedalye's daughter who hadn't come down even to look around after her father's death. Passersby stared gloomily at this house, which stood empty and had no heir:

—Reb Gedalye's well and truly dead, eh? There's nothing left.

Meanwhile, Avreml the rabbi drew on community funds some-

---

*A mezuzah (Hebrew, "doorpost") is a piece of parchment contained in a case, inscribed with the Hebrew verses Deuteronomy 6:4–9 and 11:13–21, and affixed to the doorpost of Jewish homes.

where and used them to erect a small mausoleum over Reb Gedalye's grave. He quarreled with those shtetl householders who thought this inappropriate, and insisted on having his way:

—It's fine, it's fine . . . It's entirely fitting and proper: Reb Gedalye bequeathed thirteen hundred rubles to the community, and the community erected a mausoleum over his grave—the one thing has nothing to do with the other.

Thereafter the rabbi didn't leave his house for days on end, spending his time studying the Mishnah in Reb Gedalye's memory.* When the mausoleum over the grave was finally completed, the rabbi had almost reached the end of one of the tractates, so he went down to the cemetery with some twenty men, completed his study of the last chapters at Reb Gedalye's graveside, and recited Kaddish there. Later that morning, after Avreml the rabbi and his study group had returned, the noonday hour in the old Husyatin study house seemed to drag on much longer than usual; all felt faint with hunger, and took a drop of whiskey for the ascent of Reb Gedalye's soul.

Everything in the study house was quiet and routinely commonplace. The first dust of the approaching spring lay on the lecterns and the benches, and the caretaker had already breakfasted at home somewhere. Discussion focused on the white shirt in which Reb Gedalye had asked to be clothed before his death:

—That shirt was probably inherited from a great-great-grandfather.

Holding his glass of whiskey, the rabbi spoke to those assembled about Reb Gedalye of blessed memory:

—This is what happened . . . Right at the end, this is what happened: he said to me, Avreml, he said to me, why are you weeping? . . . Foolish fellow: if I felt I were leaving anyone behind me, I'd make the journey there as readily as going to a dance.

All those who stood round heard and were silent. Only one man, an

---

*In memory of the dead, it is customary to study chapters from the Mishnah, a third-century collection of rabbinic debates on the Torah. The Mishnah consists of six orders, each containing seven to twelve tractates. There may be many chapters of Mishnah in any given tractate. In the presence of a prayer quorum of ten adult men, a special Kaddish is recited upon the completion of this study.

emaciated, timid sycophant who was unemployed, edged unobtrusively closer to someone at the back and smiled foolishly in consequence of the liquor he'd drunk. Wanting to make some allusion to the many young men whom Mirel had always dragged around with her as she wandered over the shtetl and to the fact that she'd not come down to the shtetl here after her father's death, he remarked snidely:

—Evidently Reb Gedalye knew his own daughter, eh? Evidently he knew very well what she was.

Only during the intermediate days of Passover did Tarabay's children come down to the village, bringing with them Heler's friend, the student at the polytechnic. He encountered the midwife Schatz, who was now living near the sugar factory, and on Heler's behalf related to her the exact nature of the illness Mirel had suffered there in the city at precisely the time Reb Gedalye had been lying on his deathbed here in the shtetl.

At the same time, those in Avrom-Moyshe Burnes's house were made aware that Mirel no longer lived with her husband but apart, in a hotel with the midwife's friend Herz; that she was somehow both divorced and not divorced; that she refused to receive any of her husband's relatives except one, a cousin who was still a bachelor and was, so the rumor went, an immensely wealthy businessman. One Sunday afternoon all this became the subject of discussion in the dining room:

—What's there to think about? Velvl can certainly praise and thank God that he escaped.

But when Velvl suddenly came out of his father's study into the dining room, silence fell, and in the general discomfiture no one was able to look him in the face. Both daughters slipped out of the dining room one by one, and only his mother put her feet up and settled herself more comfortably on the sofa.

All was quiet.

—Velvl—his mother asked—when will all this come to an end, Velvl? . . . When will you make us all happy?

Scowling, Velvl turned to her:

—What?

He crossed angrily to the window and gazed out. He couldn't understand what they wanted from him or why they kept on nagging him, so he stared at the house of Reb Gedalye's relative, the bookkeeper, and at the furniture that was being carried out and piled into two heavily laden wagons:

—Now Reb Gedalye's relative was also moving to the provincial capital, and soon no one would be left here in the shtetl . . .

Here in the shtetl, the long hot days would soon stretch out endlessly with all the tedium of summer. The place would be deserted, and there'd be no one left to respect. And he, Velvl Burnes . . . Yes, there were the three hundred *desyatins* of rich, loamy earth near the river on Miratov's land that he was now being offered:

—He should certainly lease them, these three hundred *desyatins*.

4.3

Shortly after Shavuot a letter arrived from the crippled student Lipkis:

He'd undergone a successful operation on his leg.

On Friday night, after the Sabbath service, this was discussed in the Husyatin study house:

—What's special about this news? The tendons in his leg had grown together, so it's very likely he'll now start walking straight like everyone else.

People were also standing around a prosperous householder whose seat was against the eastern wall[*] and who'd only that evening returned from the provincial capital, listening as he discussed the Zaydenovkis, who lived in a suburb over there, and one of their relatives, with whom he'd spoken personally:

—Mirel's still living in a hotel, and it's a lie that her husband's supposed to have divorced her.

Then with infinite tedium the summer week stretched out over the shtetl, and a humid and boring Friday arrived, as purposeless as the solitary peasant wagon which had unloaded all its produce and been left in the deserted marketplace from early morning on.

By noon, the memory was still vivid of the many housewives who'd

---

[*]This wall of the synagogue, which faces east toward Jerusalem, is where the Ark housing the scrolls of the Torah is located and where seats are reserved for the rabbi and other dignitaries.

shoved and jostled around several carts loaded with vegetables as soon as the sun was up, and from various places, through open doors and windows, came the delayed but rapid pounding of choppers preparing fish on wooden boards, merging with the words shouted by one neighbor to another from inside the houses. A Jewish shopkeeper was carrying an interest-free loan* to someone, and the pharmacist's assistant Safyan, returning to the pharmacy from elsewhere, couldn't bear the smoke that belched from household chimneys and hung low and heavy in the air; he was furious at the shtetl:

—The devil only knew what kind of filth they used to heat their *tsholnt* over there.

Suddenly the tinkling of bridle bells on an out-of-town hackney carriage could be heard, and a driver fresh from the railway station sped through the shtetl terrifying a cock and several hens, turned, and came to a halt before the steps of Avreml the rabbi's house.

This was very strange:

Alone in the carriage sat Mirel Hurvits, her head with its straw hat swathed in white tulle, nodding and smiling affably at the rabbi's wife who'd just appeared in the doorway.

For appearances' sake, Libke the rabbi's wife received her with flattering courtesy:

—What a question . . . She'd take her daughter Hanke into her own bedroom, and Mirel could have Hanke's room to herself.

And hand in hand, she and Mirel went into the house, with Mirel taking everything she said at face value:

—Yes, she'd known before she asked that she'd be able to live here for a few weeks—in any case, not more than a few weeks.

Returning from their walk that Sabbath afternoon, some smartly dressed young women made a detour and deliberately strolled down the side alley that ran past the windows of Avreml the rabbi's house.

The alley was clean and quiet. Houses there threw their Sabbath shadows before them in friendly rivalry:

---

*In the Jewish tradition, helping people to help themselves with an interest-free loan is regarded as the highest form of charity.

—My shadow's bigger.

—And mine bigger still.

Through the open door floated the comically enthusiastic chant with which Avreml the rabbi was reading those passages from the Talmud he was studying. In her red ritual wig, Libke the rabbi's wife sat on the front steps yawning, her face puffy with sleep, and without looking around called out to her eleven-year-old daughter who was inside the house:

—Hanke, bring the fruit out here, Hanke!* There's a plate in the dresser, Hanke!

And at her side, leaning her head against her hand, sat Mirel, staring bleakly out into the alleyway.

—Yes—she said—she greatly regretted the fact that even their relative and former bookkeeper had also moved from the shtetl to the provincial capital.

The shtetl soon knew that some sort of scandalous scene had taken place between her and her husband in the corridor of the hotel, with the result that she'd been forced to flee from the metropolis.

By this time Nosn Heler, the young man with whom she'd once spent her time wandering all over the shtetl, had squandered his entire inheritance on his penny newspaper. He now worked somewhere in the vicinity for sixty rubles a month and was again speaking all manner of ill about her. On one occasion he'd buttonholed the photographer Royzenboym there and shown him a very distasteful note that Mirel had sent him by city messenger the previous winter. And the photographer Royzenboym, a lean, powerfully built young man with the sunburned face and wide embroidered shirt of a Gentile, had subsequently returned home to the shtetl here and had tickled the infuriated Safyan under both armpits every evening:

—Turns out no one can know whose child Mirel was carrying, Safyantshik! . . .

Once, wholly without warning, Montchik suddenly came down from the provincial capital to visit her, but stayed no longer than the interval between one train and the next.

*It is customary to snack on fruit during the Sabbath since it requires no cooking.

In the shtetl it was soon common knowledge that although Montchik himself was by no means indifferent to Mirel, he'd come down not on his own behalf but on that of her husband, his cousin, who was begging her to return to him; that Montchik was a rich young bachelor and that in general, so people said:

—He was a person of refinement, this Montchik.

While he was in private discussion with Mirel in one of the rooms, Libke the rabbi's wife stood eavesdropping behind the door and heard Mirel give him a categorical answer:

—That'll never happen . . . Do you hear, Montchik? . . . Never!

Afterward they both sat in the dining room. Preoccupied, Montchik stared in front of him with huge round eyes, every now and then making a dismissive gesture:

—He'd say no more . . . He wouldn't speak another word about this again.

A spark of deeply wistful sorrow flared in Mirel's eyes; her face was flushed and she bit her lower lip. All at once she recalled that Montchik had spent eighteen hours traveling on the train, refused to believe that he wasn't hungry, and, smiling, began frying eggs for him here at the table.

At the same time Libke the rabbi's wife set out to demonstrate that she too was quite capable of entertaining worldly people. She sat politely at the table and affectedly addressed Montchik in the diction used in Warsaw:*

—Did he have any desire at all to inspect their shtetl?

Glancing at Mirel, Montchik rose distractedly from his chair:

—Yes, certainly . . . This would be the first time in his life that he'd seen a Jewish shtetl.

In the shtetl, people stood in their doorways watching him and Mirel walk down the street: he in a new light-colored suit and the gleaming

*The rabbi's wife tries to appear sophisticated by using not merely Polish Yiddish, but a dialect specific to Warsaw. Its affected sing-song intonation can sound pretentious and vulgar. For Bergelson's characters, as for Bergelson himself, high culture was associated with Russia and Germany, not with Poland.

white collar and cuffs of a big-city sophisticate, and she in a simple white, elegantly tailored dress with her head uncovered. From a distance she pointed out to him where Avrom-Moyshe Burnes lived, led him to her father's deserted house, and showed him:

—This was my room.

They paused on the verandah and peered inside through the broken window panes. Mirel raised both her hands to her head to prevent a little comb slipping from her hair, but it fell to the ground nevertheless, and when Montchik restored it to her, she very slowly took it from his hand. For a while they stood smiling at each other.

Darkness was falling, yet she continued to lead him along the side streets. It grew chilly. Montchik remarked:

—It's strangely cheerless . . . so utterly and completely cheerless. And yet . . . Who could know? Perhaps the experience of this moment alone was sufficient to justify the twenty-six years that he, Montchik, had lived in the world.

Looking at him, Mirel stretched out the cold fingers of her left hand for him to press.

With the total darkness of night had come the coolness of a summer evening. Fresh, round, and pale, a new moon rose over the alley at the back of the rabbi's house where more young women than usual were taking the air, and the coachman from the railway station had already drawn up outside the rabbi's open front door, the same coachman who'd brought Montchik into town only a few hours earlier. Inside the house, the rabbi's wife had set a lighted lamp on a windowsill and thus made the little street seem even more festive.

Mirel hastily packed Montchik's satchel.

—Montchik, look here . . . Isn't this your towel?

Montchik was preoccupied and barely heard what was said to him. When two boys from the Talmud Torah approached him for a tip, he took five gold coins from his pocket, looking questioningly at Mirel as he did so, under the impression that this was perhaps too little.

Mirel escorted him out of the house quickly, afraid that he might miss his train.

—He oughtn't to have come down here—she said.—He'd caused her such strange pain, Montchik had; he'd wrung her heart so sharply.

Were he to stay just a little while longer, she might very well do something foolish and not allow him to leave.

She took both his hands and led him to the cab, then stood there with Libke the rabbi's wife watching the coachman suddenly whip up the horses, turn so abruptly as almost to topple the vehicle, and gallop swiftly off down the road to the railway station.

—He'll easily be home by tomorrow—she said.—He has so many business affairs there . . . It's better that way.

For a short while longer she looked in the direction in which the cab had disappeared, evidently thinking that this was for the best.

Three days after Montchik's departure, two telegrams suddenly arrived for her from the city suburb. Even while they were still sealed, they told her that Montchik was in his own home again, spent much time there thinking about the day he'd spent with her here, and was once again conducting his business at the banks and on the stock exchange; that Shmulik had already called on him at home and heard the categorical answer she'd sent him through Montchik. Libke the rabbi's wife was desperate to know what was written in the telegrams, but Mirel had merely glanced at their office of origin and returned them, unopened, to the postman:

—The only answer need be—she told him—that she'd refused to accept these telegrams, that was all; she refused to accept them.

She stayed on in the shtetl as a boarder in the house of Libke the rabbi's wife, and was noticed every day when she went to the post office to send a great many telegrams and letters to someone who seemed to have no fixed abode. She'd also acquired an unsavory reputation thanks largely to Nosn Heler, who didn't stop speaking ill about her across the entire district. Safyan, the pharmacist's assistant, saw her passing as he was standing alone in the pharmacy, earnestly affixing labels to the prescriptions; later he spoke about her to a customer, one of the local intellectuals:

—Would he be so good as to look at her . . . She was an example to all idlers. And generally speaking, could anyone tell him for what purpose such a person still occupied a place on the earth?

And ordinary people standing about bareheaded inside the pharmacy listened in silence: for a while they forgot about their children lying ravaged with illness at home in their respect for Safyan, who exuded an odor of medicaments, examined the prescriptions with great earnestness before he let them out of his hands, and couldn't abide idlers.

4.4

Mirel received no answer in response to her telegrams and letters.

She wandered aimlessly about the shtetl, growing sadder and more despondent by the day.

People here openly distanced themselves from her. There was no longer any honor in knowing her, and she knew this and never spoke of it. One evening, however, when she'd wandered along the main street feeling deeply unhappy for longer than usual, she stopped both of Avrom-Moyshe Burnes's two daughters, inquired after every member of their family, and fell into conversation with them about Velvl, who because of her had given up coming to his parents' home from his farm.

—Frankly, it was difficult to understand why Velvl was hiding from her. After all, she knew perfectly well that he was the truest of good friends to her, and she was even aware that he'd traveled out to the railway station on purpose to bid her farewell.

The second time she met Burnes's daughters she greeted them amiably and inquired:

—Did they perhaps have a mind to hire a carriage the next day and take a drive of some eight or ten versts out of the shtetl?

This happened at about three in the afternoon of a hot Sunday, shortly after Velvl's mother had left on a trip abroad in search of relief for her asthma, and the farm buggy, in which Velvl had arrived a few hours earlier to see her off, was still stationed next to Burnes's verandah.

With all its windows wide open, Avrom-Moyshe's house stood gazing somewhat forlornly at the saplings growing in a straight row before it, and consoled itself:

—Before the windows of every parvenu's house, apparently, the trees are always young and small.

All the rooms were cool and quiet, the stillness broken only by the gentle rustling of the leaves outside. There was a strong sense that the mistress of the house had only just left for what would be an extended absence; that the household would now be run by the two daughters who'd forget where they'd left the keys and as a result a jollier and more liberated atmosphere than usual would prevail, that the young people's guests would linger on until late at night, and that if one of the smaller children had a tantrum about something, there'd be no one to rebuke him and he'd have to be bribed with five kopecks to be quiet.

Avrom-Moyshe Burnes paced about in his study exhaling cigarette smoke, his brow as always furrowed above the regretful expression on his unlearned face. Opposite him, next to the desk, holding a map of the three hundred *desyatins* of rich, loamy earth he'd leased not long before, stood Velvl, who was consulting his father about what should be sown there:

—Down here near the marsh perhaps it might be better to sow millet?

Suddenly the elder daughter came in to report that Mirel was now in the house and was sitting in the smaller salon. Overcome by guilt, the young woman felt obliged to justify herself:

—What a situation . . . How could one be so discourteous? . . . What was one to do when she started peering in through the open windows from outside and asking whether she might call? . . .

The young woman soon returned to the salon, leaving behind both father and son in a situation so highly unpleasant that they couldn't bring themselves to look each other in the face. At any moment, it seemed, Mirel would open the door and set foot in the study. Velvl turned pale and started breathing as rapidly as though he'd only just demonstrated some fairground trick and lifted a mass weighing ten pood. He looked across at his father, waiting to see what he would do, but his father's expression was so shaded, so wreathed in smoke, and so impassive that not the slightest alteration was evident in it. He simply furrowed his unlearned brow even more deeply and exhaled more cigarette smoke; at length his father slowly and silently made his way out through the back door of the house, seated himself in Velvl's harnessed buggy, and instructed the coachman to drive him to the brick factory where he had business to attend to.

Velvl followed him out through the same back door and strode off through the side streets to the licensed liquor store* where he had to change some money.

Those in the salon, meanwhile, sat around talking about the sounds made by a gramophone, which were very tinny and soon bored the listener to death; about little Ziamke, who knew who Tolstoy was but felt bashful now and wouldn't say; and about the impoverished gentlewoman who owned land in the village of Pritshepa, an old maid of forty who'd lost her wits again; she'd used the last of her money to buy an automobile and was telling everyone that the local count's only son would marry her.

Apart from Mirel and Velvl's sisters, others seated on the velvet chairs were their relative the young external student at the university† who taught the children Hebrew, and the niece of the widow who ran the local inn, a young woman from out of town who was studying dentistry and seemed to be of limited understanding. Standing silently to one side all the while was another young university student, recently brought in as the family tutor from one of the provinces deep in the Russian interior, who'd studied in a yeshiva as a boy. This was the first time he'd seen Mirel in person, but he already knew everything that had happened to her, and not knowing her by sight had often quarreled with both Burnes sisters and with the pharmacist's assistant, Safyan:

—What nonsense were they speaking? To judge by the picture they themselves painted of Mirel, it seemed to him that she was an interesting person, and there had to be something to her.

---

*Because taxes gathered on the sale of liquor were a key element of government finance in tsarist Russia, the liquor trade was strictly regulated by government decrees. Purveying liquor as innkeepers and publicans became one of the traditional occupations of Jews in the Pale of Settlement.

†In tsarist Russia, external students were permitted to attend lectures, but were not officially enrolled in the university and were therefore not entitled to graduate. Often these were students who had not passed the matriculation examination at a *gymnasium*, which required proficiency in both Latin and Greek. In the later years of Romanov rule, to become external students was the only way many Jews, restricted by the discriminatory quota system, could attend university courses.

Now he was captivated by her young, slightly weary face, and was by no means indifferent to her smile, to the fact that, seated on the red plush sofa, she held her head high and thrown a little back, or to her voice, modulated by the enervated tones of one who'd lived through a great deal yet remained stubbornly loyal to some private ideal and paid no mind to the opinions of others. Hence he held his peace throughout and thought of her as a bridegroom might think of his bride. He kept forgetting that the external student, the family's young relative, didn't smoke, and kept approaching him with an outstretched hand and the mien of a beggar:

—Would you please be so kind as to give me a cigarette?

The elder of Velvl's sisters was the first to hear the buggy driving away from the house and, forgetting where she was, craned her neck like a hen terrified that someone was menacingly following her on tiptoe, and foolishly strained to listen more closely. And for some reason Mirel, who was now aware that there was no longer anyone in the study, asked the external student for a pencil and a sheet of paper.

She seemed to do nothing with this writing equipment, holding the pencil in one hand and the sheet of paper in the other as she smilingly prepared to leave. Yet later, in the pocket of his dustcoat, Velvl found this sheet of paper. On it, in Mirel's handwriting, were two words in Russian:

—*Ty khoroshi*—You're a good person.

He read it again and again all the way home, carried it about among the banknotes in his wallet for several days, and finally hid it in a separate little drawer in his safe.

Mirel finally succeeded in carrying out her plan here in the shtetl.

Quite unexpectedly one morning she received the reply for which she'd been waiting all this time and was greatly pleased with it. On her way back from the post office with this response, she stopped the pharmacist's assistant Safyan in the middle of the street, told him that his new horn-rimmed spectacles suited his face very well, and firmly declared that he ought to get married:

—She hoped Safyan would believe that she meant every word: he had a profession, so why would he want to drift through life all alone?

A nervous tic spontaneously afflicted the left side of Safyan's face. He entertained quite definite opinions about getting married and genuinely wished to start airing them, but she interrupted him almost immediately to ask when the nineteenth of the month would be:

—It was essential for her to know this . . . when exactly the nineteenth of this month would fall.

4.5

The nineteenth day of the secular month happened to correspond exactly to the first day of the Hebrew month of Av, a day on which the heat of the bright sunlight hours of summer seemed to intensify.

The melancholy of the approaching Nine Days lay heavy on the shtetl.* In order to escape its oppression, men took an afternoon nap, cocks crowed either by mistake or out of a sense of desolation, and women couldn't understand the feeling of wretchedness that prevented them from knitting their socks in peace, and drove them instead from the cover of their own porches to those of their neighbors.

Around three o'clock that very afternoon, a cab driver from the railway station stopped his buggy in front of the inn at the entrance to the marketplace, and down climbed a tall, clean-shaven young man whose throat was swaddled in cotton wool and a great many bandages.

On closer scrutiny he was recognized:

—This was Herz, the midwife's acquaintance Herz.

Mirel had finally succeeded in getting him to come down here.

From all the surrounding dwellings, people stared at her as she sat beside Libke, the rabbi's wife, whiling away the tedium on the verandah of the rabbi's house, and ridiculed her:

—She certainly knew the right time to bring him down . . . She made him come just in time for Tisha B'Av.

---

*The ninth day of the Hebrew month of Av (corresponding to July/August in the secular Western calendar) is Tisha B'Av, an annual fast day commemorating the two Destructions of the Temple in Jerusalem in 586 BCE and 70 CE, respectively. The days leading up to Tisha B'Av are known as "The Nine Days," during which the strictly observant refrain from eating meat and from pleasurable activities such as listening to music.

From somewhere she soon learned that Herz was suffering from tonsillitis, so she stopped the local *feldsher* in the side street next to the rabbi's house and told him of this illness:

—He was regrettably the kind of person who'd sooner die than admit he was suffering any kind of pain. But if the *feldsher* were to call on him now, unbidden, he'd certainly let him treat his throat.

The *feldsher* did as he was asked and went off to the inn.

She herself returned to the verandah of the rabbi's house and sat down beside Libke the rabbi's wife to resume whiling away the tedium. She looked sad, and complained to Libke that the day was passing with extraordinary slowness:

—When the shadow of this house reaches the middle of the street, it's invariably six o'clock, but now . . . now this seems to be a particularly long day. There doesn't seem to have been another day as long as this all summer.

Later, when the shadow of this house had started merging with the shadows of all the surrounding houses, she left the verandah and went off along the road that led to the post office. There she met Avrom-Moyshe Burnes's two daughters who were out for a stroll with their tutor, the student. Looking sad, she paused opposite them to inquire about the shortcut across the fields to the railway line, and about a certain well-to-do young woman, an orphan from the local district, who'd been engaged for many years but hadn't yet married her fiancé:

—Didn't they remember? Many tales had been told about this young woman once.

Looking at her, both Burnes sisters called to mind their older brother who'd remained unmarried because of her, and knew also that because of her, Herz had now come down here. So they answered: "No, they couldn't remember."

—They'd never heard of such a person, they were sure.

The student, however, was greatly excited by this unexpected meeting, and was fully prepared to walk up and down the road with Mirel in the big-city manner. For this reason he tried to continue the conversation:

—Be that as it may . . . The story about this young woman must be very interesting, whatever the case.

Mirel, however, pretended not to hear and soon took her leave. Walking on beyond the outskirts of the shtetl, she wandered about there alone through the long twilight.

That evening, when people were sitting down to their meal in all the shtetl's houses and it was difficult to recognize anyone on the dark and deserted streets, she slipped into the inn at the entrance to the marketplace and spent a considerable time with Herz in his room.

The red curtains that hung over Herz's illuminated windows had been drawn, and no one was wandering about in the street outside except the young woman studying dentistry, the niece of the widow who ran the inn. Intensely curious to know what Herz and Mirel were speaking about in there, she quietly slipped into the empty room adjacent to theirs, huddled close to the gap between the warped double doors with their knotholes, and heard them reopening old wounds:

—Herz—Mirel started to say—I've waited such along time for you here; I'm sure no one's ever waited for you as long as this.

There was silence in the room. Herz was angry and made no reply.

—Herz—Mirel went on—recently I've understood so little of what's been happening with me; I don't know why I've thought about you so much; I don't even know for what reason I came back here, to this shtetl.

She paused in thought for a moment and then added:

—She'd thought that things would be better for her here in the shtetl. She still thought that *somewhere* things would be better for her.

Herz tinkled a teaspoon in a glass as he prepared a solution of boric acid* for his throat with boiling water from the samovar.

—All well and good—he interrupted her—but why on earth had she so stubbornly insisted that he come down to meet her here, in this shtetl of all places, where everyone knew her and where prying eyes stared out at him from every house? Even the midwife Schatz lived in the vicinity . . . Now he felt like some kind of brainless provincial bridegroom, all thanks to such colossal idiocy as her self-indulgent whim.

---

*Boric (also called boracic or orthoboric) acid, often used as an antiseptic, exists in the form of colorless crystals or white powder and dissolves in water.

Mirel made him no reply: her voice simply started sounding more worn out, as though she'd come to beg alms from him:

—Herz, it still seems to me that you know much more than I do.

Generally speaking she still imagined that somewhere there were still a few such individuals who knew *something* but they kept their knowledge secret . . . She begged Herz's pardon for having summoned him down here . . . So little was left to her in life outside her imaginings. And now she was living in this shtetl again . . . she whiled away the tedium thinking of these things. For whole evenings on end she sat on the verandah next to Libke the rabbi's wife looking west, toward the red sky aflame with the setting sun. During one such evening she'd imagined that, from this ruddy extremity of the sky, an alternative fiery Mirel was staring back at her, beckoning to her from a distance: "No one," that beckoning gesture seemed to say, "knew why Mirel Hurvits blundered aimlessly around the world, and I, the Mirel burning on the horizon in this fiery extremity of the sky, I too once blundered about and I too had no idea why."

As Herz had no idea what she wanted, a barely perceptible smile flitted across his ironic expression and stayed there all the time she was speaking. He was frustrated by this discussion and finally interrupted her:

—Quite possibly, but what was the use of spending their first evening talking about such high-flown things?

He could tell her that on one occasion her husband's cousin Montchik had called on him at his hotel . . . He'd come wearing a black frock coat. Yes, and her husband himself as well:

—They'd informed him in the hotel that her husband had inquired for him on two separate occasions.

Then Mirel stared across at him, and spoke not a single word more. His last remark had deeply insulted her. She turned pale and did not so much as bid him good night. For a moment she stopped and stood indecisively in the darkened corridor of the inn, but made no attempt to turn back. She merely adjusted her scarf and disappeared into the darkness outdoors.

When the young woman who was studying dentistry left the inn, Herz was standing at the open door of his brightly lit room asking for pen and ink and another kerosene lamp. Outside, the young woman walked past the inn, peering down the street. The night was dark and cool, the shtetl was asleep, and Mirel was nowhere to be seen. To determine in which direction she'd gone was impossible: left, to the rabbi's house, or right, taking the road that led to the post office and the fields on the outskirts of the shtetl.

In the early hours of the morning, Libke the rabbi's wife raised her head from her pillow in the darkness, leaned over to the second bed in which her husband was sleeping, and began calling to him in a muffled, sleepy voice:

—Avreml?! . . . Avreml?! . . . Are you sleeping, Avreml?

The whole house was dark, silent, and forlorn. The night had utterly enveloped it, had everywhere coiled itself around the extinguished shtetl and far beyond, encircling the surrounding fields where the desolation of all those asleep beat quietly on the ground.

The rabbi jerked slightly and started awake with sleepy alarm and a half-strangulated question:

—Eh?!

Later they both lay half-awake in their beds, raised their heads in the darkness, and heard Mirel weeping behind the locked door on the other side of the wall. The sounds she made were gagging, stifled, and full of yearning. Every now and then they were intensified by a fresh rush of full-throated sobs that recalled her childhood years as an indulged only child. Under the wracked shuddering of her body the bed could be heard creaking, as though someone standing over her had seized her by the throat and was choking her while uttering the repeated reminder:

—You've destroyed your life . . . And it's lost now, lost forever . . .

Befuddled with sleep, the rabbi's wife sat up in her bed and adjusted her nightcap.

—She's been to see him—she remarked, referring to Herz at the inn.—She's spent the whole evening with him.

Then she quietly opened a shutter and saw:

The gray light of dawn was already creeping over the shtetl. In all the neighboring houses, people were still asleep, and only farther off, where the marketplace began, were lights still burning in Herz's room in the inn where the red curtains were still drawn, concealing him and the writing at which he'd gone on working through the night.

4.6

Two nights before Tisha B'Av, rain fell steadily and for a long time. It beat down on sleeping roofs but was unable to wake them, and drenched a solitary peasant wagon dragging its way slowly over the muddy shtetl, directing it toward the single, restless, illuminated window ahead that stared out of the rabbi's sodden side street.

Something disturbing had befallen Mirel again, with the result that the rabbi's wife slept badly in her bedroom, conscious of the incredulity aroused in the shtetl that she and her husband permitted Mirel to live in a rabbi's house while at the same time keeping an unmarried man at the inn here. The rabbi's wife had no idea what she'd done to deserve all these troubles, and kept opening her eyes and sighing to her husband loudly enough for Mirel to hear in her own room:

—Oh, how trying this all is! . . . But how does one tell someone: Pack up your things and get out?

The next morning was hot, humid, and tedious. Among the drying clods of earth, puddles of rainwater and a few shards of glass glared too brightly in the sunlight, and the newly rinsed houses dried rapidly for the sake of Tisha B'Av, uncertain of whether the rain would sweep down to soak them again.

Behind the locked door of Mirel's room the agitated pacing of the night before could still be heard.

Around eleven o'clock in the morning she left that room in haste and went straight to the inn where the hired buggy was already waiting for Herz. The blue shadows under her eyes were as dark as bruises, and the angle of her back spoke clearly of the fact that her situation both here in the shtetl and everywhere else was now irremediable and irrecoverable and had to be terminated as quickly as possible. She looked straight ahead at the buggy next to the inn, her mind working too rapidly and with too much tension because of her sleepless night.

She still had to remind Herz of something.

But drawing level with the façade of Avrom-Moyshe Burnes's house, she suddenly regretted this decision and stopped:

—There was nothing more than foolish self-delusion in her long-standing wish to believe that she'd be able to live with him abroad somewhere.

Next to the verandah of Burnes's house she saw Velvl's younger sister and turned to her:

—Could Brokhe perhaps tell her what day of the month it was? . . . She, Mirel, had already stayed far too long here in the shtetl.

Leaving the frightened girl a vivid impression of her fasting, exhausted face with its bruised-looking eyes, she strode rapidly over the dried-out clods of earth toward the post office to send someone a telegram, hearing behind her the stationary buggy suddenly pull away as the cab driver enthusiastically whipped up the horses:

—*Viyo!* . . . We need to hurry back home in time to read Lamentations!

Libke the rabbi's wife was waiting for her in the dining room and stopped her:

—Yes . . . she and Avreml had wanted to speak with her . . . They'd wanted to tell her that of course she'd been very welcome all the time she'd stayed with them . . .

Her hands were folded stupidly over her belly and her eyes had an odd gleam. Mirel had no wish to hear what she had to say:

—She knew, she knew . . . the next day she, Mirel, would no longer be here.

And she went immediately to her room, chained the door behind her, and drew the shutters closed from within.

She urgently needed to sleep, even if only for a few hours, to relieve her splitting headache and calm the anxious turmoil in her mind about what she'd do a few hours later. To think about this was pointless. If the narrow strip of wearisomely blazing sunshine that split the darkness through a crack in the fast-drying shutters made it difficult to doze off, it was still possible, lying on the bed, for her swiftly to pull off her blouse, throw her bare, tingling arms over her burning head and imagine that her twenty-four desolate years of life hadn't issued solely in a void . . . This made her feel a little more at ease, and for a moment she ceased fretting about the following day and the fact that she'd have absolutely no place to which she might go. In the swirling confusion that preceded deep sleep, having once had Gedalye Hurvits for a father here in the shtetl seemed so very far away and long ago, and her weary dozing mind summoned up the image of a half-forgotten late Friday afternoon some seven or eight years earlier: the setting sun had cast a rose-red glow over everything, and at a window inside the house stood Gitele, her mother, already dressed for the Sabbath, staring out down the road that led into the shtetl from the provincial capital and complaining anxiously, as she did every Friday:

—Just look: it's already so late, and there's still no sign of Gedalye!

She left the house early on the first morning after Tisha B'Av, and did not return to the rabbi's side street.

In the afternoon she was seen wandering about the deserted promenade next to the post office, and then on the road that led out of the shtetl. Meeting the young man who used to buy two small wagonloads of flour every week from Reb Gedalye's mill, she asked him to book a cab in the shtetl to take her to the railway station, and to ask at the rabbi's house that her belongings be sent with it.

When the cab driver drove up to meet her outside the shtetl just before sunset, she was in great haste, but after the first few versts she no longer reproached him for continually slowing down; instead she instructed him not to drive directly to the railway station but to make a slight detour, to the solitary Jewish inn that idled away its days under its red roof at a little distance from the overgrown cottages of the railway workers, waiting day and night for a bridal couple to use it as a rendezvous.

She stayed there more than a week, waiting for someone.

Four times a day people from the shtetl saw her coming to the railway station with her face drawn in sorrow. She wandered along the entire length of each stationary train, peering into every carriage without speaking a word to anyone, and then returned to the inn with her sorrowful expression unchanged. People clustered in a group at the end of the platform and watched her retreating:

—Mirel's really come down in the world, eh?

At length she left by herself on the train that traveled to the border.

This was reported in town, but knowing where she'd gone was impossible.

4.7

Once on a quite ordinary Thursday, when every trace of her had long vanished from the railway station, Velvl Burnes made his way there from his farm after the last trains had departed and drove directly to the inn that stood under its huge red roof.

Smartly clad in a new black suit and brand new linen under his traveling coat, he ordered a room prepared for him and sent his buggy back home:

—His driver was to call for him here tomorrow at noon, did he hear? Not a moment before noon.

All the rooms in the inn were unoccupied, and there were no houses nearby. In his room, where each minute seemed longer and more protracted than in his own home, a silent desolation swept up and over him. He sat on the chintz sofa, wandered over the unfamiliar red floor, stopped at the window and looked out at the geese feeding on the grass beyond.

He went down to the platform twice: in the evening, after both goods trains had left, and very early in the morning when the entire deserted platform was still asleep and the red eye of the distant, white-painted signal boom still gleamed in the rising sun together with the first platform lamp, next to which a ladder had been left the day before.

He also set out along the path that led from the inn to the little wood close by, and stood there on the high bank of a newly restored trench.

Silence reigned in the little wood. High up, the branches barely rustled; from time to time a yellow autumn leaf dislodged itself and drifted down through the air; and the unspeaking trees knew something: they stood all around with their tall clean trunks listening to the barely perceptible rustle of their own branches and thought about Mirel, who'd once lived for more than a week in the nearby inn:

—Yes . . . Mirel once wandered about over here during the day . . .

She spoke to no one here, but without any need to do so she once wandered slowly about among us, we young tree trunks.

Late in the month, as Elul was approaching, the student Lipkis, no longer crippled, returned home, and while he was still on the road he learned from the cab driver:

—Well, well, well! It's certainly almost a month since Mirel left us.

In his mother's house he slept through the whole night as well as all the following morning and all the next afternoon, and had no reason to get up. He snored away comfortably, but his sleepy mind recalled that Mirel was no longer here, that she'd been in his thoughts when they'd anesthetized him for his operation, all the time he'd been convalescing during his summer teaching job, and afterward, when he was already making his way home here and had repeatedly slipped out into the corridor of the train carriage to examine yet again the mended leg he was bringing back for her.

That evening, feeling as deflated as though a wedding he'd been looking forward to had been canceled, he drifted aimlessly about the deserted shtetl with no one in whom to confide that he harbored no resentment against Mirel, that during the summer he would rise with the morning star to resume his medical studies and would repeat over and over together with the contents of his textbooks:

—I'm no enemy to Mirel . . . no enemy, no enemy.

He stopped next to Reb Gedalye's abandoned house and regarded it, then strolled slowly down the broad side street and viewed the rabbi's house from a distance. He found it strangely fresh and novel to saunter slowly and effortlessly through the very same streets along which he'd clumsily swung his hips from side to side for fully twenty-six years and along which he'd bent his entire body back and forth with every stride like a the deputy caretaker of a synagogue during the recitation of the Eighteen Benedictions.*

---

*The Eighteen Benedictions are recited in silence while standing and facing Jerusalem three times each day, at the morning, afternoon, and evening services, respectively. Rocking back and forth while reciting this prayer is regarded as a mark of piety.

Recognizing him from where she sat on her verandah, the rabbi's wife rose and began slowly walking toward him:

—So indeed, so indeed . . . How else? Now you're whole and healthy, may no evil eye afflict you, like everyone else.

She fell into conversation with him about his operation, about his brother who, report had it, had started prospering and was becoming a rich man, and about the fact that her daughter Hanke must certainly have forgotten everything she'd once spent almost a year studying with him. She'd greatly appreciate it if Lipkis would specifically check up on this:

—Could Hanke still write from dictation?

So Lipkis went into the house and checked up on whether Hanke still knew anything.

Everything was quiet and the rabbi's wife was no longer standing at his side. Hanke sat at the table writing as he walked about, dictating slowly, glancing up at the ceiling and across at the walls of the room in which, for six weeks, Mirel had lived. Several bits and pieces that she'd left behind lay scattered about in the open closet, among them a small crumpled sheet of paper half-covered with writing. Plucking it out, Lipkis recognized it as a letter Mirel had begun but never completed. It read:

—Again, Montchik, nothing has come of any of the plans I'd thought to make. Everything I think of always comes to nothing. Herz is very unjust to me. Earlier, I used to find this distressing: I spoke to him about those things that pained me, and he responded with reference to some remnants of a generation that no longer had any place in life. But now all this is over too, and it is difficult for me to speak of it. I can no longer stay where I am at present. I have no idea where, but I must go far away from here. Yellow leaves are already falling from the trees, and this fall season is replicated in my heart. I'm living through the autumn of my life, Montchik; I've been living through it since the day of my birth, and I've never known a spring. The thought that someone else has lived through my springtime grows more and more obvious to me from day to day: even before I was born, someone else had lived out my springtime.